D0285701

Meji

BOOK TWO

A NOVEL BY

MILTON J. DAVIS

This story is a work of fiction. Any references to real events, persons and locales are intended only to give the fiction a sense of reality and authenticity. Any resemblance to actual persons, living or dead is entirely coincidental.

Copyright © 2005
Milton J. Davis

Published 2009

All Rights Reserved.

ISBN 13: 978-0-9800842-4-5
ISBN 10: 0-9800842-4-5

Edited by Jana Wright
Cover Art by Thomas Richard Davis III
Layout/Cover Design by URAEUS

Manufactured in the United States of America

First Edition

Meji

BOOK TWO

Introduction

Storytellers are part of society's life blood. They sing the songs of what-might-be, what-could-be, and remind us that dreams come at a cost to the characters in their stories, as it does in real life. We travel to places known and unknown, reside in the lives of others and find amusement and affirmation through the imagination of storytellers. In the course of reading these stories we are lifted, entertained and often times surprised.

You hold in your hands Book Two of the Meji series by skilled storyteller Milton Davis. In Book One Milton weaves an original and intriguing story of twin brothers, Ndoro and Obaseki, finding their way in a beautiful and dangerous world. Milton has created a fantastical version of Africa where in the grasslands of the continent of Uhuru the twins are separated at birth by necessity. They are raised in different societies. One of the brothers possesses a gift that shapes the destiny of their world.

I enjoyed the journey through Meji Book One because of Milton's ability to draw the reader into the intricate lives of his powerful characters. Now in Book Two the cost of the twins' destiny is heightened as they travel on separate paths. The unique magic created by Milton in this series held my complete attention as the brother and their abilities mature.

Allow yourself to relax into this book, into the travels through treacherous and divisive lands as Ndoro and Obaseki make their way to fulfill their purpose. Milton will paint on your mind with his imaginative brush creatures that don't exist but could. You will recognize the human ego manipulating people in the characters around the twin brothers and enjoy the fictional lives unfolding. I rejoiced in the ending of Book Two and look forward to more tales of Meji. This is the true magic of storytellers.

-**Linda Addison**, award-winning author of Consumed, Reduced to Beautiful Grey Ashes and the first African-American to receive the Bram Stoker award

To Brandon and Alana
My wonderful children

1

The quiet village nestled on the banks of the Nyoka River was nothing special; it was a simple community that ebbed and flowed with the rhythm of the river. Its people labored under a clear blue sky common in the dry season, their easy voices free of the strains of the busy rainy season. The women worked in the compounds, repairing roofs and patching walls damaged by the rains. The men tended the animals, sitting in groups to discuss the village business as men do. They called themselves Diaka, which in their language meant 'the good people.' Anyone observing them would agree with the claim.

Ndoro peered down at the village from his hiding place in the hills. For days he'd watched the Diaka go on about their lives, trying to decide the best way to approach them. He had no doubt about meeting them for he was starving. After fleeing Selike, he wandered about the grasslands, refusing to take the advice of Jelani to head south to his grandfather's land. It would be the first place his father would look, and Ndoro was not certain the grandfather he had never met would protect him. Instead he headed east, hunting small game during the day, while hiding from simbas and hyenas during the night. He had no purpose or plan; dealing with the events of the past weeks were enough to fill his mind. He had killed a medicine priest. It was a stain on his ego, a blemish that covered the triumph of bringing the old simba to his father. He would have to erase it somehow; when and where he had no idea. His first task was to stay alive; atonement would come later.

A few weeks from Selike he spotted a Sesu impi running

across the grasslands. He spent the night in a baobab cradled between two large branches like a leopard. The impi did not see him, but throughout the day he was wary, keeping his journey close to areas where he could escape to cover quickly if seen. The next day confirmed his suspicions; Sesu impis crisscrossed the area, some running, others creeping about looking for his sign. His days of wandering were over. He had to set out in some direction, any way that took him away from Sesuland. He'd wandered too far away from Selike to get his bearings toward Mawenaland and the supposed safety of his grandfather, so after a long sleepless day he decided to follow the Kojo River. It was said the river ran through the bordering hills and into the forest. Stories told to him as a boy spoke of trees so dense a man would have to cut himself in half to pass between them. It was believed to be the home of lost spirits, the place where the souls of those forgotten by their descendents fled to suffer, torturing others that came across their path.

Waiting for the cover of darkness, Ndoro slept in his wooded sanctuary invisible to the wandering Sesu. The absence of heat woke him; he opened his eyes to the reddish sky of a setting sun. He also spied a frightening sight in the branches below him. A leopard lounged, gnawing on the leg of an antelope. The smell of fresh kill covered Ndoro's scent, making him invisible. The leopard finished its meal and proceeded to fall asleep. For hours he waited for the leopard to leave but the beast apparently had no intention of doing so. As the moon peaked over the horizon Ndoro decided he had been patient enough. He gingerly came to his feet, steadied himself, then jumped up and down on the branches. The startled cat howled and scrambled out of the tree, disappearing into the darkness. Ndoro waited to be sure the feline was gone before climbing down and heading for the river's edge.

The full moon's luminescence unveiled the teeming

savannah. For Ndoro, it was a blessing and a curse. The muted light made it easier for him to see the river and the animals that made crossing the region treacherous. The glow also made him more visible to anything or anyone searching for him but he had to take the risk.

The riverbank bristled with movement. Crocodiles dragged themselves in and out of the murky liquid while hippopotami waded with little interest. Both were dangerous to Ndoro, so he stayed away from the edges unless the shoreline proved desolate enough that he could move closer without harm.

Ndoro did not realize the monumental task he was undertaking until it was too late to turn back. The river he assumed was the Kojo did not lead to Mawenaland. This was the Nyoka, which wound its way across the grasslands then turned south into the savannah. It was there, after two weeks of night-trekking, that he found himself staring down into the village below.

He could wait no longer. Leaving his weapons in the bush, he emerged from the dense foliage and scrambled down the hill onto the road leading into the village. He timed his appearance to meet the old man he'd seen coming down the path every day, driving a herd of goats from the grassland to the village. Ndoro lost his balance and stumbled, falling on the road at the old man's feet.

The old man looked down at him, smiling with broken teeth.

"So you finally decided to show yourself."

Ndoro could say nothing, the wind knocked out of him.

"You must be weak if a little fall like that hurts," the old man said. He reached out, grabbing Ndoro's arm with surprising strength and lifting him to a sitting position.

"My name is Jabulani. Who are you?"

Ndoro coughed, eyes downcast. "Ndoro."

"Hmm…are you Sesu?"

Ndoro looked up at the elder, feeling slight comfort in the fact that Jabulani knew his origins.

"Yes, baba, I am Sesu."

Jabulani nodded his head, reaching into his waist pouch. He handed Ndoro a yam.

"Here. You are very hungry. I will take you to my home."

The sight of the yam brought the pain of hunger back to Ndoro. He took it as politely as he could then bit into it voraciously. The firm sweetness made him close his eyes with joy.

Jabulani laughed. "Slow down, son. That's your yam. No one's going to take it from you."

When Ndoro finished Jabulani helped him stand and gave him another yam as they walked down the narrow path to the village. It was larger than Ndoro expected, occupying a large field at the edge of a stand of trees. As they passed curious onlookers, Ndoro got the impression that Jabulani was more that a goat herder. Intense stares at him were followed by respectful nods to Jabulani.

"It seems I am in noble company," Ndoro commented.

"The worm cannot tell the difference between a rich dead man and a poor dead man," Jabulani replied.

Two young men pushed their way through the crowd towards them. One was as tall as Ndoro but with a heavy, muscular frame. The second man was a mirror image of the other but a head shorter. The resemblance to Jabulani was unmistakable.

"Baba, where have you been?" the taller one asked, a hint of anger in his respectful tone.

"I took my goats to the hill pastures, Jawanza."

"The hills are not safe with the man-killer about," the

other son said.

Jabulani frowned at his son. "Kamau, you're afraid of a donkey's horns."

The two looked at their father with exasperation, and then turned their attention to his companion. Ndoro lowered the yam from his face, standing straighter as his eyes met those of the brothers.

"This is Ndoro," Jabulani said. "He is a lost Sesu. He will be staying with us for a while."

The brothers' expressions transformed from distrust to awe.

"A Sesu," Jawanza replied. "Then you were in no danger."

"A shumba hunter," Kamau whispered. "You found a shumba hunter!"

"Your baba didn't find me," Ndoro corrected. "I came here on my own."

"You must admit, you presence is good for the Diaka," Jabulani said. "A shumba stalks our village and has killed two, both of them children. We are not hunters, but I remember stories of the Sesu and their skill at hunting. Now come, you will rest and build up your strength, and then you will kill the shumba."

Ndoro's anger was not tempered by the old man's generous smile. He'd been tricked, but he could not refuse after accepting Diaka hospitality.

"What is this shumba, baba?" Ndoro asked. "Is it a simba?"

Jabulani shook his head. "I wish it was so. A shumba looks like a simba, but it is much different. It hunts alone, and it prefers the forest to the savannah. Some say they are spirits of the old gods, forced to roam the earth for some transgression no one remembers. They are very dangerous, and they have no fear of men. In fact, they prefer us."

Ndoro was beginning to regret coming to the Diaka. Hunting the shumba would be difficult even with experienced Sesu. Of course he'd killed Old Simba alone, but it was something he didn't wish to do again. Simbas were obvious in their ways; this shumba seemed to behave more like a leopard. This would be a far more dangerous hunt.

As they approached Jabulani's compound Ndoro pushed back his concerns. A low stone wall encircled the group of wooden homes inside. Outside the entrance two women surrounded by children stopped their basket-weaving and jumped to their feet.

"Baba!" They rushed Jabulani with hugs and cries, followed by the children. From inside the compound others came, their joy just as passionate. Somewhere a drummer began to play and the family sang and danced. Ndoro stepped aside as Jabulani's family celebrated their patriarch's return.

A shrill scream pierced the singing, emanating from within the compound. The drumming and singing ceased. Jabulani's children turned in the direction of the compound, whispering among themselves. Jabulani let out a sigh and rolled his eyes as Jawanza and Kamau snickered.

"What's wrong?" Ndoro asked.

"Mama is coming." Jawanza smiled.

The woman was as tall as Jabulani and almost as wide. Her chubby face was contorted into a frown as she marched toward her husband, a narrow tree branch in her hand.

"Talana," Jabulani began, "I…"

Talana swatted Jabulani across the arm.

"Woman, what is wrong with you?"

"If you wish to act like a child I will treat you like one!" Talana retorted.

"I was gone only for a week."

Talana's anger subsided. "No one knew where you were. I thought the shumba killed you."

Jabulani touched his wife's shoulder and she smiled. "I went to the temple on the lake to ask Kikuba for help. He accepted my gift of goats and sent this man to help us." Jabulani put his hand on Ndoro's shoulder. "He is a shumba hunter."

"I was not sent by any god to help you," Ndoro explained.

"If Jabulani asked Kikuba to send help then it is why you are here, whether you know it or not." Talana looked him up and down. "You need to eat. Come."

She took a step then turned back to Jabulani, hitting him again with the branch. "I don't care if you did talk to Kikuba. You tell me where you're going the next time."

Ndoro covered his mouth to hide his smile. Jabulani's grandchildren were not as modest, laughing at their grandfather out loud. Even Jabulani smiled despite his best efforts to appear angry.

Talana led Ndoro through the gates of the family compound and into her house. His eyes burned from the smoke, but the smell of the stew simmering on the pot over the fire was worth the pain.

"Sit here." Talana pointed at a woven straw mat on the floor. Ndoro sat and Talana handed him a bowl of stew and a spoon.

"Thank you, mama," Ndoro said respectfully. The stew was the best food he'd eaten since fleeing Selike. A wave of serenity passed through him as he ate, followed by a sudden tiredness. He barely finished the stew before the bowl dropped from his hand, Talana catching it before it hit the ground. He was sound asleep before he collapsed on the mat.

When he awoke he felt better than he had in days. Strips of sunlight penetrated the thatch roof of the hut, illuminating the cramped interior. Talana and Jabulani sat opposite each other, enjoying a meal that smelled as delicious as the stew he ate before sleeping.

Jabulani looked at him and smiled. "Good, you are awake. I thought Talana killed you."

Talana punched Jabulani's shoulder. "I don't know anything about Sesu. The potion was just right for a Diaka man his size."

"You drugged me?" Ndoro asked.

"You needed to rest. You feel better now, don't you?"

"Yes, I do," Ndoro admitted. "But from now on, I would like to know if I'm about to be helped."

Jabulani nodded, and then handed Ndoro a bowl. "Eat now. We must meet the elders today to discuss the shumba. It killed Shuka yesterday in his millet field. It is growing bolder every day."

Ndoro nodded. "It has become used to man flesh and it senses your fear. We must kill it as soon as possible."

Jabulani smiled. "So you will help us?"

"Of course," Ndoro replied. "It is true we Sesu hunt simbas. But it is no easy thing. Many warriors have died during simba hunts. Planning and experience are very important."

"Have you killed a simba?" Talana inquired

"Yes," Ndoro answered.

"How many warriors did it take?"

Ndoro hesitated, not wanting to seem boastful, but refusing to lie to his hosts.

"I killed him alone."

Jabulani sprang to his feet, clapping his hands. "Kikuba

has truly blessed us! He sent us a great simba hunter."

Ndoro raised his hand. "Baba, please listen to me. What I did was stupid. I was trying to prove myself to gain my father's attention and almost died doing so."

"But you did not die. Your wisdom will help us succeed," Talana finished.

Ndoro sighed, giving up his attempts to dampen the couple's expectations.

Jabulani finished his food and stood. "Come, Ndoro, it is time to see the elders."

Ndoro and Jabulani exited the house into the bright sun. Jawanza and Kamau waited for them by the compound gate. Ndoro smiled when he saw Jawanza carrying his assegai, sword and shield.

"I brought these for you," he said. "You will need them."

"Thank you." The four men set out to meet the elders. They walked through the twisting crowded streets, following the narrow alleyways separating family compounds until they emerged on the wide avenue leading to the center of town. Everyone they passed stared at Ndoro hopefully and he was embarrassed by all the attention. It was odd how bold and confident he had been in Selike when nothing was expected of him. Now that he was getting the respect he deserved, he was nervous and unsure. Maybe this was a spell of Mulugo's doing, even though medicine priest was dead. Could his spirit be following him? He would ask Talana once he returned from his meeting with the elders.

They made their way to a grove of trees in the center of the village. Under the huge canopy of the largest tree sat eight elderly men deep in discussion. As they walked closer the men halted their conversation. They all stared at Ndoro, their faces a patchwork of emotions.

They halted before the elders and sat. Ndoro watched his companions for any sign of ceremony, waiting to follow their movements. But there were none, only the simple nod of acknowledgement. Ndoro nodded as well.

"Elders, I bring you Ndoro of the Sesu, the Shumba hunter," Jabulani announced.

"Your influence on Kikuba is impressive, Jabulani," one of the elders said. "There has never been a time you have visited the oracle and not succeed."

The elder stood. "I am Shaihi, speaker for the elders. Your arrival is a true blessing, for the shumba is killing every day. I see you have your weapons."

Ndoro nodded.

"Good. Once you kill the shumba, you must hide them. The dendi-fari does not allow weapons in the village unless issued by him."

"Excuse me, but who is this dendi-fari?"

Shaihi cut his eyes at Jabulani, who looked away. "The dendi-fari is our master."

Ndoro's eyes went wide. "You are slaves?"

"Our village belongs to the dendi-fari of Galadima, servant of Askia Diallo."

Ndoro could not stay among these people. If the dendi-fari appeared while he was present he might be considered a slave as well. However, he was obligated to help them when he accepted their hospitality. He would have to leave as soon as he killed the beast.

"The shumba hunts you because he is old. I need help tracking him; I am not familiar with the signs of the forest. Once we know the pattern, we can plan where to bait him."

The elders nodded. "How many men will you need?"

"As many as possible."

"We will ask our families for volunteers. We will meet again this evening to discuss our plans for hunting the shumba."

Ndoro looked puzzled. "Volunteers?"

"We are elders, not Askia. We can only ask."

"I will help," Jawanza announced.

"I will, too," Kamau said, although his voice betrayed his uncertainty.

Shaihi smiled. "You have two so far."

Ndoro shrugged his shoulders. The Diaka were definitely not warriors. Sesu men and boys fought for the chance to join the simba hunts, the highest praise going to the warrior that struck the first blow. Among the Sesu, killing a simba was the highest form of bravery.

The elders dispersed to their clans. Ndoro said nothing as they walked back to the family compound. He went straight to Talana's hut, Mulugo's spirit still on his mind despite his situation. The matriarch of the Osseni clan was tending her yams, humming a song as she weeded the rows.

"Mama Talana, I must tell you something."

Talana ceased her gardening. "What is the matter, Ndoro?"

"I think a spirit is haunting me."

Talana put down her hoe and approached him. She traced his body with her palms, keeping her hands a few inches from his skin.

"I sense no spirits about you."

Ndoro sat before Talana. "You must know how I came to be here. It had nothing to do with Baba Jabulani's prayers." Ndoro told Talana his story. After he finished, she sat beside him.

"You've caused a lot of trouble for one so young, boh-boh.

Let me tell you a secret. Spirits exist among us. Some are peaceful, yet some are angry and use their second lives to seek revenge on those that harmed them while they were alive. This Mulugo was a medicine-priest, so he could be especially dangerous. Pray to your ancestors for protection, Ndoro."

Ndoro smiled. "The ancestors have done nothing but cause trouble for me. I have chosen not to listen to them."

"That is your decision," Talana replied. "Remember; if you choose to live your life without respecting the ancestors do not expect them to respect you."

Talana handed him a yam. "Now eat. You will need your strength for the days ahead. I think you will find the Diaka are not the bravest of men."

Talana's prediction was sadly true. When the elders met again that afternoon, no clan had sent men to join the hunt. It would be Jawanza, Kamau and himself.

Shaihi's face was a portrait of disappointment. "I am sorry, Ndoro. It seems our young men have no taste for hunting shumba."

"But the shumba has a taste for them," Ndoro snapped. "Jawanza, Kamau, and I will kill the shumba." With that Ndoro stalked away. Jawanza and Kamau ran to catch him. Jawanza was excited, but Kamau's face drooped with worry.

"What do we do first, Ndoro?" Jawanza asked.

"We bait him before he attacks again."

They returned to the compound, discussing their plan along the way. They found Jabulani sitting before Talana's hut, enjoying a snack of kola nuts.

"Baba," Jawanza said, "we need a goat."

Jabulani frowned but didn't argue, leading the trio to his goat herd and giving them a sickly grey animal. They led the goat through town, a parade of children and adults trailing them. Ndoro scowled at them all, still ill tempered from the Diaka reaction to the call for help.

The impromptu parade ended as they left the village and entered the surrounding clearing.

"Jawanza, where have the attacks taken place?" Ndoro asked.

"There, there and there", Jawanza answered, pointing out the directions.

"He hunts along the river's edge," Ndoro commented. "Animals are distracted when they drink, or people when they fill their calabashes."

Ndoro walked to the river, searching for crocodile sign.

"The trees come close to the river on the south," he said. "If we leave the goat too close to the shore crocodiles will surely make a meal of it."

"There is a trail that leads from the bush to the river there," Kamau said. "Elephants use it when they come to drink."

He led them to the trail. "This is an excellent ambush spot," Ndoro said. He pulled his knife, grabbed the goat and slit its throat.

Kamau was not happy. "You killed baba's goat!"

"What did you think I was going to do?" Ndoro asked. "Shumbas kill only when they have to. He will take an easy meal over a difficult one. That's why he hunts you."

Ndoro placed the goat's carcass downwind from where he thought the shumba might approach.

"We will wait in the trees. Jawanza, we need bows and poison arrows."

Jawanza ran immediately to the village. Ndoro looked at Kamau, sensing his uncertainty. He placed his hand gently on his shoulder.

"Kamau, a shumba is no different from any other animal. If you stand your ground and show no fear, he will respect you and give way."

Kamau nodded but still looked worried.

"Come," Ndoro said. "We will sit here until Jawanza returns."

Jawanza returned an hour later with the weapons.

"The both of you will hide on opposite sides of the goat," Ndoro explained. "When the shumba appears you will shoot him and I will attack him. The poison should slow him enough for me to make a quick kill." He looked at the both of them, careful to hide his fear. "Jawanza, you take first watch."

The three men separated, Jawanza and Kamau taking their positions. Ndoro sat across the path opposite the goat. Clouds slowly gathered overhead and raindrops pattered the path, quickly transforming it to a muddy mess. Ndoro frown in discomfort as he went over the plan. Sesu hunters would have taken the shumba with spears, but Ndoro did not trust his raw companions at close quarters with such a beast. Jawanza was too eager, which would make him careless, and Kamau was afraid. They were all he had; they would have to do.

Ndoro jumped from sleep, a sense of dread in his mind. He grabbed his assegai and shield and sprang to his feet, looking about desperately for Jawanza and Kamau. A scream cut through the rainy night, a sound Ndoro felt in his bones. Jawanza and Kamau emerged from their hiding places.

"What was that?" Kamau asked.

"I don't know," Ndoro replied.

"Baba Keffi!" Jawanza shouted. "His farm is near!" Jawanza sprang from the brush and ran down the road toward the sound.

Ndoro and Kamau went after him, catching him moments later.

"What is wrong with you?" Ndoro shouted. "You think you can kill this beast alone?" The three splashed down the muddy path until Ndoro spotted movement in the distance through the sheets of rain.

"Jawanza, Kamau, go to the woods quickly. Remember our plan!"

The brothers disappeared into the wet trees. Ndoro raised his shield, his assegai braced in his right hand. He stared as the image took shape as it drew nearer. It was the largest simba he'd ever seen, carrying something in his jaws. As it came closer, Ndoro saw it was a man, probably Baba Keffi. With a jerk of its massive head it tossed the body aside and fixed its eyes on Ndoro. Ndoro realized he was not confronting a normal simba. It seemed to smile as it bared its teeth and stood on its hind legs.

"Ndoro," it growled. "You did not think you would escape me so easily, did you?"

Ndoro was startled. "Mulugo?"

The shumba laughed. "I have followed you since the day you struck me down, waiting for my chance for revenge. It is time for you to die, abomination!"

Shumba Mulugo stepped toward Ndoro then roared in pain, an arrow protruding from its right shoulder. The beast reached for the arrow as if its paw was a hand. Another arrow whizzed by, missing it by inches. A third arrow struck the beast in its left paw. The beast roared again, turning his head toward Jawanza's hiding place.

Ndoro shifted his assegai and threw it as hard and as straight as he could. The projectile struck the beast in the chest and it yelped. It grasped the shaft with both paws as it stumbled away. Ndoro charged, raising his sword over his head for the killing blow. A hard blow to his jaw staggered him, the world turning dark as he flew backward and smacked into the hard mud path.

No sooner had he hit the ground was he lifted again, his shoulder on fire. The Mulugo-beast had his shoulder in its jaws, raising him from the mud. Ndoro slammed his wrist-knife from his free arm against the beast's head, but it only tightened its grip. He struck again and Mulugo dropped him. He blacked out for a moment, and then opened his eyes to see Jawanza on the creature's back, stabbing frantically with his knife.

"Kamau!" he called out. "Help us!"

Ndoro tried to lift his left arm, but it would not respond. He pushed himself up with his right arm and crawled to his assegai and shield. As he turned, Kamau stepped out onto the trail. He looked at Ndoro, then at his brother struggling with the beast, and turned and ran away. Ndoro shook his head, disappointed but not surprised. He struggled to his feet, assegai in hand and staggered back into the battle.

The Mulugo beast managed to grab hold of Jawanza and threw him into the bush. He was about to follow and finish off the Diaka when Ndoro blocked his path.

"Is this all?" he shouted. "Is the spirit of a great medicine priest weaker in death than in life? Come so I can kill you again!"

The beast let loose a roar that shook the trees. It half ran, half-stumbled toward Ndoro, apparently weakened by the poison. Ndoro crouched low, bracing himself for the attack.

"Die, abomination!" it roared. The creature leapt at Ndoro, who rolled backward onto his back. As the Mulugo-beast filled his vision Ndoro raised his assegai, bracing it as well as he could in the mud. The blade cut a path through the creature's lower jaw, tearing through the roof of its mouth and penetrating the skull to the brain. Its weight fell full on Ndoro and his right arm snapped as the breath was knocked out of his lungs. Blood and rain flowed over him as he gasped for air.

"Forget about me!" he heard Jawanza say. "Ndoro is under the shumba!"

The pressure of the shumba's body eased then was no more. Above him a circle of Diaka men stared down at him.

"Is he alive?" one asked.

Ndoro nodded his head and saw stars.

"Put him in the cart with Jawanza. The rest of you get the shumba's body. Mama Talana said we must bring it, too."

The voice giving the orders was that of Kamau. The men tried to be gentle, but Ndoro had felt less pain fighting the Mulugo-beast. They laid him down in the cart, beside Jawanza.

"You killed him," Jawanza said.

"No, we killed him," Ndoro replied.

Jawanza smiled, and then passed out. Ndoro wished he'd been so lucky. The cart ride back to the village was a terrible affair. The jostling cart amplified the shooting pain of his injuries. His rescuers were just as rough removing him from the cart and carrying him to Mama Talana's house. Two beds waited for him and Jawanza. As soon as they were eased into the beds the room crowded with the curious. Ndoro was in so much pain he was beginning to wish the shumba had killed him.

There was a sudden commotion followed by smacks, yelps and curses. The crowd fled and Talana stood alone before them, breathing heavily with an old dented orinka in her hand.

"Damn fools!" she said. "What do they think this is?" Her expression softened as she looked at Ndoro and Jawanza.

"It looks as though Kamau was the smartest of the three of you."

She pulled up a stool and sat between the beds. "Well shumba slayers, let's get on with it."

She shoved a foul-smelling ball of fat into each of their mouths and ordered them to chew. Ndoro was on his second chew when the pain in his body disappeared with his consciousness. He fell into a deep, restful sleep briefly interrupted by questions and answers he couldn't remember. When he finally awoke, his wounds were bandaged and his broken bones set. Jawanza lay beside him, still unconscious. Ndoro struggled to sit on the edge of the bed and was pleased. There was pain, but nothing he could not handle.

"What are you doing?" Talana shouted.

"Sitting."

Talana pushed him back down on the bed and he winced.

"You shouldn't be awake," she complained. "You should still be asleep. It's been only three days and the poultice was made for one week."

"I've been asleep for three days?"

Talana lifted his bandages. "Your wounds are healed!"

She removed the remainder of the bandages but left the splint on his arm.

"You have a magic about you, boy. Your wounds have mended too quickly for a normal man."

"I am Sesu," Ndoro boasted.

Talana moved the shoulder of his broken right arm and he grimaced. "Your arm is still broken, O Great Sesu. You will be with us for a while yet. Besides, you are a hero now. There are many people waiting to celebrate you and to offer their daughters for marriage."

"I can't stay," Ndoro said.

"Is it time to leave the company of slaves?"

Ndoro fell silent, embarrassed by Talana's question.

She inspected Jawanza's wounds, her back turned to Ndoro. "No need to be ashamed. You are a free man from a noble people. You should not be here. Jok created a place for everyone in this world; the Diaka are here to serve. But I feel a change coming for us. I think you are at the center of this change."

"I respect your words, Mama Talana, though I don't put much trust in feelings."

"It doesn't matter. Your bones will heal slowly. You will have to stay until the dry season."

As Talana predicted, Ndoro's rehabilitation lasted the length of the rainy season. During those damp days Ndoro gradually became a part of Jabulani's family, taking on the chores he could manage with his injured arm. He became the buffer between Jawanza and Kamau, easing the tension that developed between the brothers after the shumba hunt. Ndoro had no doubt Kamau fled in fear, but he had at least gathered himself enough to bring help, however late it had been. By the end of rainy season the brothers were speaking to each other again, much to the joy of the entire family.

That joy ended during the beginning of the dry season. The rains dwindled as the days grew shorter; soon the cloudless skies dominated the Diaka lands. Ndoro sensed a change in the attitude of the village with the season. Uneasiness replaced the dreariness of the rainy season; the villagers seemed agitated.

Ndoro sat with Jabulani in front of the walls of the compound, enjoying a snack of kola nuts.

"Baba, the village has changed since the rains. Everyone seems nervous."

"It's dry season. The dendi-fari will come soon."

"Is there a problem with the harvest?"

Jabulani took the kola nut from his mouth. "No, the harvest will be fine. Dry season is war season, and the dendi-fari is always at war."

"That should be no concern to you," Ndoro said. "Your people are not warriors."

Jabulani stared at Ndoro. "We are whatever the dendi-fari wants us to be." The old man rose and shuffled into the compound. The reason for the change in mood was obvious now; if the Diaka were called to fight, they would be slaughtered.

The dendi-fari arrived the next day during the afternoon. Ndoro was helping Mama Talana dig yams when a commotion caught their attention. Kamau came running up to them, stumbling to a stop and resting his hands on his knees, his mouth wide and gasping for air.

"What's wrong, boy?" Talana asked.

Kamau looked up. "The dendi-fari, the dendi-fari is here. I saw his camp near the river when I went to check the fish traps."

Talana froze, dropping the yam she held. Ndoro watched her trudge to the bell hanging near the front of her home. She struck the bell with a mournful rhythm, its shallow sound calling all the family members to the compound. Despite its size, the courtyard filled in moments with the extended family. They gathered about Jabulani's home, waiting for their patriarch to appear. But Jabulani was nowhere to be found.

"Ndoro, Jawanza," Talana called. "Go find your father."

The two set off immediately. The village streets emptied as other families were called to their compounds to prepare for the dendi-fari's arrival. Ndoro and Jawanza ventured outside the village and found Jabulani tending his goats at the village pasture.

"Baba," Ndoro called, "Mama sends for you."

Jabulani turned to look at the two, his face sad. "The dendi-fari is here?"

"Yes he is, baba," Jawanza replied.

Jabulani followed Ndoro and Jawanza back to the compound. The family was gone, so they made their way to the meeting tree.

"You don't have to come," Jabulani said to Ndoro.

"You have accepted me as your son. I will respect you as a father," Ndoro replied.

They hurried along, joining the family and the others as they gathered in the courtyard surrounding the meeting tree. Ndoro looked over the crowd and saw the dendi-fari sitting before the large tree on a gilded stool. He stood and the Diaka fell to their knees in unison, sprinkling their heads with dirt. Ndoro remained standing, staring at the dendi-fari. The master of the Diaka was a tall, strongly-built man with intelligent brown eyes that focused on Ndoro. Multiple topes covered his upper body to increase his girth, the outer garment a deep blue robe decorated with finely woven white patterns. Two servants stood beside him, each holding an elegant ebonywood staff capped with ivory and gold. Behind him his warriors posed, fierce men covered in dark robes and leather helmets, armed with studded shields and tall lances.

"You have his attention," Jabulani whispered. "That is not a good thing. Be careful, my Sesu son."

The Diaka were all present. Without hesitation the dendi-fari stepped to the edge of the gathering, standing before the elders crouched at his feet.

"The Diaka have served my family faithfully for many years, and I have done my best to answer your service with kindness. We accept your gifts of the harvest, the abundance a sure sign that the ancestors are content."

The dendi-fari's face changed from benevolent to serious. "As you know, I am a proud servant of the Askia and as his servant I am subject to his will. So it is with gratitude that I respond to his call in time of peril. As we speak the enemies of the High One conspire to do him harm within the borders of Bordu. The Askia has asked that I serve him by raising an army to deal with this threat and, as his servant, I have agreed. Today I ask the Diaka to do the same for me. The time of farmers has ended; as you rose to slay the shumba that hunted your own, you must rise to slay those that hunt your Askia."

The Diaka responded with utter silence. They clutched each other, their mouths moving in silent prayer. The dendi-fari paused for a moment, letting his words settle.

"In a month's time, Sanafaran Otuhu will come to accept our Diaka brothers into our ranks. We will dance together in victory when the Bordubu are destroyed."

The dendi-fari remained standing as his servants gathered his stool, placing it in its gilded chest. The Diaka dispersed; many mumbling at the misfortune the dendi-fari had placed upon them. Ndoro remained where he stood. The warriors approached him, their swords in hand. They walked up to him, forming a semi-circle about him.

"Who are you?" the closest man asked.

"I will give my answer only to the dendi-fari," Ndoro replied. "Men of equal status must speak face to face."

The warrior frowned and motioned for Ndoro to follow. They escorted him to the dendi-fari, who stood between his servants with a curious smile on his face.

"Who is this free man living among my slaves?" he asked.

"I am Ndoro kaDingane."

The dendi-fari's eyes widened with his smile. "A Sesu!" He circled Ndoro, looking him up and down. "Ndoro son of Dingane, is it? You seem to be a true warrior of the grasslands. But I ask myself, what is the son of an inkosi doing among my slaves?"

The warriors laughed at the dendi-fari's insult. Though his throat burned in anger, Ndoro held his posture. He would not lose his temper or his life because of an insult. The dendi-fari seemed to be waiting for a response, for a disappointed frown came to his face.

"You need not answer my question," the dendi-fari finally said. "No one knows the changing favors of nobles better than I. A trusted brother one day becomes a hated enemy the next."

The male servants arrived with the dendi-fari's litter.

"I am Biton Sangare, dendi-fari of the Diaka. You may stay among them if you wish, although I think you would find the hospitality of free men more comfortable."

"I am Sesu," Ndoro replied. "The simple life suits me fine. Besides, I will be on my way soon."

Biton raised an eyebrow. "Really? I wish to ask you a favor before you leave us, young Sesu."

He stepped closer to Ndoro, looking about as if concerned about being heard.

"I do your friends a great wrong by asking them to fight. They are not warriors and I fear the only benefit they will be is to catch the arrows and spears of the Bordubu. I need fighting men."

"There are brave men among them," Ndoro replied.

Biton smiled. "True, but bravery cannot stop a spear. The Sesu are trained from birth to be warriors, is that not so?"

Ndoro didn't like where this conversation was going. He nodded in response.

Biton's smile grew wider. "I have a proposal. Stay here as my representative, my koi for the Diaka. Train them in the warrior ways of the Sesu. You will be paid well, of course."

"There is no time to train them," Ndoro replied.

"I give you till next dry season. The Diaka will be spared this season's campaign if you agree to train them for next season. I can wait for trained warriors."

"That is still not enough time," Ndoro explained. "Sesu are trained from birth. No one can learn so much in so little time."

Biton's smile faded. "My Sesu friend, you must do this. Every season I raise an army in hopes of defeating the Bordubu and every season I fail. The nobles are more concerned in duels and praise-songs and the foot soldiers are no better than the Diaka. They break like twigs against the shields of the Bordubu army. The only reason that the Bordubu are not our masters is that they have no interest in subduing us. But with a trained army victory could be ours. Besides, the lives of your friends depend on your decision. Whether you agree or not, the Diaka will fight. They have a better chance of surviving if they had the skills of a Sesu."

Biton climbed into his litter. "Please consider my request. If you decide train them, send a runner to me. The Diaka know where to find me."

Biton waved a hand and the litter bearers set off down the main avenue followed by his bodyguard. Villagers prostrated as the litter passed, remaining on the ground until the entourage disappeared into the surrounding brush.

Ndoro watched the dendi-fari leave and contemplated his

words. Training the Diaka to fight was a tremendous burden to place on his young shoulders, no matter what his heritage. Though he was the son of an inkosi, he had never been trained to be an induna because of the stigma placed on him and his mother. The responsibility he craved as a Sesu had been granted to him among strangers.

Jabulani interrupted his thoughts. "The dendi-fari spoke to you. What were his words?"

Ndoro looked at his adopted father and realized the wisdom of the dendi-fari. He knew Ndoro would help the Diaka not because he was asked, but because he truly cared for them.

"I have until next dry season to make you fighting men."

"Ayha! Ayha! I praise the spirits for sending you!"

Diaka ran to them upon hearing Jabulani's shouting. Ndoro attempted to calm him down.

"Baba, listen to me! You still have to fight."

"But we will fight like warriors and bring honor to our families," Jabulani sang.

Jawanza and Kamau were the first to reach them. Before they said a word Jabulani raised his hand.

"Gather the elders and bring them to the grove," he ordered. "Come, Ndoro. We will wait for them."

Jabulani grasped his arm and almost dragged him back to the largest tree. Ndoro sat under the heavy branches, his head reeling as the crowd gathered again, but this time in optimistic expectation. The elders appeared soon afterwards. There was not a happy face among them. Shaihi's voice was tense when he spoke.

"What is going on, Jabulani?"

"The dendi-fari has postponed our service until next dry season. He has made Ndoro our koi. He is to train our men in the Sesu warrior way."

Shaihi's eyebrows rose as he looked to Ndoro. "Is this true?"

"Yes," Ndoro answered.

Shaihi exhaled. "The ancestors truly listen to you, Jabulani." Shaihi prostrated before Ndoro and sprinkled dirt on his head. The other elders repeated the gesture; Ndoro reached down to pick each man up.

"Please, don't do this. I agreed to train you, nothing more."

"You are the son of a chief, are you not?" Shaihi asked.

Ndoro nodded.

"Then you were born for this responsibility."

Jabulani touched Ndoro's shoulder.

"Shaihi and I are old enough to remember the last time the Diaka marched off to war for the dendi-fari. We watched our fathers and brothers leave this village, never to return. They, like us, were farmers, not warriors. They were never trained to fight. Your knowledge will give us a chance at least to come home."

"I can't promise you that," Ndoro said.

"With your training, we can at least hope," Shaihi replied.

Ndoro felt trapped. The Diaka and the dendi-fari were depending on him. Maybe what little he knew might help his adopted tribe, but he doubted it. Still, there was hope among the Diaka and he would not rob them of that.

"We don't have much time," Shaihi warned. "The seasons will pass like a cheetah. Koi Ndoro, what do you wish us to do?"

Ndoro was speechless. This was happening too fast. He needed time to understand this sudden change in status.

"Everyone, return to your homes," he finally said. "I need time to organize. Shaihi, Jabulani, can I depend on the wisdom of the elders?"

"Of course you can," Jabulani answered.

Drumming erupted in the distance and the city exploded in celebration. Ndoro watched the Diaka dance as the weight of responsibility crashed down on his shoulders. There was so much to do, so much to plan and he had no experience at all. For the first time in his young life Ndoro felt like praying.

Jabulani made his way to Ndoro. "There is a house in the compound we will prepare for you until your own compound is complete."

"I don't need a compound!"

"Of course you do. You are a koi now. You will need a compound for your personal needs and to hold the homes of your officers."

There was no stopping Jabulani. Ndoro nodded and followed his family in a jubilant parade back to the compound.

The house Jabulani gave him had belonged to one of his daughters who married Shaihi's eldest son two years before Ndoro's arrival. Talana had kept it in good shape, the conical thatch roof recently rewoven with fresh grass and the interior floor swept smooth. Ndoro had nothing except his weapons, but that was soon remedied. Gifts came from every family; cooking pots, stools, bed boards, ceremonial masks and even livestock and grain. Jabulani was right when he said he would need his own compound.

Ndoro had little time to be grateful for his fortune, for his every waking moment was filled with his new duty. Since he had no idea what to do, he began by using his own training as an example. A week after his dubious promotion he gathered the elders to explain his plan.

"Each family will establish a group of young men, an intanga. The oldest male, the induna, will act as leader of the group," he began. "The group males will be given their own section of the family compound where they will live together. The eldest male will report to me every day for training. When he returns to his compound, he will instruct his group. Once a week, all the males will meet in the village pasture to train together. We begin training today."

The elders returned to their homes to convey the orders. Ndoro walked with Jabulani, his eyes downcast.

"What is wrong, Ndoro?"

"Nothing." Ndoro realized his plan was not the best, but it was the only way he could train every man in time.

His mood lifted when he entered his house. Mama Talana was cooking, the smell of her delicious stew thick in the air. Someone else was with her, a young woman Ndoro did not recognize. She was obviously Talana's daughter, possessing the same intense eyes. Unlike other Diaka women who braided their hair, her hair was short. It reminded him of the women of his homeland.

Talana noticed him staring at the woman and laughed.

"Sit down and eat, boy," she ordered. "These stupid men act as if you've grown ten years in a day."

Ndoro took the bowl from Talana eagerly and ate. The stew was tasty and soothing as always. As he finished, Talana brought the woman to him.

"This is my daughter Sarama. She had come back to us from the Diarra clan. Her husband died of sickness six months ago. We were finally able to return the lobola given for her marriage."

"It had to be a very large lobola for such a beautiful woman," Ndoro said.

Sarama and Talana smiled. "You have a sweet tongue, koi-boy," Talana said. "Be careful how you use it."

Talana took his bowl and scooped out more stew. "Sarama

will help maintain your compound when it is complete."

Ndoro placed his bowl down. "I accepted this duty because of my debt to your family. Don't look at me as a master. Look at me as your son."

Talana laughed. "Don't worry about that, boh-boh. Mama Talana can see the child in your eyes. The time will come when you are truly the master of the Diaka, but not now."

Ndoro turned his attention to Sarama. "I thank you for your help."

Sarama shrugged. "It's nothing. You honor my family with your presence, and I can see you are loved by them. It will give me a chance to see if you are worthy of such admiration."

"You are truly your mother's daughter." He finished his stew and handed the bowl to Sarama. "I must meet the men at the village square. We begin training today."

Ndoro grabbed his weapons and left the house, jogging to the village pasture just outside the walls. The soon to be indunas waited for him, Jawanza and Kamau among the chosen. The group was a disappointing sight. Their shields and spears were barely sturdy enough for hunting, let alone fighting. Old rusted swords hung at their sides, more useless than the spears they carried. He would have to meet with the elders to see if there was a nearby village or town possessing a blacksmith skilled in weaponry. If not, they would have to ask the dendi-fari for help.

The men and boys fell silent as he drew a line with the tip of his assegai in the dirt.

"Take a place at the line," he ordered.

The Diaka formed a ragged line, their eyes wandering. Only Jawanza gave his full attention. Ndoro charged forward, attacking an older man who chatted with a friend. Some of the others yelled, but it was too late. Ndoro slammed his shield into the man, knocking him into the dirt. In a fluid motion Ndoro stabbed the man in the thigh, not deep enough to maim him but enough to draw blood. The man yelped and grabbed his thigh as he scrambled away. The others, including Jawanza, fell into shocked silence. Ndoro walked back to his place on the opposite side of the line.

"It can happen that quickly," he explained. "One lapse and you are among the ancestors. If you wish to have a chance to live, you will remember everything I teach you today and now on. You will go back to your compounds and teach your brothers, and all of you will practice during every spare moment. If you are lucky you will learn enough to bring glory upon yourself and your ancestors."

Ndoro began with simple blocking and thrusting drills that lasted until dusk. They trudged back to their compounds, Jawanza, Kamau and Ndoro returning together in exhausted silence. On his way he received word that the elders had sent a message to Jehnay requesting new weapons. They did not know when the weapons would arrive. When Ndoro entered his house, Sarama was there, preparing his evening meal. He collapsed on his bed.

"The drill went well?" she asked.

"It went long. They picked up well enough, but this is impossible. I had my entire life to learn what I know."

"A bull grows his ears before his horns," Sarama replied. "Be patient, they will learn."

She handed him his bowl and he ate slowly, watching Sarama as she put away the cooking pots. She had the soothing spirit of her mother, but her body was more than just a distraction. She moved as if she wanted him to notice her, though he also knew it just might be him imagining an invitation. The turmoil of his life had never given him the time to get to know any woman. Had Talana paired them together for just that reason? He looked away from her and into his bowl. Ndoro decided he was reading his own thoughts into Sarama's motions. Besides, despite everything, she was still a slave. He knew Sesu custom well; a clear line separated free men from slaves, a line even the inkosi could not cross. But he was not in Sesuland.

The weeks ran by like the Nyoka as Ndoro trained the Diaka. His days were filled with drills, sparring, mock battles and weapon training, leaving him exhausted by nightfall. Sarama was always there when he returned, preparing his food and listening to him recount the day. Her replies were always encouraging and her advice full of wisdom. Ndoro became more and more impressed with her as time passed.

As Sarama foretold, the bull began to grow its horns. The Diaka took their training to heart and it began to show. Each family's intanga became adept at the drills, impressing Ndoro with their precision. A sense of pride emerged among the groups, each clan creating a family totem that they carried to training displayed atop a staff. Jabulani's clan chose the goat in honor of their patriarch and his love of goat herding.

The rains came and the drills continued despite the planting season. With training constantly interrupted, Ndoro spent less time with the men. He occupied his time with the elders, trying to find out as much as possible about the style of fighting in this land. What he heard disturbed him. The Sesu style of the swift mass attack was not done. Instead, large armies met face to face in flat fields of grass, following the ritual of exchanging insults and watching nobles duel in individual combat. Sometimes a battle never occurred, especially if one side realized the nyama of its opponents was too strong to overcome. But when a battle did occur it was often brutal and bloody. Ndoro trudged back to his home, his mind heavy with this new revelation. As always, Sarama was waiting.

"What did the elders say?" she asked.

Ndoro collapsed on his stool. "Everything I've done is wrong. It's all wrong!"

Sarama handed him his bowl. "I have waited on you for four months, Koi Ndoro. You have never done anything wrong."

Ndoro shrugged. "How can you be so sure?"

Sarama gave Ndoro one of her gentle smiles. "You are too young to be the man the elders wish you to be. But you did not walk away; you stayed to teach what you could. You did not do anything wrong; you did something different. Now you must change."

"Change to what?" Ndoro fell back onto his cot. "I know nothing of this way of war."

"That is your strength." Sarama sat beside him. "When a people follow a tradition, they never question it. They obey because it is all they know. But you, Koi Ndoro, have the advantage of being free of these traditions. You see our ways from the outside with no care of right or wrong. What is obvious to you is invisible to us. There is strength in our ways, but there may also be weaknesses."

Ndoro sat upright. "Strengths and weaknesses."

Sarama stood. "Eat your stew. It will help you think."

"Thank you, Sarama."

Sarama smiled. "See. A Diaka man would never thank a woman for her advice."

Sarama began to leave when Ndoro stood.

"You don't have to go," he said.

Sarama smiled again. "One change at a time, Koi Ndoro."

Ndoro finished his stew then spent the rest of the night analyzing the words of the elders. He drew diagrams in the floor of his house, trying his best to visualize the patterns explained to him. Look for strengths and weaknesses, Sarama advised. Slowly the patterns emerged. Chaos became coherent; the patterns became clear.

The next morning a sliver of sunshine escaped through the constant clouds and fell on Ndoro's face. He sprang from his cot, gathered his weapons and rushed out of his house to the training field. Splashing to the top hill in the center of the field, he banged the muster drum. The warriors charged the hill moments later.

Ndoro gazed down upon them, barely able to contain himself.

"Diaka, we have trained hard and you have done well. I have given you all I know, and you have honored me by learning with all you have."

"But I have taken you down the wrong path. Today we will begin again not from the very beginning, but taking a different path. When we are done, the word Diaka will strike fear in our enemies and the griots will sing our song for generations!"

The Diaka cheered but Ndoro waved them silent.

"We have a lot to learn in a little time. Our transformation begins today."

The rainy season ended with a violent storm that damaged crops and destroyed a few homes outside the village. Everyone was involved with repairing the damage when the dendi-fari and his entourage entered the village that afternoon. The council drum summoned all to the meeting tree. Ndoro was with Sarama inspecting his new compound when he heard the summons.

"The season passed too quickly," he said.

Sarama place her hand on his shoulder. "We are ready."

Ndoro grabbed her hand. "I don't know how long we will

be gone, but when I return I would like to spend more time with you."

Sarama smiled. "You are a young man, Ndoro. There are many younger women in this village that desire your time."

"My time belongs to you."

Sarama's face became serious. "I don't deny my feelings for you, but I will not be anyone's concubine. As a slave, that is all I can be to you."

Ndoro decided to show Sarama how serious he felt. He kissed her.

"You told me yourself that I could change what I wished. When I return the Diaka will no longer be slaves."

"A young man's dream," Sarama replied. "Go now. The dendi-fari awaits you."

The dendi-fari sat on his gilded stool beneath the meeting tree, flanked by his bodyguards and another group of men Ndoro did not recognize. Their rich garments signified noble families, and the presence of griots confirmed his thoughts. The Diaka surrounded them, prostrate, their head covered with dust. Ndoro walked before the dendi-fari and assumed the same position.

"So Sesu, you have remained to fulfill your promise," Biton commented. "Rise and show your face."

Ndoro stood. "I gave my word."

One of the noble warriors came forward. He was a head shorter than Ndoro, but powerfully built.

"What good is the word of a Sesu?" he said. "They say your people are cattle thieves with delusions of greatness."

Ndoro looked at this intruder into his conversation and frowned. It was an insult that demanded a response, but Ndoro was not about to kill this man with so much at stake for the Diaka.

Biton raised his staff for their attention. "I see only you, Ndoro. Where are your warriors?"

Ndoro raised his orinka and the muster drums answered. A chant rose in the distance, deep male voices resonating in time with the drums. Down the avenue they trotted, five hundred strong, marching in family groups. Once they reached the plaza the rhythm changed. The family groups broke into ranks of archers, spearmen and heavy infantry. Ndoro jabbed his orinka in the air and the drumming ceased. He turned slowly to face Biton, cutting a glance at the arrogant nobleman.

"The Diaka await your command."

Biton smiled broadly, apparently pleased. The nobleman stepped forward again.

"They can march, but can they fight?"

"There is only one way to find out," Ndoro replied.

"Koi Ndoro, this skeptic is Otuhu, a Soninke horseman and Sanafaran of my army," Biton explained.

Ndoro was not impressed. He bowed, but did not give Otuhu the same respect he bestowed on Biton.

"Don't assume your claim of Sesu lineage makes you my equal," Otuhu warned.

Biton stepped in before Ndoro was able to reply. "We will spend the night here, and then march to the other villages in the morning."

With that the dendi-fari retired to his litter. Otuhu followed, glaring at Ndoro. Biton's bearers lifted him and carried him to Ndoro.

"Our camp is only a few miles from the village. Join us."

"Thank you for the invitation but tonight must be for my men and their families."

Biton nodded in agreement. "Celebrate well tonight. I

find it is the best way to build courage in men who are about to die. I will send two bulls for your feast."

To a Sesu, it was an expensive gift. Ndoro could barely hide his gratefulness. "Thank you, dendi-fari."

Biton waved his flywhisk and the entourage departed. Ndoro needed to say nothing, for all had been heard. The streets filled with jubilant hordes and the warriors broke rank to dance with their families. Ndoro was swamped by Jabulani's clan. He smiled and hugged and kissed them all, but inside he was in turmoil. He searched the throng for Sarama and found her standing too far away, her eyes meeting his, her smile bringing a similar smile to his face.

The feast began immediately. The village center was quickly decorated while cooking pots were rushed from family compounds to prepare the food. A group of excited men attacked the ground with shovels and picks, rushing to dig the cooking pit to roast the bulls. Chickens and goats were slaughtered, while Talana, using a special magic just for such an occasion, brought hundreds of fish to the surface of the river for the children to harvest. Two of the dendi-fari's guards arrived with the bulls soon afterwards. The only break in the celebrating occurred as Jabulani gave praise to the ancestors and offered the bulls in sacrifice.

By nightfall everyone sat in a circle around the meeting tree, the area illuminated by wavering torch lights. Drummers played while groups of dancers from different families took turns performing under the broad branches of the meeting tree. Ndoro occupied the honored position closest to the tree with Jabulani, Jawanza, Talana and the rest of the clan close by. He was served the choicest meat from the bull as well as given the honor of sampling every item first before it was served to the rest of the celebrants. Never in his life had he eaten so much food. His stomach was as tight as a water bag. Sarama was also there, sitting among her sisters. Ndoro saw them talking as they looked at him. Sarama chatted and laughed, keeping her penetrating eyes on him at all times. Ndoro felt his skin warm from the heat of her gaze.

Jabulani slapped his back. "Never have I seen such a feast! The Diaka are truly blessed this night."

"When we return from battle, there will be no other feast grander than this," Ndoro replied.

Jabulani put his fingers to his lips and shushed Ndoro. "Don't dwell on the future. A warrior must live for the day, for it is all he has."

Ndoro laughed. "You talk as if you're the warrior!"

A swarm of Jabulani's grandchildren appeared, their little hands pulling at Ndoro.

"Dance, dance!" they shouted. "You must dance!"

Ndoro laughed as they pulled him to his feet. "I know no dances. At least not Diaka ones."

"The cattle raid dance!" Jawanza chimed. "Show them the cattle raid dance."

Ndoro never imagined the training movements taught to all Sesu boys as a dance. As he felt the rhythm of the drummers, he decided to give it a try. He took the dancers spot under the branches. As the drummers played he fell into the movements, his body moving sharp yet fluid as he crouched low, performing the sleeping simba form. He closed his eyes to feel the music while he walked, ran and thrust imaginary spears at empty enemies. The roar of the crowd forced his eyes open to see the indunas, his officers, joining him. They chanted his instructions in time and Ndoro finally heard the music in his words. This was how the Diaka learned what he taught them. Behind the walls of the compounds the training had become a dance, his words a song.

As family members joined in, Ndoro saw the effect these new warriors had on the other Diaka. He realized even if all of them died tomorrow, the Diaka would always have this moment. It was the night they stood as men. They would march away the next day not as conscripts, but as warriors.

The celebration did not end until well into the night. Ndoro staggered to his house, more from a full stomach than the insanely potent millet beer served throughout the night. He waved his companions good night as he entered his house. He barely sat on his bed when Sarama entered.

"Sarama? What are you doing?"

Sarama put her finger to her lips. She undid the wrap around her waist and quickly removed her top. Her body was as beautiful as her knowing smile, lighting the room with her aural light. She moved up to him slowly, placing her hands on his shoulders and pushing him down on the bed.

"I will not be your concubine," she whispered. "Promise me, Ndoro."

"I promise," Ndoro replied, his voice tight with longing.

Sarama disarmed him with another of her smiles. "Now let me show you why my lobola was so generous."

Ndoro awoke alone. If Diaka customs were like the Sesu, it would be an embarrassment for Sarama to have spent the night with him as a single woman. He was glad though; the time had come for the Diaka to march off to war. He dressed carefully, donning the uniform crafted by his adopted sisters. As he placed his plumed helmet on his head Talana entered his house.

"The Great Koi is ready to begin his legend?" she asked.

Ndoro could not match her jovial mood. "Mama, you bless me with your company."

"And what of Sarama's company?"

Ndoro eyes widened as he was flushed with surprise and embarrassment.

Talana shuffled toward him as she spoke. "Do you think I would not find out, boh-boh? Sarama is my favorite; we have no secrets between us. I suggest you begin gathering your lobola. She's very valuable."

Talana then reached into her pouch. "It is said we all come into this world possessing a certain amount of nyama, or spirit strength. Some men possess more than others, which is why some men are obas while others are slaves. But a man can increase his nyama by gathering that of other men or animals."

She handed him a necklace of cowry shells with two simba fangs in the center. "I know you have the hairballs of your first Shumba kill. Add to that the killing teeth of the demon-shumba. They will increase your nyama."

"Thank you mama," he replied. He bent down and Talana tied the necklace around his neck.

"Now, you fight and come back home. My daughter need not lose a husband before she marries him." She kissed his cheek, hugged him then opened the door.

Ndoro stepped outside and the muster drums rumbled. He set out at a warrior pace to the village pasture, the warriors of his intanga falling into rank beside and behind him. They ran from compound to compound, with the other intangas joining them until they all ran together through the town. Very few villagers came out to see them go. Many were still recovering from the night's celebration while others saw no joy in their leaving. Though Ndoro promised to bring all the warriors home, no one in the village would hold him to such an impossible vow. Some men would die, it was certain, but at least these Diaka had the chance to come home. Ndoro had given them skill and by doing so, he gave them a chance to survive.

The dendi-fari's camp was five miles north of the village. As Ndoro led the warriors up the steep road leading to the site, he scanned the woods filled with warriors from other villages. They were obviously conscripts, all clothed in whatever they possessed, their spears old and worn, their leather shields ragged. They looked upon the Diaka as they did the Songhai horsemen. It was a look that did not go unnoticed among the ranks.

Ndoro called the Diaka to a halt before a ring of tents in the center of camp. The flap of the largest tent opened and Otuhu emerged.

"You are late," he accused.

"I was not told when to arrive," Ndoro retorted.

"Don't take Biton's fondness of you as a sign of acceptance, cattle thief," Otuhu warned. "This is the second time you have insulted me. There will not be a third."

Ndoro said nothing, his every effort focused on keeping him from throwing his orinka at Otuhu's head.

Otuhu spun and strode back to the tent. "Come, the others wait."

Biton stood in the center of the tent beside a huge canvas map that hung from the center. The noble leaders of the cavalry sat in front. Behind them sat the leaders of the infantry units. They were less finely dressed, bearing few amulets on their old uniforms.

Biton looked away from the map as Otuhu and Ndoro entered.

"I see you found him," Biton said.

Otuhu said nothing as he took his place among the cavalry. Ndoro sat beside the infantry captains.

"Most of you are not aware of the situation in Jehnay, so let me update you. The interregnum has lasted almost eight months and the city is in chaos. Askia Kasali's death was a great loss. The elders have yet to select a successor among his sons, for they don't think any of them have the strength to lead. The rumor is that they wish to ask Kasali's cousin, Jafaru, to rule. But Jafaru is not Songhai and does not deserve the title of Askia.

"I have pledged my loyalty to the Askia's eldest son, Sudetu. He informed me that word of the elders' preference has reach Jafaru and that he is preparing an army to march to Jehnay to receive the blessing of the elders. One road leads from Nala to Jehnay, and that road runs through Galadima. Last season, we attempted to take Jafaru from Bordu and failed. This season, we are charged to keep Jafaru and his army in Bordu until Sudetu has made his claim to the Stool. Once that has been secured, he will send his warriors to help us."

Otuhu stood and joined Biton. "The Nala road is most narrow here." He pointed at the map. "Jafaru's army is larger that ours, so we must meet them where their size will be at a disadvantage."

"What about the river?" Ndoro asked.

Otuhu glared at him. "As I said, we will position ourselves here, where the road is narrow."

Ndoro stood. "What about the river?"

Otuhu grabbed his sword hilt and advanced toward Ndoro. Biton placed a hand on his shoulder.

"What about the river, Ndoro?" Biton asked.

"If you know he has a larger army, I'm sure he knows as well. He can engage our forces at the gap and send his reserves through the forest to outflank us. If we make a stand at the bridge we lessen the chance of being flanked. If we destroy the bridge, we will force Jafaru's army to ford the river. Our archers could drive them back."

"What you suggest is not honorable!" Otuhu shouted. "I should expect as much from a cow thief."

"It is your decision, Dendi-fari. I would follow Otuhu's plan if you wish to die with honor."

The nobles came to their feet and stood beside Otuhu, showing their support.

"We have always trusted the wisdom of Otuhu," Biton replied. "He has led us to many opportunities for honor and praise-songs, but not many victories."

Otuhu looked stunned. "Dendi-fari! You don't mean to listen to the Sesu?"

Biton approached Otuhu and placed a hand on his shoulder. "These are different times, my friend. This is no battle for honor. We must stop Jafaru."

He looked at Ndoro. "Take your Diaka to Ingera. Hold Jafaru at the bridge as long as you can. We will position the remaining warriors at Otuhu's point. When you can hold no longer, send a runner to tell us you are falling back. Jafaru will think we are retreating and drop his guard. Then we will smash him."

Ndoro was impressed with Biton's solution. Not only had he come up with a suitable compromise, he'd combined both tactics into an unbeatable strategy.

"It is a sound plan," Otuhu admitted. "I doubt the cow stealer and his slaves can hold the bridge long enough to make much of a difference."

"If we are not capable of holding the bridge, you won't have to worry about us anymore," Ndoro replied.

Otuhu smiled. "Let them go."

Ndoro bowed to both men as he exited the tent. Otuhu's arrogance challenged his patience. In Selike a stick fight would have been inevitable, giving him a chance to beat some respect into the haughty Soninke. He pushed that emotion aside as he reached the Diaka camp. His warriors had separated themselves from the other clans, huddling around weak fires. Jawanza and the other indunas gathered around him as he entered the camp.

"What is the word?" Jawanza asked.

"We march to the Ingera Bridge. Our task is to hold the bridge as long as possible."

"We will do this alone?" Kamau asked.

Ndoro felt the uncertainty among them all except Jawanza, who was brave beyond common sense. Jawanza believed in him totally and would do whatever he asked. But Jawanza was not the only Diaka.

"We trained two seasons for this moment," he said to them. "We cannot run away from this responsibility. We must face this battle like men, as Diaka. The others are conscripts, forced to fight by the nobles. They will be no help to us. We stand a better chance standing together at the Ingera Bridge."

"I have no idea how large Jafaru's army is, but I do know the heart of everyone before me. We will make our stand at the bridge and Jafaru's army will not pass."

Ndoro grabbed Kamau by the shoulders. "I need you to take the archers back to the village."

Kamau looked embarrassed. "Why, Koi Ndoro?"

Ndoro knew what Kamau was thinking, what the others thought. "I need you to meet us at the bridge, but I want you to come by the river."

Kamau's eyes brightened. "As you wish, Koi Ndoro." He bowed and left immediately, gathering the archers for the march back to the village.

"The rest of you go back to your units and form ranks. We leave immediately."

The Diaka departure broke the quiet tension of the camp. Kamau and the archers were the first to leave; Ndoro and the remaining Diaka pulled out an hour later. They headed northeast on the Nala road, marching through a gauntlet of Soninke conscripts who yelled insults and laughed. The Diaka showed no response; each man's face was an emotionless mask, eyes locked forward. Ndoro was stoic as well, although inside his mind swirled in a storm of emotions. The excitement in his heart was dampened by uncertainty of what lay ahead and the fear of the battle's outcome. Would the Diaka fight as they had been trained? Would he stand strong as their leader? The questions faded into his mind as he concentrated on the march.

The Ingera Bridge stood fifty miles northeast of the camp, four days march at a warrior's pace. The road they followed meandered through dense woods, occasionally interrupted by tall grasses and low trees. Ndoro pick a small clearing for the first night's camp, preferring the safety of the open field to the closeness of the forest. They ate and rested that night, rousing before daylight to continue their trek. By nightfall of the second day they were in forest again, slowed only by a passing herd of elephants sauntering across the path. Another short night and the Diaka were on their feet again, running down the wooded slope to the bridge.

Ndoro ran the last miles of the road cautiously. For three days the road revealed no signs of life other than the elephant herd and the canopy birds. They'd passed no one traveling the well-used road. To Ndoro it was a sure sign Jafaru knew their plans and might be on the move. He chose not to share his thoughts with the rest of the Diaka. He would get them to the bridge first; after a good rest he would deal with his misgivings.

That respite was not to be. As they came about the last bend in the highway leading to the bridge, Ndoro saw what he dreaded. An advance party of Jafaru's army had reached the river first. Tents stood on both banks, the Bordubu warriors going about their daily business. Ndoro raised his hand and the Diaka halted. They moved quietly back out of view. Without his summons his indunas came forward.

"Jafaru is here," Ndoro stated. "Jawanza, come with me."

Ndoro plunged into the bush with Jawanza close behind. Together they crept through the dense foliage, cutting a straight path to the road's edge. Ndoro peered through the leaves at his enemy.

"They are resting. I believe they've just arrived. Come, we don't have much time."

The duo made their way back to the waiting officers.

"Bring the throwers forward. Everyone else draw your assegais."

Ndoro looked at each induna eye to eye. They were as ready as they would ever be.

"Throwers advance." The throwers moved into position, nervous faces on every man. Ndoro smiled, placing a hand of each of their shoulders.

"This is our moment," he said. "Make your ancestors proud."

Ndoro and turned and ran into the open with the throwers, their javelins in hand and across their backs. They reached throwing range undetected, the complacent Bordubu sentries resting on their shields.

The first volley rained down of the Bordubu without

warning, the silence destroyed by the cries of wounded and dying men, a sound which caused the throwers to hesitate with their second volley.

"Your brothers are depending on your actions today," Ndoro scolded. " Don't disappoint them!"

The throwers hurled another volley as the warriors scrambled for cover. Ndoro signaled and the throwers fell back, making way for the foot soldiers.

Ndoro said nothing as he and his warriors ran to the bridge. The Bordubu scrambled to form ranks before the attack, but the Diaka charge was too swift. Ndoro met the first man with a push of his shield and thrusting spear. To his relief the Diaka fell in beside him, fighting with silent efficiency. They drove the Bordubu onto and across the bridge in minutes. With space on the opposite bank the Diaka formed a solid wall of shields and spears, thrusting the Bordubu back until they faltered and ran down the road to Nala.

A cheer broke loose from the Diaka so loud it startled the birds in the canopy above. Ndoro was swept by a rush of relief and pride, jabbing his assegai in the air as he shouted. But as he turned toward the bridge, the weight of responsibility settled again on his shoulders. There were wounded and dead before him. Many of them were Diaka.

"Come", he ordered. "We must tend to our brothers."

Some of the Diaka were healers and they went to their task immediately. The wounded were treated and bandaged, while the dead were prayed over and covered with their shields. Ndoro sent a patrol down the road toward Nala, and then sent runners back to the bulk of the army waiting at the pass. As he checked the men, he glanced downriver. The archers had not arrived. He began to doubt his decision to send Kamau back to the village for the canoes.

Jawanza came to his side, his face beaming.

"We won, Ndoro, we won!"

Ndoro smiled. "Yes, but this is just the first test. We..."

Shouting burst from the trees, the ground trembling under Ndoro's feet. One of the Diaka sent on patrol toward Nala came into view, waving his hands and shouting as loud as possible.

"Horsemen are coming!

The man jumped into the bush as the Bordubu cavalry appeared. They formed a line that stretched from one side of the road to the other. Horses and riders were shrouded in quilted kapok armor, each rider carrying a two-headed heavy lance.

"Form ranks!" Ndoro shouted. The Diaka abandoned the shorter assegais for their longer lances. Ndoro formed the line at the entrance to the bridge, using the narrow way to restrict the number of horsemen that could bear down on them. The sight and sounds of the charging horses became more ominous as they neared. The riders lowered their lances in unison, their wide double blades pointed at the Diaka line. It was more than the neophyte warriors could take. Those in the rear ran for the cover of the forest. Others climbed the sides of the bridge and leapt into the river. Only Jawanza and a handful of warriors remained at the bridge. Ndoro had no choice but to pull back. They ran across the bridge following the other Diaka into the bush. As he jumped into the temporary safety of the foliage, a second plan formed in his mind. The Diaka had to retake the bridge; he would not give Otuhu the satisfaction of being the predictor of their defeat. If he had just a little time to regroup, he could turn this retreat into an advantage.

A hail of arrows stopped the Bordubu attack midway across the bridge. Ndoro ran to the edge of the road to see a magnificent sight. Diaka canoes filled with archers spanned the river from bank to bank. The bowmen fired with uncanny accuracy from the swaying boats, their missiles tearing through the Bordubu's protective kapok. It was all the time Ndoro needed to regroup. With his intanga surrounding him he charged back to the road. The Bordubu cavalry milled about on the bridge, some throwing spears at the archers while others attempted to regroup to renew the assault.

Ndoro ran into the confusion, throwing his spear into the nearest horseman. He pulled his sword as he grabbed another rider and toppled him from his mount. The other Diaka followed his technique, swarming around the cavalry men and dismounting them. The riders on the opposite side of the bridge turned and rode away.

Again the Diaka celebrated and again Ndoro checked their enthusiasm.

"Regroup!" he shouted. Ndoro sprinted to the edge of the bridge and called the archers. Kamau was the first to the bridge.

"Well done, brother," Ndoro said. Jawanza ran to his brother and hugged him.

"Fall in with the others. We must follow the Bordubu immediately."

"Biton ordered us only to hold the bridge," Kamau said.

"The Bordubu are broken," Ndoro replied, annoyed that Kamau mentioned Biton's name. "If we wait for Otuhu and the others we will lose our advantage. We must move now or die."

The Diaka pursued the Bordubu, leaving a few warriors behind to tend to the wounded and the dead. Ndoro was wary of ambushes along the way, but the Bordubu seemed to be in full retreat. They came across scattered bodies; the Bordubu abandoned their wounded to increase their pace. The cruel tactic did not work. By dusk the Diaka saw Bordubu stragglers before them.

The highway grew wider as they advanced on Nala. The thick brush scattered into the grasslands and small abandoned farms appeared on the darkening horizon. By nightfall Ndoro could see the outer walls of Nala. The Bordubu fled across the field surrounding the city, never stopping to defend. They ran into the city gates which closed quickly behind them.

Ndoro waved his shield. The Diaka stopped before the bleached stone walls, panting but maintaining formation as they awaited orders. Though they proved themselves in open combat, they had no experience in siege warfare. Ndoro himself had no knowledge of such fighting. As much as he hated to admit, they would have to wait for Otuhu and the rest of the Soninke army before advancing further.

The Diaka put on a belligerent display, beating their shields and yelling insults before retreating to the safety of the woods to set up camp. Ndoro ordered sentries at the wood's boundary, rotating the guards throughout the night. He fell into a heavy, dreamless sleep, totally exhausted from the victorious day.

He awoke to the light of dawn as it weaved its way into the forest. The sentries had kept their watch during the night, reporting no movements outside the walls of Nala. The men were awake and eating when they heard the approaching rumble of Otuhu and his noble cavalry. The sanafaran wasted no time, galloping through the bush to Ndoro's tent. He leapt off his horse and marched to Ndoro, who sat before his fire roasting a freshly killed rabbit.

"You were told to hold the bridge!" Otuhu shouted.

"I did," Ndoro replied.

Otuhu trembled as he spoke, his hand seeking the hilt

of his sword. "You have no respect for my authority. When this campaign is over, you and I will deal with this, cow stealer."

Ndoro stood, looking directly into the sanafaran's eyes.

"We stand before the ramparts of Nala, a goal that was unattainable until this day. Only a wall stands between you and Jafaru, and you complain about respect? If you wish my respect, earn it."

Ndoro glanced down at Otuhu's hand. "The next time you touch your sword hilt before me be prepared to draw your blade."

"Will we fight the Bordubu or each other?"

Biton made his way through the bush accompanied by his bodyguards, stepping between Ndoro and Otuhu.

"Ndoro is correct about one thing, Otuhu. You should be thankful we are here. Though I must say his tactics concern me, especially the lack of respect. But what matters is what has been accomplished. Well done."

Otuhu glared at Ndoro. "You disobeyed orders and moved forward without the support of the rest of the army."

"The Bordubu fell apart," Ndoro repeated. "We had to pursue them to prevent them from regrouping."

Biton looked at Otuhu and the nobleman looked at the ground.

"It was a good decision," Otuhu admitted. "Now that we have Jafaru trapped we can lay siege to the city. I'll instruct the men to begin building a siege town immediately."

Biton wave his hand. "I have no time for a siege. Once the elders make their pronouncement, Songhai support may sway in Jabaru's favor. We must return to Jehnay with his head now."

"Now is the time to honor tradition," Otuhu urged. "If I challenge Jafaru to duel he must accept. It would be a great dishonor to refuse me. His griot would sing his shame the rest of his life."

"Be careful, Otuhu," Biton warned. "Jafaru is a skilled warrior. He's slain many nobles to reach the position he holds among the elders."

Otuhu mounted his horse. "If he kills me he deserves to be Askia. My death will be honorable and the praise-songs will record my valor."

Biton's expression showed unhappiness with Otuhu's decision.

"Losing you is not a situation I look forward to, honor or not."

"You have the cattle thief," Otuhu replied. "Maybe he and his slaves will find a way to fly over the walls of Nala and carry Jafaru to you."

Despite the insult, Ndoro gained a grudging respect for Otuhu. A challenge between two talented warriors was well known among the Sesu. It was the future he envisioned for himself once he returned to Selike to confront his father.

"I wish you well," Ndoro said.

Otuhu scowled. "Wishes have no place on the battlefield."

"You will need the parley sword," Biton suggested. The dendi-fari sent his servants to fetch the ceremonial weapon.

Otuhu summoned his squires. "Bring me my father's sword."

The squires hurried to Otuhu's pack horses and returned with an ebonywood box decorated with intricate carvings and cowry shells. They placed the box down at the sanafaran's feet and then backed away. No sooner had they retreated did Otuhu's griot appear. He knelt before the case and sang as he passed his hands from end to end. His song completed, the griot stepped away and Otuhu took his place. He opened the box and revealed the most magnificent sword Ndoro had ever seen. The metal blade shone like light and reflected like the clearest water, the blade long and sharp. The hilt was carved from ivory, with gold inlaid throughout. Otuhu took the sword from the box, handling it like a precious lover. His servants hung the elaborate leather baldric from his shoulder. Though Dingane was a great chief and possessed untold wealth in cattle, Ndoro was sure the sword at Otuhu's side was worth more than all the treasures of Sesuland. The world outside his homeland contained wonders it seemed he was just beginning to experience.

Biton interrupted is thoughts.

"Pick you best men. You will accompany Otuhu." The dendi-fari leaned close to Ndoro's ear. "Otuhu seeks honor in death, for you have shamed him by accomplishing what he could not. He is no value to me dead. Don't let him throw his life away because the ancestors granted you luck."

Ndoro nodded. He called the Diatanee to him. They were his best, selected before leaving the village from among the hundreds of Diaka. These were the men Ndoro felt possessed the true spirit of the Sesu. Their ranks included Jawanza, Kamau, the indunas and other select warriors. The Diatanee formed ranks behind Ndoro, who led them to stand behind Otuhu and the Songhai cavalry. The sanafaran led the group from his horse, the parley sword held high.

They were halfway to the city walls when the gates opened and the Nala cavalry raced toward them at full gallop.

"Kimbia, Diaka!" Ndoro shouted. The Diatanee surged past the trotting horses and locked shields before Otuhu.

"Get out of the way fools," Otuhu bellowed. He turned to

Ndoro. "This is only a show. They will back down as soon as they recognize the parley sword."

Ndoro wasn't convinced. He wasn't sure about Nala tactics, but deception was the root of Sesu warfare. "Hold your positions," he ordered.

Otuhu glared at Ndoro before turning his head toward the approaching Nalans. He raised the parley sword higher, stabbing it into the sky for emphasis.

The Nalans continued to advance. "Lances ready," Ndoro commanded. He glanced at Otuhu as the Diatanee braced their horse slayers into the earth, their broad spearheads aimed at horse breast height.

"What kind of treachery is this?" Otuhu said. "Warriors, swords ready!"

Otuhu flung the parley sword to the ground and freed his glorious sword from its jeweled scabbard. Waving it over his head, he led the Soninke cavalry forward to face the Nalans, disrupting the Diaka formation. Ndoro cursed Otuhu as he rode by. The Sesu signaled the remaining army, waving his shield and sword. The Diaka responded immediately, running to him from the bush. The conscripts followed in ragged formation, urged by Biton to go forward.

The horsemen crashed into each other with a thunderous roar. Ndoro instructed the Diatanee to spread out as they attacked the Nala cavalrymen with their lances. As the other Diaka arrived, they fell into battle, instinctively surrounding the Nalans. The fighting was fierce, the desperate Nalans trying to break the spear-tipped ring imprisoning them while dueling with Otuhu and his cohorts. They fell one by one; soon only one remained. The warrior sat upon a menacing black stallion that moved defiantly, snorting and pounding its metal-shod hooves against the ground.

The rider held a sword just as dazzling as Otuhu's, swinging the blade with deadly precision as he drove his attackers back. His intense face revealed no fear, only anger.

Ndoro called the Diaka away. The cavalry fell back, forming ranks behind Otuhu. The sanafaran advanced, stopping at sword length before the lone man.

"Jafaru, your time to join the ancestors has come," Otuhu announced.

"You cannot deny me my right!" Jafaru retorted. "The elders chose me!"

Otuhu smiled. "But Fate has not," he said.

Jafaru attacked Otuhu in a furious assault. Otuhu parried desperately, but it was obvious he was no equal to Jafaru. The other cavalry men saw this as well, but they did not interfere. Ndoro remembered Biton's words and snatched a javelin from a nearby Diaka. Hefting the weapon to his shoulder he ran headlong toward the dueling nobles. Jafaru slammed his horse into Otuhu, knocking from his mount into the grass. Otuhu struck the ground hard, his sword flying from his hand. Jafaru pulled back on the reins of his stallion, and the animal rose onto its hinds legs.

"If Sudetu wishes me dead, he will have to kill me himself!" Jafaru declared.

Ndoro leaned back and threw the javelin with all his strength. The missile streaked through the air and into the head of Jafaru, the impact knocking him from his horse to the ground before Otuhu. The stallion tumbled onto its back, righted itself and fled toward the walls of Nala. Ndoro had no time to dwell on his action. As the cavalry rushed to Otuhu and the body of Jafaru, Ndoro summoned the Diaka and they fell into defensive formation, anticipating a second assault from the Bordubu. As he surmised, the gates of the city swung open. Instead of disgorging a mass of warriors, one man emerged mounted on a donkey. His head was half shaven and he appeared naked except for a simple loincloth. He carried a ceremonial sword similar to the one Otuhu discarded.

"A royal messenger," one of the conscripts said.

"Maybe they will truly talk this time and we can go home," another said.

"Don't hope too soon," Ndoro replied. "The Nalans don't seem to respect this custom of parley unless it suits them. Maintain formation until we know their true intentions."

Ndoro knew the conscripts were under the command of the cavalry, but their masters were occupied with the spoils of Jafaru and his doomed cohorts. A few of them glared at him, including Otuhu. Ndoro ignored them, his attention on the approaching messenger.

The rider halted before Ndoro. He dismounted and immediately touched his head to the ground.

"Honorable High Chief Mamadou Sekou sends these words for all to hear. Jafaru you came for and Jafaru you have. This matter between Nala and Jehnay is settled. Leave now and we offer safe passage. Stay any longer and the ground will shake with the horses of Nala as they trample the bones of Soninke and Diaka."

Ndoro stepped forward. "Does the chief of Nala guarantee our safe passage home?"

The royal messenger smiled. "The chief does not wish to taste the fury of the Diaka again."

"Tell your chief we will leave immediately."

The messenger knelt again, mounted the donkey and rode away. He was a small image in the distance by the time Otuhu and Biton found their way to Ndoro.

"What did the messenger say, and why did he say it to you?" Otuhu demanded.

"The chief of Nala will not attack us if we leave now," Ndoro answered. "His loyalty to Jafaru ended with his life."

"It was not your place to accept his message," Biton added. "You are not the leader of this expedition!"

"I apologize for my error," Ndoro replied. He fought his urge to tell him everything the messenger said. Whatever he had done set both men against him. His concern was to get the Diaka back to their village.

"Gather your warriors, Sesu," Biton ordered. "You will form the rear guard. Otuhu, secure the head of Jafaru. Sudetu will be pleased with our proof of his rival's death. The elders will have no choice but to name him Askia now."

Otuhu marched away, calling his cavalry and conscripts to order. The horsemen responded but the conscripts remained with the Diaka. One of them, a tall man with small features approached Ndoro. He wore a red band of cloth on his upper arm, a sign of rank.

"What do you want us to do, Koi Ndoro?"

"Go back to the Soninke," Ndoro replied. "I am not your master."

The conscript officer smiled. "But you are, Koi Ndoro. You are the master of this field." Before he could stop him the conscript knelt and touched his forehead to the ground, sprinkling his head with dirt. He backed away a few feet, stood and returned to his men. He barked at the others in a language Ndoro didn't recognize and the conscripts returned to their position with the Soninke.

Ndoro watched Biton and Otuhu as they made final preparations for the return. He was disappointed with his first taste of organized war. Gone was the celebration of victory, the looting of the vanquished. There were no cattle to take home, no loot to fill his knapsack and no woman to soothe his psyche and help clear his mind. Although he understood Biton's eagerness to return to Jehnay, he was disturbed by the sour mood of the dendi-fari. He called his officers to him.

"Let the Soninke and their men get far ahead. Keep your units in battle formation."

"Do your think the Nalans will attack?" Jawanza asked.

"I don't fear the Nalans. I'm concerned about the jackals before us."

They looked at Ndoro and he saw the uncertainty in their eyes.

"We will march to the bridge. Kamau, if the canoes are still there you will take them back to the village with as many of the wounded you can carry. Take the archers with you as well. When you get back to the village tell everyone to stay in their compounds until we arrive."

Kamau's face betrayed his fear. "Why would they attack us? Aren't we allies?"

"It is my fault," Ndoro replied. "The dendi-fari asked me to make you warriors. He didn't expect me to succeed."

The Diaka went silently to their units. Ndoro walked ahead of his unit, his shoulders drooping with the mental burden riding them. In order to save the Diaka, he may have doomed them.

The Diaka slowed their pace until the Soninke disappeared. They marched silently, eyes shifting back and forth. Ndoro felt the uneasiness biting the back of his neck, so he straightened himself and picked up the pace. The road became hazy the closer they came to the bridge; Ndoro smelled smoke and his hands tensed around his assegai.

The Soninke conscript ranks rustled nervously at the far end of the bridge obscured by smoke rising from the river below. They had set fire to Kamau's canoes, blocking a Diaka escape by the river. The cavalry stood behind the conscripts, Otuhu in the center, the sword of Jafaru in his grasp. Biton sat upon his stallion beside him.

"Archers forward!" Ndoro commanded. The archers rushed to their position, forming a line just before the entrance of the bridge. Ndoro didn't have to call for the indunas. They appeared at his side immediately. The mounting smoke from the burning canoes masked the far side of the bridge, reducing the vision of the archers.

"Otuhu thinks he's taken away our advantage with the archers. At this distance we will get one volley at the most. We'll position the spearmen directly behind the archers. Make sure to leave gaps to allow the archers room to pull back. Have them regroup on both sides of the bridge. They can fire at will once they are in position. If Otuhu sends the conscripts we will signal the lancers to switch to swords and orinkas."

The indunas returned to their units to pass on his orders. No sooner had they done so did the smoke begin to rumble like thunderclouds.

"Swords!" Ndoro shouted. In practiced unison the Diaka dropped the spears; swords sang as they were freed from their scabbards. The Diaka archers loaded their bows and waited for the first sign of the charge. Midway on the bridge the Soninke emerged like ghosts from the smoke. It was a mixed charge; two columns of warriors followed by a company of horsemen.

"Archers, fire on the foot soldiers only!" He raised and dropped his orinka and the arrows flew, bringing down the conscripts with lethal alacrity. The archers fell back to the banks, as the cavalry became tangled among the sudden mass of dead and wounded warriors.

Ndoro watched the cavalrymen shouting at the conscripts, trying to restore order. The faces of the conscripts told him what he needed to know. He ran to the lances, grabbing a lance from the ground.

"Follow me!" he yelled and ran to the bridge. The spearmen quickly caught him, forming a shield line. Ndoro sensed fear among the conscripts and pressed the attack. By the time the Soninke realized what was happening, the Diaka were only strides away, the closest conscripts already falling to the bold attack.

The conscripts ran. Otuhu and his cohorts struck at them with their swords but the exodus continued. Some slipped past the cavalrymen while others jumped over the sides of the bridge, disappearing into the rising black smoke of the burning canoes. The Diaka attacked, Ndoro at the lead. His target was Otuhu. The Songhai nobleman had betrayed him; he was not fit to live. Ndoro jumped over a falling conscript and struck at Otuhu with his assegai. Otuhu, still carrying the gilded sword, sliced the spear in half. Ndoro ducked a vicious swing at his head then leaped onto the horse with Otuhu. They struggled, hands locked as they wrestled for the advantage. A passing Diaka drove his lance into Otuhu's horse and the animal jumped to its hind legs, throwing both men. Ndoro landed on his back, the impact knocking him into darkness. He opened his eyes to see Otuhu looming over him.

"Did you think you could dishonor me and live?"

He raised his sword. "It ends today, thief."

Ndoro rolled as the sword came down, sparks flying from the blade as it bounced off stone. He grabbed a broken lance from the ground and plunged it into Otuhu's gut. The noble dropped his sword as he fell backward. Ndoro stood with his lance in his hand.

"No one betrays me and lives," he said. He stabbed Otuhu again, this time driving the lance point where he knew the heart should be. Yanking the broken weapon free, he ran toward the growing horde of Diaka. He took Otuhu's life; now he had to save Biton's.

The dendi-fari was surrounded by angry Diaka. He swung his sword frantically as his bodyguards tried to drive back the attacking horde.

"Diaka back!" Ndoro yelled, but not one man heeded his order. A few Diaka running to the fray gave him a menacing look. This was revenge no less than his own against Otuhu but more justified.

The last bodyguard went down under flailing swords. No sooner did he disappear that Biton's horse toppled. The dendi-fari fell into the midst of his slaves, his body beaten and hacked without remorse. The Diaka backed away, revealing his mutilated form to Ndoro's angry eyes.

Smoke swirled around Ndoro as he approached Biton's body. The ground was littered with the dead and dying, Diaka and Soninke. Warriors walked among the carnage, finishing off the wounded Soninke with orinka blows. Ndoro was disturbed by their efficiency; the former farmers were now ruthless warriors. He didn't know whether he should be proud or ashamed.

The Diatanee came to him slowly, their faces solemn yet unremorseful. In their eyes they had done what had to be done, but they had also opened a door of unknown consequences. Otuhu's death could be explained; the death of Biton was another matter.

"What do you wish, Koi Ndoro?" Jawanza asked, looking away from Ndoro's eyes.

"Now you ask what to do," Ndoro replied. "Maybe I should be the one asking the question."

The indunas remained quiet, all looking at the ground expectantly.

"Gather the wounded that can travel. Use the horses to carry them if you can. We must return to the village as soon as possible."

The Diaka limped back to the village, arriving by dusk on the fifth day. A runner had been sent ahead and they were met by family and friends. Mothers, sisters, fathers and brothers found their warriors, welcoming them with hugs and tears of joy. Others relieved the warriors of the injured, rushing them back to family compounds to be cared for. Then there were the most unfortunate, wandering the fields searching the faces of those returning, slowly realizing their men were not coming home. Their painful sobs mixed with cries of relief as more Diaka warriors streamed into the village.

Ndoro, Jawanza and Kamau were among the last to arrive. They were swarmed by sisters and brothers. Ndoro saw Sarama running to him, tears running down her face. The wall he'd erected in his mind came down; he dropped his weapons and met her, arms open wide. Their embrace was full and deep.

"My shumba slayer has returned," Sarama whispered.

Ndoro didn't reply, his joy all too brief. There were other matters to deal with.

"I need to talk to Jabulani," he said.

"Now?" Sarama looked puzzled.

"Yes, now."

"Come, I know where to find him."

Sarama took his hand and he followed her to the village pasture. Jabulani sat on the hill watching his prized goats graze on the verdant grass. Sarama was about to take him closer but Ndoro stopped her.

"I need to speak to him alone."

Sarama eyes became suspicious. "What is wrong, Ndoro?"

He didn't answer. Ndoro walked calmly despite the anger boiling inside him. Jabulani sat cross-legged, his eyes closed.

"Baba," Ndoro said.

Jabulani opened his eyes. "You return victorious?"

"Yes."

Jabulani looked at Ndoro, fatherly admiration in his eyes. "You wish to talk to the elders. You wish an explanation."

"I deserve one," Ndoro replied, his anger evident in his voice.

Jabulani slowly stood. "Come."

They met the elders under the great tree. The village seemed deserted, everyone cloistered in family compounds celebrating or mourning. Ndoro sat with his back to the tree, the position of leadership among the Diaka. The elders formed a crescent around him. Jabulani leaned on his staff, his place halfway between the elders and Ndoro.

Shaihi spoke first. "I know you are angry, Koi Ndoro, but there is a reason we did not tell you everything."

"You were younger than we expected," Jabulani said. "We believed if we revealed too much you would leave us to our fate."

"You knew your sons would kill Biton. You counted on it," Ndoro said.

"It is as it should be," Jabulani replied. "Since you are our koi you should know the full story of the people that chose to follow you."

"This land is not our home. We Diaka come from the south, from a land of forests and valleys. We came to Galadima as refugees from war, a war we instigated but lost. Our enemies, the Tacuma, possessed the land of gold dust that we coveted. So we attacked them, not knowing they were under the protection of the river spirit. Every river we crossed on our way to battle struck out with fast currents, hungry crocodiles and protective hippopotami that crushed our canoes. When we finally reached Tacumaland, we were no match for their well-rested and well-armed warriors. We were driven from our homeland. Those who fell behind were taken as slaves.

"When our ancestors came here, they discovered they had fled one war for another. Jehnay and Nala were at war then as they are now. Tired and desperate, our ancestors accepted the yoke of slavery in return for protection by the Soninke. That yoke has chaffed our shoulders for three hundred years."

Shaihi leaned toward Ndoro. "It was foretold by the Oracle that a shumba slayer would come, that he would make us warriors again and free us from the Soninke. Our medicine priests prayed to the ancestors and the spirit of the lake, offering our precious goats as sacrifice. Jabulani is the blood of our priest, the most talented of our healers. It was his prayers that were finally answered."

Ndoro looked at each of the elders, their eyes reflecting their belief. Though he knew the circumstance of his arrival, nothing he said would change their minds. He killed the shumba, he made them warriors again and he led them from slavery to freedom, if only for a moment.

How could he judge them when he had been dishonest as well? The Diaka were an answer to his vow of revenge against his own. They were a seed, a beginning that if nurtured properly could bring him everything he desired.

"We cannot stay here," Ndoro finally said. "As soon as the word of Jafaru's death reached Jehnay, Sudetu will claim the title of Askia, and then he will send the bulk of his army to find the slayers of Biton."

"We considered this, Koi Ndoro," Shaihi replied. "It is time we returned home."

"We have prepared canoes for the journey," Jabulani said. "The people are ready."

Ndoro nodded his approval. "We need a few days rest," Ndoro said.

"Then it is settled," Shaihi announced, relief evident on his face.

"Ndoro," Jabulani said. "Are you still our koi?"

Ndoro smiled. "If you will have me."

Jabulani smiled back. "You were given to us by the ancestors. It is not our choice to make."

Ndoro left the elders to make plans for the exodus. The days were catching up to him, his wounds aching and his body tired beyond anything he'd experienced. The family greeted him quietly as he entered the compound, their emotions subdued until he smiled. They joyfully assaulted him, pulling and hugging and kissing him the entire walk back to his home.

As he went to the door, Talana emerged.

"You don't live here anymore," she scolded. Sarama emerged behind her, a sly smile on her face.

Talana turned to Sarama. "Take this boy home."

Sarama sauntered to Ndoro and took his hand, sparking a roar of laughter. She led him out of the family compound down the narrow alleyways to his completed home. He'd been so distracted by his revelations he didn't notice the structure was complete.

"We only have a few days to enjoy it," Sarama whispered. "Make them count, Askia of the Diaka."

"The free Diaka," Ndoro replied.

*　*　*

Ndoro helped load the canoes for the journey south. Sarama worked by his side, helping him with the provisions. Jabulani leaned on his staff as he watched the Diaka prepare for the journey home. They had no idea where they were going, only the sketchy details of a legend. Ndoro selected fifty of his best warriors to man the lead canoes. They would leave three days ahead, guided by Jabulani's directions.

His canoe was finally ready. He looked at Sarama, her constant smile tainted with a hint of worry.

"You're risking your life for a story," she said. "You don't even know if it's true."

"Your father believes it," Ndoro replied. "That is good enough for me. Besides, the Diaka must leave this land. There is no turning back now."

Sarama placed her head on his chest. "Be careful, Ndoro. Come back to me."

Jabulani interrupted them with a growl. "There will be enough time for that nonsense once we find Diakaland. Sarama, go help your mother."

Sarama departed, glancing back at Ndoro.

"Are we ready?" Jabulani asked.

Ndoro looked down at this adopted father and smiled. "Yes baba, we're ready."

"Then let's go!" Jabulani shouted.

Ndoro laughed. "You've waited three hundred years. You can wait a little longer."

Ndoro signaled the drummers and they pounded out the cadence to assemble. He helped Jabulani into the lead canoe and boarded himself. There were five canoes, ten men per boat with provisions loaded. A small group gathered about the shore, waving a brief farewell.

They were ready. Ndoro gave the signal and they launched the canoes into the Kojo, placing themselves at the mercy of Jabulani's memory and the river's secrets. As Ndoro looked out on the expanse of water before him, he realized he was again embarking on a journey into the unknown, his vow of revenge his only guide. But at least this time, he was not alone.

2

The city was named Alamako, which in the tongue of its inhabitants meant God bless. To Obaseki's eyes it was anything but blessed. As he led Eshe, Pajonga and Olushola down the wide dilapidated avenue separating the family compounds, he was struck by the fear in the eyes of the people watching them from behind the decrepit walls. At first he thought it was because of Pajonga, whose towering height and fierce expression always brought stares. But he soon realized he was the one who caused the stares. It was as if they saw his gift and feared it.

Their journey had begun months ago during the dry season. Though Obaseki had chosen to depart Abo, Noncemba refused to let his grandson leave in shame. He held a celebration, inviting all those that did not agree with the elders' decision. There was another reason for the celebration; Obaseki and Eshe were to be married. Noncemba presented Eshe's family with a thousand head of Zebu cattle, a treasure of ivory, cowry shells, gold dust and salt. The grounds of his kraal came alive with celebrants honoring the young apprentice and his beautiful wife throughout the day and most of the night. On the morning of their departure the mood was more subdued. Their families cried and hugged them goodbye. In a final gesture, Noncemba presented Pajonga and Olushola to the couple. The intimidating Pajonga had served the royal family as a faithful bodyguard for years and was eager to accompany Obaseki on his journey. Olushola, a short, slight woman with a round face and shy smile, was a treasure in disguise. Her purpose was to help Eshe with cooking and other chores, but more importantly,

Olushola was Malinke. She knew the way to Alamako.

The final words he heard spoken in Abo came from Fuluke.

"This is an important journey," he said. "Ndoki is a powerful medicine-priest, more powerful than I could ever be. It is said he also wields a mayembe possessing a fallen spirit. He can teach you how to control Moyo and how to tap into its power. But be careful, for Ndoki can only be trusted so much. He may see you as a rival, and he is a very jealous man. It will be up to you to choose your time to leave."

The words rang in his ears as they made their way to the empty marketplace on the far end of Alamako.

"These people are afraid." Olushola whispered. "See the walls? Those talismans and gris-gris are to ward off evil spirits."

"The city is cursed," Pajonga said. "We should leave. I'd rather camp in the forest."

"We'll stay one night," Obaseki replied. "We need to rest, our donkey needs good feed and we need to find someone to lead us to Ndoki."

The avenue opened into a wide circular plaza. High mud walls, similar to those in Mawenaland, enclosed the area. The plaza was void of life. Millet fields grew untended, weeds and other invaders strangling out the remaining crop needed in times of siege. Piles of spoiled bananas lay below their former perches, rotting in the intermittent sunlight. Above them the oba's compound loomed over the mud walls surrounding its hilltop perch. The building appeared abandoned as well; thick vines surrounded the terra cotta figurines decorating the pillars that accented the corners of the wall.

"You don't want to go there," a child-like voice warned.

They turned to see a small boy standing behind them.

His head seemed too large for his small neck and he wore only a soiled loincloth and a golden necklace much too valuable for his appearance.

Pajonga stepped forward, his hand on his sword hilt. "Leave us thief, before I cut off your head and return that necklace to its true owner."

"No, wait," Obaseki interjected. There was something about the boy's eyes that told Obaseki what he needed to know.

"Are you a guide?"

The boy smiled. "It depends on where you wish to go."

"We wish to find Ndoki."

"Ndoki does not live here. He lives in Infana."

"Well then," Obaseki said. "Can you take us to Infana?"

"I am not your guide there, not today," the boy replied. "Today I will take you to the inn. Tomorrow I will take you to Infana."

"Did you hear my master?" Pajonga demanded. "He wishes to go today!"

The boy glared at the bodyguard. "As I said, you will rest today, for the journey to Infana is arduous."

Pajonga was flustered by the boy's arrogance. "Why you...!"

Obaseki grabbed Pajonga's sword arm before he drew the blade. "You'd be wasting your time striking him, my friend. He is already dead. Save your zeal to protect us when it will matter."

Pajonga's eyes widened as he looked at the smirking boy. "I am sorry, master." Obaseki turned his attention back to the boy. "Thank you for your help."

The boy bowed slightly and trotted from the plaza, gesturing for them to follow. They retraced their steps for a moment and then plunged into a confusing maze of alleys and passageways, emerging suddenly before a large plain rectangular building at the edge of the city. Smoke floated from the mud-brick chimney; like the other buildings of Alamako its walls were plastered with talismans.

"Rest well," the boy said. "I will meet you tomorrow morning. There is food, water and bedding inside."

"Will you come inside and show us where to find these things?" Obaseki asked.

The boy flashed his sly grin and ran away, disappearing into the alleyways.

Pajonga ran after him for a moment. "Insolent monkey!" he growled.

Obaseki laughed. "Let him go, Pajonga. He couldn't enter the building if he wanted. The gris-gris was placed here to keep him and his kind out."

"He is a demon," Olushola said. "We should not go into this place."

"She's right," Pajonga agreed. "This could be a trap."

"No, the inn is fine," Obaseki decided. "He was probably sent by Ndoki to welcome us."

Eshe, who had been silent since they entered Alamako, walked into the building without hesitation. Despite his assuring words, Obaseki rushed after her, his chest tight with dread.

The inn was in perfect order, a stark contrast to the outside. Low chairs sat neatly around worn mahogany tables. Yellow calabashes filled with water rested on each table surrounded by ceramic cups. The smell of cooked meat drifted from the open kitchen, reminding Obaseki how hungry he was. On the opposite side of the room were sleeping quarters, five in all. The largest had been prepared for the donkeys, fresh straw covering the stone floor.

Eshe grabbed a calabash and went to one of the rooms. Inside were a low table and two beds, complete with blankets and head rests.

Obaseki cursed. "I should have seen it sooner. You are sick."

Eshe smiled as she sat the calabash down on the table. "You were leading us here, Seki. You can't be aware of everything."

"When it comes to you I should," he replied. He eased her down onto the bed and examined her.

"You have a fever, but I don't feel the presence of any spirits." He reached into his herb pouch, selecting a special blend of leaves and bark. "Chew this with your water. It will break your fever and ease your aches until I can discover the reason for your sickness."

Eshe obeyed and in moments was fast asleep. Obaseki stepped back into the main room. Pajonga and Olushola were unpacking the donkey, whispering to each other as they looked about furtively.

"Is there something wrong?" he asked.

"No, master," Pajonga replied. "We are grateful for the rest and the food."

"You are worried about Eshe?"

The duo looked at each other, giving him his answer.

"She will be fine," Obaseki assured them. "Now is not the time to worry. It is time to rest."

Obaseki joined them in a meal of cooked chicken and yams. They ate voraciously, remembering only at the last minute to save a meal for Eshe. Afterward Pajonga and Olushola slept, preferring blankets and the dirt floor to the bedchambers.

Obaseki paced, unable to sleep. Fuluke warned him of the power of Ndoki, but he didn't expect what they encountered today. The sight of the dead boy disturbed him; maybe this was wrong. How could he protect Moyo from a medicine-priest that raised the dead and knew he was coming before he arrived?

"Fuluke thinks too much of me," he whispered.

"Fuluke believes in you as I do." Eshe was awake, her smile bright but her eyes groggy. She stood and walked to the dining hall, kissing him on the cheek as she passed. She sat at the table with the rest of the food, Obaseki joining her.

"I have no idea what I am to do," he said. "I sense strangeness about this place. Not just among the living, but among the spirits as well."

"Maybe that is your purpose," Eshe replied. "You must bring balance here."

"I don't have the power to do so."

Eshe looked up from her meal. "You don't now, but you will."

Obaseki smiled. She was weak with sickness and still encouraging him on his unclear quest.

After she finished her meal Obaseki helped Eshe back to bed. He lay down and fell quickly to sleep. Instantly he found himself standing before Fuluke although he knew his mentor was hundreds of miles away. The ground was cold beneath his feet, the wind teasing the white robes gathered about his cold body. They stood on a high precipice with the entire world below them, people and sprits living their lives unaware of the silent observers above them.

He saw himself sleeping beside Eshe, Pajonga and Olushola resting in the lobby. He pulled away, seeing the ring of fear surrounding them like a sinister moat, kept at bay by some unknown glow. Whatever it was, Obaseki was certain it was no spirit.

"Where are the souls?" he asked.

"Stolen," Fuluke replied, though his voice seemed unfamiliar. "They were taken to serve Ndoki. Such is his power."

"Will he see me as an enemy or a friend?"

"Neither if you are lucky. It is best he thinks of you as someone of no consequence."

Fuluke turned his head to Obaseki. As he looked into his mentor's eyes he realized it was not Fuluke to whom he spoke.

"But then you are no mere priest."

Obaseki sprang erect from his bed. He was cold, just like the image in his dream. Warmth came with the early morning light, creeping into the inn through the uncovered windows as the light cast long shadows across the floors.

The morning quiet was shattered by thunderous drumming. The rhythm reeled about the walls, driving Obaseki angrily to his feet. He stormed to the entrance of the building and saw the boy prancing about as he struck the drum.

"Wake up, my friends!" he sang. "We have a long journey and a short day!"

Obaseki returned to the inn and woke everyone. Pajonga and Olushola grumbled as they packed. Eshe stirred and smiled as Obaseki place his hand on her forehead. The heat was gone and the color of her eyes was brighter.

"We must travel far today," Obaseki warned. "Are you up to it?"

"I am ready," she replied. "Don't worry about me, Seki. I'll be fine."

Obaseki looked skeptical, aware how Eshe never wished to be a burden.

"Still, you will ride the donkey until we need to walk."

"We need the donkey to carry our supplies."

"We will split the load among ourselves."

Eshe smiled. "Pajonga and Olushola will not be pleased."

Obaseki laughed. "They are never happy. Come, let's go."

They set out a few hours after daylight, following their guide through the city and outside into the surrounding forest. The heat rose with the sun, summoning steam from the foliage. They followed the strange boy in silence, the sounds of the forest their only distraction. The road became steep, snaking upward through a ridge of hills blanketed by forests and mists. Climbing into the hills was more difficult than Obaseki expected. The road was muddy and narrow, his feet sinking into the mud with each step, sapping his energy. The donkey had no better time of it, braying and grunting in protest, moving forward only because of the pulling and cursing of Pajonga.

"Hurry up!" the boy admonished. "We must reach the top of the ridge by nightfall."

Obaseki stopped. "Those of us that still breathe are tired. We have no talisman to give us strength."

The boy smiled. "If you don't make the top of the ridge by sundown, even my master's powers will not protect you. There are many dangers in this forest beyond his control."

The words spurred the travelers. They struggled with the steep hill all day, reaching the crest as the sun receded below the summits along the western horizon. A house stood in a small clearing before them. A circle of staffs protected the house, each one crowned by animal figures carved from ivory. As with the inn, the boy did not step within the staffed perimeter.

"Now you will rest," the boy sang. "Tomorrow we go down the hill. It will be much easier."

Flashing his grin, the boy disappeared into the bush. The quartet trudged into the house after tethering the donkey to an ironwood tree nearby. The house seemed larger inside though still modest in comparison to the inn. Olushola quickly set about starting a fire while Obaseki and Pajonga unpacked provisions. Eshe sat down hard by Olushola, attempting to help with the fire.

"Mistress, please," Olushola said. "I will tend to the fire. You should rest."

"I'm fine," Eshe replied.

Olushola edged closer, lowering her voice as she spoke. "I am an old woman, despite the youth of my skin. I know a pregnant woman when I see one."

Eshe's eyes widened. "You know?"

Olushola looked away smiling. "Your secret is safe with me."

Pajonga unpacked his weapons and hurried outside. Obaseki was concerned and followed him. He came up to the bodyguard staring into the forest.

"What is it?" he finally asked.

"The donkey is gone," Pajonga replied. "I think the boy stole it." He looked about, his hands tight on the sword.

"Listen," he said.

"To what?"

Pajonga looked into the trees. "Something is coming."

The quiet was shattered by the wail of the donkey. Branches before them exploded and the donkey sailed through the air, crashing at their feet. The animal lived despite its broken body.

A low, ominous moan wafted from the dark. A sinister chorus answered, the entire forest reverberating with the foreboding sound emanating from unknown throats.

Olushola stuck her head from the house.

"Come in now!" she urged. "They are coming!"

Obaseki grasped his mayembe beneath his robe. It was hot to the touch; a sure sign that whatever came was more than normal.

They ran for the house as the source of the sound emerged from the damp leaves. Obaseki glanced back to see the hulking figures, human-like in their gait but much larger and wider. Their bodies were covered with black coarse hair; their chest, face, and hands were swathed in leathery black skin. One of the creatures opened its mouth and moaned, exposing a ragged row of sharp teeth and elongated fangs.

Obaseki looked away, daring not to look again until he was in the safety of the house. He rummaged through his belongings and found his sword.

"What are those things?" he asked Olushola as he armed himself.

"Ghoulas," she replied, her voice trembling. "They look like mountain apes, but they are not. They hold the souls of evil men, witch doctors who gave up their human bodies for the powerful bodies of the apes. It is said they go mad when they transform, hunting in the high mountains for human flesh."

Pajonga went to the door and stood with his sword ready.

"They will come to eat us, then," he stated.

"They cannot pass the staffs," Obaseki reminded them. "They will come no closer than the ring. The magic from them is too powerful. It will keep the ghoulas out."

"And the ghoulas will keep us in," Olushola said.

Obaseki watched the ghoulas encircle the house, their human-like expressions showing they were not happy with the staffs. They looked at the mangled body of the donkey and became more agitated, grunting loud and pounding the ground with their massive fists. More ghoulas emerged from the woods, summoned by the howling of their brethren.

"What is happening?" Eshe asked, eyes wide with fear.

"They want the donkey," Obaseki replied.

"Then we must give it to them," Olushola urged. "They tasted its blood and won't be satisfied until they have it… or us."

Obaseki looked at Pajonga. "We must give them their kill."

Resignation conquered Pajonga's face briefly, replaced by his stern frown. He secured his armor, picked up his lance and shield, and then strode to the door. Obaseki followed with his sword in his left hand, Moyo in his right. The mayembe glowed green, passing the aura of confidence into Obaseki as it did during the battle of Abo. Together they stepped through the door and the ghoulas fell silent. As soon as they neared the donkey carcass the ghoulas went into frenzy, pounding their chests and the ground, hitting each other violently as they glared at the duo approaching their kill.

"Let's do this quickly," Obaseki said. They lifted the donkey, Obaseki grasping the front legs as Pajonga lifted with the rear legs. They swung the body back and forth, gaining momentum as the ghoula protest grew heated. On the third swing they let go, the corpse passing through the barrier. As it passed through the invisible shield two nearby ghoulas fell through.

Obaseki wasted no time. "Moyo zuka!" he shouted, uttering the words that unleashed the essence of Moyo. The painful blinding light consumed him, blurring his sight of the ape-men and Pajonga.

"Pajonga, get behind me!" Obaseki managed to say before the deadly tendrils flew out in all directions. Pajonga managed to dive for the safety of the house; the ghoulas were much less fortunate. Jagged streams of power pierced their chests, dragging out the souls of the witch doctors that corrupted the animals' bodies. Screams filled his head as the bolts breached the barrier, spearing the ghoulas that tore at the donkey. The other ghoulas fled into the bush.

Obaseki slowly exerted his will on Moyo, forcing the malevolent force back into the mayembe. The smell of burned flesh and hair invaded his nostrils, bodies of the ghoulas at his feet, the others strewn about beyond the staff ring like broken branches. Fatigue consumed him and he fell into darkness.

Obaseki awoke inside the house, his head resting on Eshe's lap. His forehead felt damp, so he tried to touch it. Pain jolted him and he quickly put his hand down, fighting the urge to pass out again.

"Relax, Seki," Eshe whispered.

"What day is it?" he asked.

"It is still night," Eshe replied as she changed the cloth on his forehead. "You slew the ghoulas a few hours ago."

"So it was as bad as the last time."

Eshe was quiet for a moment. "In a way, no."

Pajonga rose from his cot and came close to the couple. "How is he?"

"Awake," Obaseki replied.

Pajonga fell to his knees immediately, pressing his head against the ground.

"Again I am privileged to witness your power!"

Obaseki closed his eyes with the next wave of pain. "Get off your knees, Pajonga and get some sleep. We should be safe now."

Olushola cowered on the opposite side of the house. She stared at Obaseki, eyes wide with fright. He struggled to sit.

"What is wrong, Olushola?"

She did not reply. Olushola closed her eyes and hid her face behind her hands, a muffled whimper escaping between her fingers.

"She's been like this since you drove the ghoulas away," Eshe said.

Obaseki struggled to his feet and approached the woman. "Olushola, it's alright. The ghoulas are gone."

Olushola flinched when he reached toward her.

"This place is cursed. We will die here," she whispered.

Obaseki felt what Olushola feared. He wondered if Ndoki had passed judgment on him and sent the ghoulas to kill him. He regretted bringing Eshe and the others along, though he would have never made it as far without them. It was not his place to put the lives of others in danger, ancestors or not.

Obaseki went to his medicine bag and removed a soothing herb blend. He shared it with Pajonga and Olushola who both fell asleep. When he offered a portion to Eshe, she refused.

"I am fine," she said. "I am just tired."

Obaseki sat near his wife. "Tomorrow I want you and the others to return to Alamako"

Eshe's eyes widened. "Why?"

"Olushola has a right to be afraid. If this medicine-priest is responsible for the ghoula attack I fear what he might do to you in order to control me."

Eshe sighed. "We may be in just as much danger in the village."

"You'll be welcomed without me. Olushola will help convince them that you are my servants."

"You will face this man alone?"

Obaseki nodded.

Eshe grasped his hand. "At least take Pajonga with you.

You might need his strength."

"I dare not leave you and Olushola unprotected."

"Pajonga will come with us to the village," Eshe decided. "If the villagers accept us, we will send him to you."

"If I do not return in a month, go back to Abo," Obaseki said.

Eshe turned away. "I don't want to think that way."

"Promise me you will go back," Obaseki insisted.

Eshe hesitated. "I promise, but not before I try to find you first."

"I can't convince you otherwise, can I?"

Eshe looked into his eyes and smiled. "No."

"Then I will have to accept as much. Now get some sleep, sweet flower."

They did nothing of the sort, making love throughout the night, both aware it might be their last moment together. As the sun forced its way through the dense foliage they lay side by side, pleasant weariness settling in.

Obaseki sat up, and dressed slowly. He crawled to his herb bag and made a quick blend of ginseng root, coffee beans and other herbs, a concoction sure to sustain them both through the day.

"A clever blend, but the local taba root is more effective."

Obaseki looked up to see the door blocked by a huge man, the sun reflecting off his gold-capped teeth. A jeweled mayembe hung from his neck. The talisman pulsed with the familiar green glow, the sign of an active spirit inside. The intruder's small eyes, black skin and broad nose resembled those of the ghoulas. A brightly colored sash held the tunic around his waist and the dagger at his side.

Pajonga sprang to his feet, sword in hand. As the intruder slowly turned toward the bodyguard, Obaseki hastily stood between them.

"Thank you for your advice," he said. "May I ask your name?"

"Ndoki," the man answered. "Welcome to Infana, Obaseki of the Mawena."

Ndoki sat cross-legged on the ground. "I take it your journey was pleasant?"

Obaseki glanced at Pajonga, signaling him to put away his sword. He sat before Ndoki. "Except for last night, it has been uneventful."

"Oh yes, the ghoulas. I have no control over them, although they can be useful without knowing."

"Such as keeping a person in one place?" Obaseki asked.

Ndoki let loose a deep rumbling laugh that shook his necklaces. "I didn't expect them to attack you, but I protected the house just in case. You were perfectly safe."

"Tell that to our donkey," Pajonga said. "They killed it and came through your barrier."

Ndoki's eyes narrowed as he looked toward Pajonga.

"Pajonga is my companion," Obaseki said. "I would appreciate it if you would refrain from casting spells his way."

Ndoki jerked his head to Obaseki. "He doesn't deserve our attention, let alone our friendship."

"I am no different from him," Obaseki said.

"Oh, you are, young Mawena. Your place is not among these pets, I assure you. You have much to learn about what you possess."

Ndoki sprang to his feet with surprising agility for a man of his girth. "We're wasting time. Your companions are welcomed to stay here until you return. I do think, however, they would find Alamako more to their liking."

"Will the ghoulas return?" Pajonga asked.

Ndoki smiled. "One never knows about ghoulas. It's

possible they were satisfied by your donkey, but they might seek revenge for their unfortunate brothers. Either way, you are safe here as long as you stay with the staffs."

"We will only be here one more day," Eshe said. "We have decided to return to Alamako. But we will need a donkey."

"The boy will bring you another," Ndoki promised.

"No, not him," Eshe said. "Send a real boy."

Ndoki looked at Obaseki and smiled. "She must be good, for she steals secrets from your lips."

"There are no secrets between us," Obaseki replied.

Ndoki frowned. "So be it. You will have your donkey. Come, Obaseki, I have no more desire to be on the trail at night than you do."

There was nothing else left to say to Eshe. Obaseki packed quickly, hugged and kissed his sweet flower, then followed Ndoki down the narrow path leading away from the house and into the woods. The dense foliage made quick work of his view. In moments it was if the house never existed. The forest spoke around them, monkey calls and birdsong competing for their place in the chorus. Ndoro found himself almost running to keep up with Ndoki.

"Infana is not far," Ndoki said. "You will love it. It is the perfect city for ones such as us."

"And why are we so alike?" Obaseki asked.

Ndoki stopped suddenly and Obaseki almost ran into him. Ndoki lifted the mayembe about his neck.

"My mayembe contains the soul of a fallen spirit as well, though she was not as powerful as Moyo. She is Delu and this land was once her realm. I discovered her mayembe in Infana, so I have made it my home."

Obaseki saw an image in the distance. As they drew closer

he recognized it as a spirit, sauntering down the trail as if carrying a basket upon its head. It stopped upon seeing them, turned and ran into the bush. Ndoki sprang forward, chasing the spirit into the bush. The pursuit was brief. The sorcerer emerged from the brush smiling, the mayembe glowing brightly.

"The first fact you must accept is that Moyo must be fed," Ndoki stated. "He is starving; that is why you fight to control him when he is released."

"But he consumes spirits," Obaseki said.

Ndoki's face became solemn. "I sense your talent. You have affinity with souls and you wish not to harm them. Your destiny, however, depends on the mastery of Moyo. Moyo must be controlled. You must feed him to control him."

Obaseki clinched his eyes, the image of consumed souls flashing in his head.

"Can you hear it?" Ndoki asked

"What?"

"The sea! We are almost home!" Ndoki exclaimed.

Ndoki ran ahead of Obaseki, disappearing around a bend in the path. Obaseki sighed, too tired to chase his strange companion. He trudged around the bend then rolled his eyes at the sight of the steep hill before him. Ndoki stood on the crest, waving his hands like an excited child.

"Come, come! Infana waits!"

Obaseki's thighs burned as he climbed the hill. A roaring sound came to his ears and the smell of water, fish, and salt filled his nose as he struggled to the top of the hill. At the crest of the hill he was struck by the view below him. Infana, the city of Ndoki, sprawled among broken cliffs that plunged into the churning waters below. It was a collection of circular white washed buildings crowned with blue tiled roofs. The decrepit structures clung to the sea cliff edges, peering into the blue sea below and beyond. Towering waves crashed against the base of the cliffs, tossing sea spray high over the cliff edge. The water stretched as far as he could see and Obaseki was amazed. The stories he heard as a boy had not prepared him for the reality of the ocean's vastness.

He broke his attention from the sea long enough to look down into Infana. There was movement below in the streets, but it was not human movement. The city was filled with spirits, more that he could count. There had to be thousands of them, he thought.

"It is beautiful, isn't it," Ndoki said, startling Obaseki.

"Yes, yes it is." Obaseki looked at Ndoki, the questions in his mind making him wary of his companion. "There are spirits but no people."

"Only some of the spirits are of those who lived in Infana. The rest are from everywhere; Kossa, Sesuland, the Sahel, even as far as the Talsa Mountains. I brought them all here from around the world to serve me."

"I guess there are many spirits from Alamako as well."

Ndoki ignored his comment. "Come. We will go to my home and rest."

They descended into the city together. Obaseki observed spirits tending invisible millet fields, cooking over empty fires and herding long dead cattle. The Zamani was powerful here among the cliffs; the spirits appeared as clear as the living despite their translucence. Above all, he saw the terror in their eyes as they looked at Ndoki. They looked back at him in curiosity and fear, a few faces drawn in despair. Obaseki took their looks as warnings. He would have to be careful with Ndoki so as not to end up among them.

Ndoki's house was modest for one who claimed to be the

master of the Ifana's spirits. The rectangular structure rested on a low rise outside the city walls, surrounded by its own brightly colored wall. There was no physical gate, only the familiar totems placed on either side. As they neared they were greeted by two boys, each wearing necklaces similar to that worn by the boy sent to lead them to the house camp. To Obaseki's surprise, they came directly to him and took his belongings.

"They can touch?"

Ndoki chuckled. "Infana is a special place. The physical and spirit world are one here, if you choose to experience it. The city was the home of the old gods in the days when the gods lived among men. Moyo lived here, as did Delu. The buildings stand the same as they did thousands of years ago. Even the plants and animals of the forest dare not intrude upon this sacred ground."

"But you live outside its walls," Obaseki commented.

"The city is for the spirits and gods," Ndoki replied. "I am not ready yet but I am close, as you will be."

"I'm not sure that is my fate," Obaseki replied. "I came here to learn to control Moyo, not to become a god."

Ndoki turned, his face angry. "You do not control a god spirit! It is not your place to choose your fate."

Obaseki studied Ndoki with both forms of sight. Though the man stood before him, the spirit was something again.

"You are correct," Obaseki replied. "I am tired and not thinking clearly."

Ndoki smiled. "It has been a long journey. Rest here and I will have the servants bring you food. You will find it very satisfying."

Ndoki left the house grinning broadly. Obaseki sat on a gilded stool before a low stone table. He was in danger, no doubt. His sight revealed that Ndoki's soul was being slowly consumed by the spirit within his mayembe. He had to leave this place.

Two boys entered the room with trays of food and placed them before him on the table. Despite the delicious smells and sights before him, Obaseki noticed the warning in their expressions. There was obviously something in the food other than spices, but Obaseki was too hungry and tired to care. He ate until his stomach hurt, and then he lay on the plush pillows and slept.

Ndoki jostled him awake. Darkness filled the room, his host's golden smiled illuminated by the torch he carried.

"Are you rested?" he asked.

Obaseki nodded.

"Good. Come with me."

Obaseki stood, startled by the strength in his limbs. He grasped Moyo and felt the heat rising inside. He tensed, expecting the uncontrollable surge of power. Instead the flow remained gentle and constant.

He stared at Ndoki.

"What did you do to me?"

"It is a potion," Ndoki said. "It links you with Moyo, but it is only temporary. That is why we must go now. You will need Moyo's strength for this task."

Ndoki handed Obaseki a torch and lit another for himself. Together they walked the undulating roads of Infana, the sound of the ocean louder with each step. A full moon emerged from the horizon, the city walls incandescent from its light.

The road became rocky as they neared the cliffs. The smell was overwhelming, but Obaseki managed to calm his stomach and continue forward. The full moon rested directly above them, the ocean's surface shimmering under its pale blue radiance. Waves thundered against the broken rocks as sea spray drizzled down on them.

"This trail leads to a cave below the cliffs," Ndoki shouted. "On a night like this, moonlight reflects into the cave, lighting it like the sun.

"On the far end of the cave grows seaweed that is necessary for you to gain the power of Moyo. Pick as much as you can and bring them back."

Obaseki started and Ndoki halted him.

"You will need this," he said.

He handed Obaseki a gilded double-pointed spear. Obaseki felt the weapon's weight and could tell it would have been too heavy to lift without Moyo's energy. He waved to Ndoki and descended the trail, torch in one hand and spear in the other. The rocks rose on either side of him, the trail narrowing as he progressed. Darkness engulfed him save the light of the torch. The sound of the ocean was deafening in the corridor as Obaseki inched forward, sucking in his breath to pass. Just when he thought he could go no further the path widened. Light crept in from ahead, gradually overpowering the flickering torchlight.

Obaseki stumbled into the cave. It was large, long stalactites extending from the ceiling toward the swaying sea. Directly across from his position the mysterious weeds thrived, broad-leafed plants emitting an eerie light. He searched the edges of the cave for a path to the weeds; he was a poor swimmer and had no intentions of entering the water unless he had no other choice.

He walked gingerly between the broken stalagmites, keeping his balance with the spear. The waves roared inside the cavern, so much so that he didn't hear the explosion behind him. A column of water slammed into his back, knocking him forward into the rocks. He threw his hands out, losing the spear but sparing himself serious injury among the jagged stones. Before he could turn he was struck again, crashing painfully against the cave floor. Moyo's contact dulled the pain, but he knew he was injured. As his eyes cleared, he saw the source of his pummeling. The creature towered above him like the branches of a baobab, its serpent-like head glistening in the moonlight as it swayed back and forth with the rhythm of the sea. Its jaw swelled and then tightened as the creature spat a wide stream of water toward Obaseki. He spun away, the water slamming into the stone beside him. The serpent dove into the sea and Obaseki struggled to his feet. He stood still for a moment to regain his balance then ran for the cavern entrance. He was only a few steps away from safety when the serpent emerged from the water again. He fell to the ground and pulled himself into a ball, taking the brunt of the water against his back. His cry was drowned by the voice of the sea reverberating throughout the cavern. He lay stunned, gasping for breath as the serpent plunged back into the water again. Obaseki groped for and found the spear, turned about then sat up. He had one chance to kill the serpent and he had to take it. Obaseki stood, wishing he'd paid more attention to his weapon training as he braced himself for the next emergence of the serpent.

The creature rose again. Obaseki brought the spear to his shoulder as the serpent came to its full height. The moment it hesitated, its mouth full of seawater, Obaseki hurled the spear with all his strength. The projectile flew from his hand with a speed that startled him, striking the serpent below the jaw and bursting out the top of its head, ending its flight lodged into the cave ceiling. The serpent's mouth sagged open, releasing a waterfall of bloody liquid.

Obaseki sprinted to the narrow pass as the serpent fell forward, the ground trembling as its bulk struck the rocks. The force threw him into the gap, bashing his head against the narrow rocks. Blinding pain sent him into unconsciousness.

The light of the rising sun filled the cavern and Obaseki opened his eyes. His head ached; he licked his dry lips and tasted blood. A wave of nausea enveloped him and he coughed and vomited. He was weak; whatever Ndoki gave him to tap into Moyo's strength had dissipated. The mayembe lay stagnant against his chest.

Obaseki pulled himself up against the rocks, giving his eyes time to adjust to the stronger light. As they focused he realized the brightness did not come from the outside of the cave. It emanated from a mysterious orb hovering before him. As he watched, the orb took a featureless human form. It was some sort of spirit, one like he'd never seen. Instinct told him he should fear it, but he was too tired and hurt to care.

"You are well," it said in a deep, soothing tone.

"No," Obaseki replied.

"If you fought a saba and lived, you are well. Can you heal yourself with the mayembe?"

"I don't know," Obaseki answered. "I have not yet mastered it."

The spirit reached out with a line of light and touched the mayembe. It responded by glowing with a red, angry light.

"Moyo," it said with disgust. "His essence cannot heal you. He was a destroyer."

The light expanded, swallowing him in brightness. He felt himself mending, his strength increasing. The light contracted back to a thin line and pulled back into the spirit.

"What are you?" Obaseki asked.

"You have forgotten me," it replied. Obaseki detected sadness in its voice.

He focused his eyes on the shimmering image as it took

form. His eyes went wide as he recognized who hovered before him, his heart leaping with joy.

"Lewa!"

Lewa drifted down before Obaseki. "Hello, Seki."

Obaseki reached out to his friend. They touched and he felt her love flow into him, healing his wounds.

"You moved on?"

Lewa nodded. "It was the only way I could watch you and keep you safe."

"Thank you." Obaseki's mood changed suddenly as he remembered his situation.

"Fuluke said I would find my destiny here."

"Fuluke thought Ndoki would help you, but Ndoki no longer exists as your mentor knew him," Lewa explained. "Celu used him to hide from us. Ndoki revived her and has paid with his soul."

"Where is Celu?"

"Waiting for you. She was Moyo's lover once and wishes to be so again. We cannot take her from this world, so you must send her to us."

Obaseki's heart raced as he realized what he must do. "I can't destroy Celu! I am too weak to battle an orisha!"

"You have no choice." Lewa's image flickered with the sea breeze. "You must use what she desires to defeat her."

Obaseki looked at the mayembe as he came to his feet. "Why must I do this? What purpose does it serve?"

"The path is not always clear when the destination is true. Celu will tell you where your purpose lies."

Lewa faded, taking the light away.

"Lewa, wait!" Obaseki shouted. The cave fell back into its unusual radiance and Obaseki was alone again. He heard his name echo down the passage, bringing him back to his dilemma. He couldn't go back on the path knowing Celu waited to destroy him. The only other way out was the cave, although he did not know where the currents would take him. He decided uncertainty was safer. He crept to the water's edge and lowered himself in. The warm buoyant liquid soothed him as he struggled toward the cave's mouth. The cave floor gradually descended beyond his reach, forcing him to swim. He stayed as close to the jagged rocks as possible despite the dangerous swells and eddies.

The waves grew stronger near the mouth of the cave, forcing him to strike out for deeper water to avoid the rocks. He was not a strong swimmer. The distance was short, but to Obaseki it seemed like miles. The waves hammered the rocks ahead, swallowing them in foam. Obaseki took a deep breath and swam.

A wave surge lifted him, pushing back into the cave. Obaseki thrashed toward open water to avoid being thrown against jagged stones behind him. As the waves retreated he followed them, his crawl becoming a sprint to the sea. Obaseki fought the water and himself, his breath threatening to burst out, his arms and legs burning as he struggled to the opening.

Blinding light signaled his escape into open water. Obaseki stopped swimming and waited for the waves to carry him to shore. The water lifted him and he rode the crest at the mercy of the waters, bracing himself for the impact sure to come. He hit the rocks hard, letting out a gasp. The roaring water masked his panting; he flailed about to anchor himself among the stones so as not to be dragged back out to sea by the receding waves. His breath came back to him as the water disappeared and he dragged himself away from the sea edge. When he finally reached higher ground, he felt as if he had been beaten like a drum. He ached everywhere.

"Obaseki! Obaseki!"

Ndoki's urgent call reminded him his plight was not yet over. He peeked over the rocks and spied the rotund witch-doctor pacing about, wringing his hands as he peered down the narrow trail into the cave.

"He must be dead," he whispered. "He has to be dead by now."

Ndoki jerked, the desperate look on his face transformed into an angry glare.

"I did not want him dead!"

Fear took hold of the face again. "I would rather see him dead than suffer as I have."

Ndoki's face changed again to anger. "I have no use for you. It is time you join your brother. Moyo and I will be together again. He will take me to his city in the Mahgreb, where we'll rule our lands together."

Ndoki's face returned to fear, then pain. His skin glowed red, smoke rising from his head and limbs as he fell to the ground screaming. His skin boiled as his clothes burst into flames. Light spilled from his mouth and ran down his chin, flowing over him until it covered his entire body. Obaseki watched Ndoki's body burn and shrink into a charred husk in the shape of a woman. The burnt form broke open and Celu emerged from her human cocoon, her face featureless except for wide amber eyes that burned like fire.

Obaseki wanted to stay hidden among the rocks and for Celu to disappear into the city. But he knew she would not go to the city. She would follow the path into the cave and discover his escape. She would hunt him down, forcing him to summon Moyo from the spirit world, condemning him to the same fate as Ndoki. Then she would destroy all those he loved and the ancestors would not stop her.

Obaseki remembered Lewa's words.

"You must use what she loves the most," she said. His fingers tighten around Moyo. More and more he found himself depending on the power within, realizing he had to find a way to truly control it. But it was not to be that day, nor was Alamako the place. Before he came to his feet to confront Celu, the Lewa's voice emerged in his head again.

"Celu will tell you where you need to be."

He gathered his remaining strength and stood. Celu turned to him, her molten eyes expanding.

"You live?"

"Ndoki's attempt to kill me failed."

Celu moved toward him. "You don't have to end as Ndoki did. Moyo is weaker than I imagined. In order to revive him, the two of you must merge into one."

Obaseki tightened his grip on Moyo. "And what becomes of my body, of my spirit? Does my flesh burn away to reveal your lover? Is my soul consumed by Moyo's hunger?"

"You are a fool, Obaseki!" Celu reply harshly. "I offer you immortality and power, and you whine about your frail flesh. You are no better than Ndoki."

Obaseki unleashed Moyo just as Celu spewed a stream of flame from her eyes. The torrent collided with the light tendrils and Obaseki cowered from the heat as the flow soared over his head and exploded into fire and steam as it hit the ocean surface, throwing a plume of steam into the air. Unlike his other releases, Obaseki fought Moyo to exert control over the random violence. Celu sent another stream at him and Obaseki concentrated, bending a tendril to meet it. Instead of deflecting it, the tendril absorbed the stream, knocking Obaseki back onto the rocks.

"Don't make me kill you!" Celu shouted.

Obaseki pushed the pain aside, continuing to concentrate. But suddenly he realized his error. He was fighting Moyo and it fought back, refusing to be controlled. So he stopped, wiping his mind blank with thoughts of dark solitude. The tendrils ceased thrashing. They swayed with the rhythm of his heart.

"Moyo?" Celu said.

Obaseki was oblivious to Celu's words. The tendrils retracted into him, forming about him and outlining him as Celu's essence had done Ndoki. Opening his eyes, he observed Celu approaching him warily. He tensed, not knowing if what he was about to do would work. It was his only chance. He had to throw full concentration on Celu, sending all of Moyo's energy at her.

Celu edged closer. "Moyo?"

Obaseki attacked. The energy rushed from him in one solid beam, striking Celu in the head and lifting her into the air. Obaseki screamed, his body being ripped apart, every particle separating from another. Celu struggled against the onslaught, the stream of light lifting her higher, pulling rocks and water with it, sucking the life from every living creature surrounding it. Through his pain Obaseki heard the howls of spirits as they were dragged upward into the vortex of his attack.

Then suddenly there was silence, followed by a sound like the origin of all thunder. Obaseki became whole again, falling hard onto the rocks. He would die soon, he thought. This was his task then, to destroy Celu before she revived Moyo to fight the ancestors again. He used the god-spirit against her and prevailed; now his time was over. He closed his eyes, waiting for eternal peace. Instead he heard the familiar voice from the cave.

"You did well," Lewa said.

Obaseki lay still, waiting.

"Your journey is not over," she continued. "We are not ready for you yet. There is yet one more task for you to perform."

"I must go to the Mahgreb?" Obaseki managed to say.

"Yes."

"I will not go." Obaseki whispered. "I wish to die."

"Those who love you will come soon. You will live for them."

Obaseki was finished talking to spirits. He closed his eyes and waited for death, descending into peaceful oblivion until another familiar voice caught him.

"Seki?"

Eshe's warm, soft lips touched his forehead, lifting away his death wish. Pain rushed back into his body and he screamed.

"Hold him tight!" an unfamiliar voice ordered.

Unseen hands locked him down, his body struggling on its own. He felt a liquid pass his lips and through his teeth, forging a warm stream down his throat. The pain followed the liquid downward, congregating in his abdomen and dissipating. He dared to open his eyes and was rewarded with Eshe's lovely face.

"Sweet Flower," he whispered.

Eshe lifted his head gently and kissed him.

"Thank you, Lumumuba."

The dark-skinned masked man nodded. "It is the least I can do. We have our ancestors back because of him. We can live in peace again."

"I thank you as well, Lumumba," Obaseki said.

Lumumba lifted his healing mask, fell to his knees and touched his forehead on the floor. "Your words honor me, master of Moyo."

Pajonga and Olushola entered the room. They knelt as

well, a gesture Obaseki found embarrassing.

"Please, everyone rise. This isn't necessary."

"Pajonga found you," Eshe said. "He insisted on searching for you after a week passed and we did not hear from you."

"You are a true friend," Obaseki said. "A friend should not be a slave. Before these witnesses I grant you your freedom."

Pajonga jumped to his feet, his eyes glistening. "What did you say, master?"

"I am no longer your master," Obaseki replied. "I was never comfortable with the situation, and after this journey, you deserve to be free."

Obaseki looked into Olushola's expectant eyes. "This is your home, isn't it?"

"Yes, master, yes it is."

"Then stay and keep an eye on Pajonga. I grant your freedom as well."

"Thank you, Obaseki," she stammered.

The two embraced and hurried from the room. Obaseki looked into Eshe's eyes and met her approval.

"You are a good, brave man, my husband," she said. "Will Alamako be our home as well?"

Eshe's question triggered Lewa's last words in his head. His face turned somber.

"My path does not end here, sweet flower."

Eshe's face remained peaceful, though Obaseki sensed her disappointment.

"Where do the ancestors send us?" she asked.

"North," Obaseki replied. "North to the Mahgreb."

3

Ndoro and the Diaka stared over the cliff, watching the Nyoka River plunged into the misty gorge below. The descent was dizzying, the deafening voice of the river rising from the base of the falls as tons of water smashed into massive rock. The powerful waterway emerged from the spray into an expansive valley, its wide banks crowded with towering trees. Ndoro was in awe; surely no other Sesu had stood where he stood, witnessing the artistry and power of Unkulunkulu.

He turned to Jawanza. "It is beautiful," he said. Jawanza stood behind him, his assegai at his side, his face and arms glistening with sweat and spray..

"This land is truly a gift from the ancestors," Jawanza replied.

"It is home," Jabulani declared, "just as the legends describe it."

Ndoro scratched his chin. "Now how do we get down there?"

Jabulani extracted the weathered map from his pouch and sat on the ground, spreading it out before him.

"We will have to go further east. The cliffs are not so high there. I estimate two or three days."

Ndoro squatted beside him. "Good. We will camp here and continue on in the morning."

They made camp a safe distance from the cliff's edge, building a large fire to keep away the chill of the approaching darkness. Ndoro did not worry about the blaze being spotted;

from what he could see the land was empty and probably had been so since the Diaka fled. There were thirty of them total, the group a week away from the temporary village established further down the river. For three months the Diaka traveled down the Nyoka, facing the dangers of the swift currrents, cataracts and animals as they followed the map to their former homeland. Some were lost along the way, never to reach their destination. Now they were only a few days away from the prize, and a feeling of anticipation swept through the weary tribe. If old Diakaland was anything near what the legends described the arduous journey was well worth the cost.

Ndoro, Jawanza, Kamau and Jabulani sat before the fire, eating dried buffalo and yams. The trees bustled with sound as night creatures became active, continuing the struggle to survive in the shadows. Ndoro watched Jabulani and was concerned. He was sullen, which did not bode well.

"What is wrong, baba?"

Jabulani chewed his food slowly. "I thank the ancestors for guiding us so far. Despite those who have died, this has been an easy journey."

He looked into Ndoro's eyes, his expression turning grim. "But our ancestors fled this land for a reason. I wonder if that reason waits to drive us away again."

"That will not happen," Jawanza said. "We are strong now, and we have Shumba."

"Jabulani is right," Ndoro agreed. "From now on we must be on our guard. We will post sentries tonight."

Everyone nodded in agreement. Ndoro stood, stretching as the rigors of the day caught up with him.

"We are tired," he said. "We should get to sleep now for tomorrow's surprises."

The shrill calls of a troupe of passing vervets woke them to muted sunlight. They broke camp, Jabulani leading the way into the valley on a path that tumbled down into dense forest. Everyone became wary, remembering the conversation of the other night. Ndoro walked with measured confidence, fully in tune with what was happening around him.

The path narrowed and they were forced to leave their provisions behind. Ndoro checked each man to make sure they had all their weapons, including the poison-tipped arrows. They clambered down the steep slope, Jawanza leading the way. Moisture from the vegetation covered them every time they brushed it; by the time they reached the valley floor they were drenched. The view ahead was in great contrast from where they stood hours ago. A green wall of trees, vines and bushes loomed before them, allowing only a few feet of visibility. Ndoro clutched the amulet around his neck, the one given to him by Sarama. He whispered a prayer before taking the lead and plunging into the thicket. He did not know the gods of this land, nor the countless spirits that obviously dwelled in such a place. He only hoped that Ukulunkulu's strong hands would extend its protection there.

A few miles into the bush they came upon what looked like an elephant trail. Jabulani grasped Ndoro's shoulder.

"Something's wrong. We should be there by now."

Ndoro moved beside him. "Maybe the map is wrong. It's been hundreds of years."

Jawanza walked pass them. "Maybe we should keep going."

He walked through the underbrush and disappeared. No sooner had the leaves enveloped him did they hear him yell.

Ndoro charged through the bushes, his assegai held high. Blinding light struck him and he stopped in his tracks.

"Jawanza!" he shouted.

"Ndoro!" his brother replied. "Come, come see!"

He found Jawanza, a broad smile on his adopted brother's face. Before him, about one thousand feet down, was the valley of the Diaka. The Nyoka snaked between high mountain ridges, a wide and gently sloping plain on either side that ran to the base of the tree-covered peaks. There were no signs of any other humans. The banks teemed with animals of all kinds; antelopes, buffalo, elephants and others could be seen from their height.

Jabulani bumped into Ndoro, closely followed by the others. He saw the vision before him and fell to his knees.

"We are home," Jabulani whispered.

"Jawanza, go back to the village and spread the news," Ndoro said. "I will take Jabulani and the others down into the valley. We will set up camp and wait for you."

Jawanza looked disappointed. Ndoro smiled and patted his shoulder.

"Just one more week, my brother," he said. "Now go; the longer you wait the longer it will take you to return."

Jawanza selected his party and left quickly, all of them with dejected looks on their face. Ndoro turned to Jabulani, but the old man was gone. He was sprinting down the trail to the valley.

"Jabulani, wait!" Ndoro called out.

He and the other warriors laughed as they ran to catch up with Jabulani. Their laughter turned into effort when they realized the old man was faster than they thought. By the time they caught up to him he was at the base of the hill, standing motionless.

"Baba!" Ndoro said. "You've been saving your energy."

Ndoro fell silent when he saw what held Jabulani's attention. A stone pillar the height of a man blocked the path. It was triangular, crowned with the carving of a crocodile. Writing ran down the length of the pillar. Jabulani shook as he read.

"What does it say?" Ndoro asked.

"Those that once lived here are cursed by the river god Ngwena," Jabulani read. "Those who follow will suffer the same fate."

Ndoro pushed Jabulani aside. Bracing his shoulder against the stone, he dug his feet into the damp ground and pushed. The others came to his aid and they strained against the stone as if opening a forbidden door. Slowly the base of the obelisk tilted, leaned, and then crashed to the ground.

Ndoro looked at his adopted father and smiled. "Let us tempt fate."

He stepped over the obelisk and entered the Diaka's' homeland.

The remaining Diaka arrived the following week. They set about their task quickly, building a makeshift village on the edge of the river. As the women and children built homes and cleared fields, the men hunted the woods for the abundant game. Ndoro called the first elders meeting after two weeks, greeting the learned men under a modest ironwood tree near the new village.

A joyful feeling radiated among the old ones sitting in the semi-circle about Ndoro. They jostled about like young boys, smiling and joking while Jabulani tried to call them to order. They finally calmed down when Ndoro stood.

"Welcome home," Ndoro said. The elders clapped and touched their heads to the ground before him.

"We have come far for this day. Homes have been built and fields are planted. Our hunters bring in game and our fishermen fill their nets daily. But there is much more for us to do."

"Tell us what you wish, Shumba," Shaihi asked. "You have led us to freedom and to our homeland. It is obvious the ancestors have chosen you."

Ndoro was still not used to the admiration of the Diaka, especially these older men who held more wisdom among them that he could ever wish to have. He hesitated before revealing his plan because he knew it was selfish. But if he were to one day return home, he would need these brave people to help him.

"I wish to make the Diaka strong. I wish for all the tribes between our valley and Songhai to fear the warriors of this land."

The mood changed sudden like a rainy season storm. The old men looked among themselves with knowing expressions before Shaihi spoke.

"You are a young man, Shumba," he said. "The path before you seems new, but to us it is old and worn. It is good enough for us to sit here and see our people free. But a fire burns inside you. We saw it the day you first came into our village. We used your fire to free us. Do not use it to destroy us."

"I am only asking you to be what you can become," Ndoro replied.

"Your dream is a Sesu dream, not Diaka," Shaihi replied.

"The Diaka are warriors," Ndoro replied. "Do you think the Songhai lick their wounds and forget the Diaka? Do you think the Tacuma will welcome us back when they discover we have returned?"

Ndoro regretted instigating the worry he saw in the elders' faces, but it was necessary. He had no idea what the Songhai planned; he did not even know if the Tacuma still existed. He did know that by bringing up these hated and feared enemies, his argument would be heard.

"You are Ndoro, the Diaka-koi, our Shumba," Shaihi finally responded. "If you tell the young men your dream, they will follow you. But we ask that you wait. We have much work to do. We have no wealth but the land we farm and the food we raise. We have no cattle, no items to trade, and no iron to make weapons. We need time, Shumba."

"Patience is the key to all good things," Jabulani added.

The elders' point was well made, Ndoro admitted to himself.

"Your council comes with wisdom," he said. "We will concentrate on what we have. But we must be mindful of our defense. The Songhai is a distant enemy but the Tacuma are a present worry."

"We agree as much," Shaihi said.

"I think we should build a stone city closer to the mountains," Ndoro said. "The river village is vulnerable to attack. A walled city against the mountains would provide a sound defense."

"The river is also the home of the Tacuma's totem, Ngwena," Jabulani added. The further away we are from this bad omen the better."

"Again you show your wisdom," Shaihi said. "We will gather our stone smiths and find a quarry. We will begin work immediately."

The gathering broke up with everyone in better spirits. Ndoro retired to his home where Sarama waited, stirring the pot of stew as she hummed.

"So, my warrior returns triumphant?"

Ndoro came up behind her and wrapped his arms around her waist. She was plump with child, her fullness a welcomed sight to everyone in the family. Ndoro was now a true Diaka.

"No one triumphs over the elders", he corrected. "We agreed."

"But you got your way."

"Of course."

"It won't be so easy when this little one comes," Sarama said as she rubbed her stomach with his hand.

"He will be a fine warrior," he said.

"She will be a proud Diaka maiden," Sarama retorted.

Ndoro eyes went wide. "You know this?"

"Mama told me so. She is never wrong."

Ndoro went to the stool and sat hard. "So I must wait for a son."

Sarama hit him on the head with her spoon. "And be happy for your daughter."

Ndoro reached out, grabbing her around the waist and pulling her onto his lap. They laughed and kissed and forgot about the stew until much later in the evening.

The following weeks hummed by to the rhythm of a busy multitude. Fields were planted and the farmers waited while the hunters continued to harvest the bounty of the valley. Unlike the lands to the north, the rain seemed to spread itself evenly throughout the seasons, allowing for longer growing seasons and bigger harvests. The stonecutters found their quarry and began the arduous task of cutting stone for the new city. The mysterious brotherhood of blacksmiths located a source of the rock from which they summoned the metal essential for tools and weapons. Though it seemed a time for peace, Ndoro, Jawanza and Kamau kept the Diaka men sharp with drills and mock battles. Patrols were organized to keep constant vigil, sometimes staying out for weeks as they surveyed the valley and the surrounding hills. A new generation of boys was coming of age and Ndoro organized them into the peer groups he remembered as a child. Sesu stick fighting was taught to develop their martial skills, and competitions were arranged to foster unity among the peer groups and the boys as a whole.

It was during the first full moon of the sixth month when the Diaka discovered they were not alone. Night came early to the valley as it always did, the sun disappearing behind the verdant peaks. Ndoro and Sarama enjoyed each other's company in the compound, chatting over an intense game of oware when they were interrupted by an urgent rapping on their door. Ndoro opened it to reveal the worried face of Jawanza.

"Shumba, you must come quickly."

"What is it?"

"The night patrol captured someone breaking into the granary."

"Who is it? What family does he belong to?"

Jawanza hesitated. "He is not Diaka."

The two men ran through the streets to the granary at the center of the city. A crowd gathered, people pushing to get closer to the warriors before the granary door.

"Move aside!" Jawanza shouted. "Make way for the Diaka-koi!"

The crowd parted immediately, revealing the intruder. He sat cross-legged on the ground, his hands tied behind his back. His head shaven, the man looked about angrily at his captors. He was thin, his ribs showing through his scarred skin. His chest was covered by a large ngwena brand, a ragged loincloth his only clothing.

Ndoro walked to the man and squatted before him.

"Who are you?"

"I am a beast," the man replied. "Kill me and be done with it."

Ndoro tried again. "What is your name?"

"I have no name," the captive replied. "I am a beast, and my masters will come for me soon."

"Who are your masters?

"The people who will be your masters soon; the Tacuma."

Ndoro kept his face stern despite the crowd's collective gasp. "The Tacuma know we are here?"

The captive smiled. "They suspected, but now they know. They will come to kill your men and take your women and children. This land has been cursed since the Diaka were driven away. You have condemned yourselves by coming here."

Ndoro smiled back. "I see you didn't mind stealing a little condemned food."

He stood erect. "This land is not cursed to us. It was ours before; it is ours again."

The man's smile melted away. "Diaka? No!"

"Diaka, yes," Ndoro replied. "Take this man and hold him in the empty storehouse," he said to the patrollers. "Make sure he is fed."

He faced the terrified man again. "Sleep well, beast. We have much to discuss in the morning."

Ndoro spent a restless night wondering about the captive's words. If the Tacuma knew they were in the valley, how long would they wait before attacking? Did they know they were the Diaka, or did they think they were a wandering tribe that knew nothing of the curse? The questions spun about in his head as he fell in and out of sleep through night, the last awakening made final by the emerging daylight. Ndoro was the first to the stockade. The sentries greeted him with a sharp bow. They opened the door to the empty granary and he entered.

The air burned with the smell of decaying grain and rodent droppings. The captive sat upright on the opposite wall, his face passive.

"Do we have a name today?" Ndoro asked.

"I am a slave. Tacuma slaves have no names as you will

discover soon."

Ndoro did not like the arrogant words of this man. He would have killed him by now if not for the information he sought.

"You speak of the Tacuma as if they are gods, but gods need no slaves."

"The gods have men to serve them in respect and fear," the captive replied. "The Tacuma have men to serve them as slaves."

"If you praise them so much, why did you run away?"

The captive smiled. "I did not run away. I was sent to find you."

Ndoro's eyes narrowed, focusing on the ngwena brand on the captive's chest. There was something about the eye that bothered him.

"Yes, the eye of the ngwena sees," the captive said. "It sees what I see. My masters know where I have been and where I am. What I see, my masters see."

Ndoro stood upright, the captive laughing. "Yes, yes, you know now, don't you? You will meet the Tacuma very soon."

Ndoro snatched his sword and stabbed the man in the chest where the eye of the ngwena stared. He ran from the granary to his compound.

"Sound the attack drums!" he shouted. "The Tacuma are coming!"

No sooner had the words escaped his lips that cries were heard coming from the river's edge. Ndoro and the guards ran to the river as the attack drums rumbled through the village. Other warriors streamed out of their family compounds. The Diatanee came one by one, forming ranks around their leader. The army was full force as they came to the river.

They met a crowd of women running for their lives. They all had been washing along the river when the canoes appeared. There were bodies on the ground, arrows protruding from their backs. Ndoro was hit by a wave of terror; Sarama had left earlier to wash with the other women.

The Tacuma warriors rowed to the banks, covering their landing with a shower of arrows. They poured out of their canoes with short broad swords and wooden shields, their heads covered by wooden masks carved in the shape of the ngwena, the long snouts brandishing jagged white teeth. Ngwena hide protected their torsos and legs.

The Diaka locked their shields, covering the fleeing women and themselves as their archers fired back. Ndoro charged forward, followed by the other Diaka. He threw his orinka high with his men and the Tacuma raised their shield in response, falling for the diversion. The Diaka hurled their assegais at the unprotected midsections, cutting down scores of Tacuma. Ndoro led the attack as they crashed into the warriors.

It was a vicious battle. Ndoro was blind in his rage, swinging and hacking with unbridled fury. The Diaka swarmed over the Tacuma, killing those on the banks and driving the others back to the canoes.

"Don't let them escape!" Ndoro shouted. "Kill them all!"

The Diaka ran into the river, tackling the fleeing Tacuma and stabbing them in the water. Those that reached the canoes found only a brief respite as the Diaka archers joined the fight again with their deadly volleys. The distracted Tacuma did not notice the Diaka swimmers. They capsized the war canoes, spilling the warriors into the river and the waiting blades of their brothers.

The battle ended as quickly as it began. The Tacuma were wiped out to a man, but the Diaka suffered as well. Women and children ran to the river, searching for their loved ones. The wailing echoed from the riverbank as families found their dead sons, fathers and brothers. The wounded were taken to the village center to be tended.

Ndoro heard a familiar voice cry out. He stood motionless, daring not to move until he heard the cry again and knew he had to face what waited for him. He walked slowly to the riverside and to the circle of his family on their knees. The crying sunk into his chest as he neared. Everyone saw him approaching and parted, revealing the sight he expected. Strength left his legs and he fell to his knees, dropping his weapons as he reached out to the body of Sarama. Talana held her daughter in her arms, cradling her as well as she could. Ndoro could go no closer. He looked into Talana's eyes and saw the loss to them both.

Rage exploded inside him and he stopped crying. The pain found a place to hide, escaping the fury that coursed through him like a flooding river. He picked up his weapons and stood.

"Take care of her, mama," he said. "I have something I must do."

The family warriors came to their feet, the meaning of Ndoro's words clear. They followed him back to the main village where Jabulani, despite his loss, performed the necessary ritual to appease the souls of the slain Tacuma. The sight of Sarama's father chanting among her killers drove his rage to a higher level.

"Stop!" Ndoro commanded. Jabulani looked at him with angry puzzlement.

"You know what must be done," Jabulani replied. "Their souls must be honored to rest in peace."

"Let their ngwena spirit give them peace," Ndoro replied. He turned to his warriors. "Throw them into the river!"

The Diaka swarmed past Jabulani and set about the task.

They flung the bodies of the Tacuma to the river.

Ndoro smiled. "Now their spirit has the choice of saving them or eating them."

He turned his back to the river and strode way until an odd sound emanated from behind him. He turned to see the river churning with the bodies of the Tacuma warriors. The carcasses rose to surface jerking and twisting, arms and legs shrinking as torsos became extended. Their heads stretched as jagged triangular teeth burst from their mouths. Leathery scales encased their skin as tails emerged from their backs.

Jabulani appeared at his side, yanking his arm. "Come, Ndoro! The Ngwena comes!"

Ndoro snatched his arm away. "Let him."

Jabulani gave up and fled into the woods with the other villagers. The warriors remained, though their shifting eyes betrayed them. Their fears were answered as the Tacuma warriors returned, this time in flesh of ngwenas. They moved fast, driving back the Diaka, pushing them away from Ndoro but not attacking. Ndoro seemed oblivious to the reptiles as they swarmed around him, growling and snapping. He looked down at them, a smile creasing his face. Sarama and his unborn child were with the spirits. He would soon be with them.

The water churned again. A huge shadow approached, weaving its way to the shore just under the surface of the river, its large eyes focused on Ndoro. It climbed from the water onto the bank and slowly approached the reptilian circle. Even in his sorrow and rage Ndoro was moved by the size of the beast. The perimeter of the circle opened and the bull ngwena entered. Ndoro's hands clenched about his assegai and shield, anticipation coursing through him. The ngwena let out a long bellow as it transformed, standing on its hind legs as its body took shape. Its hind legs extended as its fore limbs took the shape of massive human arms. The crocodile man's eyes sparked as it looked down on Ndoro.

Ndoro charged the beast and was knocked aside by the sweep of its tail. He struck the ground and almost rolled into one of the ngwena, blocking its snapping jaws with his shield. He was coming to his feet when the beast struck at him with his claws. Ndoro ducked as he swung his sword. The blow glanced off its scales. It swung its tail again but Ndoro jumped over it, slipping behind his attacker. He threw his assegai and watched it bounce off the thick back scales.

The beast spun about. "What are you?" it hissed.

Ndoro extracted his sword again as his answer. The beast moved toward him then stopped, turning its head from side to side.

"You are no man," it said. "A man would be dead by now."

The ngwenas surrounding Ndoro rustled, edging closer to him. The beast was summoning them to attack, Ndoro thought. It could not defeat him alone. Ndoro smirked. This river spirit was not much to fight, let alone fear.

He charged the crocodile-spirit and it lunged at him, mouth wide and teeth glistening. Ndoro stepped aside and stabbed low, striking the beast in its underbelly. It howled and its servants fell still. The beast grabbed the blade before Ndoro could pull it out and dragged him toward the gaping jaws. Ndoro brought his shield about and jammed it between its teeth. The beast bit down, tearing through leather and wood. Its grip loosened on the sword and Ndoro snatched it free. As the beast reached for the shield in its mouth, Ndoro gripped his sword with both hands and struck beast's wrist. The blade hesitated then sliced through the joint, the paw falling to the ground. A cry came from the beast that tore at his ears. The crocodiles spun on the ground as they did when tearing a victim apart, but this time in pain. They fled to the river, transforming back into the still bodies of the slain Tacuma. The river-spirit held its damaged arm against its body with its good paw and ran for the safety of the water. Ndoro was not about to be denied his kill. He chased after the beast and grabbed its massive tail, lifting its hind legs from the ground. The Ngwena-beast fell to its front legs, tearing at the mud with its claws and stub in a vain attempt to reach the murky river.

"Hold him Ndoro!" Jabulani shouted. Ndoro twisted his head about to see his foster father pick up the severed paw and drop it into a gourd. He placed the gourd on the ground and drew a series of patterns on it. The beast attempted to twist free but Ndoro's grip was unyielding. Jabulani placed the gourd on the ground as he chanted then clapped his hands.

The beast ceased struggling and fell to its knees, breathing heavily. Ndoro let the tail go and picked up his sword.

"Thank you, baba," he said as he raised his sword over the beast's head.

Jabulani scampered forward and stepped in between Ndoro and the beast.

"No, Ndoro, you don't have to kill him."

"Of course I do," Ndoro replied.

"You don't understand," Jabulani said. "His paw and his soul are trapped in the gourd. As long as you possess a part of a spirit it must obey you. It cannot return to the spirit realm without it. You are its master now."

"I have no faith in magic, Baba," Ndoro replied. "This beast is better off dead."

"You can kill him, but by doing so you destroy your revenge," Jabulani said. "If you control the beast, you control the Tacuma."

Ndoro looked at the beast. "Is this true?"

The beast did not answer.

"Answer me!" Ndoro shouted. He saw the beast struggle

against opening its jaws.

"Yes. It is true."

A grin came to Ndoro's face. "Can we build some type of cage to hold him?"

"This is the only cage you need," Jabulani replied. He tied a leather cord around the mouth of the gourd and handed it to Ndoro. Ndoro tied it around his waist.

"He is yours now," Jabulani said. "You are his master."

Ndoro frowned at his captive river-spirit. "Stay here until I return."

A moan seeped from the beast's jaws.

"Come, baba", Ndoro said as his rage ebbed. "We must mourn."

They walked together in silence, the cries from their compound growing louder with each step. As they passed through the gate tears trickled from their eyes as well. The women gathered outside Ndoro's home, their mourning ritual loud and aching. They came to him, wrapping their arms about his neck and crying into his chest, their words incoherent in their sorrow. Ndoro pushed them aside as politely as possible. The doorway was clear; he opened it and went inside.

Sarama lay on the floor as if asleep, her body covered with a white cotton sheet. Talana knelt beside her, rocking back and forth, singing softly. Ndoro dropped to his knees and laid beside his wife, wrapping his arms around her coldness and burying his head into her arm. Sobs shook him and he did not fight to keep them inside. Together he and Talana cried for Sarama, pleading for her spirit to stay close to them and accept this new land as her home. They cried for the unborn child, the daughter that was never named, one of the first victims of the war that was about to begin.

Ndoro lifted himself from the floor. He had allowed himself the luxury of mourning; he would never do so again. He stepped away from Talana and nodded, making way for her to perform a last task for her daughter. Ndoro left the house amid the constant wailing of not only his compound, but also that of the entire city. The sounds became too much for him so he walked away, ignoring the urgent words of other villagers asking for a council. He followed the main road out of the village, the road that led to the stone mines in the eastern mountains. He walked through the sunlight and the night sky, oblivious to the animals scampering in the canopy of the high forests and totally ignoring those that threatened him on the ground. Two days after he began his trek he passed the camp of the stonecutters. The men recognized him, but Ndoro ignored them, stepping into the woods at the end of the path. Ndoro began to climb the ridge. Digging his feet into the soil with each step, he fought his way upward, using the hanging vines to pull himself up the steep slope. The dense foliage engulfed him; darkness prevailing where light had no right to be. He continued to climb, lungs burning with each step, until he reached a granite outcrop. A path worn by the gait of men snaked its way ahead of him and he followed it. By dusk he was at the top of the highest peak on the ridge. Ndoro stopped and spread his blankets on the stone. He removed his weapons one by one, laying them next to his blanket. As he began to lie down he heard human sounds and he grabbed his assegai. The crocodile-spirit appeared and sat opposite him.

"I wish to be alone," Ndoro said. "Leave me."

The crocodile man stood. "As you wish. I would not want to see you mourn like a woman."

Ndoro came to his feet. "Your mouth will get you killed."

"Better death than be a servant to a weak fool," the beast

replied.

Ndoro smiled. "You wish I would kill you, don't you? Why should I make your end easy?"

"If you won't kill me, at least make my service worth the humiliation."

Ndoro sat, ignoring the Ngwena's words.

"You come here to understand your place," the beast replied. "Your wife is dead. There is nothing you can do about it. You can run as far as you like and she will still be dead."

"What do you know of humans?" Ndoro shouted.

"You can't imagine how long I've lived," the beast replied. "I've been hunted and worshipped by your kind for thousands of years. I've come to know you very well."

"I'm tired of talking and I am disgusted looking at you," Ndoro replied. "I need to think. Leave me."

"Think of this," the beast replied. "You defeated a spirit, something a man should not be able to do. The ancestors have a plan for you whether you believe so or not."

The beast closed his eyes, transforming into a human form more disturbing because of its perfection. He smiled and sauntered away, disappearing into the foliage. Ndoro dropped his weapons and lay back down, although he did not sleep. He thought of his journey since fleeing Selike, of his adoption by the Diaka, his training them and making them warriors, of their trek to the new homeland and his defeat of the river-spirit. Buried under it all remained the promise he made to himself, the promise to return to Selike and claim the Royal Stool as his own. The river beast claimed the ancestors had a plan for him. As far as he was concerned, the ancestors did not figure in his life. Every triumph in his life he'd accomplished on his own. Life with the Diaka had distracted him from his purpose. If he were to see Selike again, he would have to take control of his life again.

As the morning sun peered over the eastern peaks Ndoro stared down on the valley. In the distance smoke of the morning fires rose from the Diaka villages. He heard the clattering of the stonecutters at the quarry below him. Somewhere to the north the Tacuma waited in vain for the return of their warriors while their priests called on a god that would not answer. He heard the rustling of branches and the river beast appeared.

"Do you have a name?" Ndoro inquired

"Nakisisa," the beast replied.

"You know where the Tacuma live?"

The beast nodded.

"You will lead us to them, Nakisisa."

Nakisisa smiled. "The night's rest has done you well. Maybe you will serve the ancestors purpose."

"I could care less about the ancestors," Ndoro replied. "I have my own reasons."

The ngwena man grinned. "As you say, master."

The two of them returned to the village after the mourning ceremonies were complete. A pall hung over the village, the people lethargically performing their daily chores. Ndoro went to Jabulani's compound and found the same mood. His adopted family barely noticed his return as he walked through the compound to his home. Ndoro stopped and opened the door. The house was empty. He closed his eyes and imagined Sarama squatting before the fire, stirring her delicious stew, the smile that pushed away his worries on her beautiful face. The shadows of grief reentered his mind, swallowing Sarama's memory and he closed the door. Ndoro stepped away and went to the house of Jabulani. The old man sat before the door, slowly chewing on a kola nut. He smiled.

"You have returned," he said. "Many thought you went back to your people."

Ndoro sat beside his foster father.

"We would have understood if you did," Jabulani continued. "Sarama was special. It is difficult to lose someone you love."

Ndoro refused to contemplate Jabulani's words.

"Baba, I require council with the elders."

Jabulani's smile disappeared. "Why?"

"We need to discuss war against the Tacuma."

Jabulani nodded slowly. "I will send Jawanza."

The council meeting was short. Ndoro made his intentions clear and the council did not stand in his way. The stonecutters were summoned back to the village to help build war canoes. The ironsmiths went to work creating spear tips, wrist knives, swords and other weapons of war. Life flowed back into the veins of the Diaka in a grim form. They were no longer fishermen and farmers; they were warriors again.

Three weeks after Ndoro's return the village rang with the sounds of celebration. Women and children danced to the drummers who stood on rooftops beating out praises as the army ran through the streets. Ndoro, Jawanza and Kamau, dressed in full Diaka battle dress, waited at the docks with the elders. Nakisisa languished in the water in his reptilian form, his eyes just visible over the rippling surface.

Ndoro raised his assegai and the drummers changed the rhythm, summoning the warriors to the canoes. The army marched into the shallow mooring and climbed aboard. Kamau led the archers into the lead boats; Jawanza loaded his warriors into the boats to the rear. The largest boat rested ahead of the others, an enormous canoe with metal plating on the bow, a platform rising over the edge. Fifty Diatanee boarded the massive craft in single file, chanting as they took their places. When the last had entered, Ndoro boarded, taking his place on the platform. Nakisisa remained in the water, awaiting Ndoro's signal.

One hundred canoes filled with warriors undulated upon the river. Diaka lined the banks of the Nyoka, an entire nation present to witness its new beginning. Pride resonated in their voices as they sang; their arms raised high as they danced. Ndoro scanned the war fleet and smiled. This was his monument to Sarama. He promised to make her a wife and he did, but he was never able to make her a queen. Ndoro circled his assegai over his head, the same assegai that slew Old Simba. In unison the rowers pushed off and the crowd cheered. Nakisisa swam before Ndoro's canoe as ordered, leading the Diaka army to Tacumaland.

According to Nakisisa, Tacumaland lay two weeks south. Once they reached the borderlands, it could be another two days before they reached the capital city. The river spirit warned Ndoro of the size of Tacumaland, convincing him the Diaka could not defeat them in a long war. Ndoro decided to make a decisive strike at the center of the kingdom itself, the city of Jinja. He hoped the show of force would keep the Tacuma at bay long enough for the Diaka to build their strength and complete construction of the stone city. There was also Nakisisa. The Tacuma's reaction to their fallen god was critical to the success of the attack. If it did not go as he anticipated, the Diaka would march back to their homeland only to be destroyed by the same people that drove them away centuries ago.

The days were spent rowing, the nights resting along the banks. The river held few cataracts to slow their progress; their biggest obstacles were the groups of hippopotami scattered along the river. The fearless beasts blocked their progress numerous times, ignoring the threats of the warriors. Nakisisa was no help; being part crocodile he held a great respect and fear of the animals. Only the constant beating of the water with the oars forced the beast to move, more in annoyance than fear.

With only a half day's rowing from the borders of Tacuma, the Diaka settled into their last camp before making the run for the city. There would be no rest the next day. Ndoro's orders were clear. The canoes would not stop until they reached Jinja.

Ndoro sat by a small fire with his brothers. They ate silently, each deep within his thoughts. Ndoro hated idle moments such as this, for it gave his mind a chance to wander back to memories of Sarama. Nakisisa sat just beyond the light of the fire, his eyes glowing. Ndoro rose and walked away, headed for the war canoes. Nakisisa followed him. As Ndoro inspected the canoes, the crocodile-spirit slid into the black waters. He listened to the beast splash about as it found and devoured its prey, hoping a man was not the victim. The beast returned in human form, his face bright red with blood.

He looked at Ndoro and smiled. "It humors me when humans look at me that way. You act as if you've never seen blood, yet tomorrow you will spill much of it yourselves."

"We are not much different from you," Ndoro said.

"You are the first to admit it," Nakisisa replied.

"I have no reason to lie," Ndoro replied. "I know the only way to survive is to be stronger than those that oppose you. My father was weak and allowed me to be driven away. If he were stronger, he would have defied the elders and stopped the smelling out that condemned me."

"Tradition is a powerful force," Nakisisa replied. "The Diaka follow you only because of tradition. Power alone is nothing; power within tradition is everything."

"You are a wise slave," Ndoro replied.

"And you are a fast learner," Nakisisa said. "It will be an honor to kill you one day."

The Diaka rose before first light and boarded their war canoes. They abandoned their supplies at the campsites, making for faster travel. Ndoro arranged the boats in attack formation, the archer boats near the river edge protecting the warrior boats in the center. At the front of the formation was Ndoro's armored canoe flanked by two smaller canoes manned with fire archers. They penetrated the borders of Tacuma before dawn, pushing forward as fast they could row. They passed scores of fishing villages, their inhabitants harvesting the river's bounty along the banks. Some waved at them, apparently thinking they were returning Tacuma. It was well into the day before the response to their advance transformed from friendly waves to angry glares and shouts. Ndoro knew runners were outpacing them to warn the villages upriver.

"Increase the pace," he ordered. The drummer beat faster and the rowers responded. Ndoro scanned forward and saw the villagers of the upcoming town pushing their boats into the river.

The lead archers loaded their bows. The fishermen were attempting to block the river, pushing their boats out and lashing them together end to end. Some tied the boats together while others ran to the banks with armloads of sticks and filled the boats.

Nakisisa swam beside Ndoro's canoe. "They are building a firewall," he said. "Look behind us."

Ndoro strained his eyes and saw a mass of canoes filled with Tacuma warriors rapidly approaching their rear.

The boat barricade came into bow range. Diaka arrows

jumped from the bows in a chorus of twanging bowstrings, the iron-tipped missiles falling upon the blockade workers with devastating accuracy. Another volley cut down the torchbearers attempting to light the straw-filled canoes. Though the canoes did not burn, they were still tied together. The Diaka would have to cut the boats free in order to pass. Three Diatanee jumped into the water without urging, swimming for the boats. Arrows flew toward them from the banks and the Diaka responded, driving the Tacuma back behind the trees for protection. The warriors reached the canoes and cut them free with their wrist daggers, clearing the way to move on.

The pace drummer renewed his rhythm and the fleet surged ahead, pulling away from the pursuing Tacuma canoes. The water-bound Diatanee clamored onto Ndoro's canoe as it sped by, and they took their place among the others. They raced upriver through a gauntlet of arrows and spears as the Tacuma responded to this bold attack. Warriors ran along the riverbanks trying to anticipate where the Diaka would make landfall, none suspecting the objective of the attack until the granite walls of Jinja rose over the horizon.

The Tacuma unleashed a torrent of arrows at the Diaka canoes. The deluge was too much for the Diaka to return; they raised their shields and hid under the protection of wood and leather. But still they rowed, headed for the island. Tacuma warriors jumped into the river, swimming for the canoes under the cover of the arrows. Nakisisa attacked them, blood swirling in the currents as he struck them one by one. The Tacuma on the banks looked on in terror as their river-god betrayed his worshippers. They fell away from river's edge, many of them dropping their weapons and falling to their knees.

The canoes approached the banks of Jinja unopposed.

They ran aground and the Diaka poured out, the Diatanee first to set foot on the sandy banks. A massive spiked iron gate sealed the towering walls, a formidable barrier between the Diaka and their prize. Tacuma warriors stood along the ramparts like statues, their faces locked in disbelief as they watched Ndoro stride to them, Nakisisa trailing behind him in obvious servitude. The Diaka-koi continued forward until he was within shouting distance of the walls, ignoring the fact that he was also well within arrow range.

"Tacuma! I have come for what is mine!" Ndoro shouted. "Your god stands beside me, master to my will. We stand before your walls because your ancestors have forsaken you. Your warriors flee like children upon the sight of true men. Open your gates and live; raise your spears against us and die!"

Ndoro watched the ramparts of the city walls for signs the Tacuma might fight. He dare not look behind; he knew the Tacuma warriors pursuing him upriver now stood behind him. He was surrounded. They all waited for a signal from the city, Diaka and Tacuma alike. A lone figure appeared on the walls. The man stood for a moment and then disappeared. The gates of the city swung open.

Ndoro and Nakisisa walked through the metal portal into Jinja. A broad avenue extended before them bordered by squat reed homes with high pointed roofs surrounded by shrub fences. Jinjawa peered from windows and doorways, their eyes transfixed on Nakisisa in his ngwena shape. The duo was deep into the city before the warning horns sounded, sending the Jinjawa scrambling into their homes and emptying the streets with amazing speed. The primal fear they held for the river-beast spread like fire on dry grass. Those that did not flee stood paralyzed, their eyes following Ndoro and Nakisisa as they made their way up the main avenue toward the inner city gates. Ndoro spotted armed men peering at them from behind buildings but none made a move to block their path. He knew eventually someone would marshal his fear and challenge them; he hoped their procession would be over by then.

Ndoro and the ngwena approached the heart of Jinja. Ndoro held his shield and assegai at the ready, constantly scanning for anyone brave enough to try to stop their advance. He searched for a building of significance, a place where he and his companion could confront the inkosi of the Tacuma. Ahead of them lay the central city surrounded by a bleached white stone wall painted with geometric shapes and patterns unfamiliar to Ndoro. The immense iron and wood gate was open.

What Ndoro had seen of the outer city did not compare to what he gazed upon as he stood in the midst of the royal compound. The city brimmed with spacious gray stone dwellings crowned with ochre tiles. Each home was encircled by a wooden fence and possessed a stone tower attached to the house. The home towers grew in height as they came closer to the city center. Ndoro guessed that the height of the tower might signify the status of a family. If the inkosi's palace resided in the city center, then those closest to the palace would be the homes of the chosen clans, hence the higher towers. Over the door of each home rested a gilded staff carved with totems unique to each home. At the right end of the staff an ivory carving of an animal's head was attached. Ndoro noticed that groups of homes contained the same animal head, be it elephant, gorilla, or monkey. Apparently the animal totem designated the clan the house members belonged. The doors were richly carved, scenes of heroic feats and religious faith depicted in ebony. Despite the opulence, there was still no sign of life. The ngwena's presence was working too well. Ndoro realized if he did not find anyone to deal with he could not complete his plan.

He finally focused on the imposing building in the center. A wide pyramid formed the core, bisected by a stone stairway ascending to a square chamber at the pinnacle. Two rectangular buildings with tile dome roofs flanked the pyramid, each one punctuated with a thin minaret equal in height to the pyramid. Ndoro surmised it was either the palace of their inkosi or some type of temple; either way, it was a structure which would probably be protected.

"We will go there," he ordered the ngwena.

No sooner had he pointed at the building than his assumption proven true. Scores of warriors emerged from the chamber and charged down the steep stairs, forming a spear tipped barrier at the base. Behind them came three elderly men dressed in red robes, each holding golden staffs similar to the ones before the homes just passed. They stood stoically, their eyes void of emotion. Ndoro sensed he was in a situation that hinged on his next words.

One priest stepped forward. His wrinkled faced edged with a white beard marked him as the oldest of the three, but he moved with the confidence of one much younger. The warriors made way as he came forward; the man halted well within the protection of the Tacuma spears.

"Why have you come here, Nakisisa?" he asked with a deep, resonant voice, his eyes locked intensely on the river-beast. There was no fear in his voice, only curiosity and annoyance.

The priest continued to speak. "When my father's father first confronted you, it was agreed that you would spare his life if he made sacrifices to you. We have not broken our promise; why have you broken yours?"

"He is not here of his own free will," Ndoro replied. "He is here because I command his presence."

The elder raised an eyebrow. "Nakisisa, is this true?"

"Do not talk to him!" Ndoro roared. "Look at his right paw."

The elder looked and his eyes widened. He stumbled away, falling as he scampered up the stairs. The warriors, seeing the fear on the priest's face, broke their positions and began to scatter.

"Stop, all of you!" Ndoro commanded. The Tacuma halted, their backs turned and shoulders hunched as if expecting death to strike at any moment.

"No longer will you fear Nakisisa," he announced. "From now on, you will fear me!"

Ndoro turned his attention to the eldest councilor. "Step forward," he said.

The elder turned slowly toward Ndoro, tears running down his cheeks.

Ndoro almost felt sympathy for the man, but reality would allow him few luxuries.

"Do not fear, old one. You will not die this day." Ndoro spoke loud so those around him could here. "Your inkosi is weak like a sick child. Despite the gris-gris he has gathered about him, he could not stop me from marching before the steps of his palace. I am Ndoro of the Sesu, son of inkosi Dingane, Koi of the Diaka. Ask your ancestors who would better lead the Tacuma; a warrior who has conquered that which you fear, or an inkosi that hides behind priests and women to spare his own life?"

A roar rose from the top of the temple. More Tacuma warriors spilled out, running down the stairs like an angry flood. Ndoro smiled as he and Nakisisa prepared for the onslaught. At the head of the Tacuma warriors was the inkosi himself, his gilded shield held before him, his sword raised high. It was his last chance to keep his bloodline in control of his people. Killing

Ndoro would surely restore his right and erase the shame of their city's violation. If he failed, he would die by the hands of his people. Any strong people would not allow an inkosi defeated in battle to rule them. It was a sure sign that the gods did not favor him, that his place among men was now low.

Ndoro felt something brush his shoulder, knocking him sideways. He turned back in time to see the ngwena in mid-air, its claws and fangs bared, suspended over the inkosi. The man had only a moment to see the creature before it fell upon him, the two of them crashing to the stone steps. The Tacuma warriors froze, backing away from the horrible scene as the river-beast tore at their leader, the inkosi screaming as he struggled against the beast. The priests fell to their knees, crying out to their ancestors to stop the bad fortune that was destroying them.

The river-beast stopped and stood, its muzzle drenched with blood. The inkosi lay still at his feet, his eyes locked in a lifeless stare into the cloudless sky. Everyone watched as the creature loped back to Ndoro's side, licking at the blood on its claw. It turned toward Ndoro.

"They will listen to you now," he said.

Ndoro looked away from the river-beast to the people surrounding him. They all looked at him, faces contorted by fear and uncertainty. The old priest came to him, his eyes mournful and desperate.

"What must we do to rid ourselves of the fate that is upon us?" he asked.

"Accept me as your inkosi," Ndoro replied, "so that the gods see you are led by one of strength. Deliver those of noble blood to me, so that their weaknesses will never shame you again."

"And what of the Tacuma?" the priest asked.

"Take your place below the Diaka," Ndoro replied. "Your time as masters has ended. Resist and you will perish. Serve me well and the Tacuma will live to see the Diaka take their place as the true masters of this valley."

The priest nodded thoughtfully. "We cannot deny what we have seen. Duma has shown us your strength; by mastering the river-beast you have proven your favor among the ancestors." The priest rose to his feet. "What shall we call you?"

"Shumba," Ndoro replied.

4

A bonfire blazed in the center of the royal kraal, built from the limbs of the Sesu meeting tree. A mournful sound rose over the crackling flames, the sound of female voices lamenting a loss so deep the consequences couldn't be imagined. Below the royal kraal the drums spoke in a steady sonorous rhythm, echoing the sorrow filling the breast of every Sesu man, woman and child. Dingane, the Bull of the Sesu, was dead.

Inaamdura cried into the hem of her long skirt, thankful for the concoction Cancanja gave her to stimulate tears. A portion of the Great Wife's mourning was sincere; there was a time that she loved Dingane fiercely. She had defied her obligations as a Bonga wife and given up her Shamfa heritage for him, immersing herself into her new tribe. It was for those memories she cried, those times when her future for the Sesu was clear. Her feelings changed when Ligongo was born. A mother's love dampened the flame for her inkosi, and his indifference to their son doused it. Though outwardly Dingane followed the restrictions set upon Ndoro, inwardly she knew he admired the abomination. She'd hoped Ndoro's murder of Mulugo and flight from Selike would confirm his curse but the opposite was the case. Weeks after his disappearance the rumors began. Ndoro the disgraced transformed into Ndoro the perfect warrior, a man sent by the ancestors to judge the Sesu. She found it easy to ignore the stories among the common folks; it was the rumors of the Royal Kraal she could not tolerate. The other wives whispered of impis sent to find Ndoro and bring him home, of Dingane growing tired of his foreign wife and longing for the embrace of Shani. But the lies against Ligongo stung the most. He'd grown into a fine man in her eyes, but in the eyes of the Sesu he was just as foreign as his mother. He was tall and lean where the Sesu were thick; his narrow nose and thin lips looked anemic compared to the proud wide Sesu noses and lips. Where the Sesu men were often challenging and sparring in the stick fights, Ligongo preferred less martial pursuits. Dingane never asked him to accompany him on his hunts and he barely took him along on the mandatory royal raids. Ligongo was just as brave in battle as the best Sesu, but respect for his skills came grudgingly. To the Sesu he would never be one of them.

It was the frustration of rejection that drove her to Cacanja once again. The poison was subtle, requiring months of ingestion to do its work. To the victim the gradual weakening would be taken as the natural decline with age. A man like Dingane would never admit his failing skills. On that fateful day he went into the bush with his most trusted indunas, intent on bringing back the skin of a lion. Instead he and three of his companions fell victim to the pride, slain in proud Sesu fashion.

She waited until the Royal Stool Room was empty before hurrying to her study. The most crucial time was rapidly approaching. Once the mourning days passed the Sesu kingdom would be without an inkosi, which meant it would be without laws. The empire she worked so hard to build would briefly fall into chaos, remaining so until the elders selected a new inkosi. Inaamdura labored over the years to insure the interregnum would not last long. She had deliberately dispersed her bribes unevenly among the elders, hoping to cause discord. A unanimous decision would be too suspicious, and the disunity among the families would work to Ligongo's favor while he consolidated control.

She sat at her desk, extracting the scrolls from her drawer

and began writing. Her first messages would go to the elders, confirming and denying her support as she planned. The next messages would go to her allies beyond Selike, those whose loyalties were bought with gold and cowries. The final message would go to Bikita. Her sister was now ruler of Shamfa, her mother and father shells of formality. Under Inaamdura's secret supervision her younger sister rebuilt the Shamfa army, leading it over the mountains into the Barrens and ending Amadika and Twaambo's ambitions once and for all. Inaamdura's help was in the end selfish; she needed an army she could count on just in case the Sesu rejected Ligongo's right to rule and revolted. Her mercenaries would be effective only if she had an army. That army waited at the foothills of Shamfa.

A servant entered the room, a thin girl covered in a leather tunic; her hair braided and beaded Shamfa style.

Inaamdura rose from her desk, the scrolls tucked in an elaborate leather pouch.

"What is it, Thembeka?"

Thembeka fell to her knees, touching her head on the floor. "Great Wife, the elders wait for you by the bonfire to lead the general mourning."

Inaamdura walked past the girl, handing her the bag.

"Take these to the Shamfa messengers," she commanded.

"Yes, Great Mother."

Inaamdura was leaving the palace when she met Ligongo. His face was long with grief, his red eyes despondent. He was dressed in formal Sesu warrior garb, covered in fine brushed cow tails; a leopard headband sporting two stork feathers adorned his head.

"Momma," he pleaded. "Let me go with you."

"It's not safe, my son," she replied. "This is a delicate time, especially for you. There are many who don't wish to see you become inkosi."

"And how will hiding in the palace during my father's mourning strengthen my support? They will say I hide like a bush mouse from my enemies while my mother faces them like a simba."

She couldn't deny the truth in his words. "Come then, show your father the respect he never showed you."

Ligongo ignored the barb and accompanied her outside. The household waited for them, every servant, wife and child present, everyone except Jelani and Shani. Inaamdura covered her mouth, hiding her smile. It was no matter. Once the mourning bonfire took its last breath, Shani's time among the Sesu would be done.

On other side of the Royal Kraal Shani knelt before her small fireplace, her tears genuine. Dingane's death was a blow to her, a pain surprisingly deep. Only recently had he begun to see her again, visiting the hut usually during the evening. They would sit outside and talk of old days, the days before the twins were born. Their relationship had never been settled, roiling like a rock filled river. They eventually grew accustomed to each other, and they were becoming close again. His sudden death shattered any hopes she may have nursed of reconciliation.

A light touch interrupted her mourning. Jelani looked down at her awkwardly. "We must go, inkosa," he urged. "Inaamdura will come for you as soon as the bonfire dies."

"I know, Jelani," she sighed. "Where is Themba?"

Jelani looked disappointed. "She refuses to go. She says we will be caught and killed."

Shani smiled. "She has lost the bravery of youth. Does she think she has a better chance here?"

"She may be smarter than the both of us," Jelani said.

"No. Inaamdura has no use for me. She hates me more than Ndoro because I created him. Dingane's attention didn't help, either."

Shani laid out a wide wool cloth and filled it with her belongings. As a Great Wife she would have needed a wagon to hold her possessions. Though Dingane began to show her favor shortly before he died, she still held the lowest-wife status. She filled the cloth with a few items, treasured objects she brought from Mawenaland.

She pulled the corners of the cloth together and secured it. Jelani stood before her, his travel pack thrown over his shoulder, his black skin flickering before the firelight.

His shield covered his broad back, resting beside his assegai, bow and quiver of fletchless arrows. A broad Mawena sword rode his hip. He watched Shani as she tied the blanket. She looked at him when she was done.

"Come, we must hurry," he said.

Jelani exited the house first, his keen eyes scanning the darkness for interlopers. He opened the door wider and Shani emerged, her eyes darting furtively from side to side.

"It's too dark," she whispered. "We cannot leave now. We should wait until dawn."

"Dawn will be too late," Jelani replied. "Follow me."

They skirted north of the city, avoiding the light of the bonfire and the knots of mourners surrounding the enclosure. The route took them away from Mawenaland, but it was necessary to avoid any sentries. Jelani's night vision was like the hyena; they barely stumbled as they ran away from Selike. They continued north for half the night, resting briefly whenever they found a small rise. By dawn they were heading east. Jelani wanted to make sure they were far from Sesu borders before heading south toward Mawenaland. They ran the risk of encountering enemies of the Sesu, but it was worth the risk to escape Inaamdura's wrath.

The sun was high overhead before Jelani allowed them an extended break. Again he chose a small hill as refuge, a high point that allowed him to see any approaching animals or Sesu well before they were close enough to threaten them. Shani opened her blanket, removing two loaves of bread. They sat together and ate.

"How are you?" Jelani asked.

"I am good."

"The pace is not too swift?"

Shani looked up from her bread. "The pace is fine."

"I can slow down if you wish."

"No, you cannot slow down. If we do, we'll be caught."

Silence entered between them again as they finished their bread, a tension building for more reasons that the threat of death.

Shani folded her blanket. "Themba was right not to come. She would not have been able to keep up."

Jelani nodded. "What puzzles me is how you have been able to."

Shani wrapped the blanket with the leather strip and hung the bundle from her shoulder.

"My son and my husband are dead. All the family I have left is in Mawenaland. I will not let the Sesu deny me my father and my living son."

Jelani scanned the landscape. Wildebeests languished in the distance, huge herds gathering for the migration signaling the beginning of the dry season. Simbas lurked in the shadows, constantly looking for the weakness that spelled opportunity to a hungry pride.

"We have another hard day ahead before we can relax," he said.

"Will we be far enough away?"

"No. You have impressed me with your endurance, inkosa, but a determined impi would catch us. We have the advantage of a head start, but that is not enough. I'm counting on Inaamdura's joy when she discovered we've fled. If we are lucky she will be happy to be rid of us, or she may decide testing Noncemba's wrath not worth the possible consequences."

"I don't care what she decides, as long as she doesn't send an impi after us," Shani concluded.

They ran until nightfall. Jelani made camp under an acacia and they slept soundly until a group of foraging giraffes woke them.

Jelani gathered his items and went to gathers Shani's. She pushed him away.

"You don't have to serve me, Jelani. I am no longer the wife of an inkosi."

"You are still Noncemba's daughter," he replied.

"Not out here," she announced. "Here I am just a woman, and you are just a man. We will both do what we need to do to survive until we reach Mawenaland."

"So I am 'just' a man?" Jelani folded his arms across his chest in mock anger.

Shani smiled. "You are just a brave, handsome and good man."

Jelani nodded. "And you are just a beautiful, strong, caring woman."

They shared a brief smile. Jelani gazed across the

landscape, the serious look returning to his face.

"We will walk today. The sun will be hot and we need to conserve our strength. There are few waterholes here so we must watch our water supply."

Their walk was leisurely but wary as they kept a close eye on the wildlife filling the grasslands. The simbas of this region learned the lesson of the Sesu long ago and avoided the duo, even though the prides contained enough females to quickly overwhelm them. The elephants proved more difficult. Twice they found themselves charged by a large female protecting her herd. Luckily the matriarchs were satisfied by bluff; neither of them could have outrun a female in full fury.

For the first time in all the years as Dingane's wife Shani took a long look at the land that had become her home years ago. She spent those years adjusting to the Sesu way of life, never taking the time to really see the domain her husband ruled. It was truly a beautiful place, rolling hills speckled with sparse acacias and fat baobabs, grasslands undulating with massive herds of animals of all types. Its gentle appearance hid the harshness of its core, a quality that created the Sesu. She realized despite her miserable last years she would miss this land. It had been her home; it was the place where her sons were born.

The thought of the twins sent sadness racing through her. Ndoro was lost, probably dead, his body rotted away in the swaying grass, his bones bleached by rain and sunlight. Tears filled her eyes and she forced them away. She had mourned longer for Ndoro than she had for Dingane, for Dingane's weakness was the reason Ndoro had to flee. He had driven their son into the bush to die.

Then she looked at Jelani, his gait still easy despite the miles they had traveled. He had come to Sesuland a young warrior, but now he walked with the confidence time bestows on those who survive its ravages and uncertainties. He performed Ndoro's initiation rites and taught him how to fight the Mawena way. He taught her son the secrets of men and women and finally risked his life to insure Ndoro's escape. Shani realized then that she was looking at Ndoro's father, not by blood but by deed. He had performed everything Dingane had not. Every quality Ndoro exhibited as a man he learned from Jelani. Ndoro had been so focused on proving himself to Dingane and the Sesu that he never realized who truly made him the man he was. In truth, she had been just as blind as her son. Dingane's presence had overshadowed Jelani's work. The Mawena never complained once. He did his duty for her and for her son.

She remembered the day Jelani exposed his feelings for her. Her cheeks warmed as she recalled his words. "I wish I could do more," he said. He didn't realize he had done far beyond anything she expected. Ndoro's father had not died days ago; he walked before her, leading the way home.

Shani hurried forward to walk beside him, brushing her hip against his hand. He jerked his hand away instinctively.

"I am sorry, inkosa," he said automatically.

"I told you, Jelani, out here I am neither inkosa nor princess. I am just a woman and you are just a man, a man that deserves the woman he desires."

Jelani dared to look in Shani's eyes. She saw the want clouded by confusion, so she decided to clear the matter for him. She reached up, placing her hand behind his neck and pulling his lips down to hers. After a brief kiss Jelani pulled away, his eyes clear, his smile joyful.

"Shani," he said.

"Jelani," she answered.

They walked side by side for the rest of the day. By nightfall Jelani had found another tree to rest under for the night, situated by a clear lake. No sooner had they finished their meal did they unleash the feelings that had been denied under the eternal starlight. They fell asleep in each others arms.

Jelani awoke in a dream. He gazed into Shani's sleeping face wondering why the ancestors brought this unbelievable moment upon him. So many obstacles stood in the way between what occurred that night, insurmountable barriers of caste and customs. He held no false hopes. They were in between worlds in the bush; once they arrived in Mawenaland life would once again place its rules upon them. She would be princess and he would be servant.

Shani opened her eyes and saw the questions in her new lover's face.

"It will be different," she said.

"How can it be?" Jelani asked. "Your father will never agree to it. The elders will never allow it."

"They cannot deny what happened between us."

Jelani sat up, surprised. "You would tell him what we did? You'll be dishonored!"

"I don't care about honor anymore, Jelani. I married a man I didn't love for honor. I gave up my child for honor."

Jelani stood. "We shouldn't talk about this now. We must eat and move on. The day is passing us by."

Shani nodded. She wanted to talk, but she knew Jelani was confused. There would be plenty of time before they reached Mawenaland.

Shani walked in front of him, her hips swaying hypnotically. Jelani's mind was filling with amorous intentions when a stern voice interrupted his thoughts.

"They are coming."

Jelani stopped, shaking his head. Shani turned to look at him, her face puzzled.

"Jelani, what's wrong?"

He held up his hand to silence her, his head tilted awkwardly.

"They are coming. They are close."

Jelani recognized the voice reverberating in his head. A sad smile formed on his face.

"Shani, keep walking forward." Shani obeyed, her hands trembling.

"Jelani, tell me what's going on."

"The Sesu have found us," he answered.

Shani stumbled as she heard his words but she continued to walk.

"How do you know? I haven't seen anyone."

Jelani shifted uncomfortably. "I was told."

"What are you talking about? We are the only ones here. Who could tell you?"

"Husani," Jelani said.

Shani stopped and spun to face him. "Husani? Don't play with me this way!"

Jelani grasped her shoulders and turned her back around. "Husani has warned me of the Sesu, as he should. He is my older brother; it is his duty."

"I don't understand," Shani confessed. "How could Husani...?"

"There is no time to explain, Shani. Listen to me very carefully. The Sesu haven't seen you yet. When I tell you to stop walking you must lay down in the grass. I will cover you with my shield. Do not stand until you hear me yell, then run as fast as you can. Don't look back."

"Jelani, don't do this. We can outrun them."

Jelani hesitated. "No, Shani. We can't. Please, lay down now."

Shani descended to her knees then lay in the prickly grass. Jelani knelt behind her, placing his shield and assegai by her side.

"Take them with you," Shani said. "I don't need them."

Jelani chuckled. "These are Sesu tools. I will meet them as I am; a Mawena."

Jelani stood and spun around. He walked away from Shani and any chance of them having a future together. His brother had come from the Zamani to remind him of his duty. He drew his sword, swinging it back and forth to test his grip. The blade was sharp, the point keen. He extracted his dagger in his left hand, holding the hilt so the blade rested against his protected forearm. He was ready to fight.

The impi bobbed over the horizon as his brother foretold, ten Sesu warriors with bare headrings. They were young ones, probably running ahead of the older warriors to claim their first kill. They would be eager, reckless and tired; all qualities that would be in Jelani's favor. But they were still Sesu; he would have to be very precise in his attack.

They spotted him and let out a triumphant yell. Their pace increase and they glided across the grass toward Jelani. The wise Mawena kept walking, studying the charge and calculating his plan. He watched them shift their assegais to their left hands with their leaf shields then reach across their shoulders to extract throwing spears from the quivers across their backs. At least they had the patience to wait until they were in range before throwing in unison. Jelani trotted forward and the spears fell harmlessly behind him. The Sesu line was ragged; some of the warriors seemed to be breathing hard. This was good. He waited until he could see their eyes before he attacked.

"Mawena!" he yelled, hoping Shani recognized the signal. He rushed the warrior in the center of the line, deliberately exposing his chest. As the young Sesu raised his assegai in triumph Jelani spun away and struck the man beside him with his dagger, burying the blade in his throat. He kept spinning through the line and ended behind the warriors. His sword was in and out the back of the first warrior in an instant. The warrior before him managed to raise his shield and block Jelani's dagger. The Mawena let the man's assegai graze his torso while he hooked his sword behind the shield and stabbed the Sesu in the head. He turned in time to deflect another assegai, striking it so hard the Sesu lost his grip, the spear flying from his hand. He reached for his orinka, exposing enough of himself for Jelani to run his sword into the man's shoulder. He wanted to finish the man but the other Sesu were attempting to respond to his swift assault by forming a line behind their shields. He jumped between two of them, stabbing the men simultaneously with sword and dagger. The remaining three managed to lock their shields, their assegais protruding between the gaps as they advanced toward him. Jelani dropped to the ground and swung wide, cutting each man across the shins. They fell in unison, their shields and spears tangled. He killed them before they could rise.

Jelani looked at his grim work with no emotion. They were brave men, but they were inexperienced. He went to each one, cutting the head ring from their scalps and sticking them in his waist belt. He was about to turn to find Shani when he heard the war chant of another impi.

"We are coming; we are coming for you."

Ten more warriors approached him in a uniform line, shields locked and assegais raised. Each man wore adornments with their head rings; stork feathers, leopard headbands and eagle plumes. They were seasoned warriors, veterans of cattle raids and military campaigns. They would not succumb so easily to his swift, deceptive skills. Jelani wiped his sweaty hands on his kilt and walked towards the impi, singing a Mawena song of valor and death.

The second impi slowed as it spotted the bodies of their comrades strewn around the arrogant Mawena. They advanced in unison, careful not to make the mistake their younger comrades committed. Still the Mawena's furious assault took them by surprise. Two of them were dead before they regained composure and attacked. The Mawena knew he was trapped, but he fought despite no chance of surviving. There was no pattern to his assault; he fought on instinct, moving, striking and blocking with the desperation of a cornered simba. He felt pain, wounds that would take their toll, but he battled with the energy of a fresh man. He struck until there was no one to strike; he stopped, surprised by the bodies of ten more warriors lying at his feet. But this victory came with a price. Blood flowed over his body like little rivers; an assegai protruded from his thigh like an odd branch. These were wounds he would soon heal from if it were not for the deep pain in his abdomen, a wound that sapped his strength like poison.

He heard the chant rising from the distance. Another impi was approaching, another group of Sesu determined to fulfill Inaamdura's sentence. He could not stop them. He would be dead before they reached him.

"You have done well, brother," Husani said.

"They will find her and kill her," Jelani gasped.

"They will not," Husani replied. "Others are coming."

Jelani turned to look behind him. Warriors approached, running with shields and assegais, their faces grim and determined. He read the shield pattern and managed a smile. A promise made long ago was being fulfilled.

The kaShange sprinted pass Jelani and attacked the impi. The Sesu fought honorably but were no match for the numerous kaShange. Jelani watched on his knees to be sure that no one survived to threaten Shani. As the kaShange approached him Jelani let go, collapsing into the grass. He rolled onto his back; his eyes wide open to the sun and sky.

Shani swayed nervously as she waited for the return of the kaShange impi. Mayinga stood beside her, his personal warriors a few steps behind. They watched the remaining kaShange warriors return with Jelani. He was lying on his shield, his arms hanging over the edges. She ran to the warriors carrying the shield, tears running down her dirty face.

"Jelani! Jelani!"

The inyanga came to her, placing a hand on her shoulder. "I've done all I can do. He is not dead yet, but he will be."

Shani's eyes widened with relief. "We must get him to Mawenaland. The healer there can save him."

The inyanga looked skeptical. "The wound to his stomach is a fatal one. There is too much damage."

"He will not die!" Shani shouted.

Mayinga came forward. "We will take him to Mawenaland."

He looked at Shani with sympathy. "Ndoro brought my father home to die among us and I have not forgotten. We are not far from the borderlands. Can you run?"

Shani looked back at Mayinga, her face resolved. "I will run."

They reached the borderlands by dusk, approaching the ragged tree line cautiously. The kaShange warriors placed Jelani down and stepped away. Shani knelt beside him as Mayinga approached her.

"This is as far was we go," he said. "We have no quarrel with the Mawena, but we are kaShange. If we cross into Mawenaland our actions might be seen as hostile."

Shani looked concerned. "How will they know we are here?"

Mayinga grinned. "Believe me, inkosa. They know we are here. The Kosobu are very diligent."

The kaShange warriors place water and food beside Shani and Jelani. Mayinga raised his assegai and the kaShange trotted back to their kraal. The inkosi hesitated, bowing to Shani one last time.

"When you see Ndoro again, tell him Mayinga of the kaShange still considers him a friend."

Shani looked away. "Ndoro is dead."

Mayinga smiled. "I do not think so." He turned and ran away to catch up with his men.

The Kosobu appeared in force soon afterward. They gathered about the two, covering Shani in blankets and picking Jelani up from the ground. A wagon arrived and both were placed inside for the ride back to Koso. Jelani was taken to the medicine priest's home while Shani was led to the house of the chief. His wives dressed her in Mawena finery, transforming her in moments from the wife of a Sesu inkosi to the daughter of Oba Noncemba. The difference was jarring to Shani; only moments ago she was running for her life; now she was surrounded by strangers treating her like the princess she had been many years ago. Her mind was still reeling when the Kosobu chief, Olatunde, entered the main room with the village elders. They bowed and sat on their stools before her.

"Thank you for saving us," Shani said.

Olatunde nodded again. "You are Mawena. We would have come for you even if the kaShange had not brought you to the border."

"You knew we were being hunted?"

"Only recently," the chief admitted. "Our spies could not get close to the Sesu sections of Selike due to the restrictions imposed during the mourning period. Things became easier after the bonfire died. The interregnum worked to our advantage and we heard of your escape. You made good time."

"Jelani would have it no other way," Shani said. "How is he?"

"He is not dead," the chief said. "Our medicine priest says he may recover, but he won't be the same. Too many spirits are involved."

"Spirits?"

"The souls of the Sesu he killed wish to drag his soul with them into the Zamani, but Husani fights to keep him alive."

Shani stood. "I wish to see him."

Olatunde's eyes reflected sympathy. "We have prepared a boat and an escort for your return to Abo. It is not safe for you so close to the borderlands. The Sesu may attack if they know you are here, but they will not if they hear you are in Abo."

"I will not leave until I know Jelani is fine," she said.

"There is nothing you can do, princess. I promise I will send word on his condition."

Shani stood in defiant silence. Olatunde sighed.

"I will take you to him. I hope you realize you are putting us at a great risk."

The medicine priest's home was next to the chief's. Olatunde knocked on the door and the medicine priest appeared. He was younger than Shani expected, his body more suited for a warrior than a healer, his tunic festooned with the customary talismans and gris-gris. He bowed, and then stepped aside.

"Welcome, princess. I've been expecting you."

"Where is he?" Shani asked.

"Straight ahead in the back room."

Shani hurried to the room. Jelani occupied a small bed, his head propped up on a worn headrest. Healing candles burned in low iron lamps in each corner. A small table heaped with jars sat next to the table, accompanied by a stool. Shani sat in the stool and grasped Jelani's hand.

"The princess wishes to stay with him until he is better," Olatunde said.

"Good. It will help his spirit fight to stay among us," the medicine priest answered. "I am Jumoke. I will provide whatever you need."

"Thank you, Jumoke." Shani gave Olatunde a nod to dismiss him. The chief frowned and left the house.

"Olatunde is not happy," Jumoke commented.

"Neither am I," Shani retorted. "Olatunde is a chief and my father is Oba. I suggest you concentrate on Jelani's needs and mine."

"Yes my princess, of course," Jumoke stammered.

Shani spent the next three weeks at Jelani's side, administering his medicines while Jumoke performed the rituals to aid his healing. Olatunde grew more impatient with each passing day, sending his servants to ask Shani daily when she would leave. She ignored them, concentrating only on Jelani. When the Jelani finally opened his eyes, it was as much a relief to the Kosobu as it was for Shani.

"Hello, man," Shani whispered.

Jelani managed a smile. "Hello, woman."

Shani bent over him and kissed his cheek. "I knew you wouldn't leave me."

Jelani reached up and touched her cheek. "But you must

leave me."

Shani straightened. "I told you I don't care."

"You should," Jelani replied. "You are home now, and you know what that means. You must be a princess and I must be a warrior. It is our way. It is what makes us strong."

Shani wanted to defy his words, but she knew in the end she would be overwhelmed. She kissed him one more time.

"Jumoke!" she shouted. The medicine priest came quickly.

"What is it my…By the ancestors!" Jumoke folded his hands and bowed.

"Tell Olatunde I am ready to depart," Shani said. "Today."

"Of course, princess. I will tell him."

Shani stood. "Thank you, Jelani. Thank you for saving me. Thank you for raising Ndoro. Thank you for loving us both."

She turned and walked out the house, fighting to maintain her dignity before the Kosobu. Jelani's words were painful but true. They were in the world again and protocol must be followed. She was the oba's daughter; he was her servant. She would wear the mask, but inside she would hold on to their love. It was all she had that truly belonged to her.

5

Zimfara stirred as the rising sun chased away the previous night's chill. Perched on the northernmost edge of the Mpanda savannah, the city was a rest stop for caravans completing the trip across the vast and terrible Mahgreb desert. A towering stone wall enclosed clusters of mud-brick buildings lining narrow roads that meandered to the sprawling marketplace at the city's core. Unlike the homogeneous villages of the interior, Zimfara was composed of many tribes with no one group holding dominance over the other. The Grand Merchant held sway here, a man whose skill, reputation and wealth gave him the right to control such a vast and diverse place. It was a city filled with dreamers and wanderers, the wrong and the righteous. It was also the home of a young man seeking answers to unknown questions.

Obaseki awoke and had no idea where he was. The bed in which he lay was simple yet comfortable, the headrest padded with expensive silk. A large storage chest loitered against the wall opposite him; its surface covered with jewelry and etched brass clasps. An intricately woven carpet decorated the wall above the chest, its abstract calligraphy unfamiliar to his eyes. Along the other walls were shelves filled with gourds of various colors, shapes and sizes. He slowly realized they belonged to him, containing the herbs that were the tools of his profession. Despite the clarity of the previous night's dream, he was still in Zimfara.

He donned his turban and robes, then went into the next room. Eshe knelt before the cooking pots; her loveliness was hidden by a white Zimfarian dress, her hair covered by her elaborate blue headscarf. The Zimfarans wore too much clothing for his taste, even though the garments were essential to protect the body from the harsh sun. Eshe fell into the traditional dress quickly, but Obaseki drew the line when she talked of wearing the veil that would hide her face. He did not like the ways of the Zimfarans and would be happy the sooner they were on their way. But Eshe resisted, insisting that they stay a few months more to make sure they had enough provisions for their journey. Obaseki acquiesced, but he knew Eshe had other reasons for wanting to stay.

She looked up when he entered the room, her smile as effervescent as ever.

"You did not sleep well, Seki," she said. "Was it the dream?"

"Yes." He went to her and sat. "It is getting stronger. I think it is time for us to leave."

Eshe's warm smile waned as she served Obaseki his food. They ate in silence, the tension present as always. He knew what the problems were; with Moyo her feelings and thoughts were no secret to him, though he would never let her know. It was time he spoke up.

"You do not wish to leave, do you Eshe?"

"No." She continued to look at her plate. She had become quite the merchant of late, selling and exchanging fabrics and decorated leather for clothing and other goods. It was one of the reasons she did not want to leave Zimfara. The old Eshe would have stared him in the face, arrogant in her response.

"Maybe this is the destiny planned for you, Seki. You are well respected here. People come from many towns and cities just to receive your healings. We can become wealthy here."

"I did not agree to banishment just to become wealthy,"

Obaseki said harshly. "There is something beyond this, Eshe? Something far greater than being a healer."

"What else can there be?" Eshe looked him in the eye then, her face a mixture of anxiety and confusion. "You dream of a place that might not exist, a land that buries the bones of gods. Maybe your dreams are only dreams."

Obaseki flinched as if struck. Eshe? The one person who had long known of his inner self seemed to have finally lost her faith. The reasons were clear. The loss of their child during the journey from Alamako had wracked both of them. Though his pain was dulled by his knowledge of the beyond, Eshe had no such solace. And then there was Zimfara, its citizens constantly scrambling to accumulate wealth with no sense of tribal honor. The two were a sickness that fouled her mind and spirit.

"You above all else should know better," he said. "You know the power I possess. The ancestors have not led me this far just to become a healer."

Eshe said nothing as she wiped her plate with her bread.

"You no longer believe, do you Eshe," he asked.

"I do, yes I do Seki, but..."

They heard the chimes in the shop, indicating a customer. Eshe rose abruptly and ran down to the shop below their room.

"We will discuss it later," Obaseki called out. He sulked back to his meal though his mind was miles away. He had to go. Every day in Zimfara took him farther away from where he should be. He would ask Eshe one more time, and if she refused, he would go alone.

Eshe reappeared, a concerned look on her face.

"Seki, there is someone here to see you."

She was shoved aside and a man entered the room, filling the doorway. He was covered completely in dark blue fabric, a large *sheska* wrapped around his head, robes that draped to his scuffed brown boots and a veil that hid every facial feature but his eyes. A sword hung from his shoulder, his ring-crusted hand resting on the hilt. The stranger stared at Obaseki in a way that made the young medicine-priest feel inferior in his presence.

"You are the healer?" the man asked, his voice strong despite his covered mouth.

"Yes I am," Obaseki replied.

"You will come with me," the man ordered. "My master is sick and needs your help."

"Who sends you?" Obaseki asked.

"The Grand Merchant," the man replied.

Obaseki frowned while Eshe grinned. He had no respect for the nobles of this city, people gaining status not by ancestral right but by wealth. It was the reason Obaseki never saw spirits here; the dead were treated like so much trash and never honored. No spirit would linger in a place so foul. But disobeying the Grand Merchant was a death sentence.

"What is his ailment?" he inquired.

The man's eyes narrowed. "How should I know? You are the healer; you must come see for yourself."

Obaseki went to his gourds, selecting a wide range of remedies since he was not completely familiar with the ailments of this land. He packed them in his saddle bag and threw it over his shoulder. "I am ready."

The man turned and walked out. Obaseki followed, pausing briefly to look at Eshe.

"We will finish our conversation when I return, sweet flower," he said smiling. Eshe smiled back nervously.

Obaseki followed the envoy into the busy streets and to another shrouded warrior standing with three camels. The excess of wealth, Obaseki thought to himself. The Grand Merchant's villa was surely not far enough to warrant the use of camels. They mounted, the envoy taking the reins of Obaseki's camel before setting off. But they were not heading in the direction of the villa; they were heading for the city gate.

Obaseki stuck his hand into his robes and found Moyo, the horn's warmth clearing his head. Those that passed them looked at the warriors with anger in their eyes. An old woman shuffled up to the warrior leading him and spat, barking at him a language Obaseki did not understand. Something was wrong; whoever these men were, they were not envoys of the Merchant.

"Who are you?" he finally asked, tensing for their response. The false envoy jerked his head to face Obaseki, gripping his sword hilt in response.

"Do not say a word," he warned. "There is a man watching your home. If you attempt to escape your wife will die. Do you understand?"

"Yes," Obaseki managed to say. He was stunned, his mouth suddenly dry, his hand sweating. He was being kidnapped, but he did not know why or by whom. If they meant to rob him they could have done so at his home. He never denied anyone assistance and often went to the surrounding villages to administer medicines and healing to those lesser folks that served the nobles. The only people he could not reach were the mysterious Tuaregs, known for their fierceness and their habit of raiding the countryside.

Obaseki stiffened when he realized who his kidnappers were. Zimfarans were constantly on its guard against Tuareg raids, maintaining a crack mercenary guard to protect the city and patrol the major highways leading into and out of the city. There had been no attacks since he and Eshe had been in the city, but the fear was real and constant.

They rode through the gates without notice, the Tuaregs keeping a close eye on Obaseki as they passed the sentries. He thought of yelling, but the Tuaregs were too close and could take his life before the guards responded. So he remained silent, his hopes dwindling as they traveled farther and farther away from Zimfara along the road leading into the desert.

Once they were out of view of the city, his captors left the trail and headed into scrub brush and sand, the loping camels settling into a steady rhythm. After a few moments Obaseki was totally lost; every direction seemed the same to him. He was in Fate's hand now; no one could insure his return but the Tuaregs.

They spent the bulk of the day climbing a dune that seemed as high as a mountain. The crest of the dune revealed the Tuareg settlement; scores of domed shaped camel-hide tents dotting a basin adjoining a sparse oasis. The settlement came to life as the riders approached, a crowd forming about the oasis. Obaseki found them to be a handsome, regal looking people. The men looked at him with fierce, intelligent eyes, the women, unveiled, stared with equal intensity but with more subtle grace. They spoke in their own language, leaving Obaseki totally unaware of his situation. The two riders dismounted before a man dressed similar to them, but with a shesh of purple and gold threads indicating his status. One of the riders approached Obaseki.

"Come with me," he ordered. Obaseki climbed down from the camel and descended into a crowd of children that gathered around him and made a cautious procession through the settlement. They were neither malicious nor friendly, just trailing him silently, their eyes the most inquiring aspect about them.

He was led to an enormous tent located in the middle of the oasis beside the well. Two guards blocked the entrance, each holding wide ayar shields and tall iron lances. The man motioned and the guards stepped aside. As Obaseki entered he was forced to the ground, his face pushed into the sand. He struggled for a moment, but realized he was in the presence of a chieftain. He relented, remaining in his position until allowed to raise his head.

The chieftain lay in a bed of lamb's wool, his head propped by an ivory headrest. A woman sat beside him, her brown oval face a striking complement to the handsome face of the chieftain. An amber necklace encircled her elegant neck and her earlobes drooped with large crescents of gold. The tent was filled with the trappings of hundreds of tribes, the fruits of the Tuareg caravan raids. If Obaseki had any doubts he was in the presence of a chieftain, they were quickly dispelled by the opulence surrounding him.

He was also surprised to see the white glow of possession outlining the chieftain's body. At least there were some people of this land that still honored their ancestors.

The man in the rich turban came to Obaseki's side. "He was wounded in a raid. We did what we could, but he is still dying."

"There is a spirit in him," Obaseki replied. The woman jerked her head toward him, terror in her eyes.

"His body heals, but his soul is still sick," Obaseki continued. He walked to the chieftain and was about to touch him when the man grabbed his hand.

"You cannot touch him!" he shouted.

"Then he will die," Obaseki warned. "You kidnapped me to save your chieftain, so let me. It is the only way it can be done."

The man gave Obaseki a suspicious look, then let go of his hand. Obaseki pulled away the robes, revealing a wicked gash along the chieftain's right side. The wound was treated with a useless mixture of animal-derived medicines. Obaseki wiped the concoction away and replaced it with the healing herbs in his bag. The poultice would speed the healing of the wound; the spirit was another matter. Going back into his bag he extracted the herbs essential for spirit-raising. He carefully outlined the chieftain's body with the plants, invoking a silent prayer with each herb. Once he'd surrounded the chieftain, Obaseki turned back to his wealthy guardian.

"I must use my mayembe," he said. "It is not a weapon, only an object I use to heal others." Obaseki extracted Moyo from his robes and the Tuareg seemed astounded. He looked at Obaseki respectfully, stepping away with a slight bow.

"Do what you must," the man said.

Obaseki stood beside the bed, holding the gilded horn over the chieftain. He chanted, his rhythmic voice setting a compelling tone. He swayed with the rhythm of the chant, feeling a part of his spirit extend into the mayembe and descend into the blackness of the world between worlds, the abyss that years ago threatened to consume him whenever he dared use Moyo. Obaseki no longer felt fear in this void; the duel with Celu had taught him the patience and skill essential to raise spirits. Fuluke would be proud to see how his young apprentice had evolved. He was right to leave Abo, for as Fuluke foretold, his talents would have never reached the level he now possessed.

The world took shape around him and he was immediately beset by the sounds of struggle. Obaseki rushed to the scene, seeing what he suspected. The chieftain fought the spirit of the man he had slain in battle, a wild-eyed Bedouin who obviously was more than just a warrior. What this mystical assassin had not conquered in life, he was trying to accomplish in death. The chieftain, weakened by the spiritual extraction, struggled against the killer, but it was obvious that he would succumb. Obaseki had no choice; he would destroy the opponent.

Obaseki raised his hand and opened it. Resting in his palm was the essence of Moyo, the lost ka of a fallen god, the consumer of souls. Obaseki pushed Moyo away, the spirit growing as it moved toward the struggle. By the time the assassin realized something was wrong Moyo had grown into a ball of searing light. The spirit screamed as it was sucked into the consuming fire. The chieftain's spirit dissipated, released from the Zamani to return to its body. Obaseki followed, traveling through the mayembe and back into the familiar form of his body. The chieftain lay before him, his face filled with the color of life. Moyo had taken the soul of the attacker. The healing was complete.

Obaseki collapsed onto his pillow. His clothes were drenched, but he felt a sensation of serenity that often accompanied the use of Moyo. The elder was still in the room, so was the chieftain's wife.

"I've done my task," Obaseki stated. "Your chieftain will live. Now please take me back to Zimfara."

"You will be returned when El-Fatih regains consciousness," his captor replied.

Obaseki studied the man before him, tapping into the powers of Moyo to search his feelings. The man cared little for this El-Fatih; in fact he seemed disappointed. Obaseki was not surprised. The wickedness of Zimfara seemed to have reached into the desert as well.

"If I must stay, I will stay with your chieftain," Obaseki said. "If he must survive for me to leave, then I will make sure he does."

The nobleman raised an eyebrow at Obaseki's statement then turned to the woman. She nodded her head in approval. "So be it," the nobleman replied. He disappeared from the tent with a swirl of his robes.

Obaseki moved his pillow closer to El-Fatih. He was tired and famished, his stomach protesting loudly with growls like a desert wolf. It didn't help that beside the chieftain's wife sat three plates filled with foods that would be a feast anywhere Obaseki had traveled before. He dared not asked for anything, for he was unsure of what the results might be. It was always good to show strength, his grandfather had taught him long ago. Any weakness may make the difference between life and death.

The chieftain's wife rose from the foot of the bed and picked up the bowl of fruit. She sauntered to Obaseki and sat down before him. She looked up into his eyes and smiled.

"Thank you," he said.

"You saved my husband," she replied.

"We won't know that until he revives."

"With Moyo there is no doubt," she answered. "Every Tuareg knows this, even Jussien."

Obaseki almost choked on the date he was chewing. "You know of Moyo?"

"Yes," she calmly replied. "Your mayembe is the soul of the fallen god, the orisha of the Tuaregs. Every Tuareg has heard the story of his fall from grace as a child, although it has been so long since anyone has seen the mayembe or been to Yakubu."

"Yakubu?"

"It is the place where Moyo fell from heaven and where the first medicine-priest fought for the possession. It was once a holy place for us until gold became our god."

Excitement squelched any hunger Obaseki once had.

"What does Yakubu look like?" he asked.

"It sits atop a plateau, an oasis crowning a dry mountain.

I remember visiting with my clan, when a terrible sickness spread through our camp. We went to Moyo with sacrifices of goats and bread, hoping he would be generous and stop the sickness. But we did not know he was gone. Our priests cursed him and we continued to die. Many lost their faith, but I believed because my family was spared." The woman smiled at the remembrance, her eyes far away.

The chieftain stirred. His wife ran to his side, whispering to him. Obaseki turned away, giving the couple a private moment, his mind filled with what the woman has just told him. The image that had haunted his dreams since he left Infana was real. Not only that, it was close. Moyo had led him to this place, and a crisis among the Tuaregs brought him closer. But he was uncertain of his fate among them. He was promised his life if the chieftain lived. Since that seemed certain, he waited to see if the Tuaregs were true to their word.

A commotion broke his musing. The chieftain was trying to sit up against his wife's will. She tried to hold him down; he pushed her away. His face displayed the long line of Tuareg nobles, the dark skin and engaging eyes of superiority. His light brown eyes widened when he finally noticed Obaseki.

"You are the man from my dream," he said. Obaseki nodded.

"I am El-Fatih Habre. You saved my life."

"I am only a healer," Obaseki replied.

"Come closer," El-Fatih commanded. "I wish to see Moyo."

Obaseki was concerned, but the chieftain's smile conveyed his honesty.

"Only a healer possessing the fallen one could do what you did," El-Fatih said. Obaseki took the horn from his robe. El-

Fatih nodded.

"So my near-death has borne good fruit," he said, smiling. "How long has Moyo possessed you?"

Obaseki smiled at the accuracy of El-Fatih's words. "Five years, but we hold to common ground."

"We shall see," Fatih smirked. "Thuria, summon my warriors."

"You are still weak," she admonished. "It is better you rest until you are strong enough to deal with Jussien."

"If I wait too long he will be lost in the desert."

Thuria wrinkled her brow, her thick eyebrows almost meeting. "I will have the warriors search the camp. If they do not find him, they will go after him and bring him back. Meanwhile, you will rest."

"Not until I deal with the healer," El-Fatih replied. "You saved my life, so what do I owe you?"

"I wish to go back to my wife," Obaseki said quickly.

"So be it," El-Fatih declared.

"I would also like to go to Yakubu," Obaseki finished.

El-Fatih's generous smiled transformed into a look of concern. "Do you know what you ask?"

"Yes, I think so," Obaseki replied.

"Do not think, healer," El-Fatih replied earnestly. "Yakubu is the only place in Uhuru where Moyo can take his true form. If you cannot control him you will die."

"Moyo is a part of me," Obaseki replied. "It is why I am here. I don't know what will happen at Yakubu; I only know it must be."

El-Fatih eyed Obaseki cautiously. "A man seeking certain death is either foolish or brave. I think you are a little of both." El-Fatih swayed as the effect of his wound re-surfaced. He lay back down.

"I will have a tent prepared for you. We will return you to Zimfara in the morning."

The tent was a welcomed sight. The interior was almost as lavishly done as El-Fatih's, worthy of a diplomat's room in the palace of the Grand Merchant. Obaseki savored the sight of the bed most of all. Exhausted from his ordeal, he stripped off his garments, collapsed into the soft cushions and fell immediately to sleep.

But it was not a restful sleep. The dream of Yakubu was gone; in its place was something horrifying. A city burned, black smoke billowing into a sharp blue sky. Bodies were strewn about, some mutilated beyond recognition. The smell of death was overpowering. Outside on the bloody streets, a huge army marched, one larger than any Obaseki had ever witnessed. A man strode at the head of this army, a war club in one hand and a short spear in the other. The sea of warriors surrounding him chanted with the rhythm of war drums, the sound of one word bursting from their lips; Shumba. Obaseki realized this was his twin, the part of himself that surfaced in his dreams in the past. This time he knew this was not just a hint of his evil spirit. This other side of him existed; the suffering and death he caused was real. Staring into his soulless black eyes Obaseki saw his destiny. He awoke, the night still ruling the desert sky. He felt a familiar touch on his cheek and turned to see the Eshe's face. He grabbed her immediately, squeezing her in joy and relief.

He felt himself enfolded by the strong, supple arms of his wife. He savored their embrace a moment longer and then pushed her arms length.

"What are you doing here?"

"The Tuaregs brought me here." Her voice was bitter.

"I don't understand," Obaseki said. "El-Fatih promised he would take me back to Zimfara."

"There is no Zimfara!" Eshe blurted. Her head fell against his shoulders as she cried.

"What are you talking about?" he asked urgently.

"The Tuaregs sacked it, Seki. They burned it to the ground. I was on my way to market when someone grabbed me from behind and pushed me into an alley. Before I could struggle they put a bag over my head and pushed me into a cart. I was so afraid, Seki! I started to struggle, and then someone told me I was being taken to you, that I would be safe. Then they said I should be grateful I was the wife of Moyo."

She stopped for a moment, raising her head from Obaseki's shoulder. He looked into her eyes and was angered by the shock and pain he saw.

"The cart stopped and the bag was taken away," she continued. "That's when I saw what they did." She trembled in his arms as she spoke.

"They killed everyone, Seki. Men, women, children; they spared nothing."

Obaseki pulled Eshe close, stroking her hair. She had been happy with life in Zimfara. She had worked hard to establish a living for them there while he struggled to find his destiny. Now it was gone, burned to the ground by the Tuaregs.

"Come, Eshe," he said. "Let us go speak to El-Fatih."

"Who is El-Fatih," Eshe asked. "What can he do?"

"He is the leader of the Tuaregs, and I saved his life. As to what he can do about what has already been done, I don't know. But he owes me an explanation."

Obaseki led Eshe across the encampment to El-Fatih's tent. He half-expected to be stopped by the guards, but they let him pass, one guard actually holding the tent flap open for him. When they entered, they were stopped immediately by a well-armed warrior, apparently one of El-Fatih's bodyguards.

"I ask your pardon, Moyo, but El-Fatih has business he must finish," the warrior said. Obaseki nodded; puzzled by the deference he was suddenly receiving. He held Eshe's hand and turned his attention to the center of the tent. El-Fatih sat on a gilded stool, his chin resting on his fist. He was surrounded by his bodyguards and others of his entourage, every person wearing a hard expression. At El-Fatih's feet three men knelt, shackles around their wrists and ankles. Two of the men Obaseki recognized immediately.

The portly, bearded man prostrated at El-Fatih's feet was the Grand Merchant of Zimfara. He sweated profusely, his once elegant silk shirt drenched and torn. The other man was Jussien, his gilded captor, dignified even in chains. His face was battered, but he showed no signs of pain. The third man Obaseki did not know. He wore the uniform of the Zimfara garrison, but his facial features betrayed him as an outlander, most likely an ally of Zimfara or a mercenary. He attempted to imitate Jussien's stolid pose but his trembling hands gave away his true emotions.

El-Fatih glanced at Obaseki and acknowledged his presence with a slight nod of his head. He then turned his attention back to his captors, coming to his feet to deliver their sentences.

"You have conspired to bring down the noble clans of the Tuareg and have been found guilty by the tribal councils. As the Jackal clan claims highest status among the clans, I have been given the privilege to choose your punishment."

El-Fatih dealt with the mercenary first. "The mercenary will be released. Give him a day's worth of water then drive him into the desert. Let us see how his warrior's luck holds out." Two warriors stepped from the entourage and dragged the man out of the tent, striking him along the way.

El-Fatih turned to the Grand Merchant. "If we learned from our ancestors, we could save ourselves so much pain," he said. He strode back to his stool and sat, never taking his eyes off the unfortunate man.

"Every Grand Merchant thinks he is greater than the one before him. Sooner or later he imagines he will be the one to rid the world of Tuaregs. So the lesson must be taught over and over again, as it will be today."

The Grand Merchant sprang to his feet, his face desperate. "Fatih, I beg you to spare my life! I have much more than you can possibly dream; wealth ten times the worth of the entire Sudan. Spare me and I'll take you to it."

"Your gold means nothing to me," El-Fatih said. "It is as worthless as your loyalty. But you will not die, fat man. You belong to me."

The Grand Merchant lost all semblance of nobility when he heard El-Fatih's words. He prostrated himself before the chieftain, his huge bulk trembling. "Thank you, great Fatih, thank you for your mercy!"

El-Fatih turned to one of his warriors, a menacing man with a uniform of black from his riding boots to his turban. "Take this fool away and castrate him. He will make a fine eunuch."

The Grand Merchant scrambled to his knees. "No! I cannot…" The warrior struck the Merchant on the head with his sword hilt and the Merchant crashed into the dirt unconscious. With the help of two other warriors they dragged the limp body from the tent.

Only Jussien remained. El-Fatih's face took on a shadow as if the sun had fled his soul and left darkness behind. They looked at each other, Jussien's expression as emotionless as before, El-Fatih clearly upset. The chieftain seemed to be waiting for his betrayer to say something, but if he was, he was sorely disappointed. With exaggerated effort El-Fatih rose and walked to Jussien, kneeling close to whisper to his old friend.

"Why, Jussien?"

"You have no vision, Fatih. We live in the Mahgreb, our children starving, our mouths filled with sand while the Zimfarans grow fat from trade. We raid their caravans for only a fraction of their wealth when we could control the entire Mahgreb. But we do not, because you hang on to old ways and old values."

"You could not have brought this up before council?" El-Fatih demanded. "You had to conspire with Zimfarans and order my death?"

"The council would not listen to me and you know this," Jussien retorted. "They are not as rigid as you, but they would never go against you because they fear you. And what is your death compared to the lives of our people?"

El-Fatih shook his head slowly. "What did they offer you?"

"Half the tariffs collected on caravans and one thousand pieces of gold."

El-Fatih sighed. "That is a handsome price, my brother. And you would build a city as fine as Zimfara so we would no longer living in tents. You would use our camels for food instead of war. We would become as fat and as lazy and as godless as the Zimfarans. We would die as a people, but we would be rich and our children would not starve." He spat into the sand. "Better we all perish than to suffer such a fate."

Jussien closed his eyes and lowered his head by bending at his waist. He looked up at El-Fatih, his eyes fearless. "You will be the ruin of us all."

El-Fatih stood and drew his sword. With both hands gripping the ivory hilt, he brought the blade down on Jussien's neck. Jussien's head rolled free, the body tumbling into the carpets.

Obaseki watched in horror as two more warriors wrapped the soiled carpet around Jussien's remains and carried them from the tent. He and Eshe quickly opened a way for them to pass and found themselves holding the tarp for the rest of the witnesses of Tuareg justice.

"This is not the time to discuss Zimfara with El-Fatih," Obaseki whispered. He grasped Eshe's hand and they proceeded to leave with the rest of the people.

"Medicine-priest!" El-Fatih called out. Obaseki grimaced at the call of his title; he turned and immediately bowed. Eshe did also, though her response was slow and defiant. "I see you have found your wife," the chieftain commented with a grin on his face. It was as if nothing had happened. He strode over to the duo, stopping before Eshe.

"Stand up, woman," El-Fatih ordered. Eshe glared at him as she stood.

El-Fatih laughed. "You have a fine wife, medicine-priest. Full of fire and strength."

El-Fatih bowed to Eshe, which seemed to catch her off guard. Her eyes widened; she looked at Obaseki for an explanation. Obaseki could do nothing but shrug.

"You are angry with me," El-Fatih stated. "That is your right. What happened this day began long before either of you came to Zimfara. The scourge of the city always reaches out to our young ones, drawing them into a life of decadence and despair. I will not allow this to happen to the Tuaregs. I would burn a thousand Zimfaras first."

El-Fatih turned his eyes to Obaseki. "You are well?"

"Yes," Obaseki answered. "I thank you for your attention."

"Good, for tomorrow we break camp." El-Fatih strode to his stool and sat. "We will go to Yakubu to see if you are truly favored by Moyo."

Obaseki was struck silent by El-Fatih's words. Eshe looked at him, the pain gone from her eyes, replaced by a wife's fearful worry.

Obaseki took Eshe's hand in his. "We will be ready," he answered.

*　　*　　*

They were deep into the desert, a land of swirling sand and terrible heat. The Tuaregs made camp at the edge of the harsh terrain, hiding in their sturdy tents from the searing tempest. El-Fatih, Obaseki and Eshe were the only ones to continue on, heading for the place that the Tuaregs knew as the cradle of their god, the land of Yakubu.

Obaseki felt this was surely the place. Moyo burned so hot he had to place it in a leather pouch and drag it behind his camel. He felt the power of this land emanating from the sand, the sky and the constant, abrasive wind. It was a land gripped in turmoil, and Obaseki knew why. Moyo was lord of this land; his power set the balance of the spirits that called it home. Without him, there was no order. Without him, there was chaos.

The further they advanced the stronger the maelstrom became. Obaseki could barely see either of his companions; his eyes strained against the sand blanket surrounding him. Sand scraped his exposed skin, pushing into his mouth despite the scarf protecting it. Eshe rode beside him, but it was clear the journey was wearing them both down.

Obaseki's camel collapsed. He tumbled into the sand and was immediately enveloped by the churning winds.

"Eshe! El-Fatih!" Howling wind swallowed his voice and enveloped him in blinding sand. He jerked his head about frantically, desperate for any signs of his companions. A glow caught his eye; it was the horn, sitting alone in the sand, pulsing with white light. Obaseki made his way to the mayembe, kneeling down to retrieve it. The horn shifted and Obaseki jerked his hand away.

"The sand," he reasoned. "It must be the sand."

He reached for the mayembe again and this time he knew it was not the sand. The mayembe expanded, losing its shape and flowing like water. He stepped away from the flow as it widened, afraid of what might happen. Was Moyo returning? Was the closeness of Yakubu sparking his resurrection? He did not know, but he was sure this would not bode him well.

The glowing ooze grew to the size of a man, and then began to move away. Its passage calmed the air in its path, the abrasive wind dying down as it progressed. Obaseki followed the apparition, uncertain of what to do. The pool glided for a time then abruptly rose from the ground into the sky. As the shimmering shape ascended it lost its grip on the world below and the winds swelled in size and fury. Obaseki was again beset by a twisting torrent of wind and sand. He fell to his knees and groped forward, trying to find some protection. He traveled up a slope that quickly became a steep incline, forcing him to climb. Above him the light that was once Moyo hovered. His dark hands dug into the jagged rock, his feet feeling for a foothold while the circle of light moved before him. The illumination seemed to be leading him so Obaseki followed, deciding that wherever he went would be better than the torment he was experiencing. He climbed for hours, following the light to an unknown end but feeling a compulsion to go on. His future was with the light. No doubt entered his mind on this one thing.

He reached out his right arm and touched a level surface. He pulled himself up and rolled onto a bed of grass. After a brief rest Obaseki struggled to his feet, searching for the golden glow. The light hovered before him, shifting and expanding into the shape of a man. It darkened as features appeared; Obaseki found himself staring into the face of his nightmares. The altered image of himself crouched low like a lion, his eyes blank with hatred. In his right hand he held the white cowhide shield; his left hand grasped the short spear. The pelt of a simba rested on his head and shoulders, the empty skin of the head and mane shrouding his face, the arms tied before his chest. Obaseki wanted to speak, but before he could open his mouth his twin attacked.

Obaseki dodged a spear thrust but was caught by the shield. He rolled with the blow, coming to his feet when he was well away. His doppelganger spun and charged again. Obaseki ran toward it, ramming himself against the shield and grabbing the spear hand. He was immediately engulfed in pain like no other, a searing that razed every particle of his body. Obaseki grabbed his nemesis with his right arm, his mind lost in a struggle of emotions. The image spirit passed into him as he tightened his grip around it, the pain replaced by a level of contentment Obaseki had never known. It was within him; Moyo had given his soul up to Obaseki in order to survive, and through the horn led the medicine-priest to the only ground where the transformation could occur. His mind raced as it assimilated the knowledge of centuries. The onslaught made him dizzy; he staggered and fell. He lay on his back, the land around him suddenly familiar. Every rock, crevice, tree and grain of sand was known to him as it had been known to Moyo. His memory raced back to images of men and women similar to the Tuaregs living peacefully upon the raised plain, tending fields and pastures rich with cattle and crops. Above it all Moyo reigned until that fateful moment when he defied the gods, when Moyo tried to be more than those who created him. Obaseki saw chaos grip the land; the terrible winds, the rainless skies. Cattle wilted and died like leaves as waterholes dried into nothing. The grasslands became brown patches of dust. The Tuaregs prayed to a god that no longer existed, hoping for salvation that never came. So they left, migrating into the surrounding desert in hopes that they would find another fertile land. Instead only desert awaited them, the land which they now held sway.

Obaseki stood in the center of a storm. He closed his eyes, extending his arms like the wings of an eagle. He thought of calm and the wind responded. Silence surrounded him and Obaseki was pleased. He extended his hands skyward, the image of storm clouds in his mind. The sky darkened with blue-gray clouds that hung low with their cargo of water. With a wave of his hand the sky split with the lightening and the rain fell in torrents.

Obaseki felt a hand on his shoulder and turned to see Eshe and El-Fatih. Eshe froze when their eyes met. El-Fatih approached him, a solemn look on his weathered face. The ground turning to mud under his feet, El-Fatih stopped before Obaseki and prostrated himself.

"Moyo," he said. "You have returned to us."

Obaseki reached down and pulled El-Fatih to his feet. "I am not your god. I am the same man as before, but Moyo's spirit has escaped the mayembe."

"He sits on your head?" El-Fatih asked.

"Yes," Obaseki replied. "Listen to me, Fatih. Bring your people back to Yakubu. Your ancestors are here, this is your home. The land is still fertile and the rain will bring it back to life. You can build a city here."

"You sound like Jussien," El-Fatih said suspiciously.

"Jussien wanted the Tuareg to emulate others, to become something they are not. But this is your home. You know this."

"The desert made us strong," El-Fatih countered.

"The desert will always be a part of you," Obaseki answered. "Moyo drew me here to say these words to you. Moyo has returned to the land. It is time for his children to return as well."

El-Fatih regained his regal composure. "I shall go to my people and send out the word. It is time for Tuaregs to come home."

Eshe approached Obaseki timidly, touching his hand.

"Are you still my husband?" she asked.

"I am, sweet flower," Obaseki replied.

She embraced him and Obaseki smiled.

"You have changed, Seki. What does this mean?"

"It means we are finally home."

6

Sesuland languished under a moonless night sky, the air still warm from the day's heat. In the villages surrounding the grand city of Selike, the people gathered about the scattered fires to talk of the day and hear stories passed down from elders to children. Behind the city walls the time for rest came much later. Sesuland had prospered much over the last twenty years. It was still not the great city its founder Dingane had envisioned, but it was the largest city in the grasslands and the center of one of the most powerful kingdoms of Uhuru.

Three men made their way to the outskirts of Selike that night. They moved cautiously, traveling through the grass instead of the roads. They carried no shields or assegais, but the slap of leather scabbards against their thighs warned of their intent. They advanced quickly, covering the miles in short time, moving between farms and villages unnoticed, continuing until they could see the outline of the watchtowers of the city, their perpetual lights burning like ever-observant eyes. The men finally rested, two squatting in the high grass, one standing to full height as he stared at his former home.

If Ndoro had been alone he would have wept. The emotions in him were stronger than he expected. The memories of his life in the city flooded his mind; the years living as a royal outcast, the tainted son of Dingane. Images of his mother resurfaced and he felt shame for not returning sooner. She would have enjoyed the status of Shumba's mother, not the humiliation of being Dingane's lesser wife. The thought brought back the anger that fuelled his every step since the night he was driven from Selike twenty years ago.

Jawanza stood beside him. "It is a beautiful city."

"Yes it is," Ndoro replied.

Nakisisa joined them in his human form. "Do you have many enemies there, Shumba?"

Ndoro turned to the river spirit, reading his grim intent. "Yes, I do."

Nakisisa smiled hungrily.

Ndoro knelt and opened the traveling pouch strapped to his side, extracting the red warrior robes of Sesuland. He discarded his Diaka garments and donned the robes of his former home.

"If I have not returned by morning, do not hesitate to attack, Jawanza. Selike must burn."

Jawanza scowled. "I still advise against this, Shumba. If you are discovered and killed all that you built will shatter like shells against stone."

"All we have achieved has been for this moment," Ndoro replied. "I am back to claim what is mine, what my father meant for me to have. I will not be denied!"

Ndoro cursed himself for the anger. He managed to smile, placing his hand on Jawanza's shoulders.

"I must do this, my brother. It is what I've lived for."

Ndoro trotted to the main road, leaving his companions in their hiding place as he set off at a warrior's pace. After a half an hour he stood before the gates of the outer wall. He hesitated, realizing that once he stepped into Selike he would be stepping into his past.

If Ndoro was prepared for old memories, he was not prepared for what he saw when he entered the city. Nothing was familiar to him; the broad avenue leading to the city's center had degenerated into a narrow maze of cluttered huts and stands. If not for the palace light towers he would have had no idea how to find the royal kraal. Fortunately the streets were almost empty and he moved quickly through the winding roads, eventually discovering the main thoroughfare leading to the kraal. He hadn't decided how he would breach the wall surrounding the kraal; he'd handle that obstacle when he came to it.

Few guards patrolled the streets, and those Ndoro passed seemed to care less about any strangers wandering the city. But then Ndoro was no stranger. He was more Sesu than these people living in his father's city. Many of those he encountered were not Sesu. Some tribes he recognized; other he didn't. He wondered for a moment what could have happened to his father that would let his city sink to such a state. Whatever the answer, Ndoro would find out from his father himself before killing him.

He finally reached the royal kraal. It was the one place that remained intact, the only structure where his memory did not fail him. The white royal herd had been replenished, resembling bovine spirits as they grazed in darkness by the kraal wall. Dingane's palace crowned the summit of the hill; still as foreboding as it was the first time Ndoro laid eyes upon it. The homes of the wives ringed the kraal wall; Inaamdura's the first to the right of the kraal gate, the others farther away. Ndoro knew which hut held his mother, the last hut of the kraal ring. No one was present as he crept to the hut, moving in close to listen. He had not seen his mother for twenty years; she probably would not recognize him. He suddenly remembered Jelani, the brave bodyguard who risked his life so Ndoro could escape. There was so much he'd left behind, good and bad. But he had returned and it was time to end this episode in his life. He took a deep breath and entered the hut.

The woman inside leapt from the table where she sat and scrambled into the dark end of the hut.

"Wait, mama!" Ndoro called out.

"You could never be my son, warrior, unless you rested in my womb when I was born." The woman eased out of the shadows. It was not his mother.

Though Ndoro was distraught by the sight of this woman in his mother's hut, he could not help but stare at her. She was the most beautiful woman he'd ever seen, even more lovely than Sarama. She wore the full simple dress of a married woman in a way that heightened instead of deterring his attention. Her beauty deadened the shock he felt finding his mother gone.

"Who are you?" he demanded.

"I am Kenyetta Matiku," she replied with a voice as regal as her face. "You are obviously a stranger, for any Sesu would know all of Inkosi Ligongo's wives."

"Inkosi Ligongo?" A grim smile formed on Ndoro's face. Inaamdura's son was finally inkosi. "What happened to my... Inkosi Dingane?"

Kenyetta was not intimidated by Ndoro's threatening manner. She emerged into the light, her full beauty revealed to him.

"Dingane died ten seasons ago," she replied. "He was killed during a simba hunt, if you believe some."

Disappointment and shock struck him like an orinka. He struggled to keep his stoic façade.

"What do others say?" he managed to ask.

"They say his death began days before the hunt. They say every time he ate supper with Inaamdura she gave him a mild poison knowing it would weaken him enough to make him easy prey for the simba. Ligongo became inkosi and she his advisor.

It was a plan she began many years ago when she conspired with Cancanja to drive Dingane's favorite son from Selike."

Ndoro staggered back from the force of Kenyetta's words. He always suspected Mulugo's intentions to be rid of him, but he never suspected Inaamdura. The woman had destroyed his family to lay claim to the power of Sesuland for her and her son.

He composed himself before asking his next question. "What happened to Shani?"

Kenyetta's face changed from casual to curious, her questioning eyes making Ndoro cautious.

"She fled in the night when she heard of Dingane's death. The inkosi protected Shani from the full fury of Inaamdura's hatred while he was alive but with his death she was sure to suffer under Ligongo. So she and Jelani fled back to Mawenaland."

Ndoro looked away from Kenyetta, his eyes glistening in the pale light of the hut. Sadness sat heavy on his shoulders. If he'd returned sooner, he could have rescued his mother from Dingane's and Inaamdura's cruelty and showed his father the true meaning of power. But the chance was lost to time; there would be no such satisfaction. There was still the matter of Inaamdura and Ligongo.

Ndoro moved to leave the hut but Kenyetta stopped him. "Were you sent by Hondo?"

Ndoro was irritated by her question. "Who is Hondo?"

Kenyetta expression returned to its original nonchalance. "He is the conqueror of Uhuru, a warrior from the forests. They say he leads an army of slaves and his general is the ghost of a river spirit. They say the noblest of Hondo's enemies get the privilege of being eaten by the river creature."

Ndoro smiled; his spies had done well spreading the rumors of his advance. His time in Kenyetta's hut was finished;

his mother was gone. It was time for him to leave as well.

"Wait! Take me with you!"

"No," Ndoro replied. "I must move quickly."

"Take me or I will scream," Kenyetta threatened. "Take me to Hondo and let him decide what to do with me."

"And why should I? If you scream I will kill you and any guard that answers."

"I'll make a good present for Hondo," she said, a desperate look on her face. "I am a beautiful woman, the daughter of a powerful chieftain."

"You would be his slave, his concubine."

"I'd rather be a slave than spend another night under that fool Ligongo!"

"I will not slow down for you."

"You won't have to," Kenyetta replied. She ran to a wooden chest by her bed and removed a long cloak that she threw over herself. The duo stole into the night, hurrying through the winding city streets. Once they exited the main gate, Ndoro started a warrior's pace, Kenyetta close behind. The sun's rays reached for the horizon, orange-red light creeping westward across the plain. They met Jawanza and Nakisisa where he had left them, both men well rested and ready to move on.

"Who is this?" Jawanza asked.

"This is Kenyetta, wife of Inkosi Ligongo," Ndoro replied. "She is to be a prize for Hondo, leader of the slave army."

Jawanza looked puzzled. "What are you talking about, Koi Shumba? You are Hondo."

Kenyetta jerked her head toward Ndoro, who smiled back.

"I am your Hondo. My warriors named me Shumba. But to the Sesu, to Inaamdura, Shani and Dingane, I was Ndoro."

Kenyetta's eyes went wide then closed as she slumped to the ground.

"Nakisisa, can you carry her?"

"Yes."

"Good. Let us go. Tomorrow will be a very busy day."

*   *   *

Inaamdura awoke to the natural melodies of her aviary as she had done every day since Dingane's death. The room was built immediately afterward and filled with imported trees and plants from Shamfa. Songbirds from all the lands within her tradesmen's reach flittered about between the exotic branches. The garden was maintained by five slaves hand-picked for their special talents. It was her throne, a subtle symbol of her power among the Sesu.

Inaamdura always knew the Sesu would never allow a foreign queen to rule them, so she groomed Ligongo from the time he could walk to sit upon the golden stool of Sesuland. He had grown into a handsome and charismatic man but lacked the focus needed to rule a people. Ligongo spent too much time with his wives and concubines, a habit frowned upon by the elders. The old men were the least of her worries; they knew where the real power lay and were careful not to cross her. The surrounding kingdoms were less respectful. A major merchant route was developing through the grasslands, a thread of bare land that meant wealth and power to the city that controlled it. Sesuland straddled this route, but other kingdoms, such as Kesh and Bugodaland, were becoming belligerent with their claims to parts of the route that bordered their territory. And then there was Hondo and his slave horde, whose activities in the south at the forest's edge were becoming more than a nuisance. Refugees poured into Sesuland daily, taxing the burden of the cities and fueling crime in their desperation to survive.

Inaamdura contemplated these matters as a servant boy dressed in a white robe and glittering sandals appeared at the entrance of the aviary.

"Great Mother, Inkosi Ligongo wishes to see you."

Inaamdura nodded for the boy to leave. Though many seasons had passed since her arrival in Sesuland, her body appeared as if it knew nothing of the passage of time. Her beauty waxed as strong as it had the day she and Dingane were wed. She took no suitor after his death, nor did she heed Sesu tradition by becoming the wife of Dingane's brother Mpanda. With her son in power she did as she pleased and it pleased her to stay alone. An occasional dalliance with a passing dignitary was the only pleasure she allowed herself.

She found Ligongo in his stool room, sitting proudly between two of his wives. Around him his children played, their games causing an incessant clatter throughout the stool room. Inaamdura entered and all motion ceased. A dignified calm fell over the chamber as Ligongo's wives took their place behind their husband, their children following behind them like little warriors. Everyone was well aware of Inaamdura's insistence on formality and it was always exercised in her presence.

Ligongo rose from his stool to greet her.

"Mama, you look beautiful as always."

Inaamdura smiled despite herself. Ligongo had a way with her, but she only let it go so far.

"What do you want of me, Gongo?" she asked, using her pet name for him to signal informality.

"Kenyetta has disappeared. No one has seen her for two days."

Inaamdura cursed under her breath. "She has been trouble from the very beginning. She was not a good choice."

"Her sisters were ugly," Ligongo retorted.

"An ugly girl bears children just as well as a pretty one," Inaamdura snapped. "Children form alliances and alliances mean power. Kenyetta has denied this of you." Inaamdura clicked her teeth. "Better she stays lost."

"Kenyetta will be found!" Ligongo shouted.

Inaamdura was surprised by his outburst. Kenyetta was more special to him than she imagined which was not good. A chill ran through her chest. This reminded her too much of Dingane and Shani. She would have to put an end to this situation immediately.

"I will send my personal guard to search the city for her," Inaamdura offered.

"My warriors are already doing so," Ligongo replied. "I think she may have left the city."

"Have you questioned your other wives?"

Ligongo laughed. "They would not tell me even if they knew. Kenyetta has many enemies among her sisters. They are glad to see her gone."

Inaamdura frowned. She knew well the politics among wives and was disappointed none of Ligongo's wives had taken the control of the household. Even Mudiwa, his Great Wife, remained docile, preferring to be Ligongo's plaything than a true wife.

The doors to the stool room flew open, banging against the stone portal. A warrior stumbled through and fell to his knees, his body glistening with sweat. He lifted his head, exhaustion on his face, his chest heaving as he spoke.

"Inkosi, you must come quickly!"

Inaamdura was furious. "Who do you think you're talking

to, dog?"

The warrior gave Inaamdura a glare that brought her to silence. "You must come, inkosi. Hondo is approaching!"

It cannot be, Inaamdura said to herself. He wouldn't dare attack Selike, not with the allies she'd gained or the army she trained. She approached the warrior cautiously.

"How do you know it's Hondo? How do you know that this is not just a raiding party?"

The warrior came to his feet, somewhat rested and clearly irritated with Inaamdura's questioning.

"A raiding party does not cover the ground of the Simba Plains." He turned to Ligongo. "Inkosi, you must come!"

Ligongo rose from his throne, striding across the room to the warrior. He was about to leave when Inaamdura spoke.

"You are inkosi. You cannot face this renegade. Let Zuberi earn his pay."

Ligongo pulled away from his mother, catching her off guard. He charged out to the stool room, heading for the council room where Zuberi and his officers waited. His bukra servant waited patiently by the royal stool with his armor. Ligongo sat as the servant dressed him.

"What is the situation, Zuberi?" he asked.

Zuberi stood. He was Suburu, an extremely tall man with charcoal skin and piercing brown eyes. He wore the robes of his people but displayed the head ring of a Sesu warrior.

"Our sentries awoke this morning to screams. Hondo's army crossed the grasslands during the night and burned the farms along the border. They sacked Isala and killed everyone inside the outpost. By the time word reached us they were only miles away. They marched within site of Selike before halting."

"How many are there?" Ligongo asked.

"Eight, maybe nine thousand warriors. No sign of cavalry, but they may be holding them back as reserves."

"They have no cavalry," Inaamdura said. "Horses and camels cannot survive in the forest. If this is truly Hondo, he would have no knowledge of cavalry."

Ligongo seemed contemplative. "Can we get word out to our allies?"

"We sent messengers to Abo and Shamfa," Zuberi replied.

"Good. What is our current strength?"

"Three thousand warriors, including the royal guard. With conscripts we can raise another twelve thousand; if we include the mercenaries, sixteen thousand."

"So, my general, what is your plan?"

"It is best we wait them out. We have more than enough supplies in the city to withstand a siege. That will give Abo and Shamfa enough time to send reinforcements."

"Hondo will realize the odds are against him," Inaamdura finished. A great smile graced her face. This was the reason for alliances; this was the power she'd been bred to build. Zuberi's plan was the strategy she envisioned many seasons ago when the rumors of Hondo first reached her ears. She would not be outsmarted by some bush chief with grand ideas. The southern tribes had been easy conquests for him; their leadership was weak and their armies small. But Sesuland was a kingdom with a long tradition of war. Hondo and his ambitions would die beneath the feet of Sesu warriors.

"Let us see this Hondo," Ligongo said.

The warriors left the council room, making their way through the palace and out into the courtyard. Royal attendants waited with their mounts and they galloped through the barren city streets to the outer wall. The ramparts were manned by Kusa archers; their keen eyes scanning the grasslands, their quivers bulging with arrows.

The royal entourage galloped to the central observation tower on the outer wall. They dismounted and clamored the spiraling stairs to the deck. Zuberi and Ligongo leaned out over the railing, Inaamdura standing behind.

For as far as the eye could see, the grass plains were filled with Hondo's warriors. They sat cross-legged before the walls of Selike, their backs turned. It was a classic Sesu insult.

"This dog will die for sure," Ligongo said. "I will put the blade in his heart myself!"

"Calm down, my son," Inaamdura advised. "War is not ruled by emotion. Our adversary plays games to taunt. Zuberi will…"

A voice rose in the distance, and the invaders stood in unison with a thump of their shields. The voice called out again and they turned, facing the city walls.

"Signal the archers," Zuberi commanded.

Ligongo placed his hand on Zuberi's shoulder. "Look."

A group of Hondo's warriors ran down the main road outside the city walls, chanting as they trotted. They were dressed differently than the other warriors, their heads covered by lion manes, their shields raised before them. The other warriors took up the chant, a chant familiar to every Sesu warrior since the day they were first blooded.

> *Many men, many spears,*
> *Many spears, many raids,*
> *Many raids, many cows.*

Inaamdura was struck with foreboding. There was something escaping her, a wild thing that lurked in the shadows of her mind. As she watched the strange formation advance, that thing took shape, emerging from the recesses of her memory and becoming a clear, coherent thought. It was what Dingane possessed, what Ndoro thrived on, what every warrior within and without the walls of Selike was infected with. Within them all burned a sense of pride so strong it overcame common sense. That was why Hondo came despite her plans, why this war would take place despite making no logical sense. But it was Hondo's doom, not hers. When he died, he and the ancestors would have much to talk about, she mused.

The warriors halted just outside bow range. The chant ended abruptly, the warriors falling still. From within their ranks a voice called out, a sound that struck Inaamdura like an assegai in her chest.

With sudden precision the warriors snapped their shields down. They stepped away, revealing a solitary warrior. His head was down, a body of a young male simba draped across his shoulders. Terror made Inaamdura speechless; the name she could not utter escaping in a whisper from Ligongo's lips.

"Ndoro!"

Inaamdura watched the man she schemed to eliminate walk slowly to the outer wall, a nightmare image of that same scene twenty seasons ago on Dingane's birthday. He was halfway to the gate when Inaamdura regain her senses. He was within bow range.

"Shoot him, shoot him!" she shouted, but no one responded. Even Ligongo was caught in a silent trance, his angry eyes never wavering from his half-brother.

Ndoro stopped before the gates, lifting the lion over his

head, and dropped it in the dirt.

"Here me, Sesu! The son of Dingane has returned! The golden stool on which Ligongo sits belongs to me. Many seasons ago you were deceived. You were told I was possessed and drove me away. Some of you thought I was dead. But look what I have done, Sesu!"

A deafening roar burst from Ndoro's army, a war chant accompanied by the beating of shields and stamping feet. Ndoro stood perfectly still, a broad smile on his face. He waited until the chant died down before he spoke again.

"In the deep forest they call me Shumba for the fierceness of the lion. I built a kingdom that reaches from the bowels of Tacuma to the edges of Sesuland. My warriors were once slaves but now hold their head high as conquerors."

Ndoro raised his spear, pointing at mother and son. "You belong to me, Selike, you and all you possess. It is my right by my blood, by my ancestors and by my hand. I will not be denied my right!"

Inaamdura looked into Ndoro's eyes and saw her death. He returned her stare, a cold grin slowly coming to his face. He was Dingane reborn, but without his father's weakness, nor Ligongo's excesses. She realized she made a grave mistake those many seasons ago. If Ndoro had stayed in Selike time would have worn him down, rejection forcing him to accept his status. The man she looked down upon knew no such thing. No man could stop him. No army could stop him.

Ndoro called out in an unknown tongue and his warriors formed around him. They turned away from the city and set off at a warrior's pace, a cadence chant strong in their throats. As they passed the other warriors they too followed, forming two columns behind Ndoro and his guard. The entire city watched them as they trotted away, eventually disappearing into dust and horizon.

Ligongo left the ramparts without a word. He scampered down the steps, mounted his horse and galloped away. Inaamdura and Zuberi followed him back to the palace.

"Zuberi, gather your officers," Inaamdura said. "I will tend to Ligongo."

Zuberi's stern face became even colder. "Begging your pardon, Queen Mother, but I think Ligongo needs the company of his warriors."

"You forget who holds the power here," Inaamdura replied. "Now go!"

Zuberi gave Inaamdura his detached stare, turned and walked away. Inaamdura rushed to the stool room. She found Ligongo sitting alone, holding the royal orinka in his hand. He looked up at Inaamdura as she entered.

"So this is how you handle war, my son? Run away and hide like a boy?"

Ligongo looked at her clearly angry. "What did he mean?"

Inaamdura replied carefully. "What are you talking about?"

Ligongo sprang to his feet. "What did he mean about being deceived?"

"So you listen to the words of a demon? A man possessed?"

"Is he really?" Ligongo sat back in his stool. "I am no fool, mama. I know how baba died, and I know of others that suspect. I know how easily your enemies disappear. Tell me the truth."

"It doesn't matter now," Inaamdura replied. "You must hold onto what I've accomplished."

"What you've accomplished?" Ligongo laughed. "Yes,

Cancanja grabbed her hand, jerked it over the fire and slit her wrist with the blade. Inaamdura screamed as he twisted her hand, letting the blood run into the fire. A thick black smoke rose from the flame. Inaamdura grew weak and dizzy, months of her life spilling from her veins and into the flames. She felt herself giving way when a searing pain enveloped her, emanating from the wrist. She managed to jerk away, stumbling and falling onto her bottom while she looked at her wrist. The cut had been cauterized by Cancanja's heated blade, a charred band of flesh replacing the open wound.

The dark smoke ceased billowing from the fire. It hung before her, a dense blackness that pulled her toward it.

"Look into the smoke and see your future," Cancanja said.

Inaamdura saw nothing at first, wondering if she gave up her lifeblood for nothing. But then images appeared in the center of the cloud, darting colors that seemed more stable with every passing moment. A vision emerged from the dancing lights, the revelation that Inaamdura had paid the ultimate price to see. Selike burned, flames churning in a storm of destruction, ebony smoke climbing into the sky. Bodies were strewn through the devastation, broken figures of Sesu warriors. On the hill of the royal kraal victorious Diaka rallied, their shields and assegais pumping with the victory dance of their war drums. Ndoro stood on the roof of the royal palace, flanked by two men she did not recognize. Behind them, impaled on a sharpened wooden stake, was Ligongo.

Inaamdura fell to her knees, her face falling into her hands.

"He must die," she said aloud. "Ndoro must die tonight!" She looked at Cancanja, desperation full in her eyes. "Can you kill him?"

"I can," Cancanja replied. "For a price."

Inaamdura stood, a seductive look coming to her face. "Anything you wish."

Cancanja broke into laughter. "Your body does not interest me. I demand a higher price."

Cancanja lifted his closed hand, opening it to reveal a small pile of white dust. "What I want is a piece of your soul."

Inaamdura gazed into the white eyes of Cancanja. "So be it," she said.

Cancanja's grin evaporated with her words. He whispered over the powder in his hand and with a sudden breath, blew it into Inaamdura's face. Again Inaamdura's body was torn with pain. The powder plunged into her like a thousand jagged knives, tearing at her from the inside. She tried to scream but no sound came from her throat, her contorted face the only sign of the pain she experienced. A part of her was being ripped away, something so deep no human hand could have reached it. She collapsed to the floor in a final rush of fire. She lay still as the pain subsided, leaving a burning sensation throughout. Finally she was able to sit up. Her eyes cleared and she saw Cancanja standing over her, his face obscured in the smoky haze. There was something else though, a sense that they were not alone. Looking about the hut she saw movement near the opposite wall. Inaamdura rose to her feet; Cancanja grabbed her wrist and jerked her to his side.

"Look into the mirror of spirits," he said. "See yourself as you truly are."

A creature stepped forward through the smoke and Inaamdura screamed. The creature screamed with her, their voices an unnatural chorus of fear. It was a hideous distortion of her, talons where manicured nails should be, fangs protruding from where normal perfect teeth should rest, the hair matted about its malformed head. The creature stared into her eyes, its putrid breath visible as puffs of vile steam.

"Send it away!" she pleaded.

"That is your task," Cancanja replied. "You asked for a way to rid yourself of Ndoro, and I have given it to you. I have made your hate real. It is yours to command. No man can stand against it and no one else can control it. But be careful, my queen, for you will suffer whatever your hate suffers."

"What happens once its task is complete?"

"It returns to you," Cancanja answered. "Do not worry, my queen. The entry will not be quite as painful as the exit."

Inaamdura stepped closer to the monstrosity. The creature stood still, its heaving chest the only movement.

"Do your hear me?" she asked. The creature nodded its head.

"Will you do as I say?" Again, the creature nodded its head.

A smile slowly came to Inaamdura's face. "You are a part of me. My mind is your mind. You know the face of Ndoro. Outside our walls he sleeps with his warriors, hoping to dance his victory on our bones. But you will find him, and when you find him, you will kill him."

The creature nodded its head again.

"Go," Inaamdura ordered. "Rid us of this fool!"

The creature reared back its head and let out a piercing scream. It charged off into the darkness with amazing speed despite its bulk. Inaamdura turned her attention to the still smiling Cancanja.

"You've done well, very well. Once Ndoro is dead you will be rewarded as always. Until then, this will have to do." Inaamdura clasped the witch doctor's cheeks between her hands and kissed him. Cancanja wiped his mouth and spat.

"I'd rather have gold."

Inaamdura smiled as she left his hut. "You will have that, too. Soon."

* * *

Ndoro sat at the war council with his indunas, his face stern. Inside he was a mix of nervousness and excitement. Twenty years of war had brought him before the walls of Selike, ready to take his place on the royal stool of the Sesu. But around him his mood was not shared. He looked at the men surrounding him, all with serious expressions. By indulging himself, he had broken a trust that every man with him depended on for survival. He waited for the arguments to begin.

Jawanza spoke first. "Shumba, I know today gave you great pride. But we have put our army in jeopardy. We have lost the element of surprise, and we will pay for it with warrior blood."

Many heads nodded in agreement. Ndoro stood, sweeping his eyes across the circle before him.

"For twenty seasons we have marched across Uhuru, singing the warrior's song and filling our kraals with cattle. You have stood beside me and placed your lives in my hands. Now we stand before the gates of Selike, our final goal. Those of you who know me understand the importance of this day, so you must also understand why we did what we did today. I hoped by showing the Sesu their true inkosi, they would take matters into their own hands and rid themselves of Ligongo. The Sesu are my people. I do not wish to shed their blood if it is avoidable."

He stopped to let them consider his words. "Tomorrow I

will send an envoy to the Sesu to ask them their decision. If they refuse, we will attack." He paused for a moment before speaking again. "Still I am surprised by your worry. The Diaka I know need not have surprise on their side."

It was a challenge to their bravery, one he knew they would accept.

Jawanza spoke for the group again. "You know us better than we know ourselves; we are your creation. We do as you wish, Shumba."

Ndoro smiled. "Then rest well, warriors. Tomorrow will demand your full fury." The indunas stood as he left the council, flanked by his bodyguards. Making his way through the camp quickly, he entered his tent to find Kenyetta waiting for him.

"What are you doing here?" he demanded.

"I was waiting for you," she replied, a smile on her face.

Ndoro was unsettled by her appearance. She was a beautiful woman, and her intent was clear. He had not allowed himself the touch of a woman since Sarama, not willing to lessen her memory. But it had been so long, and Kenyetta was so close.

She sauntered toward him. "If you are the true inkosi of Sesuland, then I must truly be your wife."

"Ligongo is your husband," Ndoro answered, angry at the weakness in his voice.

"I no longer wish to be his wife. I wish to be yours."

Kenyetta wrapped her arms around his neck and kissed him. Ndoro's hands went to her waist and he pulled her close, savoring her sweet smell. He was removing the wrap around her waist when he heard the violent tearing of his tent flap. He spun to see Nakisisa standing before him, a wild look in his feral eyes.

"What is going on?" he demanded.

The river-beast's head jerked about. "My hand, where is

my hand?"

It had been so long ago when Ndoro had taken his companion's hand that he did not understand what he was asking. Before he could answer the river-beast transformed and Kenyetta screamed.

"Give me the hand!" There was another scream, but this did not emit from Kenyetta. It came from a distance, sounding like the cry of an angry beast, but not one Ndoro could place. He heard the scream again; it was closer. It was coming toward them.

Ndoro ran to his chest, rummaging through it for the gilded box that contained the river-beast's hand. The encampment exploded in shouts and yells that rolled toward his tent like a swelling storm.

"Hurry!" Nakisisa urged. "She is almost…"

Claws ripped into Ndoro's tent and tore the side away. Ndoro abandoned his search, grabbing his assegai and orinka. He turned to the river-beast and saw the creature standing before him. It was Inaamdura, a terrible deformation of her. Its claws dripped blood as saliva ran down its fangs. Before it could move the river-beast attacked. It dove into the beast, burying its teeth into its throat and wrapping its arms around the creature's torso. The creature roared and fell away, startled by the sudden attack. The camp was frantic, some warriors fleeing, others running to the battle, their shields and assegais ready. Ndoro felt a tug on his shoulder and turned to see Kenyetta's fearful face. Jawanza stood beside her.

"Come, Shumba!" he urged. "We must flee. This creature comes for you."

"No," Ndoro replied. "Form the men. Nakisisa will not fight this battle alone."

Jawanza called out to his warriors, and in moments the bravest gathered around them. The beast had forced Nakisisa onto his back, biting at him with bloody fangs and swinging its claws. The river-beast held onto his grip, his rear legs drawn up to protect its torso, raking his foot claws at the demon's chest. Ndoro raised his assegai and the warriors readied themselves. He dropped his arm sharply and hundreds of assegais sped toward the beast. Only inches away they shattered, the splinters returning like lethal rain. Many warriors went down, wounded or killed by the shards of wood.

"This is sorcery at work," Jawanza yelled. "There is nothing we can do. This is Nakisisa's fight."

Jawanza's words reminded Ndoro of the hand. He ran back to the chest and found the gilded box. He opened the box and took out the gourd containing the hand. With a yell he ran toward the struggle.

A roar rose from his warriors, a sound that was drowned by the growls and groans of the struggle before him. While the beast was distracted by its struggle with Nakisisa, Ndoro made his move. Like lightening he drove his assegai into the beast's side. The creature raised its head and Ndoro brought his orinka down, smashing the creature's face and knocking it back stunned. Nakisisa shoved the creature away, struggling to his feet.

"Here!" Ndoro shouted, tossing the river-beast his hand. "I will hold this thing off as long as I can."

"No! It has come for you!"

Ndoro grinned. "Then let it come. I have a score to settle with its master."

The beast turned to look at Ndoro. An expression came to its face, its teeth bared.

"Time for you to die, abomination!" it roared in voice that

resembled Inaamdura's.

Ndoro braced himself for the creature's charge. With a shriek the creature pounced. Ndoro fell to his knees, raising his assegai above his head. The beast landed on him as his assegai shattered against its breasts. Ndoro felt the weight of the beast, his body wracked with pain. Suddenly the pressure was gone. Ndoro managed to roll on his side, the pain almost causing him to black out. He looked up and saw the beast rolling away with Nakisisa upon it, slashing at the beast with both hands. The river-beast locked onto the creature, his fangs firmly embedded in the creature's throat. Despite the ngwena's weight the creature stood and the surrounding warriors ran in fear. Locking its eyes on Ndoro, the queen-beast staggered toward him, a low growl emanating from its damaged throat. Its legs buckled and it collapsed, falling on Nakisisa.

Nakisisa threw the dead beast aside and struggled to his feet, changing form as he approached Ndoro. His human form displayed terrible wounds, but it walked as if nothing had happened. He halted before Ndoro and struggled to smile.

"It is good to be whole again," he spoke, holding up his hand.

"I should have given it back sooner," Ndoro replied. "You stopped being my captive long ago."

Nakisisa swayed and Ndoro caught him.

"The beast is dead, and so is Inaamdura," Nakisisa said to Ndoro's surprise. "It was a creature made from her spirit, and she suffered what it suffered. Ligongo weeps for a death he cannot explain. The city is yours if you attack now."

Nakisisa coughed, blood seeping from his nose and mouth. He looked at Ndoro and managed a smile. "It is time for me to return to the river. Live long, Great Shumba."

Nakisisa went limp in Ndoro's arms. He held the river-beast for a moment, unsure how to feel about the creature that had tried to take his life but had become a loyal companion. Nakisisa died a warrior's death, giving his life for Shumba. Ndoro eased the river-beast to the ground then watched in amazement as its body shimmered and became a pool of water. The liquid lingered for moment and then dissipated into the dry earth. Warriors gathered about Ndoro, gazing at the place where Nakisisa's body once occupied. He felt Kenyetta's hand against his back but ignored her comforting touch.

Ndoro grasped his assegai, picked up his orinka and ran. His warriors parted before him like grass before the wind. Nakisisa told him Inaamdura was dead and Selike was his for the taking; if so he would take it this night. Behind him he heard the shouts of his indunas as warriors formed ranks and fell into place. By the time he reached the crest of the hill hiding the encampment the Diaka war chant shattered the silence of the moonless night. As he reached the base of the hill his army was with him, running the warrior's pace to the city.

Selike slept as the Diaka approached. Sesu custom forbade battle at night lest the spirits of the darkness be disturbed. As Ndoro learned among the Songhai, customs can lead to disaster. A few strides before the city walls skirmishers broke free, running ahead of the main army with ladders. Behind them rushed the archers, their bows at the ready, their quivers filled with poison-tipped arrows. They were deathly efficient; the archers fell any guard appearing on the ramparts while the skirmishers put their ladders in place. They clambered up the ladders, spilling onto the ramparts. Silent clashes broke out as the Diaka fought the Sesu sentries for control of the outer wall. Once the ramparts were secure, Ndoro called a halt. The archers reloaded, this time with arrows tipped with oil soaked rags. Torchbearers ran down the single file line, lighting the arrows as they went to the center. Ndoro, standing before the archers, raised his orinka and the missiles flew like shooting stars, arching through the sky and falling down into the city darkness. The archers reloaded as the first volley ignited the homes below them. The second volley went, and then the third before screams rose from the city.

"Diaka, Kimbia!" Ndoro shouted from below, leading the charge to the drawbridge as Sesu warriors attacked the Diaka on the ramparts. The Diaka struggled to hold them back, surprised by their fury. These were not the lazy warriors and conscripts that made up the complacent kingdoms of the interior. The Sesu were well accustomed to war; they were a people forged by metal and fire.

The Diaka neared the gate, but it was still closed. Ndoro's men attacked the barrier with axes, protected by the shields of their companions from spearheads jabbed through the gaps. While Ndoro and his men attacked the gate the Sesu reclaimed the ramparts. Sesu archers appeared, not enough to form organized volleys but enough to slow the advance. They shot poisoned arrows from their small bows, Diaka warriors falling into convulsions as the lethal concoctions took quick effect. A few ladders were destroyed and the others were being threatened. Kamau directed the Diaka archer fire to the ramparts. The Sesu fell back, allowing more Diaka skirmishers to climb the ramparts.

As the Diaka fought to regain the ramparts, their comrades below broke through the gates, revealing the inferno inside. Ndoro charged through the opening and into chaos, his destination the royal kraal. His bodyguards broke rank to follow him, forming a shell of shields about him. More and more Diaka poured into the city. Diaka archers commanded the ramparts, shooting down into the fiery confusion. Small groups of Sesu warriors appeared to meet the onslaught, but without organization they were overwhelmed by the charging Diaka.

Ndoro kept running, weaving through rows of burning homes and barricades. He and his guard met little opposition; the few warriors brave enough to challenge them were quickly dispatched by his guards. Ndoro's running had begun as a rage; it was now for a purpose. Having been taken by surprise, the Sesu would sacrifice the outer city. They would organize at the city center, surrounding the royal kraal and the elders' huts. The Diaka had to reach the inner city before the Sesu organized and retreated to the second wall.

As they swarmed the second wall protecting the inner city, the Diaka finally met the full fury of Sesu resistance. Warriors flooded the streets, throwing their light spears at Ndoro and his cohorts. The guard locked shield and deflected the deadly downpour, then quickly formed ranks to meet the coming onslaught. Ndoro knocked away a Sesu's shield with his orinka and slashed his abdomen with his assegai, jumping over the body as he continued to run to the palace. Together he and his guard cut a terrible path, battling their way through the inner city to the jewel of the center, the royal kraal.

By the time they reached the third wall, the rest of the Diaka army had joined them. But what Ndoro feared loomed before him. The walls of the royal kraal were covered with Sesu archers, their bows drawn and ready. Ndoro imagined what waited behind them; thousands of Sesu warriors, their bare chests painted with the blood of a bull from the royal herd, a sign that this would be a battle to the death. The Diaka could not defeat such a determined foe, Ndoro was sure. For the first time since laying Nakisisa to rest, Ndoro ceased running. Raising his orinka, the Diaka halted, just outside bow range.

In moments Jawanza was at his side. "What do you wish, Shumba?"

"Bring the archers and skirmishers forward," he replied. "I want constant probes under cover of the archers. We might find a weak point in their defense."

Jawanza nodded and set off to his orders.

"Jawanza, wait!" Ndoro called out. His second quickly returned to his side.

"Shumba?"

"Did Kenyetta come with us?" he asked.

Jawanza's expression went from calm to anger. "Yes, Shumba. She refused to stay at the encampment."

Ndoro smiled. She was the only person that wanted to see the end of Selike more than himself.

"Where is she?"

"At the rear with the reserve column," Jawanza replied reluctantly. "I insisted she stay with them. I assigned two Diaka to guard her."

Ndoro dismissed Jawanza and made his way to the reserve column. Kenyetta's bodyguard had constructed a tent for her near the city walls. As if by instinct the flap flew open as Ndoro neared the tent and Kenyetta ran to him. "Shumba!"

Ndoro pushed her at arms length. This was no time for amorous emotions.

"Kenyetta, does the Great Wife house still contain the bedchamber passage?"

Kenyetta closed her eyes in thought. "Yes, yes it does. Why?"

Ndoro was striding away before Kenyetta had time to finish her question. He signaled for two more squads of warriors to follow, and they set a warrior's pace, running past the ranks of Diaka warriors until they reached the section of wall where the homes of Ligongo's wives were located. Ndoro summoned the induna in charge of the warriors.

"Direct the archers to fire on my signal. Your skirmishers will advance with us."

The induna did as ordered. When Ndoro dropped his orinka, the archers fired. Soon after Ndoro's group and the skirmishers advanced. Halfway across the gap Ndoro's group broke away, running to the great wife's home. Breaking down the door, Ndoro went to where Kenyetta told him the bedchamber would be. A huge chest covered with elaborate pottery sat on the entrance. They shoved the chest aside and lifted the wooden door. Lighting small torches, Ndoro led his men into the bedchamber pass.

Time was of the essence. It would not take long for someone to figure out what was truly happening. Ndoro and his party had to be out of the narrow tunnel before the Sesu could capture them there.

The Diaka ran up the incline leading to the royal palace. Ndoro stepped aside and his men rammed the entrance door, bringing it down with a thunderous crash. Ndoro followed them into Ligongo's bedchamber. There, lying on his bed was the mutilated body of Inaamdura. Though she was dressed in regal mourning garments, the wounds showed clearly on her face. Apparently the wounds inflicted on the spirit-beast scarred her as well. Ndoro was disappointed. He wanted the satisfaction of killing his father's murderer himself.

They left the royal bedroom, headed for Ligongo's stool room. The palace was empty, which made the infiltrators more wary. They were easy prey for an ambush; Ndoro only hoped he could find Ligongo before they were discovered.

They descended a stairwell that emptied into a long broad corridor lined with soapstone sculptures, richly woven tapestries and animal hides. A commotion could be heard coming from a doorway at the end of the hall. Ndoro ran forward and his men followed.

They charged into Ligongo's stool room. Ligongo was seated, flanked by his personal guard and his wives. His officers were before him, all on their knees before a leather map in deep in discussion with their leader. It was one of the inkosi's children that spotted them first, a young boy who smiled and tapped his mother on the shoulder. She looked up at Ndoro and screamed.

Ligongo leapt from his stool, grabbing the royal sword from his servant. His personal guards charged toward Ndoro and his men, but Ligongo raised his hand for them to halt.

"So we meet, my brother," Ligongo said. Ndoro advanced also, his men close behind.

"If you had not been banished, this would be your throne," Ligongo said. "Mama told me baba Dingane favored you, despite what he led people to believe. He would have eventually made you inkosi despite what anyone thought."

Ligongo slowed his advance, taking a defensive stance. "I did not want to be inkosi, my brother. I had no such ambitions. But my mother wished it to be, so it was."

Both brothers stood before each other, weapons at the ready, Ligongo with his shield and gilded sword, Ndoro with his assegai and orinka.

"I would give the stool to you gladly, but I've grown fond of it. I do owe you the chance, though. We are blood, aren't we?"

Ligongo was much better than Ndoro expected. His sudden attack drove Ndoro back, knocking his assegai from his hand and leaving him with his orinka as his only defense. His warriors surged forward to protect him, but Ndoro held up his hand, stopping them.

They circled, each brother wary of the other's skill. Ndoro charged, catching Ligongo by surprise. As Ligongo swung his sword to decapitate him, Ndoro rolled under and came to his knees, striking Ligongo in the back with his orinka. He stood and was struck by Ligongo's shield, knocking him off balance. Ndoro felt a line of pain race across his chest, the tip of Ligongo's sword slicing a bloody crease. Ignoring his wound, Ndoro took advantage of the opening, jumping past Ligongo's swinging arm and hitting his brother in the head with his orinka.

Ligongo's bodyguards attacked. They were met by the Diaka and a melee broke out around the two. Ndoro hit Ligongo again and again until his brother no longer moved. Ligongo's bodyguard broke off their attack and ran. The Diaka ran them down, killing every man before they could leave the stool room. The sound of battle was replaced by the wails of Ligongo's wives and children, terror in their eyes as they looked at Ligongo's body and the warriors before them.

Ndoro approached them. "You will not die," he said. "You are my daughters now, and you will attend the new Great Wife when she is selected. But I warn you not to cross me. Your children are mine; if any harm comes to me or my own, your children will suffer. Do you understand?"

The women went silent. There was no use threatening their lives, only the lives of the children mattered to them now. It was a cruel threat to make, but Ndoro knew it was necessary for him to control his palace first before he could control the city.

Ndoro rallied his men, leaving a few Diaka to guard his new family. They scoured the palace, searching for any hidden warriors among the rooms. Finding none, Ndoro lead his warriors out to the royal pasture.

The Diaka were attacking the walls on all sides, but the Sesu held firm. Ndoro scanned the perimeter and found what he looked for. To his west the Sesu line was sparse, held only by archers on the ramparts. The other Sesu were massing near the main gate, preparing a counterattack.

Ndoro led his men down the hill. They were on the ramparts before the archers knew what was happening. After clearing the path Ndoro signaled his warriors. The Diaka charged the breach. They were within the walls and flanking the Sesu in minutes. The Sesu indunas yelled desperately, pulling their warriors back from the wall to meet the attack on their rear. As they pulled away, other Diaka poured over the unprotected sections of the wall, surrounding the remaining Sesu. Though hopeless, they continued to fight. Ndoro led his group, battling with spear and club until a loud booming rang out over the carnage. Ligongo's wives marched in a procession from the royal palace bearing the body of their slain husband. The Sesu warriors lowered their weapons, the fight leaving their limbs at the sight of the dead inkosi. They prostrated themselves before Ndoro, sprinkling dirt on their heads in the Sesu sign of submission. Ndoro felt a hand on his shoulder and turned to see Jawanza standing by his side.

"It seems, son of Dingane, that you have won," he said.

A smile came to Ndoro's face. "Sesuland is mine."

7

The sun rose over the Mahgreb as it had for millennia, its light shimmering over the fine, pale sand. On the crest of a special plateau the sand gave way to the lush growth of the high oasis. Life had returned to Yakubu and with it the Tuaregs. From the ends of the Mahgreb they came, bringing whatever they could carry on their donkeys and camels. Wrapped in their blue robes and turbans they returned; the proud and brave Ihaggaren, who remained in the desert rather than leave their homeland; the Imrad, who prospered in the caravan towns with their trading and farming skills; and even the subservient Iklan, who despite having escaped their lowly status at the fall of Yakubu could not resist the call of their homeland.

But all would not be as it was. Others came as well, people drawn not by the wealth of the oasis, but by the man who resurrected it.

Obaseki rose from his bed as he did every morning and gazed upon the city from his tower window. He donned his robe and went to his shrine, pouring libations to his ancestors and to those that inhabited Yakubu. He saw the spirits as always, mingling with the lives of the living, but they did not approach him as they once did. He was among them, a noble spirit in their world and the world of the living. This saddened him, for he had always found companionship among the spirits. Now, sitting alone in the tower, he felt the loss of their nearness like the death of a family member.

He descended into the dining area for his meal. As always

his table was prepared and, as always, Eshe was not there. She was probably inspecting the marketplace, making sure the day's business was honest and fair. Tuareg life suited her well; women were well respected and her status as his wife gave her the power to choose her position, which she did with relish. Many of the Ihaggaren were concerned about her decision to rule over an occupation dominated by the Imrad, but they said nothing, respecting her choice and fearing Obaseki's anger.

Once his meal was done he would proceed to the Grand Hall. There he would sit on his blankets, listening to the happenings of the day, settling disputes and healing those too sick to respond to the herbalist's cures. Later he would ride through the city, touching those who pushed through the crowd to be near him in hopes he could heal them. It was a routine obligatory of a chief and a life he was ordained to live. Obaseki despised it.

This was not his destiny. The restlessness rising in him every day was worse than in his days in Abo, Infana and Zimfara. There was still a task for him, some duty that had yet been revealed to him. The gods did things in their own time. He would have to wait.

Obaseki was finishing his breakfast when Eshe burst into the room; her beautiful smile was brighter than the sun.

"My husband, you are awake!" Her voice sounded more shocked than pleased. El-Fatih came in behind her, his eyes wide through the slit of his turban. He removed his veil, having no need to protect himself from Obaseki.

"Thank you for escorting me," Eshe said to El-Fatih.

"The city has become dangerous since the arrival of the refugees," El-Fatih replied. "Be sure to summon the city guard from now on."

"I will, Fatih."

El-Fatih bowed to Obaseki. "My lord."

Obaseki nodded his head and El-Fatih exited.

Eshe sat beside him. "The market is well, Seki. You should come and walk with me sometimes."

Obaseki looked into his wife's eyes and saw the truth despite her happy mood. He'd known for some time about her feelings for El-Fatih, but it had only been recently the leader of the Tuaregs harbored the same feelings for her. Obaseki felt no anger or jealousy, only sadness.

"I know you love El-Fatih," he said. "I know he has feelings for you."

Tears welled in Eshe's eyes and she threw her head down on her folded arms. Obaseki watched her sob, feeling sorry that he had not found a better way. He reached to her, caressing her neck. Eshe looked up at him with wide fearful eyes.

"What will you do to us?"

Obaseki smiled. "Nothing." He leaned forward and kissed her on the forehead. "You are my sweet flower."

"You are not angry?"

Obaseki rose and walked to the tower window. "There are powers I wish I did not possess, Eshe. The spirits read the hearts of men and tell all. You no longer see me as a man to love. I cannot blame you. I am no longer a man, but I am not a god."

"What are you then, my husband?"

Obaseki turned to her. "I do not know. I only know the ancestors are not done with me yet."

A servant entered the room. "My oba, the crowds are gathering in the healing room."

Obaseki nodded, dismissing the servant. "We will talk later," he said. He touched her soft cheek and for a brief moment felt the warmth he'd felt when they first touched many seasons ago. Then he was gone, walking briskly through the corridor to the Grand Hall. As he entered, the throng that had waited since daybreak fell to its knees in unison, their heads touching the stone floor. Obaseki took his place on his stool, a modest wooden seat given to him by a merchant from the northern lands beyond the Mahgreb. Tuareg warriors formed a path to him, keeping the people orderly as they approached.

The haggard conditions of the disciples worried him.

"These people are not from the city," he whispered to El-Fatih, who stood beside him.

"No. They are refugees from the south."

"Refugees from what?"

"Not what, who. Hondo's armies are on the march."

Obaseki tensed at the mention of his brother's alias. Now he occupied his waking hours as well as his sleep.

"I have a feeling that we will have our chance at this Hondo," El-Fatih said. "We shall see how he likes Tuareg steel."

Obaseki said nothing. The first refugee came to him, an emaciated woman holding an equally thin child.

"My oba, please heal my daughter."

Obaseki placed his hands on the child. She was cold; there was no telling how long she'd been dead. He looked among the spirits mingling with the people in the chamber, asking a silent question.

"Does anyone know this child?"

A male spirit came forward and sat on the head of the child's mother.

"I know her," he said. "She is Kesse, and her spirit hides in the forests with her ancestors."

"Her mother wishes her to come back," Obaseki replied.

"She will come if you summon her, but she will not be the

same."

Obaseki looked at the mother with sadness. "Is she close to the Zamani?"

"Yes." The spirit relinquished his hold on the woman, who almost fell.

"What happened?" she asked, her voice weak.

"A spirit from your village," Obaseki replied. "Your daughter dwells among your family and is content. She does not wish to live away from her home."

Tears came to the woman's eyes. "I was selfish to bring her here. I carried her body when I should have buried her with our family. But Hondo came so fast! If I could be with them..."

Obaseki placed his hand on her head, letting her grief flow into him. A mother's pain was always difficult for him, but this feeling went much deeper than before. Tears came to his eyes and with them a deep ache within his chest. His hand reached for the pain, clutching at his robe.

"Moyo?" El-Fatih asked. "Are you well?"

"Call off the session," Obaseki said. "Send everyone away. I must rest. I must..."

The pain consumed his senses, blinding him to everyone and everything. He tumbled in its wake, tossed like grass in a monsoon wind, rising upward while hands grabbed at him like a human rope in a cosmic tug-of-war. Suddenly he hurtled into the heavens, his body crushed by the terrible pressure. He screamed, a cry that ripped into the force surrounding him. His horrid ascent ceased, the feeling of foundation forming under his back. Faces stared down on him, perfect masks carved from the finest ebony wood. These were the ancestors; their countless names ran through his head in a litany of tongues alien yet familiar to his tortured mind. The voices increased in cadence, a blur of sound which at first was unintelligible, but ultimately coalesced into words he understood.

"Two must become one," the chanters demanded. With these words the restlessness that filled Obaseki throughout his life was swept away, replaced by a burning fire of purpose. He fell from his spiritual perch as rapidly as he had climbed, finding himself back on his stool, El-Fatih shaking him and calling his name. He grasped his friend's wrist firmly.

"I am fine, Fatih. I won't be able to continue the healing. Please disperse the crowd."

El-Fatih looked at him puzzled, and then did as he was told. The people were disappointed but orderly, following the Tuareg warriors out of the chamber.

Obaseki left the chamber and went back to his quarters. Eshe was waiting for him.

"My husband," she said cautiously. "What have you said to El-Fatih?"

Obaseki did not respond. He went to the ivory chest that rested by his bed and opened it, revealing the mayembe. The horn glowed with spiritual fire, confirming what he suspected. The spirits were freeing him. He no longer needed Moyo with him to use its power. With the spirit force of Moyo in both the mayembe and himself, there was no reason for him to stay in Yakubu.

El-Fatih came into his room, Eshe following close behind. "Moyoseki, I am worried about you."

"Don't be," Obaseki replied. He handed the chest to El-Fatih.

"This box contains the mayembe that holds Moyo's soul. Keep it safe and Yakubu will prosper forever."

El-Fatih took the chest, his expression one of distress. "Moyo, are you...are you leaving?"

Obaseki looked at El-Fatih and Eshe and was pleased at what he saw. The city would prosper in their capable hands, even without his healings. He was content, even though he knew the outcome of his journey.

"I must go," he finally said. "There is something I must do, something I was born to do."

El-Fatih set the chest down. "You saved me, and I pledged to protect and serve you. If your journey is dangerous I must go with you."

Eshe came and stood by his side. "No matter what you think, I am still your wife. I watched you grow from the unsure medicine-priest that healed my mother to the Healer you are now. It is my duty to be with you."

Obaseki smiled at their loyalty. "I must do this alone."

He placed his hand on El-Fatih's shoulder. "Find me a good camel and provisions, for I have a long journey ahead." El-Fatih bowed and left as commanded.

Obaseki turned to his wife. Tears ran down her cheeks, a pleading expression on her face. He gently placed his hands on her cheeks.

"My sweet flower, do not cry. You know my heart is with you and yours with me. What I must do is the final road in my journey, I am sure. When I am done, I will return as your husband, nothing more, and nothing less."

Eshe sprang to him, locking her arms tight around his neck and kissing him furiously. "Be safe, my husband. Come back to me. Come back to me."

Obaseki saw El-Fatih enter the room. He kissed Eshe once again then carefully pulled away. Without a word he walked past them both to the courtyard where the camel awaited. It was a fine beast; surely one of El-Fatih's best, if not his best.

"He is a good one, and easy to handle," El-Fatih said from behind him. Obaseki turned to see his friend approaching him, his arms carrying a bundle of blue cloth.

"You came to us as a stranger," he said. "We will not have you leave as one."

Like a proud father El-Fatih dressed him in proper Tuareg fashion, carefully wrapping his head with the blue turban with the face shroud. He stood back, admiring his work.

"One more thing," he said. He clapped his hands and a young servant appeared, carrying another bundle of cloth that he handed to his master. El-Fatih opened the bundle carefully, revealing a Tuareg takouba in a finely decorated leather baldric. He draped the strap of the scabbard over Obaseki's shoulders.

"Now you are a true Ihaggaren," he said.

"Thank you, my friend", Obaseki said. "Take care of Yakubu, and take care of Eshe."

"I will," the Tuareg chieftain replied.

Obaseki mounted the camel and it rose to its full height. Looking down on El-Fatih, he began his journey. Yakubu and Eshe were in good hands. He made his wife a promise to be careful and he would. One promise, however, he would not be able to keep. As he passed through the streets of his adopted city each step enhanced the feeling of purpose in his heart. His destination was Selike, the city of his brother. He did not expect to return.

A battle of words raged among the Sesu. The man that sat on the stool of Sesuland was of royal blood, the destined leader of their people. But another dilemma presented itself that could not be ignored. Ndoro, son of Dingane, was one of twins, an abomination in the eyes of Sesu tradition, and the murderer of the medicine-priest Mulugo. In a way, their arguments seemed a waste of time since the warriors of Ndoro patrolled the streets of Selike, his conquest firmly established. Many Sesu welcomed the change, especially the young men. Ligongo was content entertaining himself with his wives, leaving the expansion of power in the hands of Inaamdura. The Queen Mother preferred political intrigue to warfare, reducing the opportunity for a warrior to gain honor and cattle. Ndoro was a leader more suited for the fortunes of a Sesu warrior, and many were ready to serve him. The will of the young warriors would have to wait on the ruling of the elders. If it was determined the ancestors did not approve of Ndoro, the Sesu would not support him. They would serve him, but they would not claim him as inkosi.

Ndoro knew the conversations whispered among the Sesu but had little patience or time for them. The endorsement of the elders was not his concern. Sesuland was his; if the elders cause him trouble he would have them killed. His immediate concern was the indunas sitting cross-legged before him at his war council, serious looks on their faces. The conquest of Sesuland did not result in the spoils of war normally allowed to the warriors by Ndoro. The men were not happy.

"We understand your feelings, great Shumba," Jawanza said. He was the only commander brave enough to speak to Ndoro in such a way and the only person other than Kamau to have earned the right. "No one is closer to your dreams than I. But it is not good for the men to risk their lives with no reward. It will be difficult to lead them in our next march."

Ndoro felt the anger rising in him. "The Diaka fight for the honor of Diakaland and for me. Reward is secondary to their valor."

Kamau cleared his throat. Though he had grown much in courage since the confrontation with Mulugo years ago, Kamau was not known for speaking in a council. He shifted back and forth before speaking.

"What you say is true for our warriors, but not our allies. It is loot they seek. We might find ourselves fighting our own if something is not done soon."

Ndoro had heard enough. He stood before his indunas to deliver his final words on the subject. "The conquest of Sesuland was my dream, not yours. It is wrong for me to expect all of you think as I do. Go to your men and tell them this; once I have become the true inkosi of Sesuland, I will open the royal kraal to them. Each clan is granted one bull and one cow to add to their herds. This is my word before all of you."

The indunas stared at Ndoro, eyes wide and mouths agape. The proclamation had the desired effect. This was far beyond anything they expected. Ndoro thought this gesture would end the council, but he was wrong.

"There is another matter we must discuss," Jawanza said, breaking the spell.

Ndoro was irritated with his old friend. "What is it?"

"Sesuland has fallen, but Abo still stands," he answered. "A simba with one tooth can still kill."

Ndoro wished Jawanza wasn't so thorough. "We will deal with Abo when the time comes."

"Great Shumba, although we are Diaka, we are still recovering," Jawanza replied. "Abo is a strong ally of the Sesu and will not take our conquest lightly."

"Don't presume to tell me of Abo," Ndoro snapped. "I'm well aware of Abo's relationship to Selike; I grew up under its shadow. I also know that Abo will listen to diplomacy before declaring war. We are a mystery to them so they will be cautious. Besides, the oba of Mawenaland is of my clan."

"But he does not know this," Jawanza replied.

Jawanza's persistence was angering him although he knew his old friend meant well. His mood reflected that of the men, an overall feeling of restlessness that hung heavy in the Diaka camp. Fear crept among the warriors; fear that with the fall of Sesuland Ndoro's days of conquest were done. Shumba would lay down his assegai and shield and take the path of peace. It was a future for which the Diaka were not prepared.

"Send ambassadors to Abo carrying diplomacy swords," Ndoro decided. "Tell them that Hondo wishes to visit their great city to pay honors to their illustrious oba. You will keep your units in training during the rainy season. Replace the fallen with Sesu conscripts if necessary. The Diaka will march next dry season."

Jawanza smiled. "It is a good plan, Shumba. Meeting with the Mawena will give us time to strengthen our forces. I will arrange for the messengers to leave immediately."

"Good. Now go, and enjoy your victory."

The indunas touched their heads on the ground, sprinkling dirt on their heads as custom. Ndoro waited for them to leave before rising. He turned to see Kenyetta standing before him, her face disapproving.

"Why did you lie to Jawanza?" she asked. Although they'd been together for weeks, Ndoro was still not used to Kenyetta's insight.

"I did not lie to him."

"You care for Abo like I care for a rock," she said. "I am your wife, Ndoro, and though you try to keep your feelings closed, I know when you are troubled."

Ndoro gazed into the night, the smoke-like haze a sign of the approaching wet season. Kenyetta's words hung before his eyes, the truth in them clear. These feelings Kenyetta mentioned so easily were new to him. All his life he had known nothing but the anger that coursed through his veins cold and hard. It drove him to build the empire he now ruled. But with the conquest of his former home, his enemies vanquished, he saw no future before him, just like the warriors that followed him.

Ndoro sat cross-legged on the blankets of the council room, Kenyetta sitting beside him, placing a comforting hand on his back.

"The night I fled my village, Jelani told me to go to Abo and seek the protection of my grandfather," Ndoro said. "I was so afraid that I didn't listen to him. I ran into the darkness, not knowing where I would find myself.

"Sometimes, when I was alone, I would dream of Abo. I would imagine my grandfather rescuing me from the wilderness and teaching me the secrets of the Mawena warrior. I would become oba and lead a great army against my baba. But there would be no battle, for Dingane would be so frightened he would give up his stool and flee."

Ndoro hung his head laughing. "A boy's wishful dreams. I realized when I found myself among the Songhai conscripts that no one would save me but me. I had to exact my own revenge. But in my heart I still saw Abo as my sanctuary. For many years it was my solace."

"You will never march on Abo," Kenyetta stated.

"No I won't. I will make peace with Abo and my grandfather. Hopefully I will finally see my mother again."

Kenyetta snuggled against him and he welcomed her warmth. "The dreams of a boy do not die in the man. Abo will be your sanctuary. Your dream will be fulfilled."

The Diaka war drums raised the new day's sun, rumbling across the outskirts of Selike. Jawanza wasted no time acting on Ndoro's commands; the messengers had been sent the day before and the Diaka were training for the march once again. Despite Ndoro's generous gift, the young warriors were eager for the chance to earn more wealth and honor while the older men relished the chance to lead warriors into battle. The Sesu warriors did not share the Diaka's excitement. Although they accepted Ndoro's right to rule they resented the preference showed to the Diaka. They were the true people of Ndoro and expected to be treated as such. Many had not forgotten the murderous purges following the conquering of the city. Whatever soldiers coming to the Diaka armies from the Sesu were mostly former slaves seeking the freedom and wealth Jawanza offered.

Despite the resistance, Sesuland was soon swept in the excitement of a new campaign. Young boys fought mock battles with sticks and shields while the warriors prepared themselves throughout the rainy season for whatever fortunes the march would bring. Ndoro again sat with his indunas, this time pleased with their appearance. Intense training worked them into fighting shape, the fat of easy life burned away. Still, Jawanza stood out among them all, his seriousness making Ndoro proud.

He addressed his adopted brother. "Is Shumba ready to roar?"

"He is," Jawanza replied.

"Good. I wish you well on your campaign."

The statement caught Jawanza off guard. "Shumba, I thought you would..."

Ndoro stood. "It was you who brought back the spirit to us, who realized we had strayed from our purpose. You trained these warriors, so it is only right that you lead them."

Jawanza bowed his head to hide his smile. "Shumba, I am but a shadow of you. The warriors expect to see you before them, not a mere servant.'"

Ndoro placed his hand on Jawanza's shoulder. "I have achieved all that I wish on the battlefield. The fire you saw in my eyes was a reflection of yours."

Ndoro removed the lion's pelt that graced his shoulders since his first battle. He placed the robe upon Jawanza.

"As of this day, I proclaim a new rank, the rank of Shumba. The wearer of this robe shall claim the privilege of command of the Diaka and be answerable only to the ancestors and myself."

Ndoro knelt behind Jawanza, who trembled.

"You are the closest friend I have," Ndoro whispered. "Make sure you come back from this campaign alive."

"Yes, Shumba. Yes, I will."

"No, my friend. From this day on you must call me Ndoro."

Jawanza looked directly into Ndoro's eyes. "As you wish, Ndoro."

Ndoro nodded his approval and came to his feet, turning his attention to the others. "You are witness to this day. Spread the word among the people. My word is law."

The indunas excused themselves. Jawanza remained, his eyes filled with confusion.

"I do not understand what has happened, but I promise I will not fail you."

"You have nothing to prove," Ndoro replied. "Now go and gather the Diaka. I wish to see the army you will lead."

Jawanza rushed from the palace. No sooner had he left did Kenyetta appeared.

"Do you think that was wise?" she asked.

"Jawanza is a good man. He will administer well until we return. Have you finished the arrangements?"

"Yes."

"Good. Let us join in Jawanza's celebration."

The procession was glorious. Ndoro looked upon Jawanza as a father would on his own son. The army did not stop to join the revelers; they continued their march out of the city and into the grasslands, where they took up the warrior pace. They headed east, toward the boundary between Sesu territory and Ndogoland. Ndogo settlers had crossed into Sesuland, building villages and raiding Sesu livestock. Instead of raiding in return, Jawanza was marching to strike at Abija, the main trading city in Ndogoland. It would be a stern warning, one the Ndogo oba would do well to heed.

No sooner had the warriors disappeared into the distance did the celebrations begin. Dancers filled the royal courtyard as beer flowed throughout the streets like a river. Ndoro and Kenyetta slipped away from the revelry, making their way quickly to the awaiting escort at the outskirts of the city. There was a litter for Kenyetta and himself; the others would have to walk the distance as warriors. The royal duo mounted and the group set off for Mawenaland and the city of Abo.

* * *

Obaseki tethered his camel on the tree that had been just a sapling the last time he visited it. Though his final destination was Selike, he could not resist the urge to see his homeland for one last time. The hut looked the same as always, smothered with the various vines and plants that supplied Fuluke with his precious herbs. He had trouble finding the trail that led to it; the forest reclaimed what once belonged to it. He felt comfortable, yet sad.

Fuluke was obviously dead, passed away so long ago that Obaseki could not sense his ka. With no children to remember and honor him, his spirit probably did not linger long in the world. He was among the ancestors, as he should be. A medicine priest's soul as powerful as his mentor would rest no other place.

The door of the dilapidated hut had long since fallen away. Obaseki stepped inside and was shocked to find a nude man sitting on the dirt floor before a libation altar. The man moved his head slightly enough to let Obaseki know he was aware of his incursion.

"I am sorry," Obaseki said. "I didn't mean to intrude upon your home."

"This has always been your home too, Seki," the man replied. "No need to apologize." The man stood and turned, revealing himself to Obaseki.

"Fuluke?" Obaseki was startled. "But…"

"Yes, I am gone, yet I am here." Fuluke smiled and gestured for Obaseki to sit.

"I did not sense your ka," Obaseki said, obviously confused.

"I did not wish it."

Obaseki was again confused. "You can do such a thing?"

Fuluke smiled. "It is a strange thing to be in between worlds. Not among men, yet not among gods. I could be closer to the spirits, but I am selfish. I enjoy this gift."

"It is good to see you," Obaseki admitted. "I have thought of you often. There were many times I wished for your counsel."

"If you had my counsel, you would not be the man you are now. I was the forge that shaped you; it took life to temper you."

"And made me into what?" The confusion leading him back to Mawenaland rose close to the surface, cooling his mood.

"I serve a people, yet I am not their oba nor do I wish to be. Now the ancestors send me to fulfill a prophecy of which I do not know the outcome."

"Who said the tempering is complete?" Fuluke asked.

"What do you mean?"

The medicine priest grinned then vanished. Obaseki stared at the space, frustration tight in his throat. This quest did not fill his heart as surely as the others. The purpose was like a fog blurring his thoughts. Were the ancestors playing tricks on him? Was their jealousy of his powers causing them to show him their true strength?

He shook his head as he stood to leave the house. He was selfish. No matter whom he was or what he possessed, it was vain of him to think Olodumare would take him personally. Jealousy is an emotion of men. His purpose had been given to him; the uncertainty came from his reluctance to follow it through. He left, but not before pouring libations to Fuluke. Once done, he mounted his camel and continued his journey to Abo.

Nightfall found him at the outskirts of the city. It was dry season, the night air cool and soothing. Though he was close enough to enter the city before darkness, Obaseki chose to spend the night alone in the woods. Setting up camp quickly, he made a small offering to the wood spirits. Everywhere he traveled, the knowledge of his journey seem to precede him, and the spirits gave him a wide berth. Obaseki had never felt so alone. As he rested his head on his bundle, a haze appeared before him, transforming into the form of Fuluke.

"Tired so soon, Seki?" the spirit asked.

"It's been a long journey," Obaseki replied. He sat up before Fuluke.

"What awaits me in Abo?" He was not troubled to let

Fuluke hear the fear in his voice. "Do the memories of my past run deep?"

"Most who remember you are too old to care, but others have lived only to see this day."

"What about my grandfather?" Obaseki asked.

Fuluke smiled. "Your grandfather is like the coconut; hard on the outside but inside, soft. He has never forgiven himself for banishing you. But he is not the one."

"Then who?"

Fuluke grinned. "You will know when you know." With that, Fuluke slowly faded away.

Obaseki shook his fist. "Why do you tease me this way? What is the purpose?"

He was answered by the murmur of the forest. His anger wasted, he dropped his head on his bundle and closed his eyes, letting sleep find its way into his eyes.

Obaseki awoke the next morning thankful the spirits had allowed him a restful slumber. He ate and broke camp, wishing to be in the city before noon, before his grandfather made his processional. The farmland and forest gave way to the clutter of homes and huts that sprawled beyond the city walls. Soon he walked among others making their way to the city. As he drew nearer to Abo he noticed this was no ordinary trek. Whole families were traveling together, baskets of food in their arms and balanced on their heads. A certain enthusiasm flowed among the throng. This must be a special day, Obaseki thought. He searched his memory, but could remember nothing significant for this day. But he'd been gone many years; some special event could have occurred on this day during those years. After a few miles walking with the gregarious multitude the excitement finally infected him. He found himself as anxious as the others, though his emotions were dulled by the reality of his purpose.

The dense crowd became sluggish as it neared the city. Obaseki noticed the guards upon the walls, a sign that did not bode well for him. If Abo was in a state of war, strangers such as himself would not be allowed beyond the first wall. At worst he might be questioned and his identity revealed. He slowed, contemplating his choice. He decided there was no real need to go to Abo. His business lay further south in Selike.

"You must go inside," Fuluke said, interrupting his thoughts. "What you seek is here."

"Have the ancestors made you their spokesman?" Obaseki whispered, knowing his teacher was invisible to those around him.

"You have," Fuluke replied. "The word of the spirits come in a way that receiver will accept."

"So you are not the spirit of my teacher," Obaseki said.

"I am Fuluke," his teacher replied. "I speak for those whom I serve."

"So my brother is coming to Abo?"

Fuluke smiled. "Your brother is here."

*   *   *

Ndoro and his party made good time, traversing the barren roads as fast as the night's light allowed. During the day they slept, hiding in the safety of the tents that obscured their identity. This was to be a secret meeting; Ndoro did not want his enemies to suspect an alliance between Selike and Abo. Such a threat would spur some type of pre-emptive action, and the Diaka were not ready to deal with such a situation so soon. Overall the trip was going well. The warriors were in good spirits and even Kenyetta seem to enjoy the rigors of the road.

Ndoro did not fare as well as the others. Since they set out for Abo his sleep had been interrupted by strange dreams. In the beginning, the dreams were incoherent visions dominated by a sense of foreboding. As the group came closer to Abo, the dreams took form, revealing images alien to him. He saw deserts, ruined cities and terrified faces, the carnage of war. He saw a magnificent city in the midst of sand, inhabited by an endless collage of people. One man hovered in the sky over them all, one man whose face he could not make out but whose image struck him with fear. He woke suddenly, his body wet with sweat, Kenyetta clinging onto his shoulder.

"My husband, what is it?" she asked.

He came to his feet and walked away with a rush of anger. Kenyetta followed.

"I have traveled many lands, fought many battles and conquered many people," he finally said. "But never have I felt the fear that I have during this journey."

Ndoro turned to his wife. "I never cared much for the spirits. Those I knew who possessed such power abused it for their own purposes. But could it be the spirits are trying to send me a message?"

"Don't waste your time with the spirits," Kenyetta replied. "Many nights I poured libations to my ancestors, hoping they would deliver me from my tortured life. But I found freedom on my own, not through some medicine-priest's bones."

She took Ndoro's hand and pulled him to her. "Come, Shumba. I will drive away your dreams."

Ndoro was tempted, but not even Kenyetta's seductions could push away the feelings lurking in his heart.

"I must walk," he said, and left the tent.

The damp night air eased his mind. It felt good to move about in daylight. Small trees and shrubs intruded on the grasslands where they camped, a sign they were nearing the forest kingdom of Abo. Mixed herds of springbok, zebras and wildebeests grazed on the short grass while keeping their distance. Even the great shumbas, his namesake, were careful not too get too close. They knew well the difference between ordinary men and Sesu, giving the latter much respect and a wide berth.

Ndoro climbed a small hill that hid a river on its western side. He clamored down the steep slope to the river's edge, startling a flock of ostriches that fled on his arrival. Looking about warily for predators, he knelt for a drink.

"Your life has always seen change in rivers," someone said.

Ndoro snatched his head about and was shocked by who stood in the river before him.

"Nakisisa?"

"I have returned, my friend and master," the river-beast said with a grin. He was in human form, nude but for a small loincloth around his waist. He showed no scars from that terrible night, a true sign Ndoro was speaking to a spirit. Suspicion put Ndoro on edge. Although the river-beast saved his life, he was still a vengeful spirit.

"The spirits have kept you well," Ndoro said.

"And the ancestors have smiled on you, Shumba." The river-beast stepped from the river. "And to think you were to be my meal."

Ndoro tensed. "Why have you returned?"

"The ancestors wish it so."

"Since when do they intrude on my life?" Ndoro replied.

"I have no need for spirits, ancestors or otherwise. My destiny has been shaped by my shield and assegai, not by some old ngoma throwing bones."

"But what of your dreams?" the river-beast asked.

"What do you know of my dreams?" Ndoro spat back.

"Your dreams are clues to your destiny, hints of what the spirits wish you to become."

Nakisisa's eyes strayed from Ndoro. "Remember your destiny. The Diaka will march again soon, for the last time." He extended his hand, giving Ndoro a worn leather pouch. Ndoro took it warily then undid the straps. Inside was an emaciated ngwena paw.

"Do you remember?" Nakisisa asked.

"Of course I do," Ndoro replied as he closed the pouch.

"I belong to you once again," Nakisisa said. "If you summon me, I will come."

The river-beast disappeared into the rushing waters. Ndoro's bodyguards appeared soon afterward and found their leader in stunned silence.

The next morning the Sesu set out again. Ndoro rode quietly in his litter, his thoughts focused on Nakisisa's parting words. The Diaka would march one last time? The uneasiness he felt concerning the journey returned in full force.

The weak trees and sparse shrubs became more numerous as they traversed the savannah. Soon the forest towered before them, a green wall full of secrets. As they neared Ndoro heard urgent voices. His warriors were immediately on guard. Raising their shields and assegais, they formed a sharp wall around Ndoro and Kenyetta. The voices died and their source emerged from the foliage. A man walked toward them wearing a white waist robe, his chest bare. Around his neck a rectangular gold bar hung, engraved with the symbols of his rank. In his right hand he carried a ceremonial sword, signifying him as an official messenger of the Oba of Mawenaland. He was flanked by four horsemen, two on each side. Men and horses were covered in kapok quilted armor.

The two groups approached each other slowly, finally stopping a javelin's throw apart. The messenger continued to approach the Sesu, weaponless and alone. Ndoro motioned one of his warriors forward. The men met, exchanged words then the warrior returned.

"Great Shumba, these warriors were sent to escort you to Abo. They have extra horses for you and the Great Wife."

"We will not ride," Ndoro replied. "I walk with my warriors."

Kenyetta whispered in her husband's ear. "Among the Mawena, the nobles always ride to show their status. Don't insult them with your arrogance."

Ndoro bristled at Kenyetta's words but yielded to her truth.

"Bring the animals. We shall ride into Abo as your custom, so long as they honor our customs when we arrive."

The warrior conveyed the message and the horses were brought forward. Kenyetta mounted easily, coming from a people who used animals frequently. Ndoro had some trouble but managed to retain his dignity by not falling completely off the beast.

On the messenger's signal the entourage proceeded into the thick forests, the path to Ndoro's dark future.

Obaseki found shelter in the Kossi section of Abo. He was surprised to see it still existed despite their treacherous attack. There was still nervousness in their manner; they seemed even more nervous around him.

He'd just finished his libations when he heard a shuffle behind him. He turned to see a Kossi, his eyes darting to him and then away.

"May I help you?" Obaseki inquired.

"Pardon my intrusion," the man replied. "I am Kanata, the keeper of the Kossi house. My brothers and I were curious to what a Tuareg was doing so far from the desert."

"The stories of Abo's greatness have spread far into the desert," Obaseki replied. "I was curious so I came to see for myself."

"Tuaregs don't just come to see," Kanata said. "They come to scout."

"As do the Kossi," Obaseki countered.

Kanata flashed a smile. "The Kossi have always recognized Abo for the jewel it is. Long ago we tried to make it ours."

The Kossi's words sat heavy on Obaseki's chest. Images of that terrible day emerged in his head, the lives lost because of his ignorant decision.

"I am here for my own reasons," Obaseki finally said. "Good day, Kanata."

The innkeeper left quickly. Obaseki followed close behind, eager to be away from his former enemies. The sights and smells of Abo awakened old memories and he fought the urge to weep. He had no idea how much he missed the city until that moment. He moved with the flow of the people, working his way to the market.

He had reason for visiting the marketplace. He knew sometimes his grandfather would visit disguised as a common villager to determine the mood of his people. Obaseki looked into the faces surrounding him, searching for a familiar smile or gesture. As he scanned the jumble, he realized it was a foolish search. His grandfather was much older and probably left such things to his warriors. Still he found himself searching until a familiar voice caught his attention.

"Is it as you remembered?" Fuluke asked.

"It is," Obaseki replied. "It is beautiful."

"So it is fitting that your destiny is revealed here."

Obaseki wished to stop and confront the spirit of his master, but the gesture would draw attention. He continued to walk.

"What is my destiny?" he asked.

"You heard the words yourself," Fuluke replied. "With Moyo, two shall become one."

Obaseki stopped. "What do you mean?"

"With Moyo, you have the power to become what you were meant to be."

"Moyo is not here," Obaseki said.

Fuluke looked stunned. "You did not bring it?"

"Moyo serves its purpose in Yakubu," Obaseki replied. "It has brought only death to Abo."

Fuluke's face became solemn. "Then you will fail." He disappeared into the crowd.

He would not fail, Obaseki thought. The ancestors would not have sent him here to do so. Besides, Fuluke was not aware of his newfound abilities. He was part spirit, but he was not close to the ancestors.

His thoughts were pushed aside by the roar of drums. The throng at the market turned toward the sound and surged in its direction. Obaseki saw the oba's warriors moving through the crowd in their red and yellow quilted uniforms riding horses covered in matching quilted armor. Behind them his grandfather followed, surrounded by the elders. He pushed his way through, the hordes of Mawena giving way easily to the Tuareg stranger among them. The procession stopped at the center of the market. Obaseki still could not see but he knew by memory what was happening. His grandfather's retainers set his stool in place. He sat, flanked by ceremonial guards holding wide bladed golden swords. Those with disputes would be brought before him one by one to have their disagreements settled. But as Obaseki neared the edge of the crowd, he saw this meeting was different. The entourage was larger; the guards more alert. He emerged from the crowd and was hit by a wave of emotions that nearly toppled him.

His grandfather sat on his golden stool, gray haired but regal. Standing behind him was a woman he did not recognize, but who apparently was important enough to hold such a place with his grandfather. The woman bent close to his grandfather to whisper and Obaseki immediately saw the resemblance. He was looking at his mother for the first time in his life, the woman he never knew. This was the secret Fuluke hinted at earlier. Only his grandfather would speak of her and then only briefly. Whatever she'd done to deserve such treatment had obviously been forgiven, for now she stood beside her father in the position as his advisor.

His grandfather rose from his stool and the multitude fell silent.

"Mawena, hear what is to be said. For many years I have been honored to be your oba, and I have done my best to rule in a way to bring prosperity to our lands. Today I have the privilege to bring you news of great importance. The Mawena have been offered the brotherhood of a neighboring people, a tribe whose blood once mixed with ours. Today, that bond is renewed. Today, the Sesu and Mawena are united again!

The Mawena warriors parted, revealing a small group of Sesu warriors that came forward. Behind them walked the man Obaseki had seen only in his dreams. Ndoro strode to his grandfather, his lion headdress regal on his shoulders. Behind him followed his second, a man who though he wore the warrior's garb of the Sesu was surely not of the same blood. Ndoro turned to the crowd.

"I stand before you not as the inkosi of the Sesu, but as the grandson of Oba Noncemba, the son of your sister Shani. Within my veins the Sesu and the Mawena are one!"

Ndoro turned to face Noncemba. A retainer stepped forward to present the ceremonial unity sword to the most senior of the elders. The elder took the sword, walked to the pair and presented the hilt to them. Grasping the hilt together, Ndoro and Noncemba raised the blade over their heads. The market erupted with the roar of drums and voices of approval as ceremonial dancers filled the streets to celebrate the reunion of the two powerful tribes. As the crowd joined in the dancing, Obaseki saw his chance. He joined in, working his way slowly toward the royal entourage. The revelers were amused at the awkward Tuareg and made room, speeding his approach. Soon there was only a weak barrier of distracted bodyguards between him and his brother. He saw the woman who was his mother embrace Ndoro, a look of pride in her eyes. He had the privilege of her love, a realization that sparked unexpected anger in Obaseki. He shoved the Sesu warriors away to either side, clearing a path to his brother. In an instant he lunged past the guards and sprang face to face with Ndoro. Pushing his mother aside, he reached into his robes and revealed the dagger. Ndoro looked puzzled, and then his eyes went to the knife. Obaseki lunged, the knife barely piercing Ndoro's skin before Ndoro grabbed his wrist. The touch struck both men like a blow. Obaseki fell back, the knife flying from his hand. Ndoro tumbled away, his flailing hands grasping Obaseki's face veil and pulling it free.

Obaseki struck the ground. He lay stunned, the faces above him looming like dark clouds, the bewildered face of his mother and grandfather mixed with the angry glares of the elders. They were suddenly pushed aside, replaced by the terrifying countenance of the man who stood by Ndoro. Obaseki saw a flash of metal and his abdomen burned. He yelled and struck out with his right hand, the force lifting the man into the air and flinging him into the crowd. Obaseki fell into darkness as he was dragged away, the silence replaced by the clanging of metal and angry shouts. He was lifted, dropped and lifted again. Anxious hands carried him swiftly then placed him on what seemed to be a camel. He jolted as the beast ran, his consciousness spinning down into a vortex of blackness. Before the darkness swallowed him, he heard a familiar voice.

"I have you, Moyo," El-Fatih said. "I will take you home."

8

Abo's marketplace spun in chaos. The crowd was in full panic, fearing the Tuaregs had used their time of celebration to invade the city. People fled to their homes while angry Sesu and Mawena warriors darted among the throng looking for any remaining camel men. The oba's guards formed a solid wall of kapok, shields and swords around the royal entourage as the war drums summoned the army.

The turmoil that prevailed outside the ring of warriors flourished inside as well. Ndoro was surrounded by faces and hands, his ears clogged by desperate questions and the wailing of women. His wound was painful but he'd suffered much worse in battle. What gripped him was the sensation when his hand grasped his brother's. For an instant it seemed he was stabbing himself, as if he held the knife meant to bring him death. He shut his eyes, shaking his head violently to rid himself of the image.

Three healers managed to work their way to him, immediately covering his wounds with herbs and mouthing chants to soothe any angry spirits wishing to see him dead. Ndoro shoved them away and struggled to his feet.

Noncemba sat on his stool, his head cradled in his hands. Beside him Shani knelt weeping. The elders surrounded them, their voices forming an incessant chatter.

"Leave us," he ordered.

"This is the second time your brother has brought evil to this city," one of the elders said.

"He is determined to see Abo destroyed," another said.

"My son is not evil!" Shani shouted at them all. "No child from my womb could be so vile."

"Maybe the Sesu were right," a third elder commented. "Maybe the twins should have been..." The priest stopped, realizing who stood among them. Ndoro felt the rage of his past swelling in his chest.

"Leave now or forfeit your lives, old men," he growled. The elders scattered into the crowd. Ndoro watched them disappear, and then stood before his grandfather.

"Why does my brother want me dead?" he asked.

"Who knows what is in his mind?" Noncemba replied. "His thoughts don't belong to him."

"What are you talking about?" Ndoro asked.

Noncemba raised his head, his face stained with tears. "Obaseki was trained to be a medicine-priest. His teacher Fuluke claimed he was special since he was born a twin. Reluctantly I allowed this, for it seemed to be his calling."

Noncemba straightened, regaining his regal stance.

"Then the Kossi attacked. We charged out to drive them back and were surrounded. Obaseki pulled out the mayembe and unleashed a terrible spirit he could not control. It killed anyone in its path, Mawena and Kossi alike. After the Kossi were driven away, the elders met to decide Obaseki's fate. Many of them lost family to the spirit and wanted it destroyed and Obaseki banished. The decision was made; Obaseki could remain in Abo if he gave up the mayembe Moyo. If not, he was banished."

"And he left," Ndoro finished.

"I did not think he would. But I'm sure the spirit of the mayembe possessed him by then. He went to Infana, the city of spirits. It was too late to save him."

"When a man is possessed there is only one way to drive

out the evil," Ndoro said.

"Why must death always follow my sons?" Shani asked. "How can you stand before me and talk of Sesu ways, Ndoro? Sesu ways condemned you to death as well! You forget so easily, my son."

Ndoro's anger swelled again despite the recent reunion with his mother. "He tried to kill me! He brought death to your city and disgraced your traditions and you ask me why I mention Sesu ways? The demon can only be driven out by death."

"As it was to be driven out of you?" Shani retorted. "Do I speak to Ndoro, or the demon that wishes to kill its own brother? Maybe you both are lost to evil!" Shani fell to her knees, letting out a moan that seemed to come from the inside of her bones. The despair of that sound drained Ndoro's rage and he knelt beside his mother, embracing her with his massive arms.

"Mama, during my childhood you and Jelani were the only people to show me love. When I thought I was a man, I ignored you to gain the attention of my father. But during my life your love has kept me alive."

"I don't want to see you suffer again, but know this. You do not speak to a demon; you speak to your son. I believe though, Obaseki is no longer your son. He has lost his spirit to Moyo. We must stop him."

"Yes, we must," Noncemba agreed. "We must destroy this spirit inside him and hope we can rescue Obaseki's soul. Abo and Selike are not safe until we do."

Shani dropped her head and knelt beside her father. "I saved my son's life so he could be killed by his brother."

Noncemba let out a breath. "Didn't you hear me? A demon's soul possesses Obaseki!"

Shani looked past Noncemba to Ndoro. "Remember your

past, son. You are not so mighty to change that."

She came to her feet then staggered away. Her words were meant to hurt, and they did. Ndoro pushed the pain aside, making room for a feeling he thought he'd never experience again. The spark of hatred he thought disappeared with the fall of Selike flared, kindled by the face of his twin, Obaseki.

"Grandfather, this is the time for the Mawena, the Sesu and the Diaka to come together as one. The evil that once was my brother must be destroyed!"

*   *   *

The Tuaregs rode throughout the day and night, stopping long enough to rest their animals and tend their wounds. They hoped to take advantage of the chaos in Abo to put a safe distance between themselves and the city. They were well into the desert before they stopped for a full rest.

El-Fatih knelt before the pool at the oasis, removed his veil and splashed his face with the warm water. They were home now, safe in the domain they mastered. After cleansing himself, he went to the tent of the medicine-priest. Obaseki lay before the old man, his eyes closed and skin ashen. Only the slight heaving of his chest gave any indication that he was still alive. El-Fatih despaired as he looked upon the savior of his people. Obaseki never liked being thought of as a god, but the fact was most of the people of Yakubu considered him so. They came to the city for his healing and protection, but they and all their ancestors could not protect him.

"How is he?" El-Fatih asked.

"Not good," the medicine-priest replied. "He is very close

to the Zamani. The spirits are gathering to celebrate his arrival."

El-Fatih looked about the tent although he did not have the eyes of a medicine priest. "I don't understand his condition. His wound is not so terrible."

The priest stood, wringing his hands. "I cannot save him. He must save himself."

"We must get him back to the city," El-Fatih announced. "Moyo can heal him."

From that day on, El-Fatih allowed little rest on their journey to Yakubu. The Tuaregs recalled their nomadic ways, jumping from oasis to oasis, avoiding those claimed by their enemies. Still, despite their carefulness, there were clashes with roving bands of nomads. The Tuaregs finished them mercilessly despite their fatigue.

After three weeks the fertile plateau of Yakubu loomed before them. The Tuaregs picked up the pace, energized by the sight of their homeland. El-Fatih was particularly uplifted. The sooner they returned Obaseki to Moyo, the sooner his strange sickness would be broken. Outriders met them at the outskirts of Low Town. Bringing their camels together at El-Fatih's instructions, they hid Obaseki from the crowds that packed the narrow streets, the dust stirred like a sandstorm by countless feet. They were soon met by El-Fatih's second, Hussein, and the city guard.

"Did you find him?" Hussein asked anxiously.

"Yes, I found him, but I cannot save him," El-Fatih replied. He gestured to the litter holding Obaseki between two camels.

"Then it will be worse," Hussein prophesized.

"What do you mean?"

"The people suspect Moyoseki is gone. They ask for his presence and his healing. Many are threatening to leave."

"Let them," El-Fatih growled. "Yakubu is a Tuareg city. Moyo is our protector, not theirs. Besides, if they can survive the desert crossing to Zimfara, they will not survive Shumba."

The two men looked as the crowd came closer, almost too close.

"Hussein, clear a path to the palace," El-Fatih ordered. "We must get him to Moyo as soon as possible."

Hussein spun his camel about with a jerk of the reins. He took out his horsetail swatter and struck at the throng, his men repeating his actions.

"Hai! Hai! Make way!" he shouted. The human flow separated and El-Fatih's party rambled through the gauntlet of onlookers, up the narrow climb to the summit of the plateau. As the walls of the palace came into view El-Fatih raised his banner and the gates swung open. When they reached the second wall its gate was open as well, their arrival signaled ahead. Eshe appeared from the palace, running as fast as her garments would allow, her attendants struggling to keep pace.

"Did you find him?" Eshe's voice was strained and almost unfamiliar to El-Fatih. He nodded his head and the camel bearing Obaseki came forward. Eshe's servants quickly surrounded the camel, taking great care as they removed Obaseki. They rushed him to the palace temple where a bed had been hastily prepared. El-Fatih and Eshe followed, the queen clinging to El-Fatih's arm.

"What happened? Why is he like this?" she demanded.

"We followed him to Abo," El-Fatih replied.

Eshe's eyes widened. "Abo?"

El-Fatih nodded. "He went to kill a man who looked just like him."

"Oya protect us!" Eshe exclaimed. "I didn't know he was hurting so much. He knew his grandfather had no choice but to banish him."

"This was no old man," El-Fatih corrected. "This man was

a warrior, an oba in his own right."

"The evil one in his dreams," Eshe whispered.

"Moyoseki tried to stab him, but one of his warriors stepped in the way and struck Moyoseki with his assegai." El-Fatih's head sagged as he hid his eyes from Eshe.

"I was not swift enough to prevent the first blow. We rescued him and fled the city. He is not dead, but he is not alive."

They entered the temple. The room was brightly lit with torches and candles; the smell of incense and offerings heavy in the air. The servant placed Obaseki on the bed and stepped away. Eshe approached, touching his face lightly as tears ran down her face.

"Seki, please don't leave me," she pleaded. "I am not ready to respect your memory." She kissed his cheek, and then laid her head on his chest, her arms embracing his still form.

Obaseki sensed Eshe's warmth and reached out for her with arms that would not move. He was a prisoner in his own body. He suffered every jostle and bump during the hard ride back to Yakubu, heard the whispers of the men speculating on his death, the questions to El-Fatih of why he was being so foolish bringing a corpse back to the city, god or not. Obaseki expected such doubts, learning early in his life not to trust the faith of men. But his heart ached, for the ancestors had abandoned him, even after he had attempted to do what was asked of him.

"You did not do what was asked of you," Fuluke answered, his spirit standing behind Eshe.

"You can hear me?" he asked.

"You are among us now. Of course I can hear you."

"So I am dead," Obaseki stated.

"No," Fuluke replied. "Your destiny has not been fulfilled.

You will have another chance."

"How?"

Fuluke gave Obaseki his familiar knowing smile. "You will see your brother again. Of this, I am sure."

*   *   *

The rainy season came early to the borderlands of the Sahel, announcing its arrival with thin gray clouds and gentle rains. The Mawena army, farmers as well as soldiers, left the ranks of the oba to plant their fields. It was because of this that Ndoro could expect no support from his new ally for his latest campaign. It was of little consequence; the Diaka had always marched alone. They would, however, have the added manpower of the Sesu. Their warriors were full of themselves of late, the celebration drums still playing for the victory against the Ndogo. What had begun as a swift strike to establish the boundaries between the two tribes became a rout. The neophyte warriors returned to Selike not only with victory, but also with the promise of tribute from Ndogoland. The Sesu had proven themselves as equals to the Diaka, and Jawanza proved himself worthy of Ndoro's appointment as Shumba.

The Lion of Diakaland stepped out of his royal palace and gazed upon his kraal. The massive enclosure spanned from the edge of the thorn fence cattle enclosure to the stone wall surrounding the base of hill. Below him rested thousands of Diaka warriors camped outside the stone enclosure prepared to march. His indunas gathered before the gate, their leopard skins and headdress distinguishing them from the others. In the lead stood Jawanza, proudly wearing the simba mane given to him by Ndoro. Ndoro felt the burning in his chest, the fire that had fueled him all his life. His hand reached down to rub the scar inflicted by his brother, another notch on his assegai of revenge.

He slowly walked out to where the throng could see him. Immediately the air shook with the chant of his name.

"Shumba! Shumba! Shumba!"

Ndoro raised his assegai and stabbed at the air with the rhythm of the chant, the volume rising with each jab. Drummers joined in, and the warriors danced, falling into song they knew well.

Ndoro danced with them, his body surging with his rejuvenated spirit. The purpose that had been missing since he gained the Stool of Sesu returned, rekindled by the demon that possessed his brother. The fire was back in his eyes, Jawanza said, and he was right.

As the warriors danced, the people of Selike joined in, the women high-pitched voices ringing joyously with the deep serious tone of the men. Children ran about among the celebrants, singing exuberantly with the others.

Ndoro planned his last campaign during the previous rainy season. Mawena and Sesu merchant spies had fanned out across the forestlands, the Sahel and the Mahgreb, asking questions among various cities about the man Obaseki and his city of Tuaregs. The answers led them north across Mahgreb to Zimfara. From there the interlopers plunged into the desert in search of Yakubu, the home of Obaseki and his demon mayembe.

Ndoro danced vigorously as he contemplated what he had to do. The image of his brother tormented his nights, waking him with sweaty chills. It was unnatural to have to kill his brother despite the possession. Kenyetta suggested he send Jawanza to lead the campaign and spare himself the conflict. But this was something he had to do. There must be no doubt of Obaseki's death. The only way to insure it was to do it himself.

What if he was wrong? Shani's words cut deep, the doubts she planted grew like weeds in his mind. If there was any chance of him being wrong about his brother, he would not carry out his obligation. Inside he hoped time would prove him wrong.

* * *

Shani was unaware of the conflict in Ndoro's mind. Soon after her son selected the merchants to seek out Obaseki, Shani met with each one, offering a small fortune to insure that she would hear any word of her son before it was given to Noncemba and Ndoro. She cried with joy when the existence of Zimfara and Yakubu was confirmed; her dances were for her own reasons. The day after the news she prepared for her departure from Selike. Themba still attended her, though at her age there was little she could do but be good company. But she was loyal, so when Shani revealed her intention to see the son she never knew Themba set about making the desire a reality.

The rainy season unleashed its downpours while Shani was still traveling. She rode in a covered cart, a ragged thing that smelled of goat and amplified each bump of the battered road with bone-jarring efficiency. Her traveling companions, Kossi merchants headed for Zimfara, walked beside the cart. They seemed impervious to the constant drizzle, their heads protected by their white turbans. Mingled with them were the bodyguards Themba hired to protect her on the long journey. Shani was skeptical at first, unwilling to put her life in the hands of people not bound to her by loyalty and servitude. Themba assured her the Blood Men were people of their word, known throughout

Uhuru for their honesty and fighting skills. Using members of the royal guard would have revealed her intentions to others, for everyone knew there were no secrets in a royal household.

The group finally came across a modest trade village. The Kossi took refuge from the rain with their livestock in the stables; Shani and her entourage went to the hostel, the largest building in the village. The proprietor was happy to see them for travelers were rare during the rains. Pleased to be out of the rain, Shani fell onto the straw cot in her room as if it was the finest bed in Uhuru. She changed into dry clothes and lay on her back, refusing to rise. The knock on her door startled her; she quickly finished dressing and found the knife concealed in her bags before answering.

"Who is it?" she asked.

"Dike of the Blood Men."

Shani cracked open the door, revealing the hard face of Dike. Themba introduced him as the leader of the bodyguard, the one to speak to when needed. The others were not to be addressed directly. Though his face was always set in a frown, his eyes conveyed a gentleness that brought trust. Shani agreed to hire them for that reason.

"Queen Mother, may I enter?"

Shani opened the door and stepped away. Dike entered, ducking under the doorframe and sitting cross-legged before her. He placed his sword across his exposed legs, and then gave Shani a curious look.

"Is this man you seek worth your life?" he asked.

Dike's question made Shani nervous. She gripped the hilt of her knife tighter.

"He is my son," she replied. "He is worth everything."

Dike smiled with his eyes. "Then the priestess was true to give us to you."

Shani was confused. "What priestess?"

Dike's eyes shifted to puzzlement. "Themba did not tell you? Forgive me Queen Mother, I thought you were aware. The Blood Men do not accept employment from just anyone, not even nobles such as you. Money is accepted only to hear a petition for our protection. The plea is heard by our priestess, who consults the spirits for her decision. If she decides the person needs our protection, then we accept the task."

Shani relaxed and sat on her cot. "I am grateful your priestess thought me worthy."

"Do not feel this way," Dike replied. "If our priestess granted our help, it is because your life is in great danger."

Shani's breath became short. "In danger from what?"

Dike eyes smiled again. "I do not know, but don't worry, Queen Mother. The Blood Men are sworn to protect you to death, and we do not die easily." He nodded his head. "Sleep now, Queen Mother. You need your rest for tomorrow's journey."

Dike turned around in his sitting position and faced the door. He meant to stay in the room with Shani, with his men outside her door. Themba made the right choice, she realized. She lie down on her cot and quickly fell to sleep, feeling the safety of a child.

She awoke to chaos. Dike held her shoulders with his hard scarred hands, shaking her vigorously.

"Queen Mother! Queen Mother! We must leave!"

Shani cleared her head and became aware of the danger. "What is happening?"

"Slavers are raiding the inn. They have not reached this floor yet, but there is only one way out." Dike removed the leather strips from the blades of his wrist knives and unsheathed his sword.

"Come. My men are waiting." Dike opened the door to the confusion outside. The other bodyguards stood blocking the door, dead Kossi at their feet. Dike took his place before his men and they proceeded down the stairs. They made it to the main floor before the slavers saw them. Shani tensed, expecting an attack, but the slavers moved away. Their scowls did not hide the truth in their eyes. They knew the Blood Men and were afraid.

Outside the hostel, the city burned. Black smoke billowed from flaming huts and filled the streets, stinging Shani's eyes. Dike led them through the melee, crouching low to see through the smoke. He raised his hands and they stopped.

"Queen Mother, stay behind my men. Grab onto the arm of the man closest to you and do not let go."

Shani locked her hands about the stout arm of the nearest Blood Man. She stumbled as they ran, the confusion accented with the ringing of clashing steel and the grunts of struggling men. All around her people fled, fought and died. She stumbled again, almost falling; the Blood Man jerked her over the body of a dead child. Behind her she heard urgent shouts. The Kossi gained nerve in numbers, approaching the Blood Man, their eyes fixed on Shani. The Blood Man halted and turned in the direction of the voices.

"Queen Mother, there are too many. You must flee, while we fight to keep you safe. There is no one between you and the forest. Go there and hide."

Shani was terrified. "How will you find me?"

The Blood Man looked at her intensely. "I will find you, Queen Mother. Now please, go."

Shani let go of the arm and ran to the forest. The other Blood Men rushed past her and joined their brother. She turned her head to see the Blood Men charging a horde of slavers, swinging their swords over their heads. The odds were impossible, she thought. They should have run with her. Suddenly feeling exposed, she jumped into the cover of the forest. All around her people fled the village. Men, women and children scattered among the trees, desperate to escape the slavers. Shani ran and then stopped. She was exhausted and she needed to rest, if just for a moment. She found a tangle of brush and thorn and forced her way into it, ignoring the scratches and pricks. She closed her eyes, wishing away the pain in her body and the fear in her heart, concentrating on Obaseki. She held in her mind the glimpse of his face the day he attacked Ndoro. They were true twins, identical in almost every way. Had he suffered after being banished from Abo? Did he and the woman he fled with have children? The thought of being a grandmother brought a smile to her face despite the imminent danger about her.

"Queen Mother?"

Shani recognized the voice of Dike and emerged painfully from her hiding place. Ten Blood Men had come with her from Abo; seven stood with her in the bush. Those remaining showed wounds that bloodied their garments, their chests heaving.

"We must travel through the bush for a few days," he said.

"The slavers will be looking for us," she replied.

For the first time since their journey Dike smiled. "There are no more slavers here but there may be others on the road. We will move through the trees until it is safe."

They set out again. Shani didn't ask Dike how they would know which direction to follow in the thick brush. The Blood Men possessed skills she'd hardly imagined. She promised she would reward Themba generously when she returned to Abo. As the sun faded into the shadows of the forest Dike and his men set up camp, building a small hut for Shani to spend the night.

It was well constructed; the thatch roof blocked the rain and the walls were embedded deep enough into the ground to prevent the seepage of water. Such a structure had taken much time, too much for the Blood Men to build protection for themselves. As Shani watched them prepare for a night in the forest, she realized they had no intentions in building another shelter. Those not chosen for the first watch piled thick stacks of brush and leaves to lie on then covered their bodies with their shields. The others positioned themselves about the camp, disappearing into the forest as they took watch, motionless in the rainy, moonless night.

The morning brought no end to the rain. Despite their best efforts the water eventually seeped into Shani's hut; she awoke in wet clothes and with a deep cough. She covered herself as best she could before entering the downpour. The Blood Men were awake, sitting about the camp apparently waiting for her to emerge from her shelter. Dike saw her and nodded his approval. He came to her and offered her a yam with a strip of dried meat. She accepted eagerly, realizing at that moment how hungry she was.

She was almost done with the yam when she began to cough again, this time a grating cough that hurt her chest. Dike was at her side immediately, his hand to her forehead.

"You are burning," he said, his voice grave. "We must get you to a healer."

"I am fine," she answered, then coughed so violently she dropped the yam.

Dike gathered the men about him with a jerk of his hand. "The Queen Mother is sick. We must get her to the nearest town quickly. We will have to take the road."

A serious look passed among them. Taking the road meant exposing themselves to the Kossi.

"We must be diligent," Dike warned. "Do not be unaware.

You will kill us all."

Shani swayed then fell. She stared upward, her head spinning, the image of Dike above her. Her stomach churned and she convulsed, spewing the food she'd just eaten onto herself.

Dike's voice penetrated her weakness and found her ears. "Queen Mother, please be still. You are very sick. We are..."

Another voice came to her, the voice of Cheelo, the man who led her from the city.

"Dike, look!"

She felt a tug on her leg and heard Dike curse. His face reappeared, distorted by her pain. He grabbed her chin and forced her mouth open. His hand appeared, holding a small brown pouch. He tilted the pouch and a white liquid poured into her mouth. It went too deeply and choked her, but Dike clamped his hands around her mouth and would not let her spit it out. The vile liquid burned its way through her body, her screams muffled by Dike's strong hands.

"Cheelo!" she heard him call out. "Take two men into the village and bring back a cart and a donkey if you can find one." His eyes came back to Shani.

"You were wounded by a poison arrow that struck your ankle. I can't stop the poison; I can only slow it down."

He smiled as best he could. "There is another village ahead. Maybe there will be a healer that can help you."

Shani's ears exploded with sound. She turned her head towards the source and saw Cheelo with the cart and a donkey. She rose like a petal in the wind as the Blood Men placed her carefully into the cart, her body cushioned by dry straw and blankets.

"Do not die, Queen Mother," Dike urged. "You have yet to see your son."

But Shani was already drifting away, the dim light of

the cloudy sky fading into a dense and empty darkness. She felt isolated, like a leaf floating still on a lake. Silence surrounded her; she could hear her breathing and feel her chest moving, but as hard as she tried she could not stand. Then she felt something, a twinge of familiarity that blossomed into rush of joy.

"Obaseki!" she exclaimed.

"Mama!" he replied.

A faint light appeared in the distance. She began to rise, but felt an unseen force holding her down.

"Please stay where you are, mama," Obaseki said. "I must come to you."

The light grew brighter as it neared. Shani found the strength to stand, squinting to see her son come into view, a smile gracing his face.

"My son, my son," she cried. "I should have never sent you away!"

Obaseki embraced her. She felt his warm tears on her unseen shoulders.

"You saved my life," Obaseki said solemnly. "Now I must save yours."

Shani stepped back from her son. "You are too late. I know where I am. Are you dead as well?"

"No. We are both still alive."

"So where are we?"

"We are in between worlds. You are very sick. The poison was discovered late, but I will not let you die."

"Do you possess such power?"

Obaseki smiled. "I am no demon, mama. I am only a son that loves the mother he never knew. I will not let you be taken away from me."

Shani fell to her knees, her shoulders shaking with silent

sobs. "I should not have sent you away. I could have protected you."

"Dingane would not allow it. Mulugo had spoken; if I had not gone to Grandfather, Ndoro and I would both be dead."

Hearing her former husband's name stilled her tears. "Is he here?"

"Of course he is," Obaseki replied. "But some spirits do not linger near the living. When their time among the living is done, they move quickly to the Zamani. Even the memories of their loved ones cannot hold them. Baba was such a spirit."

"Even in death he is never satisfied," Shani commented. "I am content here. I don't wish to go back"

Obaseki looked at his mother with pleading eyes. "You must go back. Your journey is not done yet. You must be present when the time comes."

Shani looked at her son, a glimmer of understanding in her eyes. "The ancestors have a purpose for you both. I can see that now. You are true meji, and you are my sons."

She stood in the darkness and placed her hand on Obaseki's face. "I will go back. I'll return to Abo and wait for you to call me."

"I love you, mama," Obaseki whispered. He kissed her on her cheek and Shani opened her eyes to bright light.

"She comes back to us!" Dike exclaimed. He hovered over her as before, but now there were others around her, smiles on their faces. A woman with a calming smile placed a hand on her head.

"I wish I could say this was my doing," she said to Dike. "She was too close to death for anything I could have done." She grasped Shani's hand and squeezed. "Thank your ancestors for your life."

"No, I thank my son." Shani sat up in the bed and looked about. The Blood Men gathered about her in a splendid room, furnished with items alien to her, yet beautiful. The cloths decorating the wall spoke of travels to different lands.

"Our guest awakens," someone said. A tall woman appeared before them, dressed in fabrics that shone like water covering her from her shoulders to the floor. Her face bore no tribal scars, her hair braided and bound. Her features were sharp and severe like the buckra folk she'd seen on occasion, but her skin spoke of Uhuru.

"I am Tadalesh Badebo. Welcome to my home."

"Thank you for your kindness," Shani replied.

"Your protectors say you seek your son. If your son is truly Obaseki of Yakubu, then it is I who should be thanking you."

"Your son is Moyoseki?" the healer exclaimed, her eyes wide. She fell to her knees before Shani. "Then it was he who saved you."

"Then you know where he is," Dike said.

"Of course." Tadalesh gave Dike a sly smile then sat beside Shani. "The presence of Obaseki's mother in my house can be nothing but good for my family. I could not let this opportunity pass."

Dike's face contorted into a snarl. "You risked the life of the Queen Mother for your blessing?" His hand went to his sword.

"Dike, no," Shani said sternly. "This woman, for whatever her intentions, took us in. I don't think my son would want to see her killed."

Shani stood, her balance unsure. "Dike, we leave tomorrow. We will return to Abo."

Dike looked at Shani oddly but said nothing.

Tadalesh's face took on a look of dread. "You are leaving? What of your journey? You wish to see Obaseki. He is across the desert in the Tuareg city of Yakubu. I could raise a caravan to take you to him. Of course, I would accompany you to guarantee your safe passage to his city."

"I have seen my son. Now is not the time for us to meet. That day will come."

Shani walked toward the door. Tadalesh stood in her way, and Dike's hand again went to his sword.

"Please, Queen Mother," she said desperately. "There is no reason for you to leave today. The Kossi may be still about. Stay here in my house and rest before your long journey home. You are a noble guest and will receive noble treatment."

Shani thought on Tadalesh's offer. She did not want to go back to Abo, not as it was before her journey. Ndoro was there, planning his campaign, and the helplessness she felt in preventing him from attacking Obaseki was what drove her away. Nor could she travel to Yakubu. Obaseki warned her it was not the time.

"We will accept your offer, Tadalesh. I will stay until the dry season begins."

Tadalesh smiled and tears came to her eyes. "Thank you, Queen Mother!"

Shani turned her attention to Dike and his men. "You have performed your duty well, Blood Men. Dike, please bring me my saddle bag."

Shani reached into the leather bag and pulled out a smaller leather pouch. "Here is the remaining payment."

Dike shook his head. "The Queen Mother has not returned to Abo. Our duty does not end until you arrive there."

Shani smiled with relief. She hoped Dike would answer

so. She was tired, too tired to travel soon, but she was wary of Tadalesh.

"Can you provide care for my bodyguards?" she asked the matron.

"Of course, you are all welcomed." Tadalesh turned to the door and called out in a language unknown to Shani, and immediately servants appeared. They picked up the possessions of the Blood Men and hurried away. All the guards left except Dike.

"I stay with you, Queen Mother."

"Of course," Shani replied. "Is this fine with you, Tadalesh?"

"It is your will, Queen Mother," Tadalesh replied, her head bowed.

"Good. Now, if you don't mind, I would like some time alone."

Tadalesh smiled, bowed, and then left the room, a skip in her step.

"I do not trust her," Dike said.

"She is a strange one," Shani agreed. "But I think her heart is good."

Dike nodded his head, a far away look in his eyes. "You wish to stay until the dry season."

"Yes."

"You are waiting for Ndoro."

Shani looked away from Dike. "Yes. I could not stop him in Abo. Maybe I can stop him here. The Obaseki I saw was no demon. He was no more possessed than Ndoro was when he escaped Selike."

Dike sat cross-legged on the floor before Shani. "Our priestess tells us that your sons are involved in a great struggle, one that will change Uhuru. The spirits tell her this."

Shani was surprised. This was something new, a fact Dike had hidden from her until now. She felt cold inside as she looked at the leader of her bodyguards, a realization slowly forming in her mind.

"Why did you decide to protect me?" she asked.

"To keep you from harm, Queen Mother."

"Harm from whom?"

Dike let out a sigh, his shoulders heaving with some invisible burden. "Our priestess says what will happen between your sons must happen. They were born meji for a reason. No one must block the path before them. Even Obaseki knows this."

Shani sprang from her bed. "So what am I, your prisoner?"

Dike stood before her. For the first time since leaving Abo she feared this man.

"No harm will come to you, Queen Mother, but it is essential that you do not interfere. We will stay with Tadalesh until events take their course."

Shani managed a desperate smile. She had one chance left.

"And what will you do when Ndoro comes? What will you tell him?"

"I will tell him that I have done as he asked."

Shani felt the energy drain from her body. She sat hard on the bed, grasping her head. The ancestors were still punishing her for some unknown sin, some error she'd committed to bring their wrath. Her sons would die knowing each other as enemies. With nothing left inside her, she fell into the cushions of the bed and cried.

9

The rainy season finally ended in Sesuland, the constant drizzles and downpours diminishing into hazy sunshine. Throughout the city people darted about with anxious energy. The dry season was the time of war and the Sesu were ready to march. Under the leadership of Ligongo, Sesuland suffered too many years of peace for a people whose boys graduated into manhood through battle. So many had already passed their prime; their sulking faces visible in the throng lining the wide avenues on that hot day. But those who could march knew of no prouder moment. Not only were they going to war, but they would carry the banner of Shumba Ndoro, their true inkosi.

Ndoro's mind was on other concerns. He sat before his grandfather, watching him as he paced the floor and occasionally cast an angry glance at his grandson. Ndoro shrugged inwardly; apparently his secret was exposed. No doubt it was Themba who told; she was the only one outside his circle aware of his plan, but she did not have all the details. Shani's handmaiden agreed to help him because she feared Obaseki more than she feared Ndoro. The Mawena entourage arrived during the night, Noncemba accompanied by his bodyguards and a host of noble cavalry. It was a show of force, an example of his anger. With twenty thousand warriors camped about the city ready for the march, the Mawena troop was a weak show at best.

Noncemba stopped pacing and sat hard. He glared at Ndoro and motioned as if he was going to rise again.

"You are truly Dingane's son," he said, the tone in his voice making it plain his statement was not a compliment.

"Your own mother!" he exclaimed. "You made your mother a prisoner!"

"She is not being held prisoner," Ndoro replied calmly despite being irritated by Noncemba's words. "She is being detained until I have a chance to deal with Obaseki."

"Don't play with words before me," Noncemba roared. "Whatever you may think, Shani is your mother and my daughter. If she took it upon herself to warn Obaseki of your coming then so be it. Nothing you have planned is worth the humiliation you've caused."

Though Ndoro respected his grandfather, he was not about to be handled like a child.

"You forget yourself, Grandfather," he replied. "Outside this city are twenty thousand Diaka and Sesu warriors. That is an example of the respect you should give me."

Noncemba eyes widened. "You wouldn't dare!"

"Would I?" Ndoro rose to his feet. "I have spent my entire life fighting to be where I am today. No one-not you, not Mama-has shared my burden. I've earned every ounce of respect due to me, and I will not let anyone block my way."

Noncemba's anger drained from his face. He looked solemnly at the floor, his words low and melancholy.

"I do not know what stands before me. Since the day you both were born the world has seemed crooked, as if your lives have disturbed some type of balance. Everyone around you has tried to understand this."

Noncemba stood to leave. "You will do what you wish. I have not the strength or the will to stop you. Whatever I believe about Obaseki, I don't approve of what you did to my daughter. The Mawena will not march with you. This revenge you must accomplish on your own."

Ndoro burned inside with Noncemba's refusal. "On my own as always. But understand me, grandfather. I once asked my indunas which kingdom posed the biggest threat to Sesuland, and the answer was Mawenaland. I have not forgotten their advice."

Ndoro watched Noncemba storm away. He waited until the Mawena were well on their way back to Abo before hurrying through the palace and out of the city to his encampment beside the shaded banks of the Kojo River. Hundreds of grass huts were scattered among the acacias, Diaka and Sesu warriors moving restlessly among them. As Ndoro passed, the warriors fell to their knees, sprinkling their heads with dirt. Ndoro ignored their supplication, his eyes focused on his council tent. He burst into it, finding Jawanza and his generals sitting in a circle around a large leather map.

"Jawanza, break camp," he ordered. "We march today."

"What of the Mawena?"

Ndoro closed his eyes as his anger surged to his head, threatening to boil over.

"The Mawena choose not to join us."

Jawanza smiled. "We cannot leave an enemy behind us."

"Mawenaland is still our ally," Ndoro conceded. "They will not interfere with our march. Go and prepare the men. We leave at nightfall."

Jawanza issued the order to mobilize. The army was an impressive sight, the martial amalgamation of different cultures combined for the purpose of conquest. Each unit maintained the uniform of its people but they all wore the head ring of the Diaka, the symbol of their loyalty to Ndoro. The tents were taken down and stored on the support wagons with the provisions. There would be intervals where the army could live off the land, but the provisions provided an assurance of uninterrupted marching. Merchants had been sent ahead during the rainy season, loaded down with gold and other rare items found in the forests of Tacumaland, their task to set up outposts in strategic sites along the route that would serve as bivouacs when the army needed rest. It was a well-thought-out plan that would succeed with or without the help of the Mawena.

Sesubu lined the avenues of Selike awaiting the departure of the army. Excitement pulsed through everyone, resulting in the constant singing of the women in the throng and the incessant beating of drums. Ndoro watched from his palace as his army formed ranks; Tacuma archers and skirmishers at the front, neophyte Sesu warriors at the center, and the seasoned Diaka at the rear. The ranks stood five wide and stretched beyond the city limits.

Jawanza appeared at his side. "We are ready, Shumba."

"Then let us end this," Ndoro replied. With Jawanza's assistance he donned his lion headdress, strapped on his body armor and arm knife, and then took up his shield and assegai. Ndoro strode from his room and his indunas fell in step behind him, making their way through the palace and onto the grounds. He exited the palace and saw Kenyetta, surrounded by his servants and his adopted wives. She flashed him a wicked smile, and then with a soulful cry began the traditional wailing. The other wives joined her, striking themselves and pulling at their hair, the expression of losing their husband to war. Ndoro responded in stoic ignorance, walking past them to the brick path leading to the royal avenue. His wives followed, making sure the rest of the city knew of his coming. Upon seeing their inkosi descending the path, the Sesubu responded the opposite of the wives. The city exploded with drumming and joyous voices. Everyone danced;

women, children, men, the young and the old rejoicing the return of Sesu glory. The army took up the chant, swaying side to side with the rhythm of the drummers, beating their weapons against their shields and the ground. Ndoro felt the rhythm of his people in his heart and knew that this was his destiny. He halted before his army, observing the entire city in synchronized motion, and wished that he could die that day. An arduous path lay before him; the outcome uncertain. He knew this was the path he was meant to follow. Every moment of his life had prepared him for this day. He forgave his father, dendi-fari Biton and all those who caused suffering in his life. They were teachers, their hard lessons essential for the role he now stood to play. He raised his assegai, turning slowly as he spread his gaze over the city and then took up the warrior's trot. A thunder of padded feet erupted behind him as twenty thousand warriors took up the pace. They were heading south to the desert, and eventually to Yakubu.

Shani paced the floor of her bedroom, running scenarios through her mind to escape her soft prison. She cursed Ndoro every day, disgusted that he could do such a thing to her. The Blood Men were holding her until he arrived, which meant she would never see Obaseki again unless he killed Ndoro. She had to escape, but how could she? Although Tadalesh did not prevent her from leaving the house, she was constantly under watch by Dike and his Blood Men. Her tirades kept them at a distance but did not make them disappear. Besides, Zimfara was an alien city to her. Its narrow, crowded streets seemed designed by madmen. Some roads led nowhere, while others seemed to run endlessly. The language was totally different from the tongues spoken in the Mawena savannah and the Sesu grasslands. Sometimes after another frustrating stroll through the city, she would sit in her room and gaze toward the north, hoping to see a contingent of Mawena cavalry led by her father coming to her rescue. It was a child's fantasy in a woman's mind and she admonished herself for such thoughts. If she were to escape, she would have to do it herself.

Shani was summoned as always by Dike. The voice that once made her safe now reminded her of her confinement, and her hate showed on her face.

"Breakfast is ready, Queen Mother," he announced, his tone still respectful despite the reversal of their roles.

Shani said nothing, rising from her bed and heading to the dining room. Tadalesh was there, her ever-present smile growing more annoying each day.

"Queen Mother, it is good to see you as always," she beamed. She presented a basket filled with exotic fruit. "These came yesterday with a caravan from Jadina. It is said they grow on trees fed with the blood of bulls!" With a smooth motion Tadalesh picked up knife and sliced open the orange fruit, revealing the pulpy innards that ran with a juice the color of blood.

Shani stood. "I will walk in the market," she announced. She'd lost her appetite with Tadalesh's disgusting display and desperately yearned for the crowded streets. Despite being watched, at least there she could feel alone and free.

Shani dressed quickly and left the house. The Blood Men followed, spreading out once they exited the house but staying close enough to keep an eye on her. Shani had learned to ignore them, losing herself in the confusion of Zimfara. She headed to the market, strolling slowly through the cramped alleyways, her senses assaulted by the sights, sounds and smells that were still alien to her. She wondered how her sons had adapted to these different cultures, each going so far as to become leaders in their own rights among foreigners.

A hand touched her shoulder and she turned angrily, expecting to see the face of a Blood Man. Instead, she looked up into the intense eyes of a tall, lean man with dark skin and sharp features. A ragged robe covered his tall frame. A sword hung from his shoulder. He seemed disturbed by her direct stare and looked away.

"Queen Mother," he said respectfully. "You must come with me. Your son demands your presence."

Shani jerked away from the man. "Hasn't my son sent enough people to hold me hostage?"

The man smiled. "I do not speak of Ndoro. I serve only Moyo, the man you know as Obaseki."

Shani's hand went to her mouth in surprise. She could see it now in his eyes; he resembled the men that rescued Obaseki from Abo. Without the turban, face veil and flowing robes she'd missed the obvious. Her heart surged with joy. Obaseki was going to rescue her.

That joy suddenly transformed to dread when she thought of the Blood Men. She looked about frantically.

"You look for the men that followed you," the man said.

"Yes."

The man smiled again. "They were dealt with. Please, Queen Mother, we must go before others realize you are not returning."

Shani followed the man through the maze of the market place to a small wagon hitched to a donkey. The wagon contained various plants and fruits, typical needs of the nomads of desert. Two other men stood by the wagon, nodding as they recognized the man leading Shani. They cleared a spot in the wagon for her and she climbed in among the produce.

Shani and her saviors made slow progress through the crowded city, fighting off vendors and beggars as they approached the city gate. The guard waved them past without much notice, not wanting to be bothered with what he saw as desert rabble. They continued their silent trek into the desert until dusk. They were well out of sight of the city, climbing a low dune before the man who approached her spoke.

"We will rest when we reach the other side."

The summit of the hill revealed a large encampment bustling with activity. Her protector called out in a language she did not understand and the entire encampment looked to them. She caught the word Moyo and they all fell to their knees, sprinkling sand onto their heads.

"You are among friends, Queen Mother. You are home."

Sharif Citadel loomed over Zimfara like a jealous lover, its minarets peering down in constant scrutiny. Beyond the steep hills that constituted its perch the desert stretched out beyond the horizon. Ndoro gazed out onto the endless sands knowing that beyond his sight was a city he must conquer and a brother he must destroy.

He turned his attention back to his war room. The dining room of the citadel was normally filled with dazzling items from every region of Uhuru; exquisite vases from Ptush, colorful gourds from the southern rainforests of Kanga and numerous terra cotta figurines from the city-states of Nigera. All these items had been gathered and dumped in the wide hallway outside. The only item allowed to remain was the massive mahogany dining table, an extravagant symbol of the wealth of its former owners. Surrounding the table, however, were not the usual merchants and noblemen who frequently feasted on its smooth surface. Ndoro's indunas hunched over it instead, peering down on a large map hastily drawn by a nervous looking Zimfaran mapmaker lurking behind the Sesu officers. Jawanza stood prominent among them, his bearded face contorted in a frown. He rubbed his chin as Ibrahim the mapmaker protested, his pleas falling on obviously deaf ears.

"It is impossible!" Ibrahim stuttered.

Ndoro strode to the table. "Nothing is impossible. This land is waterless and treeless and yet your people survive. We do what we wish."

"No army has ever crossed the Mahgreb, not even an army as magnificent as yours, Shumba. There are too many of you, too many!"

"Yakubu is said to be larger than Zimfara; some say it is larger than Selike. You do not think that is impossible?"

Ibrahim closed his eyes, his fingers pressing tight on his temples. "Yakubu lies on an oasis plateau, and Moyoseki is..." His voice trailed off as he stared in fear of Ndoro.

"A god?" Ndoro finished. He felt the heat of anger behind his eyes. Everyone in this cursed place thought his brother was some deity. If they did not worship him, they either respected him or feared him.

Ndoro charged Ibrahim and grabbed his neck, pulling him close.

"He is a demon, Bedouin. He fools your people with false miracles and feeds their thirst with blood!"

Ndoro shoved the man to the floor, clearly disgusted.

"Jawanza," he barked. "How does a caravan cross the Mahgreb?"

Jawanza answered without taking his eyes from the map. "A caravan supplies itself with provisions to reach half the way to its destination. A rider is sent out to bring supplies for the rest of the journey."

"We won't have that option," Ndoro commented. He joined his men at the table. Yakubu stood out like a green jewel surrounded by a ring of sand. Scattered about the map were drawings of date trees, Ibrahim's sign for an oasis. Scattered here and there were small water droplets, the artist's symbol for waterholes. Above each waterhole was a symbol signifying the tribe that claimed it.

"How complete is this map?" Ndoro asked. This time the question was aimed at Ibrahim.

"It is as much as I know," Ibrahim replied.

"Is it everything?" Ndoro asked.

Ibrahim looked nervous. "No. Many tribes keep secret waterholes known only to their members."

"Can we persuade them?" Ndoro asked.

"They would die first," Ibrahim said defiantly.

Ndoro walked slowly back to the window, worrying his chin with his right hand.

"Leave me, everyone," he said.

The indunas exited the room, dragging Ibrahim with them. Ndoro waited until he was alone before rubbing the medicine bag strapped to his waist. Nakisisa appeared before him, his arms folded across his chest. The jinn bowed slightly.

"My friend," he said. "You have use of me?"

Ndoro stared at the spirit of his old friend. It was difficult for him to get used to the transformation and his growing dependence on Nakisisa's guidance. Magic had brought him much pain in his life; this new reliance still did not have his full trust. Faced with this current challenge, he had no choice.

"Do you know where all the waterholes of the Mahgreb

are found?" Ndoro asked.

Nakisisa grinned. "I was once a river spirit, but no more. This water is protected by local spirits."

"Can you discover where they are?"

"Will it aid your march to Yakubu?"

Ndoro folded his hands behind his back. "I need to march three hundred strides across the desert. What do you think?"

"Shumba's bell is full of thorns!" Nakisisa laughed. "You have no reason for impatience. Your path has been woven."

Ndoro sat on a stool near the table. "This is taking too long! Yakubu should be ours by now, desert or no."

"I will do what I can," Nakisisa replied.

Nakisisa vanished with a rush of wind. Ndoro looked where the jinn had stood and massaged his forehead. For the first time in his life he was uncertain of his next move. No clear path ran before him. This business about his brother, of marching on Yakubu to take the life of one demon made him uneasy. Nakisisa told him it was something he must do to fulfill his destiny; Ndoro had no idea of what destiny he spoke. All he wished for since the day he fled Selike was to become inkosi of Sesuland. That dream fulfilled, he desired nothing more until Obaseki intruded on his life. Destiny was for those foolish enough to believe the words of the ancestors. Ndoro lived in the world of men.

He left the dining hall for his kraal. Although he understood the advantage of stone buildings, Ndoro's heart was in the grasslands, preferring the open space of a kraal. The grounds surrounding the castle bustled with activity as thousands of Diaka warriors settled into their temporary homes. They parted as they recognized Ndoro, some forming a wall around him as he made his way to the kraal. He smelled meat roasting and realized he was famished.

"Inkosi, you have returned!" Kenyetta stood before him, smiling.

Ndoro feigned anger. "What are you doing here?"

"Nakisisa visited me and told me I was needed." She smiled and tilted her head, a gesture that Ndoro well recognized.

He looked about at the servants preparing the meal. "Leave us," he ordered. No sooner had they exited the tent Kenyetta ran to him, throwing her arms around his shoulders and kissing him fiercely.

"The Royal Kraal has been cold since you left Selike," she whispered. "And very quiet."

"Then we must make sure the Royal Tent is not the same," Ndoro replied. He swept Kenyetta into his arms and took her to the sheepskins.

* * *

A week passed before Nakisisa returned. A dust storm raged, blotting out the sun and covering the citadel in a sandy darkness. Ndoro and his indunas took refuge inside, covering the windows with heavy camel blankets to block the sand. Ndoro found himself back before the map with Jawanza. They were plotting a route to Yakubu when a familiar voice entered his head.

"I have returned," Nakisisa said.

"Jawanza, take the indunas and inspect the men. I will be along soon," Ndoro ordered. Jawanza gave him a suspicious look but obeyed.

Moments later Nakisisa appeared at the window. Ndoro was stunned at what he saw. The river-beast bled almost everywhere.

He smiled, revealing missing teeth, his left arm hanging useless at his side. The sight reminded Ndoro of the night the river-beast killed Inaamdura.

"My friend, what happened? Can a spirit be damaged so by men?"

"Not by men, but by jinn, yes," Nakisisa replied weakly. "The water spirits of the Mahgreb do not give up their secrets easily." He sat on the window ledge, oblivious to the sandstorm pummeling the curtain behind him.

"I have a present for you, inkosi of the Sesu," Nakisisa announced. Despite his haggard look, the river-beast strode to the table. Waving his good hand across the canvas, the number of water signs doubled. Ndoro's smile showed his satisfaction.

"Well done, my friend," he said.

"Wait, Great Inkosi," Nakisisa interrupted. "You haven't received my entire gift."

With another wave of his hand a thin blue line appeared at the base of the drawing of Yakubu. The line took on a life of its own, snaking its way across the canvas, linking the waterholes and oases before ending at the foothills of Zimfara.

"What is this?" Ndoro asked.

"A river," Nakisisa replied. "An underground river created by the rains of Yakubu. It flows from the plateau to the foothills of where we stand."

Nakisisa pointed to three points on the river. "The river can be reached at these points through caverns. All you need to do now is to find enough food to feed 20,000 warriors and Yakubu is yours."

"That will be easy," Ndoro replied. "You have put Yakubu in our hands."

The river-beast smiled weakly. "Then my task is done."

There was finality in the river-beast's voice that alarmed Ndoro.

"Nakisisa, what is wrong?"

Nakisisa rose above Ndoro, his wounds healing as he spoke. "Your destiny lies across the Mahgreb, in Yakubu. It was my duty to guide you through the last leg of your journey. I have done so; now I must go."

"You say I have a destiny," Ndoro answered. "But I say this is not it. I seek my brother only to revenge his attempt on my life and to drive the demon from his body."

"Your reason is your own, but your purpose belongs to all."

"What does that mean?" Ndoro asked urgently.

"From the day I emerged from the river to kill you, I sensed a difference in you. After you defeated me and took my hand, that feeling grew every day until I fought the witch. As I passed into this life, the truth became clear. I offered myself to the ancestors to act as your guide. I knew you would not trust this path."

"Sorcerers have their own agendas," Ndoro retorted. "I know this better than most."

"Believe this, my friend. No sorcerer guides your path. Your blessings come from the ancestors. It is their strength that flows through you and that will guide you across the desert."

"And when I reach this goal?" Ndoro asked.

"Then you will see me again," Nakisisa answered. He showed Ndoro his perfect smile, then faded quickly into the storm.

Ndoro gazed where the river-beast had been. What did he mean by seeing him again? The unfamiliar feeling of fear crept back into his mind. Was he to see his friend again in victory, or was he to join him in the spirit world in defeat, a wandering spirit far from home?

He shook his head violently. He was Ndoro, inkosi of the Sesu, leader of the Diaka, ruler of every land which he'd set foot, and, according to Nakisisa, chosen for greatness by the ancestors. He would not die by any man's hand or any demon. Ndoro threw back the lion's robe draping his shoulders and strode from the safety of citadel into the howling winds of the sandstorm.

* * *

For generations to come, griots would sing of the events in Zimfara those fateful weeks of the dry season. Ndoro's Diaka legions swept into the city suddenly; overwhelming what little resistance its militia could muster. The Sesu warriors followed, bringing with them provisions for the journey across the desert. The city was surrounded by camps; the sound of war chants constant like the desert heat. The people of Zimfara witnessed this occupation with mixed feelings; those who where forced to provide lodging for indunas and nobles found their anger soothed by the seemly endless supply of gold and cowries paid for their services. So much gold flowed through the city that it bought less than before, though no one complained of the surplus. Ndoro was careful to make sure the Bedouins understood the Sesu were not here as conquerors, for their help was vital for his plan to succeed.

The city was a human termite mound of activity, every smith's anvil ringing with the making of knives, swords and assegais, the clacking of looms as weavers busied themselves making robes and desert garb for the unprepared Sesu. The camel merchants' corrals bulged as the beasts were gathered to provide transport for the supplies needed for the coming trek. Tons of forage rolled into the city daily, supplying food for thousands of cattle held in huge kraals surrounding the Sesu camp. Cattle were brought in to supply food for the warriors, but also as a special delicacy for a population used to sheep and goat as a mainstay.

Such a build-up of forces could not go unnoticed. Word spread throughout the Mahgreb, reaching Yakubu first as rumors and whispers, then later as facts and details. The time had come for action. Ndoro could not afford to wait any longer.

Night came early to the desert. The sun escaped behind the lofty mountains, conceding the day to darkness. The mild warmth of the day submitted to the cool night, the stars bright in the dark sky. Ndoro stood on the city walls wrapped in a thick wool blanket. Beyond the fortifications to the west the horizon glittered with campfires of Sesu warriors awaiting his orders to march. To the east lay the desert and beyond his sight, Yakubu. Ndoro pulled the blanket tighter, realizing the coldness he felt was not from the night air, but from within. He would lead thousands of warriors across the sands, many of them to their deaths, and for what? He'd almost forgotten the shock he felt when his brother attempted to kill him. But was it worth a war? Maybe this was wisdom, he thought with a smile. Or maybe it was fear. He quickly shook that thought from his mind. They would march tomorrow, Yakubu would fall and he would be victorious again. But then what? Ndoro turned slowly, descending the tower stairs with a heavy gait.

The morning sun had barely struggled over the steep walls when thirteen men jumped to their feet and charged from their camps, each headed for the same destination. Each man wore the armband of his unit, his drum gripped closely to his side. They met at the main road of Zimfara. The city guards swung the doors wide and the drummers ran in, climbing the stairs to the parapets. Once in place they began to play, their sound like thunder rolling from the cloudless sky. With voices as loud and urgent as their drums they sang;

On guard! The battle is coming!
Whoever runs away will get the whip!
Diaka! Rise with your spears!
Sesu! Stand and march across the sand!
Follow Shumba to Yakubu!
When a scorpion stings without mercy,
You kill it without mercy!
Come, my brothers, the scorpion must die!

The Diaka broke camp with amazing precision. In minutes the warriors were stepping in time with the drummers, chanting the words the drummers played. The Bedouin camel herders ran about confused as they hurried to follow the Diaka out of the city and into the desert. They scurried about yelling and waving their hands, miraculously organizing themselves quickly enough to follow the warriors through the gate. Throughout the city people came out of their homes to witness the spectacle. Men, women and children clamored atop houses and each other to get a glimpse of this vast army beginning its march of conquest and vengeance. Some found themselves caught up in the excitement and danced with the marching rhythms while adding their own shouts of encouragement to the black-skinned warriors.

A whisper swept the masses as the army trotted through the gates. Though his warriors were everywhere their leader was absent. For a people with no love for their occupiers, they were eager to see this mysterious conqueror march off to what was rumored to be his final campaign. The whisper became a murmur, the murmur talk, and soon the crowd chanted his name with the rhythm of the drums. But Ndoro was nowhere to be seen. His army marched out of the city, oblivious to the absence of their inkosi. As the last warrior exited the gate the inhabitants ran behind them, clamoring to the ramparts to watch the army march into the desert.

As the first Bedouins appeared atop the ramparts they were stunned at what they saw. The Diaka shifted from a double file to a single line that stretched the length of the city walls. Before them Ndoro stood upon the dune in the distance, magnificent in his warrior regalia, his cowhide shield on his left arm, his gilded assegai stabbing the sky.

"Come, my shumbas!" he shouted. "Let us run to the walls of Yakubu and tear them down!"

The Diaka raised their assegais in unison, roaring with pride to their leader. They marched again, Ndoro waving them forward. As his army made its way effortlessly up the dune, Ndoro felt the fire rising in him, displacing the fear and uncertainty that poisoned him the past days. The march was on. The final war had begun.

The mild heat of the Mahgreb winter allowed Ndoro's warriors to cover much ground during the day. Jawanza had drilled the men for months in the sand, strengthening the already chiseled bodies for the arduous march. The Bedouins were amazed by their stamina, continuously falling behind despite their camels and horses. In three days they reached the first outcrops of stone, the home of the caves that led to the underground river. Warriors descended into the darkness, emerging with fresh, cold water, much to the delight of the others. The Bedouins made mental notes, sure to mark the spot for a future dispute among the nomad tribes.

Ndoro spent his days focused on the march and his nights contemplating the coming battle. He walked among his warriors, personally checking their energy so he would make thoughtful decisions on the rest stops and camps. Each warrior was put on strict rations to ensure supplies would carry them to their destination. The nomads were well aware of the advancing army and abandoned their oasis camps for the safety of open sand. These abandoned islands of life kept the Diaka spirits high as they supplied shade and date fruit.

In ten days of marching the Diaka had covered half the distance to Yakubu. They reached the second landmark on the map, a small collection of rocky hills, surrounded by brush and camels. The camp surrounded the hills as far as the eye could see, even on the low horizon of the desert. Ndoro walked among his warriors and was concerned by what he saw. Though they smiled proudly as he spoke to them, he saw the fatigue in their eyes and the thinness of their arms and legs. Back at his tent, he summoned Jawanza. The Diaka leader came immediately.

"What is it, Shumba?"

Ndoro looked at his companion and saw the same worn look. "How are the men?"

"They are good," Jawanza lied.

"I don't think so," Ndoro countered. "Tell me the truth, Jawanza."

"The march has been harder than we thought," Jawanza admitted. "The men are not used to the heat and the rations are low, especially meat. The Bedouins are stealing food and sending it back to their tribes, the lamb in particular. It is hard to control."

"I cannot have a weak army when we reach Yakubu,"

Ndoro said. "We will rest here for five days. Send riders, Diaka riders, back to Zimfara to secure more supplies. Once you have done so, gather the Bedouin leaders and bring them to me."

Jawanza bowed and left. Ndoro summoned his servants and put them to work. They took down his tent, clearing away everything except the royal stool. He donned his full inkosi trappings, including the lion pelt he claimed so long ago.

When Jawanza arrived with the Bedouins, Ndoro was seated on his stool, an intimidating image flanked by the Diatanee. Warriors gathered about in curiosity as the Bedouins were brought before him. Some of the nomads were clearly nervous as the crowd grew; others seemed annoyed that they had been taken away from their duties.

The men stood before Ndoro, making no attempt to show respect by kneeling before him.

"Who speaks for you?" Ndoro demanded. One of the Bedouins, a tall, bearded man with skin almost as dark as Ndoro's stepped forward. His eyes locked in a permanent squint; he spoke with a deep, clear voice.

"I do, inkosi," the man replied. Though he chose a respectful response, the tone of his voice said otherwise. "I am Hassim."

"I am told Bedouins are not subject to the rules of the march," Ndoro said.

"What do you mean inkosi?"

"Bedouins are receiving more rations than my warriors," Ndoro replied. "Are you planning to lead us into battle, Hassim?"

A low laugh passed through the crowd. Ndoro, however, did not smile.

Hassim shifted, seeming to be uncomfortable. "We have

taken no more than we have been given."

"Yet our supplies run low ahead of schedule," Ndoro mused.

"Maybe the inkosi's warriors are not as disciplined as he thinks," Hassim answered. "Those not of the desert tend to be wasteful in its midst."

Ndoro stood and walked toward Hassim. "The Diaka are not conscripts and they are not liars, Bedouin. They would march until they died if I commanded them. They do not disobey orders. If any rations are missing it is your doing. You will not jeopardize this operation, and you will not insult my men!"

Hassim was opening his mouth to speak when Ndoro slammed his gilded orinka against the man's head. Hassim fell to one knee; his hand reaching out for support as Ndoro struck him again, knocking him into the sand. Ndoro bent over the Bedouin and struck him a third time. Hassim lay motionless, the life gone from his eyes. Ndoro looked at the man for a moment and glared at the other Bedouins.

"I have treated you with respect and you return my kindness with lies, insults and deception. From this day on, all Bedouins are considered my property. Any Bedouin found stealing rations will be executed and his family driven into the desert. I will not tolerate any resistance."

Ndoro walked slowly to his stool and sat. "Leave my sight. Take your leader with you."

The camel drivers scrambled to claim Hassim's body. Hatred flooded their eyes as they dragged Hassim's body away, their heads darting about as if they expected another sudden attack. No such thing would happen. The Diaka would not attack them unless Ndoro gave the signal. He watched the Bedouins, angry that they forced him to make such a decision. There would surely be resistance among them now that their status had changed. He would have to move quickly before any organized opposition could be mounted. Any large scale conflict with the Bedouins would delay his march on Yakubu.

As if he was reading his mind, Jawanza appeared before him.

"Our situation changes," he said.

"You are right, brother," Ndoro replied. "I was hoping to strike fear in them, but it looks like I sparked a different emotion. Take five thousand warriors and return to Zimfara, but you will take a different route."

Ndoro had the desk map brought to him.

"These oases are camps of major Bedouin clans. You must destroy these clans on your way back to Zimfara. Leave no one alive."

Jawanza looked up from the map. "I will follow your command as always, Shumba. But these are hard orders. The men have no fear of warriors, but to kill everyone? It will be difficult for them to do."

Ndoro sat hard on his stool, rubbing his head. "I cannot risk fighting a two headed serpent. A message must be sent to keep the Bedouins quiet."

Jawanza's eyes brightened. "We will march to the oases as you order, Shumba. But we will take the elders with us to Zimfara as our 'guests' until you return victorious from Yakubu. The clans will find it difficult to organize without their headmen to move against us. If they do, we will hold out in Zimfara and await your return."

Ndoro was impressed. Jawanza had become a leader in his own right. If the battle went badly in Yakubu, the Sesu and Diaka would find an excellent inkosi in Jawanza.

"An excellent plan," Ndoro replied. "We must act on it immediately."

"I leave today," Jawanza answered.

Jawanza and his contingent of warriors were gone before nightfall. Ndoro stood on the dune looking toward Zimfara watching them fade into the encroaching darkness. A sliver of moon crept over the horizon, the warmth of the day fleeing quickly to leave a void for the cool night air to fill. This was a setback. The Diaka that marched away with Jawanza lacked the zeal that normally accompanied them, which did not bode well. Angry warriors responded cruelly, which could stir the anger of the Bedouins even higher. He would have to bring this business to an end quickly before they found themselves mired in this desolate land.

Something flashed in the moonlight, catching his eye. He strained to get a better look, realizing that whatever it was, it was moving toward him. He stood and looked about, realizing he wandered too far away from camp. On his own insistence, the Diatanee had remained behind in camp. Ndoro felt his hand tighten around his assegai as the image became clear. They were Bedouins, six in all, trudging wearily up the dune. Instinct made him brace for an attack, but a strange premonition kept him calm. These men did not move like normal men. They seemed to glide above the sand, showing no sign of the laborious steps deep soft sand requires.

Ndoro stepped back as he realized what he saw. This was a procession of the dead; he was being approached by spirits. He froze, not knowing what to do. He wore no charm bag to protect him. A smile came to him; the Bedouins sent an adversary he knew not how to fight.

The ghostly desert men approached him and stopped. Their expressions changed from blankness to recognition.

"Obaseki," they said in hollow unison as they prostrated

on the sand. They stood, smiled and walked through him over the dune, disappearing into the dark.

Hearing the name of his brother spill from the mouths of spirits chilled his blood. A true demon he must be to command the respect of the dead! The resemblance between him and Obaseki was such that the spirits could not tell them apart. But then another question struck him cold. Why could he see them? Had they made themselves visible to him because of whom they thought he was, or was he becoming what his brother had become?

Ndoro broke his stance and ran for the camp. The Diatanee was apparently watching him from distance, for they sprinted to him with equal vigor, weapons at the ready. The first to reach him ran past him and halted, scanning the darkness for potential pursuers. Other bodyguards fell in beside the inkosi, running with him to camp. Ndoro saw the worry in their eyes, but this was no time to console. He needed answers.

Ndoro halted at the edge of the camp. He turned to his guard, his eyes intense.

"Find me a medicine-priest, now!" he commanded.

The Diatanee faded into the camp, eager for the purpose. They returned as quickly as they left; dragging a tall, thin man with large fearful eyes behind them. He was a straggler, one of those that followed large marches, profiting off the warriors by selling exotic foods, women and charms. The man's protests fell away as he recognized who he was about to see. He dropped to the ground, prostrating himself.

"Bring him," Ndoro commanded. He spun and strode to his tent. His bodyguards lifted the medicine-priest and dragged him along. Ndoro was sitting as the guards tossed the man before him.

"Leave us," Ndoro said. The Diatanee left the tent. Ndoro leaned toward the man, studying his face.

"You are not Sesu or Diaka," Ndoro stated.

The man dared to look up. "No, inkosi. I am Giguyu. I am from the east."

Ndoro nodded. Since his flight from Selike he trusted no sorcerers, especially those from Sesuland. But he had no choice. Without Nakisisa at his side, he was blind to the spirits.

"What is you name, sorcerer?"

"Faraji," the man answered nervously.

"Tell me, Faraji, do you talk to the spirits?"

Faraji smiled. "Yes, inkosi. I see the spirits and I talk to them. But as with any such gift, the use of this talent comes with a price."

Ndoro's right hand flashed from his side, his palm striking Faraji's face. Before the man could cry out the same hand gripped his neck.

"The price is you life, sorcerer! Now I will ask you again. Do you see spirits?"

"No," the medicine-priest answered.

Ndoro tighten his grip on the man's neck.

"Wait, wait!" Faraji managed to say. "I might have a way."

Ndoro pushed the man away. Faraji fell to the ground onto his side, gagging. He crawled back to a kneeling position.

"Inkosi, I am no great sorcerer," he admitted. "My sight is weak, which is why I follow the trail of soldiers to tell them what they wish to hear."

Ndoro said nothing, letting his glare answer for him. Faraji's eyes darted about, and then settled on Ndoro again. He rubbed his temples tortuously then stopped, an immense smile on his face.

"I remember a spell from my apprenticeship long ago," Faraji said. He rummaged through his medicine bag and extracted a collection of stones, shells and small bones. Faraji studied them as he shifted them about with his index finger.

"Yes, yes, I have them." He looked at Ndoro triumphantly. "These are the ones."

Faraji selected a few bones from his hand then spread them on the ground before Ndoro. He chanted, swaying his body with the rhythm of his voice. Ndoro watched him cynically. He should feel something, he thought, some type of sensation to let him know the spell worked. He felt nothing.

He raised his hand to strike Faraji when the priest jerked still, his eyes jolted open. He stared through Ndoro, focusing on something beyond Ndoro's sight.

"Hello, my friend," Faraji said. Ndoro was startled as a familiar voice emerged from Faraji's lips. His thoughts were confirmed when Faraji's face contorted the best it could to resemble the familiar smile of Nakisisa.

"No matter where I go, you manage to find me," he said to Ndoro.

"I need a spirit to deal with spirits," Ndoro replied. "I saw ghosts tonight."

"As it should be," Nakisisa stated. "As your time draws near, you and your brother become more alike. He moves among the spirits and you are gaining the same ability."

Ndoro felt a chill of fear. "Am I becoming a demon?"

"I don't know," Nakisisa replied.

There was a moment of uneasy silence before Ndoro spoke again.

"How much time do I have?"

Faraji's face looked solemn. "The time draws near; two

must become one."

Faraji's eyes rolled and he collapsed. Ndoro stood quickly, donning his armor. The message was sent; there was no more time. The fear and uncertainty that plagued him since the beginning of the campaign were engulfed in a firestorm of urgency. His life was at stake, simply enough. If it was Ukulunkulu's wish for him to die, it would not be at the hands of a demon.

The truth teller rose groggily to his feet. "What happened? What did I say?"

"Enough," Ndoro replied. The Diatanee snapped to their feet when Ndoro emerged from the tent. "Rouse the camp. We march tonight."

The Diatanee took quickly to their task. In moments the muster drums erupted and the Diaka swarmed the camp, breaking down their tents in minutes. But Ndoro could not wait. He marched out of the camp alone, his eyes focused on the darkness ahead. His bodyguards were the first to catch up with him, falling into step beside him. The clatter of a marching army filled the night soon afterward. Ndoro heard nothing but Nakisisa's last words. It was time for two to become one. He would not stop marching until he reached Yakubu.

10

Obaseki sat among friends, some from his childhood, some he'd met on his journeys. They were all dead, passed from the world of the living to the Zamani, the land of ancestor spirits. Fuluke sat beside him, gazing admirably at his former student.

"Fuluke, I have never felt this content in my entire life," Obaseki confessed. "It's as if my life among the living has been a prison sentence."

Fuluke smiled. "This is where you belong. We will all be here eventually. But you cannot stay."

Obaseki looked at his teacher in shock. "Why? Am I not dead? Did I not die from my brother's wound?

"No, Seki, you did not die," Fuluke answered. "Your brother opened a door for you, one you could not have opened yourself."

Fuluke swept his arm around. "This is your kingdom, Seki. You have seen the spirits since you were a boy. They've always been close to show the way. But your brother gave you the key."

"So what must I do?" Obaseki asked.

"You must go back," Fuluke said. "Two must become one."

Fuluke stood and met Obaseki's eyes. "Remember what you see here. Men forget their ancestors and lose their mouth to the gods. Your purpose is to restore their faith, to lead them back to the ancestors and back to the gods. Just as men need the gods, the gods need men. Neither can survive without the other."

Obaseki was stunned by Fuluke's revelation. The gods

need men? Surely Fuluke was wrong.

"There is no reason for me to lie to you," Fuluke said, answering Obaseki's thoughts. "Remember my words."

"What does Ndoro have to do with all this?" Obaseki asked.

"He approaches," Fuluke answered, his image becoming blurry. "The closer he comes, the more your grip on the Zamani slips away."

Obaseki reached for the others but they drew away, their images less distinct. Obaseki tried running to them but instead he drifted like a feather trapped in a dark wind.

"Fuluke! Help me!

But Fuluke did not help him. Obaseki fell from the Zamani, away from the world in which he felt most at home, his spirit crashing into his body. Someone was shaking him and yelling his name.

"Seki, Seki!" Eshe screamed.

El-Fatih rushed into the room, his guards close behind.

"My queen, what is wrong?"

Eshe looked at El-Fatih, her eyes filled with water. "He spoke, Fatih, he spoke to me!"

Obaseki heard their voices, but he was very weak. The fatigue pressed down on him like a thousand stones.

"My sweet flower," he whispered.

El-Fatih rushed to his side. "Moyoseki, can you see me?"

"I see you, Fatih," Obaseki replied. "And I hear you very well."

Obaseki tried to move his head and almost blacked out. He was close to death and he felt so.

"Fatih, have Jamela make a healing broth," Eshe commanded. El-Fatih was out of the room before Eshe finished, shouting orders at the top of his lungs. She turned back to Obaseki, placing her hand gently on his chest. She smiled and Obaseki felt the chill of his body subside. It was a smile from long ago, when they cherished each other like young lovers. Was she falling in love with him again? Though his spirits were lifted by the thought, he did not wish to be. He looked into her eyes and smiled the best he could.

"I must get my strength back quickly," he said.

"It will come in time, love," Eshe replied.

"I don't have time," Obaseki said. "My brother is coming and I must be prepared."

Eshe's face became grave. "You will stay here. You have an entire army to deal with your brother."

"I could have a million men, but only I can confront my brother," Obaseki said. The message from Fuluke was clear. What the ancestors had set in motion was almost complete. Any path he took would have led to this moment, this final confrontation.

"Moyo! Moyoseki!" Eshe's head jerked to the window as the roar of Obaseki's given name boomed through. She ran to the window and leaned out.

"Seki, I wish you could see this," she exclaimed.

"I can," he replied, his eyes closed. Through the vision of the spirits he saw crowds of people filling the streets, all chanting his name. He felt the love, respect and fear they held for him. It was the lesson the ancestors created him to learn.

El-Fatih entered the room with servants carrying Eshe's items. Glancing toward the window, he smirked.

"It seems the word of your awakening has spread throughout the city."

"So it has," Obaseki replied, managing a smile for his friend. "Tomorrow I will be on my feet. I wish you to teach me what makes the Tuareg such fearsome fighters."

El-Fatih's smirk grew into a smile. "It will be difficult. You may be a god, but you are still not a Tuareg. Despite this I will do my best."

"That is all I ask." Obaseki felt a wave of fatigue rising inside him and closed his eyes.

"I must rest now. Eshe, will you stay beside me?"

"Of course, my love." Eshe smiled and for the first time in many seasons Obaseki believed her love for him was true. He closed his eyes and fell into a dreamless sleep.

Eshe watched her husband drift asleep in fear. Was he only sleeping, or had his brother's wound finally claimed him? She leaned close, placing her cheek near his nose. The faint sound of his breathing calmed her; she sat straight, gently stroking his hand.

El-Fatih's hand touched her shoulder lightly. His touch was unsure, but his voice was steady.

"He has returned to us as I knew he would."

"How could you be so sure?" Eshe asked, turning her head so she could see him. "He was so close to the ancestors."

"He is not a man. I believe he was healing in his own way."

Eshe looked at her lover, knowing the words she was about to utter would hurt.

"All I thought about while he was gone was how I failed him as a wife. He was dealing with so many things and I paid him no attention. I was too busy with my own needs."

El-Fatih removed his hand from Eshe's shoulder. "It must be difficult bonded to a man such as him."

Eshe smiled; relieved that El-Fatih saw the path she was leading him down. She expected no less of him; it was the reason she was drawn to him. Whatever selfishness she indulged with him had to end. Obaseki was her husband and would need her help to recover. But it was more than that. Looking into Obaseki's eyes took her back to when they first met. She remembered the shallowness of youth in those eyes as he clumsily harnessed his powers to save her mother. To look into his eyes now was like gazing into a deep, calming river which every twist and turn spoke of paths well known and well traveled. Obaseki's eyes showed her what she had longed to see. His wanderings were done; he had found his place. She only wished she knew what that really meant.

*　　*　　*

Obaseki awoke to a room illuminated by the soft light of early morning. The fatigue that weighed on him the day before was completely gone. He felt as if he'd only slept instead of experiencing the turmoil of the past weeks. He opened his eyes wider and saw Eshe lying beside him, her sheer nightgown covering her body like morning mist. He was aroused and surprised by the feeling; it had been a long time since they'd touched each other in such a way. He ran his hand down the crest of her shoulder, following the slope of her arm and into the dip of her waist, then rising and lingering on her hip. She stirred, moaning pleasurably as she looked up into his eyes.

"Your sleep seems to have revived more than your spirit," she purred. She reached up and grasped his shoulder, pulling herself up to look at him eye to eye. They kissed, gently at first, then stronger as they both sensed his energy was real. They made love like new lovers, the passion spilling over into frantic motion and unbelievable need.

Obaseki held Eshe for a time, joyful to have his wife back completely. He kissed her cheek, then swung his legs over the edge of the bed and began to dress.

Eshe rose up on her elbows and watched him. "Aren't you tired?"

Obaseki turned to her and grinned. "No, although I probably should be. I promised El-Fatih we would begin training today."

"It must be true what he said then," Eshe said. She made her way to him, slipping her arm around his waist. "You were not dying, you were resting."

Her words raised the shadow in his mind, reviving his purpose. Obaseki removed Eshe's arm from his waist.

"I was not resting, sweet flower. I was dead."

Eshe's eyes widened. "Dead?"

"Yes," Obaseki replied. "I was among the ancestors. I walked among them with Fuluke. There-among the souls of my friends, relatives, and ancestors-I was told what I must do."

Eshe's eyes went from bewilderment to sadness. "You must confront your brother again."

"Yes."

Eshe looked away, a tear escaping her eye. Obaseki knew what she feared; that if he challenged his brother his death would be permanent. She was right, yet she was also wrong.

Distant footsteps told of El-Fatih's arrival. "My teacher comes," Obaseki said, trying his best to lighten the mood. El-Fatih strode into the room, looked at Eshe and quickly exited to a place where he could not see her near nakedness.

"I deeply apologize, Mokoseki," he said. "I was not aware. I assumed that the lateness of the day..."

"Don't grovel," Obaseki replied. "It doesn't suit you. You have full right to expect me to be ready and my wife to be decent."

He kissed Eshe's cheek then left the room. El-Fatih stood midway down the corridor, clearly embarrassed.

"Come, my teacher," Obaseki said. "It's time to make me a warrior."

He followed El-Fatih out of the palace into the courtyard. No matter how many times he'd seen these grounds its beauty always amazed him. The lushness of it was in sharp contrast to the surrounding desert. The courtyard was usually filled with servants, but today it was empty. A rack stood at the far end, filled with various weapons. El-Fatih marched to the rack.

"Knowing that you are of noble blood, I am sure you had some weapons training. I thought we would start by seeing what you remember."

He grabbed a wooden sword from the rack and handed it hilt first to Obaseki. Obaseki grasped it and felt a rush of energy overcome him. Memories flooded his mind, thoughts he knew were not his, but felt part of him just the same. The onslaught was almost overwhelming and he swayed, grabbing the weapons rack for support.

El-Fatih rushed to his side. "Are you sure you are ready?"

Obaseki steadied himself. "Yes, I'm fine. Let's continue."

El-Fatih hesitated, and then stepped away.

"We will begin with defense." El-Fatih extended his takouba, drawing a line in the air before Obaseki down from his forehead to his crotch.

"This is your center line. It is where all power revolves. Attack and defense originate here."

El-Fatih drew another line, this one horizontal and

bisecting the center line.

'These are the four oases," he said. "Northern right, northern left, south right and south left. Each oasis is vital to the survival of the tribe. Each must be defended; each must attack."

Obaseki nodded in understanding. Though the terms were different, the concept was similar to what he was taught many years ago in Abo. The memories raced back to him and sadness accompanied them. Would he ever see his home again?

El-Fatih cleared his throat, drawing Obaseki back to his training.

"Today we will do a simple thrust and parry exercise. This will help you learn the oases and help you to become familiar with your center line."

El-Fatih took a fighting stance, slowly moving his takouba toward Obaseki.

"Attack north oases right," he said. Obaseki repeated the movement toward El-Fatih, who extended his takouba, thus deflecting Obaseki's slow attack.

"Defend north oasis right," El-Fatih said. They repeated the movement for each oasis.

"Now, let us begin the game," El-Fatih announced.

El-Fatih increased the pace. Obaseki, nervous at first, struggled to match El-Fatih's speed. But then a rush came over him, a sensation reminding him of Moyo's presence. El-Fatih seemed to slow, his movements easier to follow. Maybe he was tiring, Obaseki thought. The look on his face was clearly one of frustration as he thrust and parried in time with Obaseki. Obaseki raised his hand, signaling for El-Fatih to stop.

"Are you tired?" Obaseki asked.

El-Fatih threw down his sword. "I know who you are, Moyoseki, and I respect your power and what you have done for my people. Still, it is not right to deceive a person in order to shame him."

Obaseki was puzzled. "What do you mean?"

"This! Your skills are amazing! I begin slowly to spare you, and then I find myself struggling to keep pace with you!"

Obaseki smiled and place his hand on El-Fatih's shoulder.

"I did not deceive you, my friend. I possess no such skills. I think I am somehow tapping into the skills of my brother. He must be close."

"If that is so, your brother is a formidable warrior," El-Fatih replied. "It is good you tried to ambush him."

"I still have much to learn despite my new gift."

El-Fatih smiled. "Yes, this is true. Let us discuss more complex issues."

They continued to practice throughout the day, Obaseki's skills growing with every minute. His strength increased as the day moved on, much to the amazement and consternation of El-Fatih. As the desert winds carried the shadows of the evening over the eastern hills, the duo ended their session.

"Moyoseki, you are truly chosen by the gods," El-Fatih said. "Never have I seen such as you."

Obaseki looked at his friend and his chest tightened. The Ihaggaren leader's eyes spoke admiration and reverence, not the friendship that always eluded him. But unlike the years past, his remorse came with understanding. This was not his world, but his purpose.

He placed his hand on Fatih's shoulder. "The ancestors have blessed me with a great teacher." They walked to the palace in silence as Obaseki contemplated his next move.

11

Ndoro knelt in the shifting sand, his chest heaving as he threw his shield to the ground. His body had failed him. He was on his knees, staring into the darkness, the city of Yakubu still a distance away. A hand touched his shoulder and he knocked it away, springing to his feet with his assegai ready to strike. Kumbala fell away, dropping his shield and spear.

"Inkosi forgive me!" he pleaded. "We are awaiting your signal to march."

"We will camp here and continue our march tomorrow. It will give the Bedouins time to catch up with us." He heard the lie in his voice and grimaced.

"As you wish inkosi." Kumbala lingered for a moment then trotted off.

Ndoro sat in the sand and leaned back on his fatigued arms. Never before had he pushed himself to such a point. He could not afford to show weakness, especially when the battle with his brother was so close. He had no idea what warriors his brother had gathered around him, but he was sure they would be formidable. His brother's magic was surely powerful and its effect on his followers would be immeasurable. The Diaka had fought many foes, but none strengthened with foul magic. Ndoro would have to be the example. He had to prove to his warriors that demons could be slain and the Diaka would prevail.

Camp was set up quickly in Diaka fashion. Ndoro was soon in the comfort of his marching tent, resting on his cot. Kumbala sent servants with food and drink, much to Ndoro's surprise. He ate and drank heartily, confirming the toll his forced march had taken on him as well as his men.

His eyes heavy, Ndoro fought sleep. If he slept he would dream, and he feared where his dreams would take him. His brother was attacking his mind, but the fatigue was so great he was losing his struggle to stay awake. If he closed his eyes for only a moment, just enough for a short rest...

He plunged in blackness, a fall that he realized would never end. Images raced by him, visions of his childhood, the desperation of his flight from Selike, the heady times of Songhai, the founding of his kingdom and the building of his empire. Now it all meant nothing, a moment in the stream of life that flowed around him. The face of his brother appeared as he knew it would. How could a man filled with such evil be so much like him? His brother's mouth moved in the chant Ndoro had come to despise. The litany that drove them both to the coming battle; two must become one.

He awoke to the sounds of shouts and steel. He rolled from his bed, grabbing his weapons as his tent collapsed around him. Ndoro hacked at the canvas enveloping him, rolling to avoid being trampled by his unseen attacker. He ripped a hole in the fabric and sprang to his feet in time to avoid the downward stroke of a scimitar wielded by a camel-riding Bedouin. He threw his assegai with deadly accuracy, the thick blade striking the Bedouin in the throat and toppling him to the sand. Ndoro ran to the fallen man, jerking the assegai from his throat, and then spun about to access the situation. Bedouins charged through the camp, striking down Diaka as they rose startled from sleep. His few remaining bodyguards quickly surrounded him.

"Sound the battle drums!" Ndoro shouted. He dropped to his knees, searching for and finding torch sticks. A few yards away a lone fire still burned; Ndoro sprinted for it, the Diatanee close behind him. Battle drums sounded as they reached the flames, Diaka spilling out of their tents and into the midst of the attacking Bedouins. Ndoro lit his torch and passed it to the closest Diatanee. The others fell in line, grabbing torches and rushing to help bring light to the camp.

A group of camel-riders charged the fire. Ndoro and the remaining Diatanee fell into formation, locking shields and extending their assegais. The riders turned to avoid the lethal barrier, slowing just enough to give the rallying Diaka their chance. Riders and camels crumpled under a wave of Diaka, orinkas and assegais flailing against the flickering torchlight.

The Bedouin ambush became a Diaka rout. The remaining Bedouins fled the camp amid a hail of assegais and arrows, disappearing into the darkness. Ndoro immediately sent runners out with torches, establishing a perimeter around the camp. The wounded were tended to while the dead were carefully wrapped and buried temporarily; they would later be exhumed and sent back to their homelands. Bedouin dead were dragged out of the camp and dumped over the dunes beyond the sentries. The camels were butchered and the meat prepared for smoking.

Ndoro gathered his indunas about him at the remains of his tent.

"I expected the Bedouins to react, but not so soon. We must assume there will be other attacks. We must also assume there will be no help from Zimfara."

The indunas shifted nervously as Ndoro continued.

"We must abandon our march on Yakubu, at least for now. We cannot advance unless we know our flank is secure."

"We will make camp here until Jawanza returns. Use anything available to create a perimeter and take stock of your supplies. You have your orders."

The indunas dispersed. As the Diatanee repaired his tent Ndoro walked the camp, assessing the current conditions. He had underestimated the Bedouin response to his decree. Their attack was unexpected and from what he could see, damaging. He had no idea what was happening to his rear in Zimfara. Was Jawanza under siege, or was he marching to meet him? Ndoro cursed his brother. He was behind this, he concluded. Ndoro's miscalculation and the sudden, furious Bedouin response must be his doing; all the more reason for his destruction.

Ndoro reconvened with his officers at dusk. Sentries patrolled the makeshift perimeter, a collage of animal carcasses, wood and sand. Tacuma archers were stationed behind the perimeter, their quivers filled with poisoned-tipped arrows. The wounded were moved to the center of camp with the few Bedouins that remained.

The mood among the Diaka was one Ndoro had only experienced once before at the hands of the Tacuma and Nakisisa. He sensed the fear and it disgusted him, even though he understood its origin. They were in the center of the Mahgreb with no idea of their situation. Behind them the Bedouins were revolting; ahead of them was the unknown enemy.

Ndoro sat cross-legged by the fire, draped in his simba robe. He stood slowly, meeting the eyes of each man.

"We have traveled many miles together, my brothers. Beneath our feet are the bones of many armies that thought they knew the soul of the Diaka. The Bedouins, just like the others, have underestimated the strength of the Simba. They will come and meet our teeth. They will charge and feel our claws. Then they will truly know fear as they fall to the steel of the Diaka!"

Shields and assegais rattled in the darkness, a gesture that swept the camp. Ndoro tilted his head back and chanted the familiar war chant of the Diaka, the song bursting strong and resonant from his throat. His army joined in and the chant rose from the camp like a mighty eagle, ascending the soft dunes and hard mountains. The Diaka sang loudly, warning all those within hearing that the lion was near and he was hungry.

The Bedouins emerged on the horizon with the rising sun, the undulating line of camel riders and men advancing patiently. There was no need to hurry; the Diaka had nowhere to go. This was the Mahgreb, their domain and their greatest weapon against those who thought these harsh lands were easy prey. The sand beneath the camels' hooves held the bones of many who had tried and failed to subdue these desert people, but still they came with dreams of conquest. The people, scattered among the sparse oases, were as harsh as the land they roamed. They convened as they always had during times like these, setting aside their tribal rivalries to push out the invaders. The Diaka had overstayed their welcome. It was time for the desert to claim it's due.

Ndoro stood on a small rise of sand built for observation. Below him the camp was mobilized. Archers were in position just inside the palisade wall, bows loaded and ready. Behind them stood the spearmen with their pikes, designed to thwart camel or horse charges. Inside the perimeter the Diaka waited, assegais at their sides, shields in position.

Ndoro and his indunas watched the slow approach of the Bedouins. There was no way to escape, not that the Diaka would entertain such a thought. They watched as the trot became a gallop, then transformed into a full speed charge.

A smile came to Ndoro's face as the Bedouins advanced. The archers loaded their bows, patiently waiting for the signal to fire. Their indunas raised their swords and watched as the charging line of horses disappeared into the hidden moat with the crashing sound like thunder and a maelstrom of dust and sand. The indunas dropped their hands and the archers responded, firing their poisoned tipped projectiles into the camel riders following the hapless horsemen. The riders, trying to avoid the deadly shower, moved forward and pushed those horsemen trying to avoid the pit into the cavern despite their protests. Some of the camel riders broke rank and circled camp, waving their curved swords over their heads while they cursed the Tacuma archers. They kept their distance from the moat as they probed the boundary. After circling the camp twice, the camel riders rode away, leaving their dead behind.

"Clear the moat," Ndoro ordered. "Repair the palisades and replace the spikes."

Kumbala nodded. "It was a good plan."

Ndoro did not smile. "I doubt it will work again, but it may slow them down. Position the warriors around the moat with archers behind. The Bedouins will find a way over the pit. Have the men place torches outside the perimeter. Keep them burning all night."

Ndoro retired to his tent. The sun made its slow descent into the western hills, pulling the heat away with it. As darkness settled on the Diaka camp the sounds of Bedouins came to the ears of the sentries. It was a restless night; the torches constantly extinguished by brave desert riders dodging the poison missiles fired into the darkness. The warriors sent to relight them were equally endangered. No sooner did they cross the pit than they were set upon by hidden Bedouins waiting in the darkness. Skirmishes went on throughout most of the night until Kumbala ordered the men back. They were losing too many to the torches; he would have to concede the night to the Bedouins. By dawn an uneasy quiet possessed the camp.

The sun peeked over the distant hills bringing the yells of attacking Bedouins. Ndoro sprang from his bed at the sound of the alarm drums, running out of his tent and into the emerging light. The Bedouins were charging from all sides. His archers and spearmen responded by spreading their line around the camp. Ndoro looked into the pit and smiled.

"Kumbala, light the pit!" he ordered. At Kumbala's signal torchbearers sprinted to the pit, throwing the fire into the heaps of grass and branches the Diaka had stacked into the pit during the night. The fires caught but spread slowly.

"More torches!" Ndoro shouted.

The Bedouins were too close for his order to be followed. They veered away from the parts of the pit on fire and rode for the gaps.

Ndoro's eyes narrowed. "Move the pike men into position. Make sure the Diaka are ready." He extracted his sword and braced his shield in anticipation of the Bedouin onslaught.

The Bedouin horsemen charged across the burning pit and were met by a fusillade of poison arrows. The bowmen fell back to reload, replaced by skirmishers flinging throwing-spears. The charge was stalled long enough for the pike men to form ranks before the archers. Their long thick-shafted spears forced the horse riders to divert.

By then the entire pit was ablaze, a thick black smoke rising about the camp. Fighters on both sides struggled to see through the swirling haze of dust and smoke. Bedouin riders charged through the infernal wall, bearing down on the disorganized pike men. The Tacuma archers threw down their bows and unleashed their swords, coming to the aid of the pike men.

"Diaka kimbia!" Ndoro shouted. The Diaka drums

responded and the archers broke off their attack, running toward the man-made hill at the center of the camp. The Diaka swarmed down the hill into battle. The Bedouins dismounted and drew their scimitars, realizing their camels were a disadvantage against the seasoned Diaka.

Ndoro swung his sword with wild precision as Bedouins appeared before him like ghosts through the smoke. He had no idea who was around him, if they were losing the camp or gaining the advantage. He was alone, fighting for his life with the ferocity of his namesake. If this was his day to die, he would make sure the Bedouins remembered it well.

He was shoved from behind and spun about with a slash of his sword. The blade struck a Diaka shield blocking the terrified face of one his guard.

"Shumba!" the man yelled. He turned his head and shouted to his comrades. "Diatanee together!"

Other guardsmen emerged from the smoke, smiles of relief on their faces. They quickly formed a ring about Ndoro.

The attacks lessened though the sound of battle could still be heard in the distance. Ndoro and the Diatanee moved through the camp, gathering the army about them and forming rank. War drums called for order and the warriors responded, each induna calling out for his unit and the warriors responding in kind. Ndoro gave his orders to the drummers and the army moved together in classic Diaka formation towards the sound of battle.

They emerged from the camp smoke into the midst of the mêlée. The men that fought the Bedouins were not Diaka, Sesu or Tacuma; they were other Bedouins. Unlike the ones that attacked the camp, these Bedouins wore blue-checkered keffiyahs. The Diaka surged toward the battle and the Bedouins that attacked the camp fled. The Diaka continued to charge, heading for this new threat. With a wave of his hand Ndoro ordered the sounding of the drums. The advancing Diaka stopped instantly, though it was obvious they did not wish to. Ndoro and the Diatanee approached the blue clad Bedouins, Ndoro confident in his decision to call back his warriors. This Bedouin army was smaller that the one that attacked the camp, but their tenacity was obviously enough to draw the other Bedouins away.

The leader of the new Bedouins emerged from the horde mounted on a magnificent white camel and flanked by a contingent of heavily armed riders. He was draped in a white, blood stained robe, his keffiyah held on his head with a gilded agal. The two leaders faced each other, acknowledging each other with slight nods.

"Welcome to our desert, Great Shumba," the Bedouin chief announced. "I am Sheik Anwar Bashir, chieftain of the Madani."

"I'm grateful by your hospitality," Ndoro replied, "though your reception was not needed."

"Do not confuse our intentions," Anwar replied. "We attacked the Dulbe because they had no right on our land."

Ndoro was impressed by Anwar, despite his haughty manner. It was obvious any confrontation at the moment would result in the Bedouin's death, but he gave no indication of being in danger.

"We have no quarrel with the Madani. Our destination is Yakubu."

Anwar folded his arms across his broad chest. "A great man chooses great enemies. I have no feud with the Tuaregs and their leader. But if you seek surprise, you have already lost the advantage."

Anwar nodded toward the eastern horizon. Ndoro looked

and saw two men draped in blue robes sitting on camels. They reined the beasts and turned away, descending into the hazy horizon. The Diatanee moved to follow, but Ndoro signaled them to a halt.

He turned his attention back to Anwar. "We must talk again when our business with Yakubu is finished."

"If you are still alive," Anwar replied. "May Moyo be merciful." The Madani rode off, disappearing into the distance.

Ndoro trudged back to camp in silence. The fires in the pit had burned themselves out, columns of smoke twisting into the sky. Healers tended the wounded as the warriors worked together to gather the dead. Medicine priest hovered over the bodies, performing the proper rituals to appease the spirits of the dead on both sides. The doubts he felt before the march resurfaced, fueled by his anger with Anwar's words. To the people of the desert, his defeat at the hands of his brother was a forgone conclusion. Had he underestimated Obaseki's power? Maybe he needed more time to gather more intelligence and strengthen his forces before moving on Yakubu. As he reached his tent, he felt weighed down by doubt.

"There is no more time," the voice of Nakisisa said.

"I won't be rushed by a spirit," Ndoro replied aloud, not caring who heard him.

"If you do not attack Yakubu now, your defeat is as certain as sunrise," Nakisisa insisted.

"Death has clouded your vision, Nakisisa," Ndoro snapped. "I am at half strength and most of my men wounded. I don't know whether Jawanza will return. I have lost the element of surprise. I will not suffer obvious defeat at the whim of dead spirits."

"The fate of this world does not depend on the battle of two armies. It depends on the confrontation between two brothers."

Ndoro stared into the distance as Nakisisa's words formed truth in his mind. Obaseki had understood this long ago; it was why he came alone to Abo instead of leading an army of thousands.

"Kumbala," Ndoro called. "Gather every man able to walk and as much provision we can spare. We march tonight for Yakubu."

"But Shumba, we are not ready," Kumbala replied. "We are less than half strength."

Ndoro place a hand on Kumbala's shoulder. "We must move with what we have. Jawanza will return soon to take care of the wounded. He will follow us as soon as he can."

Kumbala's expression told Ndoro he was not convinced.

"I trust the ancestors on this," Ndoro finally said with great difficulty.

Kumbala's eyes widened. "I have protected you many years, Shumba, and never have I heard those words come from your lips. If the ancestors tell you this, then it is a good decision." The captain of the Diatanee trotted off to fulfill his duties.

Ndoro turned to face the direction of Yakubu.

"I am coming, brother," he whispered.

12

Yakubu pulsed with tension since the return of the scouts, the word of the desert battle spreading throughout the city despite El-Fatih's best efforts to prevent it. The Bedouins had delayed Shumba's advance but not stopped it. It was only a matter of weeks before Ndoro's army would stand at the foot of the plateau, banging their assegais against their shields, calling for the blood of Moyoseki.

El-Fatih forced such thoughts from his mind as he reached the outer defenses. The ancient founders of the High City chose well when selecting the plateau as their home. Two sets of dunes surrounded the heights like necklaces, each mound approximately one half mile between them. Low Town crowded the area between the outer and inner dunes; a holding area for those newly arrived to Yakubu. A second city occupied the space between the second set of dune hills and the base of the plateau. It was known as Rig 'at. The oldest of the settlements, Rig'at's mud brick and marble buildings once housed the Ihaggaren. Legend said Moyo appeared one night a thousand years ago in a roar of fire and thunder, drawing the Ihaggaren to the top of the plateau and to glory. The oldest building on the plateau, the temple of Marina, was constructed around the landfall of Moyo's spirit from the heavens.

El-Fatih's mind wrestled not only with the tremendous job at hand, but also with the growing doubt he harbored inside toward Obaseki, doubts that surfaced the day he rescued the medicine-priest from death in Abo. Why would a man with such power have to resort to a stabbing to kill an enemy? During his training, El-Fatih's doubts subsided because of the alacrity with which Obaseki learned to fight. But those misgivings resurfaced during the meeting with the scouts reporting the Diaka battle with the Bedouins. Obaseki seemed uninterested, his eyes gazing at some invisible amusement. He barely acknowledged the scouts and did not notice when they completed their report. When El-Fatih asked him of his plans, his reply was just as disturbing.

"What will happen will happen. Two must become one."

El-Fatih ordered work crews to the summits of the dunes. Legend also spoke of a stone wall built along the peaks, connecting the dunes to form a reasonable defense. He was determined to find them if they existed. The walls on the outer dunes would be used as observation only. He had to concentrate his forces behind the second dune where the maze of houses would allow them to slow down the Diaka. Those living between the walls and the old city would be evacuated to Yakubu. Boulders were set in place to block the streets that weaved up the side of the plateau in case the Diaka broke through the second wall. At best the Diaka would be driven back. At worst, the people of Yakubu would have to settle in for a long siege.

El-Fatih left the excavation work, heading back to the royal palace. The iron gate swung wide upon his approach and his personal guard immediately fell in time with his steps. As they made their way to the courtroom, El-Fatih prepared himself for his briefing with Moyoseki, hoping the medicine-priest would be more concerned about survival of the city he had revived.

He entered the courtroom. Obaseki looked up from his simple stool, flanked by Shani and Eshe. With a slight gesture he dismissed the women.

"My lord," El-Fatih said as he prostrated before his oba.

"How goes the defenses?" Obaseki asked.

El-Fatih smiled, his hope renewed. "We are excavating the old ramparts to strengthen the defense of the outer city. If Shumba's army is as large as reported, we can defend ourselves behind those walls."

"Not the normal Ihaggaren response to a threat," Obaseki observed.

"I have more serious concerns than the honor of the nobles," El-Fatih replied.

"You speak of me."

El-Fatih gazed away from Obaseki. "You have changed, Moyoseki, and I am concerned. You show great power in your healing and I know the power of Moyo. It is strong enough to destroy the Diaka."

Obaseki eyes drifted to his feet. "That is true."

El-Fatih's hands began to warm, a sure sign he was losing his temper.

"Unlike you, my lord, I listened to the report of our scouts. Although they were wounded by the Bedouins, the Diaka army is still immense. It is the largest army ever to cross the Mahgreb and they have the provisions to make the journey to Yakubu in full readiness."

El-Fatih hesitated; fearful to say what he knew was true. But if it would make Obaseki act, it was worth the shame.

"I cannot stop them."

Obaseki looked into El-Fatih's eyes and the Ihaggaren leader cringed behind his face veil. He didn't want the sympathy in those eyes; he wanted action.

"Yakubu is safe," Obaseki replied. "The Diaka will never see the inside of this city. Ndoro and I will settle our business beyond the outer dunes."

Obaseki place a firm hand on El-Fatih's shoulder, and for the first time in days El-Fatih felt confidence in Moyo's caretaker.

"Go and finish your preparations. When the Diaka appear before the first wall, send for me. I will not fail you, my friend."

El-Fatih prostrated before Obaseki, sure in the knowledge of his oba's power.

*   *   *

Obaseki waited until El-Fatih was gone before slumping on his stool, cradling his worn face in his hands. Shani appeared, gliding to his side with a mother's concern.

"What did you tell him?" she asked.

"I told him what he wished to hear. I had no choice. If El-Fatih loses faith he and his people will disappear into the desert. If the Ihaggaren leave the others will, too. Ndoro and his Diaka will turn back and claim victory. That must not happen."

"Must it be this way?" Shani's face was distraught.

Obaseki smiled. "You will not lose us, momma. Your sons will always be with you."

Eshe entered the room and Obaseki's smile grew wider. He was not sure of what the confrontation with Ndoro might bring, but at least he could control his moments before answering his destiny.

"Come, sweet flower, sit with us," he said. Eshe smiled and came to sit beside him. Together son, mother, and wife conversed, keeping at bay the clouds of the future with the glow of their present pleasure.

Chadamunda was in panic. In his first duty since passing through his manhood rites he was failing. The night before, his father's herd of goats grazed peacefully under a clear moonless night. Now he was running about desperately, gathering the goats from all corners of their small oasis, the darkening skies threatening a heavy and violent rain.

Chadamunda took a quick head count of the goats and cried in dismay. Two were still missing. He fell to his knees, preparing to ask for spiritual guidance when he heard the frantic bleating emanating from the opposite side of the dune that protected the fragile oasis from the scorching desert winds.

Chadamunda scurried up the steep side of the dune. He reached the top and cried out. As far as he could see an army advanced, running and chanting towards him, his goats standing in their path. The boy turned about and stumbled down the other side of the dune.

Chadamunda dared to look back and saw the swarm of warriors crest the dune, rushing at him like a dark sirocco. He fled, his eyes focused on the mud-brick house before him. Terror shadowed him as the warriors closed the gap and enveloped him like the night. Countless hands lifted him from his feet and carried him along. Chadamunda closed his eyes and prayed. After a terrifying eternity his feet hit the ground and he stumbled, sprawling into the sand. The soft thumping of running feet surrounded him, and then slowly subsided. Familiar arms wrapped around him tightly, the comforting smell of his mother dispersing his fear. Daring to open his eyes, his house stood before him untouched. His father stood beside them, watching the horde of warriors climb and disappear over the next dune. Chadamunda's father looked into his eyes and fell to his knees. The family embraced in relief at what passed but in dread of what was to come.

Ndoro ran with an energy that amazed him. Three days ago he began his run with the Diatanee and two thousand Diaka fit enough to make the arduous march to the outskirts of Yakubu. They had not stopped running since that day. Some strange magic was at work, pushing him to this confrontation with his brother, driving away any fatigue, thirst or hunger that would cripple normal men running such a distance at such a pace.

The plateau came into view, its pinnacle peering over the tops of the rolling dunes embracing it. A diligent sentry with good eyes would have spotted them by now, raising the alarm throughout the city. If that was so, he had no way of knowing.

They climbed the next dune before them and Ndoro called a halt to their martial marathon. The sun had long been hidden by thick clouds that were alien to the barren sand before them. They rumbled as if irritated, tendrils of lightening racing across them with each bellow. For two hundred yards a flat land of hard packed rock and sand stretched, punctuated by another dune. Ndoro spotted ramparts undulating with the crests and troughs of the sandy ridge. Beyond the fortifications rose the plateau, a pillar of thriving life amidst the heat and sand. The city perched upon the heights glowed with unnatural light, its beauty a stark contrast against the furious sky. Ndoro was impressed; it was no doubt a wealthy city, one that under other circumstances would have provided much reward after its conquest. His prize, however, lie in the death of his brother and the release from this strange force that drew him to this moment. He turned to his warriors; some were weathered Diaka who had fought with him since his days in Songhai, others that were yet blooded who waited anxiously to gain their first honor in battle.

He could find no words to inspire them. This was a personal journey; there was no city to conquer and no empire to build. He turned and ran down the dune into the valley, followed by his warriors in determined silence.

*   *   *

Obaseki sat alone in the council room. No torches lit the chamber, only the faint glow of the city lights. Outside in the skies the ancestors gathered, their dark faces blocking the sun and casting a calming darkness over the dunes and valleys. Their voices rumbled across the land, words that chanted stories of the past and present with flashes of future visions. Obaseki acknowledged their presence and drew upon their confidence and wisdom.

Fuluke appeared beside him, announcing his arrival with a warm breeze.

"My brother is here," Obaseki said.

"The journey ends," Fuluke replied. "Two must become one."

Obaseki rose to his feet. He wore his blue robes, his face veil hanging to the side. His takouba slung over his shoulder, Obaseki adjusted his daggers. He was exiting the chamber when a messenger burst into view.

"Moyoseki! The Diaka are here!"

Obaseki nodded. "I know. Where is Fatih?"

"He is gathering the Ihaggaren to meet them."

Obaseki charged past the messenger, running through the palace to the stables. He mounted his camel and rushed through the gates into the street. Thousands swarmed him, their cries of praise and fear drowning out his urgent orders to clear the way.

"You cannot reach him in time," Fuluke's voice said in his head. "He has made his choice."

Obaseki ignored Fuluke and continued to shout. To his relief, a contingent of Ihaggaren warriors appeared on camelback and began shouting and beating the crowd back.

"Follow us, Moyoseki," the leader of the group said. "We will lead you to the gates."

Obaseki followed his escort through the city streets, the crowd growing as the word of the enemy outside the gate spread. Obaseki became anxious, his anger spilling into his voice.

"Damn all of you! Get out of my way!"

The power of his voice struck everyone in sight. People fled, their faces cringing in pain. Countless eyes that only a moment ago looked on him in admiration now stared in fear as they stampeded out of the way of the riders.

They galloped down the spiraling road to the outer city. As they passed through the Yakubu gates, the signal drums boomed with the thunder from above, signaling their advance. The gates throughout Rig'at swung wide as people cleared streets before the riders as they rode through the second city to the outermost ramparts. Obaseki saw the Ihaggaren gathered about the final gate, horsemen and camels in tight formation. He spurred his camel but the animal was exhausted and refused to increase its pace. He watched helplessly as the warriors rode out to meet the Diaka.

El-Fatih heard the drums signaling Obaseki's approach, but ignored the warning. The warriors gathered about him moved nervously, their eyes unsure. No matter what Moyoseki thought, El-Fatih had taken the outriders' report to heart. The army marching toward Yakubu was formidable, their vanguard before the gates a sure sign of their strength.

"This is not just a fight for Moyoseki," he shouted over the thunder. "This is for your homes and your families. We have lost this city once; we will not lose it again. No matter who he is, Moyoseki is not Ihaggaren. The Ihaggaren do not let others fight their battles."

El-Fatih turned away from the blue-clad warriors to face the gates. He glared at the gatekeepers and they swung open the barricade amid the increasing thunder and lightening. He charged forward and smiled as he heard the rumble of hooves and the war cries behind him. Before him the Diaka stood, making no move to change their formation. They remained single file, a tall warrior adorned in a lion-hooded cape standing in the center, shield and spear in hand. El-Fatih pulled his takouba from its scabbard, pointing it at the man and focusing on him. The sounds of his cohorts were drowned out by the increasing violent sky, the lightening constant. With only a few yards between him and his target, El-Fatih smiled. His life had been good; he had lived long enough to see Yakubu returned to his people and become the great city it had once been. He had helped Obaseki restore Moyo to its rightful place. If this was his day to die, he had no regrets. El-Fatih raised his tabouka over his head.

"For Moyo! For Yakubu!" he shouted. He was turning to face his companions when his life ended in a torrent of lightening.

Obaseki reached the outer gate just as the ancestors struck down the charging Ihaggaren. The death of so many at one time hit like an orinka; he rocked on his saddle, his hand going to his head.

The ancestors answered him before the question could form in his mind; it was necessary. The proper ritual had to be observed. If El-Fatih and his outriders had reached Ndoro, they could have killed him. It was that possibility the ancestors saw and moved to prevent. Even the ancestors could not control everything, Obaseki thought with a smile. Though the path he and Ndoro walked was woven before they were born, there was no guarantee either of them would follow their destinies. Fate was influenced by choice, and fortunately for the ancestors, he and Ndoro had chosen the best path. Obaseki looked into the countless faces above him. They were silent for a moment, absorbing the new souls from the scene below. He waited until the ancestors began to chant again and then rode out to meet his brother.

Ndoro was stunned to silence. The warriors lay only yards away, the stench of their burned bodies overwhelming. He had not expected an attack so suddenly; they would have surely been wiped out. For a moment he wondered what force struck them down, but the answer was hard for him to comprehend. Had the ancestors done this? Was his brother so powerful and dangerous that those he never trusted had chosen him? If Obaseki was so powerful he had come on a fool's errand and would surely die. For the first time in his life Ndoro experienced pure fear. He looked down the row of Diaka and saw the fear in their eyes as well. He could pull back and wait for Jawanza. With the full weight of the Diaka behind him Obaseki's great power would crumble. Obaseki's strategy might not be to destroy the army, but just to kill him.

A lone rider emerged from the wall on the dunes, loping toward the Diaka as the clouds rumbled again. Ndoro stepped forward, his hands tightening on his assegai and shield. His brother was coming alone; such was his confidence in his power.

The sky heralded his approach, the thunder rolling in a rhythm Ndoro recognized. There was no doubt of the power his brother possessed, but he was also sure now that he was the only one that could stop him. Was he not his twin? Somewhere inside of him he must hold such power as well. Until it manifested itself, he would rely on his martial skills. It was all he had.

Ndoro trotted toward his brother. The Diaka moved to follow but he waved them still. This was a personal confrontation. He did not want the brave men that followed him to be struck down as dishonorably as the Tuaregs.

Time disappeared; the voices of the ancestors continued to rumble across the sky and the land, its strength shaking the buildings. Obaseki halted his camel only a few yards away from his brother and dismounted. They approached each other, and then stopped, only an arm's length of space between them. The ancestors fell silent.

Ndoro watched Obaseki as he removed his veil, his hand tight on his spear. To see his brother's face was like looking into a mirror. They were true twins, identical in every way. Obaseki smiled at Ndoro, an unexpected expression considering the circumstances.

"Ata," he said.

"Atsu," Ndoro replied instinctively.

"So it must come to this?" Obaseki asked. Ndoro began to answer but realized Obaseki was not talking to him. His eyes were cast upward, staring into the heavy black clouds overhead.

"Is there no other way?" he asked the ancestors.

The heavens roared and Obaseki closed his eyes, a sorrowful expression on his face. Ndoro realized he did not wish to kill his brother. There were so many questions to ask; so much he wanted to know. No matter how many people surrounded him throughout his life, a void existed which that had not been filled. He realized the answer stood before him, and he'd come to destroy it before he had a chance to know.

Ndoro was about to speak when Obaseki's expression changed from sorrow to serious.

"Two must become one," he said.

Ndoro caught the blow from Obaseki's sword with his shield, the force of the strike knocking him off balance. He stumbled back frantically as he beat back the flurry of blows, amazed at his brother's speed. He slowly matched his pace, finally managing to thrust at his brother, breaking his rhythm and taking away his advantage.

Ndoro and Obaseki fought at an inhuman pace. The sky rumbled constantly, the rainless storm an aural reflection of the battle taking place under its dark canopy. As the two fought the people gathered around them. Ihaggaren warriors mixed with the Diaka vanguard. The warriors were surrounded by the people of Yakubu. In the distance the bulk of the Diaka army crested the dunes, marching cautiously under the strange scene around them.

Ndoro managed to break away from his brother. He was exhausted. His chest heaving, he circled looking for an opening. Obaseki looked back, a grim smile on his face.

"Obaseki, you must fight the demon inside you! Drive him from you mind. Free yourself so I won't have to!"

Obaseki shook his head in despair. "There is no demon possessing me. After all your journeys, you still don't understand." Obaseki shrugged his shoulders. "It was not your calling to understand."

The ancestors raised their voices with a force that shook the sand.

"You are the earth," Obaseki continued. "You see with the eyes of the world. You understand only that which you can experience with your senses. I am the sky. I see beyond the physical. I understand the spirits and the shadows. We are each one half of the whole, the complete circle from which a new future will be born."

Another deafening rumble erupted from the clouds and Obaseki glanced upward.

"They are all here." Obaseki dropped his sword and reached into his robe, revealing Moyo. The mayembe glowed, the intense light making him squint. Ndoro drew back, shading his eyes with his shield. Despite his fear he felt drawn to the object, the light persuading him to look in its direction.

"Two must become one," Obaseki said with a voice that seemed to emanate from outside his body. He raised the mayembe over his head, his eyes fixed on the heavens.

Ndoro seized the advantage. He lunged forward, driving his spear into Obaseki's chest. Obaseki clinched his eyes as the assegai shattered bone and entered his heart. His hands dropped in reflex, the mayembe falling toward Ndoro, the point aimed at his chest. Ndoro raised his shield but the horn tore through the tempered leather like dry leaves. It plunged into Ndoro's chest, the same spot where Ndoro had pierced his brother. But instead of pain, Ndoro was filled with calm. The mayembe's light enveloped the world around him until there was nothing but brightness and his brother, standing before him with the assegai protruding from his chest. Obaseki grasped the spear in his free hand and pulled it out. There was no blood. He looked at his brother and smiled.

"Now do you understand?" he asked.

Ndoro nodded. "We were never two."

Obaseki smiled like a proud teacher. "We were always one person; one person, two lives. It was necessary."

Ndoro felt wetness growing in his eyes. "Our burden has been heavy."

"Birth is never easy," Obaseki replied as he looked away.

"And now?" Ndoro asked.

Obaseki looked back toward his brother, closing his eyes.

"And now, two become one."

The ancestors sang with deafening voices, their joy rumbling the very foundation of the earth around them. The future became a bright, constant stream of light that ran across their dark faces and streaked downward, striking the brothers with a jubilant force. The people - Ihaggaren, Diaka, Tacuma, Sesu, Bedouin and Mawena- prostrated themselves before the furious joy, feeling no fear but anticipation of what was to become.

A rhythm danced in the voices of the ancestors, a universal cadence known to all as the song of birth and celebration. The song was sung in different languages, but its meaning was still the same.

The ancestors fell silent. Their purpose complete, they drifted back to the Zamani, releasing the sun to touch the sands with the feeble strength of dawn. As the people came to their feet, they looked to the spot where two brothers met to see only one man standing. He was naked before them, his eyes closed as his body pulsed with his deep breathing. The people murmured; which brother had survived?

El-Fatih opened his eyes and was in the world again. He sat up quickly and studied the scene around him, the same vision he saw moments ago from above as his spirit mingled with the ancestors. Around him his men stirred, each one looking at him with knowing eyes then looking past him to the lone figure surrounded by the glass-like residue of the strike. They had been given back their lives with an obligation they were expected to fulfill. El-Fatih and his resurrected warriors stepped forward, prostrating before him and covering their heads with sand.

"Rise and be recognized," the man said. El-Fatih came to his feet.

"What do I call you?" he asked.

"Obadoro."

Jawanza saw the Ihaggaren approach the man standing. He felt tired as he watched the man accept them, confirming his worst thoughts. He raised his assegai and turned away. Ndoro asked that no revenge be taken for his death and his request would be honored.

"Come, Jawanza." The voice that reverberated in his head was that of Ndoro, but he knew it was not just him. The man that stood with the Ihaggaren was more. Jawanza looked across the distance into his eyes. The fire was there in all its intensity, the smile on his inkosi's face welcoming and familiar.

"Diaka Kimbia!" Jawanza shouted. The Diaka responded, running to him with a newfound spirit. Somewhere in the outer city a woman ululated in joy and others responded. The Diaka war drums sprang to life, singing the song of the ancestors and telling a story of rebirth. Diaka danced, Ihaggaren shouted, and the celebration spread across the desert and into the streets of Yakubu. Eshe and Shani embraced, joy and loss bringing them together. The message of the ancestors spread across the desert to Zimfara, crossed the grasslands of Selike and Mawena, worked through the forest to the wooded hills and valleys of Tacuma. Two had become one and by doing so, joined many people into one. Obadoro looked across the thousands of strides and saw his future in the million of faces of his people. Two journeys had ended; one journey was just beginning. The path of Meji lay before him. It was a path the people soon to be known as the Obana would travel for a thousand years.

Glossary

Name	Pronunciation	Meaning/Relationship
Abo	AH-boh	Mawena capital city
Alamako	ah-lah-mah-koh	A city near Ifana
assegai	A (as in at)-say-guy	spear
Ata	ah-tah	first born of twins
Atsu	AT-soo	second born of twins
Azikiwe	Ah-zee-kee-way	Obaseki's uncle
Celu	SAY-loo	Ndoki's mayembe spirit
Diaka	DEE-ah-kah	the slave people
Dingane	DEHN-gah-nee	Father of the twins
Fuluke	FOO-loo-kay	Mawena medicine-priest
Gamba	GAHM-bah	Sesu warrior
Husani	HOO-sah-nee	Shani's bodyguard
Ifana	EYE-fah-nah	City of ghosts
impi	EHM-pee	a group of Sesu warriors
Inkosi	N-koh-see	Sesu for king
Jelani	JEH-lah-nee	Husani's brother
kimbia	KEHM-bee-ah	Sesu for "march"
Kossi	KOH-see	Mawena traditional enemies
kraal	krahl	cattle enclosure
Mawena	MAH-weh-nah	Shani's people
mayembe	MAH-yehm-beh	A animal horn containing a spirit
Moyo	MOH-yoh	Obaseki's mayembe spirit
Mulugo	MOO-loo-goh	Sesu medicine-priest
Ndoki	N-doh-kee	The medicine priest of Ifana
Ndoro	N-doe-roe	Obaseki's brother
nganga	N-gahn-gah	Sesu for medicine priest
ngwena	N-gweh-nah	crocodile
Noncemba	NOHN-kehm-bah	Shani's father
Obaseki	OBAH-se-kee	Ndoro's brother
Olodumare	olo-doo-mah-ray	Mawena main god

orinka	OR-ring-kah	war club
Oya	O-yah	an orisha - minor god or spirit
Paki	PAH-kee	a boy
Selike	SEE-lee-keh	Sesuland capital city
Sesu	SAY-soo	Dingane's people
Shani	SHAH-nee	The twins mother
Shumba	SHOOM-bah	Diaka for lion
Simba	SIM-bah	Sesu for lion
Songhai	SAHN-high	people of the Sahel
Soninke	SAH-nin-kee	another name for the songhai
Tacuma	TAH-koo-mah	Enemies of the Diaka
Themba	TEHM-bah	Shani's handmaiden
Tuareg	TOO-ar-rehg	people of the desert
Unkulunkulu	oo-koo-loon-koo-loo	Sesu main god
Zuwena	ZOO-weh-nah	nursemaid

JUL 0 8 2018

formation can be obtained
Gtesting.com
e USA
18150618
V00001B/15/P

9 780980 084245

About the Author

Milton Davis poses as a chemist by day in order to pursue his true identity as a fantasy and science fiction writer in the evenings and on weekends. He is married with two children and resides in Fayetteville, GA. Meji is his first novel.
He can be reached at *mv_media@bellsouth.net*,
or by visiting *www.mvmediaatl.com*.

CPSIA in
at www.IC
Printed in t
LVHW03&2
580966L